THE SERPENT'S ORDER

THE SERPENT SERIES

SZ ESTAVILLO

OLIVERHEBERBOOKS

ONE

THE DEADLY CONTRACT

DARKNESS PRESSED AGAINST HER EYES. The air carried no warmth, only a damp cold that burrowed into her marrow. The metallic taste on her tongue sharpened. Air scraped colder against her throat. Every nerve screamed awake as the chemical fog bled out of her veins. It was easy to fend off the hazy pull of delirium when it felt like she was sitting in an ice box. Frigid salty air wrapped her in an arctic grip, numbing her body. The sound of the seas never betrayed its location, offering no clues as to her whereabouts until the blackout hood was lifted.

Her surroundings winked awake, blurring slowly into focus. Faint traces of soot and aged timber amplified the cabin's solitude. As her vision sharpened, the first thing she saw was the rugged glaciers looming beyond the drafty windows. Snow consumed the landscape, a frozen expanse as thick as packed sugar, burying the world beneath at least twenty inches of wintery silence. At a distance, she could hear how the ocean roiled, a wild, restless beast, while the bitter subzero terrain stretched in stark harmony with the gray horizon.

Groggy, her eyes roamed in search of Zeus, panic setting in, forcing her heart to quicken until she spotted him across the room in a dark corner. Her head felt like a thousand-pound weight pressed down on her skull, each pulse of pain a hammer striking her temples. She found herself passed out on a lounger that looked to be a decade old—at least her kidnappers, or rather, her new boss—had the courtesy to leave her somewhere relatively comfortable. At the sound of her steps, Zeus lifted his head, tail thumping against the rickety wooden floorboards, though not quite making it to his feet.

It looked like she wasn't the only one trying to shake herself out of the cocktail she'd been injected with, as Zeus tried to drag himself up. She knelt beside him and massaged his legs, trying to coax circulation back into his limbs. After a few minutes, Zeus soldiered to his feet, the kneading doing the trick. Von exhaled, tension ebbing at the reassuring presence of her loyal companion. She ambled back to the kitchen, taking in her surroundings while Zeus kept time with her steps. A thin film of dust coated the kitchen counters and cupboards, telling her that time had been the lonely cabin's sole friend for a long while.

She rooted around, discovering there were enough dishes for one person, and the fridge had been stocked with salads and fruit. At least her mysterious employer had the decency to respect her food preferences. They even left a bowl of dried dog food and water for Zeus. How thoughtful. She smirked at their attention to detail as she headed to the bedroom—and then she saw it.

Sitting dead center on the bed, the phone was waiting for her.

Sleek, black, and unbranded—just a smooth slab of technology with no markings or logos, nothing to indicate who made it. While it appeared to be just another typical high-end smartphone, Von knew better. This wasn't an ordinary device. It was a leash. She picked it up. Lighter than she expected. No buttons, no ports, no removable SIM card. Completely sealed.

The kind of hardware designed to be untouchable, tamper-proof. Not to be trusted. The screen stayed dark for a ten-count before flickering to life, awakened by a simple touch. The interface was equal parts minimalist and sterile.

Nothing personal. No apps. No browser. Just a lone notification, already there.

"Welcome to Black Nova."

She flipped it in her hand, examining it. There wasn't even a password prompt, fingerprint, or facial recognition scan. Von wasn't logging in. She was already in—immediate access like it knew her. Then she remembered where she'd seen one before: Jefferson Pierce. Former Marine-turned-hacker, an asset for the FBI. Asset. The word twisted in her stomach, acidic and biting. She recalled the words—"federal asset"—before her world went black. Right before they took her.

"Silent Circle—" Jefferson had called it.

"A what?" She recalled how her brows had knitted together, confused over the unfamiliar phone. "Never heard of it."

"Military-grade. Locked down tight. End-to-end encrypted calls and messages."

"Sounds a bit paranoid," Von had said.

"For what I do—I gotta be. Safest, most private phone out on the market.

She recognized it now. Its black matte finish and elegant, no-nonsense style. But it wasn't hers—it was theirs. A direct line to the people who had dragged her into this. Her permission not needed. Her choices, her next movements, her next breath would be dictated, assigned. The second she thought this, the phone rang. She stared at it, letting it ring three times before quietly answering.

"You're awake. Good. Commander Lucian Cain here, in case your memory needs a little reminder," a calm, authoritative voice began. "Let's see if we didn't make a mistake bringing you into the fold."

"Where the hell am I?"

"Kodiak Island."

"Fucking Alaska?"

"Impressed you know your geography—most people don't know where Kodiak Island is," Cain said. "Before we officially begin, you must complete our test."

"And if I fail?"

"Don't think failure's in your DNA," he said, then switched to German, "*Schlangenfrau.*"

She hadn't intended to assume the title of the Serpent Woman, not before the brutal attack that dragged her to the edge of death. Her guts shredded, body mutilated and left infertile, stripped of the capacity to bear life. A monstrous snake-like crimson keloid scar now etched its path along her abdomen, sewn back up like an object in a sterile lab—efficiently reconstructed like a modern Frankenstein experiment, an uncanny patchwork that left her hollow.

Von Schlange—*Schlangenfrau*—the Serpent Woman had become her signature.

Now, it wasn't just the LAPD and the FBI using it, but Black Nova reciting it in her native tongue. Hearing it uttered from Commander Lucian Cain's mouth somehow transformed it into a menacing challenge—a dare that promised consequences too dire to ignore.

The phone chimed with an incoming picture. It was a Hispanic man in his mid-40s with weathered, olive-toned skin and black, silver-tinged hair. He had dark, brooding eyes and a quiet intensity about him that spoke of a past steeped in danger. After studying the image, she returned the phone to her ear for further instructions.

"Elias 'Eli' Vega, former DEA agent, worked in South

America undercover until he was flipped by the cartel. Eli is compromised. Working both sides. He hasn't a clue he's been exposed," the commander began. "In the closet, you'll find a lock box with everything you need. You'll find your target at the docks. Make it clean."

"Then what?"

The phone went dead.

"Hello?—*Hello?*" Von paced the length of the room, hands knotting in her hair. "Shit."

After a minute of standing there numb, Zeus leaped to his feet. He barked once at her as if to demand directions on their next move. She walked to the closet, feet heavy, dragging as though wading through quicksand—slow, anxious. Inside, a sleek black metal box awaited her. It had no locking mechanism except for a phone-sized rectangular piece that was mounted on the lid with a small circle at the center. It looked to be a biometric security system. She leaned in and waited, wondering if it was scanning her face. When nothing happened, she placed her index finger against the circular sensor, and a gentle click sang out as the lid gradually opened.

Inside the black box lay the weapon—a custom-modified SIG Sauer P320. Its vulturine presence was the result of a matte-black finish and an ergonomic grip, contoured for all hand sizes. The streamlined frame boasted an integrated accessory rail that offered unique options, allowing for laser sights and tactical lights. It had all the marks of a precise, reliable piece, outfitted with a conventional silencer mounted to the barrel. Engineered for silence. Meant for blood.

While Von harbored genuine hate for guns, her father, who was not only a world-renowned brain surgeon, wasn't only an expert in neurology but a collector of the one weapon she despised with all her being. Regardless of his daughter's protest, her father ensured she and her little sister, Sammy, wouldn't only know how to shoot but to defend themselves with perfect marksman accuracy. Though Sammy hadn't been armed at the time, she was attacked by the very men Von had been hunting before fleeing to Brazil to escape the vengeful sins of her past. To this day, her only regret was that her methods of vigilante justice inadvertently placed Sammy in the crosshairs.

Along with the gun, there were cases of bullets and a picture of her target.

She picked up the SIG Sauer P320. It felt cool and light in her hand—a small comfort in a life darkened by violence. Back when she was hunting men who destroyed Sammy's innocence, every move had been fueled by raw, personal loss. Their brutality had scarred her forever—not only through the near-fatal attack in Wyoming snow that almost ended her life. If not for Zeus throwing himself over her, warming her body, staunching the bleeding, she'd have died right then and there.

That moment changed her.

Since then, she'd killed men who deserved it. For a time, she believed it was over, escaping to Brazil, seeking a fresh start from her former life.

The doctor in her longed to return to the path she'd once chosen, to build something clean, something good—a quiet veterinary clinic, a place of healing. But the past refused to stay buried. Every night, when she closed her eyes, the door appeared in her mind, in her dreams. Mold-green paint curled away from weathered wood, the frame splintering as rustic hinges strained against an unseen force. The handle rattled, trembling with something desperate, something alive. Blood oozed from beneath the door, creeping forward, pooling at her feet. Whatever lurked in the beyond wasn't finished with her.

Rage—too intoxicating.

Fate dragged her back in.

The serpent refused to die.

Drawn out of retirement, she returned to her relentless pursuit of vengeance. Brazil had taken more than blood. It had taken Dr. Damião Sequeira—the man who loved her and understood her in ways no one else could. She'd hunted the one behind his murder down and made him pay. More recently, Ryker's crooked cops had forced her hand again. Twelve kills total under her belt—and none of them weighed on her conscience. Every one of them had been on her terms. But today, her first assignment, her test, felt different.

Different in that it was no longer her own calculated vendetta—it was someone else's order, a directive that used her as a human death tool. How many more lives would she be required to take? It was either comply or face a prison sentence for the countless lives she'd snatched from this earth. Yet one question kept scratching at her moral conviction, clawing at her soul: even if she wasn't presently behind bars, would she ever truly be free?

She turned the SIG over in her hand, checking the weight, the balance, how it contoured to her fingers like it was designed just for her. Muscle memory kicking in. While her father was the gun enthusiast, the collector—her aversion didn't seem to block the familiarity of it. The weapon felt like second nature. Black Nova had stocked the closet with everyday wear in her size: jeans and cotton tops in dark, solid colors with no logo or branding. She spied an all-black baseball cap and pulled it on, the brim shading her gray eyes.

Von took a deep breath before reaching back to shove the gun into her waistband, the cool metal pressing against her spine. She tugged her weatherproof, black tactical soft-shell jacket over it, adjusting it for concealment. Not the most comfortable spot, but she was on Kodiak Island—fucking twenty-degrees-Alaska, with strong coastal winds that mimicked

Arctic climates. So, comfort was not a prerequisite for her new job. Readiness, however, was vital.

Wasting no time, Von clicked her tongue, and with a nod at Zeus, they were out the door. The moment they stepped outside, a blast of icy wind rudely slapped their faces, forcing her hand to defend her eyes while Zeus shut his, blinking away snow flurries. Padding beside her, his breath was visible in the frigid air. While his thick coat was built for an average winter, there was nothing ordinary about Alaska, especially with the brutal wind. She squatted to meet his height, adjusting the waterproof vest that hugged his torso, shaking her head as she recalled where she'd found it—folded neatly next to a metal lock box, waiting for them.

It was hard to remain in that unsettled feeling for long when being impressed took over, impressed that this Commander Lucian Cain and his Black Nova operatives hadn't just provided clothes for her—perfectly sized for her frame, no less—but had even thought ahead to protect her dog from the elements. They were an elite force, operating above even the FBI and CIA, and yet they were conscientious enough to ensure she and Zeus didn't freeze to death. The duplicitous irony wasn't lost on her— she was nothing short of an assassin now, whether by choice or not. Yet, here they were, caring about her comfort while sending her out to kill someone.

TWO

THE FIRST MARK

THE MORNING AIR lingered thin as a candle's last flicker, until the hard edge of daylight burned it away. Kodiak's sky was still streaked with the last bruises of night, as if the first stirring of the waterfront came alive. Deep blue and endless, a few wispy clouds drifted like Glaucous-winged Gulls coasting along the horizon—a type of seagull Von's old, retired-vet mind hadn't forgotten.

The harbor held a utilitarian charm, bustling with diverse maritime activity. Running water and electricity kept it all going, powering not only small boats and larger commercial ships, but also the fueling station that kept the boats running. Von knew that she couldn't just stand there. For a brief moment, she watched dockworkers hustling around in bright visibility vests and clad in practical all-weather gear, including knee-high boots that guarded their feet from frostbite in the winter, and hard hats to protect their heads.

Like the Rio de Janeiro coffee plantation workers she'd once gazed at for a full hour, the buzz from the dock activity held the same hypnotic effect. Longshoremen, thick-shouldered and weatherworn, moved with a steady rhythm, securing cargo nets and inspecting cranes, their voices a low murmur against the lap of the tide. On the docks, a few deckhands from seiners and crabbers huddled in their oilskins waiting for favorable tides, steaming cups of coffee clutched between fingers hardened from years of working a laborious job.

The fishing fleet was waking. Purse seiners, with their broad decks and towering reels, were being prepped for another long haul of salmon. At the far end of the large harbor, a few gillnetters idled, their nets neatly looped, the captain checking tide charts and ice holds before casting out. But the big money, Von observed, came from the crabbing boats—opilio season was close, and Bering Sea's promise of high-yield traps had skippers calculating fuel costs against the risk of storms. Halibut longliners were prepping too, their skippers overseeing the baiting of circle hooks along miles of coiled ground line.

While Von had never worked on a dock, she had studied fishery operations extensively during veterinary school, recognizing the rhythmic efficiency of boats prepping gear, crews securing weighty nets, and forklifts off-loading crates of frozen catch—all parts of a system that, like any ecosystem, had its own hierarchy, vulnerabilities, and predators. Even the processors, the tenders who collected hauls from the fleet, were gearing up. At the cannery dock, forklifts beeped as they loaded pallets of flash-frozen cod onto waiting freighters, bound for markets far beyond the island, a life on the edge of the world.

A mélange of fish, diesel, and saltwater wafted through the air, trying to reel her closer, lure her curiosity, trick her into not paying close attention to anything off. Though, her attempts to read the scene seemed clouded by the fact that nothing seemed amiss on the surface. She and Zeus walked around, casually making their way down the docks, enamored by the various commercial fishing boats and their owners dedicated to one thing—catching fish and moving them fast to market.

Her skin prickled with a sense of doom she couldn't shake, over what she must do.

After walking around for a bit and seeing no one that matched her target's face, she decided she and Zeus would need to disappear and return when it was dark. A round-bellied dock worker who had seen too many cans of his favorite beer met her eyes, his gaze flicking to her jacket and her dog's vest as if questioning whether she was warm enough for Kodiak's biting cold. Weather had dried and damaged his skin—creased in deep lines, dotted with sunspots, colored like tan leather. He had that pleasant way about him that she didn't often see in Los Angeles. It reminded her again of the humble people of Brazil she'd grown to love and now missed.

"In a town of 5,500, I know all the faces around here, and you two ain't locals," he said, thrusting out his hand and grabbing hers for a sturdy shake. Like his face, hard work had developed thick calluses on both hands. "Rory Calloway, at your service. If you're looking for a fishing boat tour—fixing to be one, our sunset tour takes off in thirty minutes. If your dog's trained, we let them on."

"Nice to meet you, Rory. Name's Von, and this is my companion—Zeus," she said directly, not bothering with an alias when hiding her identity was no longer her concern. Cain hadn't given her instructions otherwise, and she didn't feel the need to lie to the man. "Looking for a place to keep warm while having myself a little tour of the town. Any suggestions?"

"Great coffee with nice heaters at the Kodiak Cup. Little shop painted brown. Got a big ol' fish on the signage. Can't miss it, just head up on Marine Way, pass the ferry terminal—it ain't a long walk. Once you hit Center Avenue, take a right, and you'll see it tucked right before the stoplight. Best coffee in town, hands down. Tell Edith behind the counter that Rory sent you, and she'll throw in an extra shot on the house."

Von thanked Rory Calloway before nodding to Zeus. "*Los geht's*," she directed, and he jumped to his feet to go.

———

The sun had begun its slow descent, slipping lower against the horizon, staining the sky with dusky lavender and amber streaks. The docks had taken on an almost golden hue, the last ray glinting off the trawlers and crab boats still moored for the evening. The dockside life continued its low murmur, but the frenetic morning had settled into a quiet lull as the approaching night gradually swept over the town.

She followed Marine Way, the virulent wind off Chiniak Bay stinging her face. The town held that small but lived-in feeling; the streets clean yet worn by the kind of everyday foot traffic only locals truly recognized. She passed by the ferry terminal, its lot mostly empty except for a couple of rust-flecked trucks that were waiting for the next departure, their bodies corroded by salt spread by the snowplows clearing the streets. Once she reached Center Avenue, she took a right, as Rory had said. Nestled between a small bait shop and a general store, the coffee shop came into view.

Kodiak Cup looked exactly as he'd described—small, brown, its wooden-paneled exterior blending with Kodiak's rustic charm. A battered sign hung above the entrance; the painting of a fish slightly faded from years of sea spray and wind. She stepped inside, a small bell jingling overhead. The warmth hit her instantly, the scent of fresh-ground beans and baked goods cutting through the briny cold—taking her back to Rio de Janeiro, to when she had her life back. The creaky wooden floor and mismatched chairs added to the coffee shop's cozy charm. The shelves were lined with handmade mugs, local honey, and bags of fresh-roasted coffee labeled "Kodiak's Best." A blackboard behind the counter listed the menu in loopy white chalk, with offerings like Fisherman's Fuel (extra strong brew), Salty Caramel Mocha, and The Trawler's Chai.

A woman with short, graying hair and a faded "Alaska Strong" sweatshirt eyed her from behind the counter. "You ain't dressed for this weather, Hon." She added grounds to the coffee filter and started a fresh batch. "Something warm?"

"Definitely." Von's teeth chattered as she hugged her chilly body, mostly covered by the all-weather tactical jacket. Edith was right—she'd either have to start layering or demand that the commander give her a proper snow jacket. "Rory Calloway said you'd throw in an extra shot?"

Edith's laugh was dry but good-natured. "That old bastard just loves spending my espresso shots." She nodded toward Zeus. "Dog's welcome inside—long as he behaves. You stayin' long?"

"Depends." Von eyed the darkening sky through the hazy window. "Might be a long night if I can't find who I'm looking for."

"How you like your poison? Don't look like the complicated type. My guess? Black with that shot of espresso on the house."

Von's brows arched in surprise. "Well, you definitely know your caffeine addicts."

"Guess'n dark roast?"

"Shit, you're good."

Edith smiled, showing yellowing coffee-stained teeth. In seconds, Von's black with a shot was plopped right in front of her in a large to-go.

"I got mighty respect for people who pay attention to

detail," Von complimented. "Thanks for the exceptional service."

"Who you lookin' for? Might be able to help. Really—except for the occasional Mormon, looney tune Latter-Days who come up in here for my pastries but avoid my daily brew like one sip'll send them straight to hell—just about everyone comes by weekly for their coffee fix."

Von considered whether she should go around mentioning her target's name or take things a little slower, find Eli when she found him. Keep her mouth shut. "Just one of the dockworkers, no one important."

"Seems important enough," she said, wagging a finger. "Got that worry all over your face. Each and every one of 'em stops by daily. Most bring their own mugs. Like to top off two, three times a day—they work long hours, always pulling overtime."

"Appreciate the tip. That's a lot of loyal customers you've got."

"Sit here long enough, and you'll find who you're looking for."

Von nodded her gratitude and followed Edith's suggestion, taking a seat next to a window, the unforgiving chill fogging the glass. It didn't take long before dockworkers began to cycle through the quaint coffee house. She glanced down at her no-nonsense, end-to-end encrypted Silent Circle phone, wishing she could find a way to connect with Jefferson. But she knew that—while her hacker buddy had eluded the LAPD and Feds—Black Nova wasn't one to be hacked or fucked with, her gut warned her. Jefferson could find anyone in a fraction of the time it took most seasoned investigators, which had been her secret weapon.

Now, she'd have to rely on her own gut instincts and skills.

She couldn't risk getting Jefferson involved—not this time.

An hour had passed. Von stayed alert, muscles tight. So did

Edith, eyes cutting her way, tracking locals as they came and went. As if she were trying to guess Von's mark. Dockworkers drifted through the café in waves, steel-toed boots clunking across the worn deck, the air thick with diesel and dark roast. Von sat tucked in the corner, the thin windowpane leaching cold from the outside air, settling into her skin. Her posture stayed loose, but her eyes were never still.

She'd drained the first cup. The refill had gone cold.

Von nursed it anyway—black, bold with espresso.

No cream. Nothing to soften the edge.

Edith sat behind the coffee bar, working a crossword puzzle. But to Von, it felt staged—something to keep her hands busy while her nosy eyes did the real work. The door jingled open again. Von didn't move her head, but her gaze tracked the silhouette. Still not him. Time had blurred—two hours gone. Zeus had been sitting as patient as ever. She owed him a walk.

Von braced herself, zipping up her tactical jacket, steeling herself for the cold.

Outside, the frosty air stung her face. The dim remaining light of day melted away into the inky night. The stars sprinkled the horizon like brilliant diamonds, brighter than anything she'd ever seen. It was almost hypnotizing, pulling her in, giving her a moment of peace—a moment where she almost forgot the gravity of her purpose, the assignment she had to pass. Zeus padded ahead, pausing to relieve himself on a nearby tree. But it was the low, guttural snarl that snapped Von out of a magical trance only nature could inflict.

A microsecond where she was almost human. Not a killer. Not an assassin.

The first thing she noticed was the stench—aged boots soaked in dock rot. Fish guts, diesel, seaweed, and salty sweat baked into cracked leather. Long hours. Soaked socks. Skin flaked from too much sun and too little rest. "Elias 'Eli' Vega, meaner in person than the pixelated mug on her phone, stomped past without a glance—except one. A tense glare aimed at Zeus, like Eli was no longer a dock worker but a prize-fighting pit bull ready to throw down. Zeus's snarl crescendoed—low to high, sharp with memory—lips curling back to expose teeth that had tasted blood and never forgot.

Von didn't flinch. Just watched, mentally cataloging her target as he shouldered the door to Kodiak Cup before vanishing inside. She gave it a beat. Then followed. Edith immediately caught her attention with a knowing look, eyebrows raised, lips pursed, eyes flickering toward Vega without needing to say a word. The shop owner knew. Somehow, she just knew. Maybe that was how this town worked. Small. Wired. Watching. If Von's instincts were right, one question circled in her mind like a bad infomercial at 3 a.m.—loud, relentless, and impossible to tune out. In a small town like Kodiak, people talked, and she wondered how many here knew all about Jaxon Ryker. And more importantly: How many wanted to stay the hell out of his way? Whatever contraband he was running from those docks—illegal drugs and guns or worse—it had people keeping quiet.

But Von wasn't here to stay quiet.

"Eli, how's fishin'?" Edith snatched his stainless-steel tumbler he'd plunked down on the counter and began filling it with his chosen coffee cocktail—all by memory.

"Boat's leaking. Patched her up, killing my back in the process, though. That marine epoxy gotta do for now. But the halibut don't care, and they can't catch themselves," he said, voice a scratchy baritone. His eyes slid sideways, briefly glancing at Von. "Got new customers, eh? Looks like business is doing good."

"We get all kinds traveling, passin' through." Edith handed him back his tumbler, topped off with fresh coffee. "Reckon that back's still giving you hell. Go see that bone-cracker I told you 'bout."

From where Von sat, she could see Edith's hands. The coffee shop owner gave Eli a smile that didn't quite reach her eyes as her fingers felt behind the coffee bar—searching, finding, steady. A rifle. Moved into place by practiced hands. Von had assumed her identity was private, known only to Black Nova, the LAPD, and the FBI. But as Edith gripped the rifle hidden beneath the counter, Von's heart began to pound against her rib cage.

Reality set in.

You couldn't hide in Kodiak, Alaska. Not from the locals.

Eli sauntered toward her, each boot step announcing itself with hard thuds.

"Didn't think Kodiak Cup was on any federal radar." He took a sip and met Von's eyes, closing the distance between them, hovering above her, stepping too close.

Too close to Zeus.

The dog erupted—snarling, barking, saliva flying, teeth bared and ready to lunge.

"Better back the fuck up," Von warned, "or he'll have you for dinner."

Before she could draw her SIG Sauer P320, Eli popped the lid off his insulated travel mug and threw hot coffee all over Zeus, who yelped from the heat but charged forward anyway, sinking his teeth into Eli's ankle.

Von sprang to her feet, throwing a right hook to Eli's jaw.

"Bitch!" He swung back—fist cracking into her temple. "I know who you work for."

Blinding pain shot through her. Lights danced. The world winked in and out of focus.

Von braced herself against the coffee table, never having been hit so hard. For a second, she thought she might pass out.

Von didn't see her coming. Neither did Eli.

WHACK! Edith slammed the butt of the rifle into the back of her target's head, sending him stumbling back, dazed but not down. Blood streamed, matting his hair, running down his neck. She might've looked like someone's grandmother, but damn—Edith had the strength to crack a man's skull.

The coffee shop owner pressed the barrel against his cheek.

"How dare you spill my coffee," Edith said, cool and collected. "You think I keep a shotgun under my coffee bar for the bears?"

"You just made a big fucking mistake—both of you!"

"There's no walking outta here. You got until the count of three. If you don't run the hell up outta here, you're getting a bullet in your ass—*and I really mean your ass*. Right in that big ol' butt-hole of yours. One-one-thousand." Edith racked the rifle, finger on the trigger, barrel pointed right between Eli Vega's cheeks. "Two-one-thousand—"

Eli sprinted out of the coffee shop, trailing blood from the open gash in his scalp. A loud gunshot cracked through the night, slicing past him through the open door—just a hair shy of exploding the back of his head.

Edith lowered her rifle, set the stock on the ground, and leaned on it like a cane.

"If that's who you're lookin' for, he's dangerous. Loaded up with enough weapons to blow the whole dock to smithereens," she warned. "Got himself a boat by the north slip. You better move."

"Didn't mean to drag you into this, Edith. Appreciate your...help."

"If you're up to what I think you're up to," Edith began, tone clipped, "best make damn sure he don't walk back in here again. Let him savor his last catch—'cause if you don't reel him in, I will."

"Don't worry, ma'am," Von said, clicking her tongue at Zeus, who jumped to his feet. "We won't miss."

They stepped out into the night.

The cold kissed her skin like a blade, slicing every thought from fear—numbing everything but the kill.

This wasn't a test.

It was just the beginning.

THREE
THE LAST CATCH

FOG ROLLED IN THICK—HAZY against the horizon, folding into the snow like a frozen tundra. Yet, Zeus had managed to track Eli Vega's scent from the moment they left Kodiak Cup. Pale tendrils drifted low against the docks, swallowing shadows and softening sound. But her canine partner moved with purpose, alert ears shooting up to the sky, nose following a bloody trail, crimson breadcrumbs blotting the thick white cushions of fresh powder beneath their feet.

Von followed, boots crunching in the thick snow, lightly padding up the planks of the dock to keep quiet, each footstep keeping time with her pulsing heart. Eli Vega left a trail of hurt. That much was certain from the open wound in the back of his skull, leaving behind a path that led to his boat. Even with a limp, his pace was quick. Desperate. All they gave her was a name and a picture. No briefing. No context. Just a test dressed up like a mission. A kill-or-fail scenario. She'd memorized his face until it was no longer human.

No longer a man—but an order.

She didn't expect Edith's actions.

The old woman moved behind the bar like she expected this

sort of thing to go down, clued in on the secrets that lurked in the underbelly of Kodiak's criminal world. Not everything Ryker touched was hidden. Not everything Black Nova did was buried. Her first target, a part of some twisted test she was supposed to pass. Secrets cracked like thin ice. One look at her, one too-long glance at her dog, and Eli Vega's eyes blackened.

He didn't need a warning, didn't need a name.

The way prey felt an instinctual alert of danger.

The way wires hummed right before they snapped.

Somewhere ahead, a boat's engine coughed up to life—her mark knew there was a hit on his head, knew that she had already found him. Von dashed through the snow, six inches that weighed each step like trying to run in sand. Zeus used his powerful legs to leap across the frosty terrain, hopping instead of trying to pound through. Her head snapped up just as the boat jerked from its mooring. She didn't think. She ran, picking up pace. Thighs burning. Breath sharp in her lungs.

"*Springe auf das Boot!*" she ordered Zeus. He sprinted faster, picking up speed. He leapt onto the boat as instructed, just as it began to pull away. Von followed close behind, launched off the edge, and vaulted over the side rail, landing hard on the deck. The boat groaned beneath her as it motored from the dock.

She landed on her back—hard, the gun tucked there bit into her. Pain rippled up her spine, blooming in her neck, forcing her to clench her jaw. A breath punched out of her lungs as though her diaphragm had been kicked with the force of a one-hundred-pound medicine ball. An odd lull of silence settled over the night. The ocean slapping against the boat, slow and indifferent, like the sea didn't care who lived or died on the surface. Just above, the sky stretched black and empty, stars cloaked by the fog. Salt and diesel fumes wafted through the air, clinging to her nose. The engine's thrum vibrated beneath her.

She gripped the edge of the boat, pulse pounding louder than anything in her ears and struggled back onto her feet.

Von locked eyes with Zeus and gave a quick swirl with her finger, a wordless directive for him to search for their mark. She put a finger to her lips—*shhh, do it quietly.* The 32-foot Alaskan-style fishing vessel sported an open stern for gear and traps. An enclosed place for the wheelhouse near the helm was sealed behind a closed door, where the navigation and controls were located. From where she stood, she noticed that this compact and rugged fishing boat, built for tumultuous weather, had a narrow galley below deck. It had to be where Eli was hiding, though the Alaskan fishing vessel appeared abandoned as she slowly padded toward the helm. Doubt crept in as the quiet consumed every tense second. Had they gone on the wrong boat? Von drew in quick, shallow breaths as a steady hand reached for the cold steel of the semi-automatic pistol resting in the holster tucked against her back.

Zeus reached the closed door that led to the wheelhouse, sniffing intensifying. He'd found their mark. As he scratched at the door, it flew open, smacking her dog across his cheek, forcing him to stumble back. Out of nowhere, Eli exploded from the navigation area—rage in his eyes, a blade in one hand, and a steel-toed boot swinging with lethal aim. The kick connected hard against Zeus's ribcage with a sickening *crack.* The dog yelped, body twisting in midair from the blow, then hit the deck. Though he quickly recovered, back on all fours like a spring uncoiling, growling low, eyes locked as anger fueled Zeus's will. He charged forward, jaws clamping onto Eli's calf with bone-crushing force. Blood spilled instantly—hot, fast. She watched it flood his mouth. Zeus held on, jaws squeezing tight.

Eli screamed and staggered, dragging the dog with him.

Von whipped out her gun and tried a shot in his direction, but Eli ducked, whipping out his knife. He swung at Zeus, and the dog lost his grip on the man's leg. Zeus stumbled back, struggling from the pain to his side. Von knew his ribs were likely fractured. Eli was already on the move. He came at her fast—no time to recover. A fist crashed into her jaw, sending her stumbling sideways, ribs slamming into the rail. Metal bit her back. Pain flared. The boat rocked harder now, the waves lapping against the hull.

He staggered but didn't fall, gritting his teeth. "You can tell Black Nova they ain't taking me down," he said, and ran toward her. Zeus struggled to his feet and powered after him, but missed his ankle by an inch, the boat rocking causing him to lose balance and slide back.

"Wrong move, asshole," she muttered, wiping blood from her mouth, eyes narrowing.

She aimed for another shot, but he was already there. Eli had closed the gap fast, swinging his knife with deadly precision. It sliced across her jaw. The pain hit like a warning flare—brief, hot, ignorable. The boat rocked with sudden turbulence as a massive wave slammed into its side. Eli careened forward, the knife nearly driving into her gut. Von dodged, knocking the knife away. The unsteady dance of the boat wrenched the gun clean out of her hand, sending it skidding across the floor.

The sound of another boat close by announced itself, and before Von had time to decipher her surroundings, loud footsteps thundered across the deck. They weren't alone. Could it be one of Eli's henchmen? A tall man stood across the way, dressed in black cargo pants and a snow jacket, still as stone. He raised his weapon and fired a shot that missed Eli's head by an inch. The bullet snapped past. His hands flew over his head as he braced himself.

The man didn't speak.

He looked like former military. Broad-shouldered. Arms like tree trunks. A chest built from shouldering war. His face was all harsh angles and quiet threat, handsome in a way that didn't feel safe. His hair was dark, his eyes the color of amber whiskey—hard to read, harder to ignore. Zeus scrambled upright, still dazed—but when the stranger stepped closer, the dog didn't bark. Didn't growl. He sniffed the man's boots, then his outstretched hand.

He passed the test.

Von didn't need to ask.

Black Nova.

With one fluid motion, he kicked something across the deck—her gun. It slid toward her, cold metal scraping against the floor.

Von snatched it up. Rolled. Fired.

Eli jerked, blood soaking through his shirt. His body rocked stubbornly on his feet before collapsing in a heap on the ground.

The operative crept closer, each step a heavy thud against the deck.

"You nearly got yourself killed," he said, voice a deep baritone.

She didn't look at him. "I didn't need you."

He walked up and stopped a few feet away. "That's the problem."

She finally met his mysterious eyes. "Name?"

He didn't answer right away, just watched her like he was still deciding if she'd earned the truth. Then: "Xander Holt."

"Black Nova?"

He gave her a small nod. "And you just passed—*barely*," he said, handing her a towel. "He got your face. It looks superficial. Don't think you'll need stitches."

"I was supposed to do this solo," she said, clenching her teeth.

Von kept the towel pressed against her jaw until the bleeding stilled, the frigid cold narrowing the blood vessels, dulling pain, coaxing the cut to close. Xander strode to the helm of the boat and began steering it back toward the docks. She followed after him.

"The real test was never to do the mission solo," he said.

She narrowed her eyes. "Then what was it?"

"Seeing how you'd react when the mission didn't go as planned. When someone showed up unannounced. Whether you'd fall apart—or adapt. Whether you'd be able to work with someone you didn't trust—even if all I did was slide your gun back," he said, pausing to pet Zeus on the head. Her dog, who rarely let strangers near, allowed it. Calm and unmoving. "And whether you'd still finish the job."

Blood pooled from Eli Vega's extinguished body, spreading across the dock, creeping toward her boots like death's fingers from beyond the grave. Von knelt down and inspected her first assignment with clinical precision, strangely aware that Vega had become just that in her mind—a target. A human mark, though the humanity within her, the conscience that should've left her with some sort of remorse, never paid a visit.

That's what bothered her the most. It wasn't so much the kill as it was the ease of it.

When had she become so cold, so robotic? A shell of her former self—the kind, animal-loving veterinarian who donated to charities, who became a vegan out of her passion for the lives of all living things. One fateful night—the attack that nearly killed her—had transformed her. The raw, endless emotional pain, the trauma of it, refused to let her forgive. Refused to let her heal. Instead, every single kill on her terms had meant something.

Given something back to her—something she lost: control.

But now, she was no longer calling the shots, no longer able to walk away. No return to normalcy. No chance to leave the dead buried, the spirits that once tormented her, terminated from this earth along with her righteous sins. In the absence of conscience, what had she become? Who had she turned into? Would Frau Doktor Katrine Adele Friedrich—her famous psychologist mother—consider her a psychopath or a sociopath? She could excuse it away now.

It was a job, nothing more.

She could still choose to go to jail, turn down Black Nova's deadly ultimatum. But Von could never bring herself to do that. She would rather kill—and with her first assignment behind her, the absence of any emotion to process was the hardest part. Von was stable, for now. Dead inside. A perfect case study—her mother would be proud. She told herself it was strength, being in control of her emotions. But even silence had weight. Even glass shattered under the wrong pressure. The spark she thought would flicker was gone. No flames. Just smoke curling deep in her gut, waiting to burn through.

Xander's voice cut through her thoughts. "You okay?" he asked. "The first time is always the hardest."

"It isn't my first time."

"How're you feeling?"

"That's the problem." She stared down at her mark, milky death eyes, glassy and dull. "I feel nothing."

"And that's why you were selected," he said. "But even the strongest of us—don't have an immediate reaction. It doesn't hit you right away. But it'll start building over time."

"Sounds like this is coming from experience."

"Well—yeah. Former Navy SEAL. Sniper. Multiple deployments: Iraq, Afghanistan. You know, same song and dance you've heard before." He raked a hand through his thick, dark hair. The story was indeed familiar. Von couldn't help but think of Jefferson Pierce—former Marine, also a sniper, but instead of choosing the operative path, he'd become a cyber asset for his hacking abilities. "Like magma beneath the crust.

You won't feel it just yet. Not at first. But it's coming. And when it erupts, it burns everything. How's your dog by the way?"

She touched his ribs, pressing lightly with two fingers. He flinched under her touch. "He's probably got bruised ribs, maybe a mild fracture. It'll heal on its own," she said, then pivoted back to his analogy. "So, what happens after Mount Vesuvius blows?"

"Well, like any job, you might actually start to get sick of all the kills." Xander smiled—cagey, secretive. The kind of smile that said he knew more than he was letting on.

Despite a brooding edge she couldn't quite place, he was exceptionally handsome—and unlike anyone she'd met. Von had always gone for the law-abiding good guys: Dr. Robert Chua, who co-owned their veterinary clinic in Casper, Wyoming. Then there was Dr. Damião Sequeira, the trauma surgeon who had performed her emergency hysterectomy and bilateral salp-ingo-oophorectomy after her attack. He'd fallen in love with her.

But she'd become detached. Asexual since then. Nonbinary.

After the first kill, her emotions coasted on neutral. Yet standing near Xander, breath still rising from the fight, some-thing stirred within her for the first time in years. A charge. Electric. Unwanted. Like static crawling under her skin. She shifted from foot to foot, too aware of the space—or the lack of it —between them.

Von wondered if he felt it, too.

There was already a war within her. She both respected him and hated him: for having to supervise her and for working alongside her when she preferred to operate alone.

Xander's gaze lifted, hooded beneath dark lashes. He folded his arms, the massive mounds of his chest bulging. Studying her for a beat, the former Navy SEAL chose his words carefully. Instead of answering her question, he pointed at the corpse. "Your part's done. We leave it to our cleanup crew."

"Really? Leave it? We just...*leave it*, leave it?"

"Yup." Xander walked off the boat, stepping back onto the deck.

She lingered at the stern, eyeing a couple of large, empty crates.

"Your part's done. Mine too. Gotta get my boat back, debrief the commander, and meet up with Sasha Redhawk. Haven't met her yet, but you will. She's Cain's shadow—runs the cleanup crew, but also does tactical destruction, infiltration, things like that. Cold as hell. Don't say too much unless it's to him." He glanced over his shoulder. "You okay to walk back to the cabin?"

"Pretty sure I can survive the thirty-second journey," Von said dryly. "I'm only what, fifty yards away? It's not the Yukon."

He laughed. It cracked through the SEAL exterior, and for a second, he looked unguarded, less like a weapon—and more like a man. Von tried to stifle the heat creeping up her neck, but it clawed higher. Slow. Invasive. A rogue impulse hijacked her focus, dragging her from blood and ice to something primal.

A carnal urge swept her imagination from her, leading her down a dimly lit room. Meant for lust. Shadowed walls swallowed the light. Bodies stripped bare. Skin against skin. Xander above her, a body like a Greek God, hard-muscled and honed. Large, calloused hands that knew where to touch. Hands that claimed. She imagined the weight of him, their professional discipline breaking apart under the strain of want.

"My number's listed in your contacts," he said, forcing her to blink hard. Fantasy vanishing like steam. He took out his phone, identical to hers, and wagged it in the air. "I'll be in touch."

She cleared her throat. "I'm sure you will."

Von watched Xander disappear in the fog, fists clenched at her sides—like she could beat desire into submission. But the erotic vision lingered. Vivid. Obscene in its clarity. The way he'd feel. The way he'd make her feel. How he'd handle her like he'd memorized every inch, knew exactly how to undo her, carry her to another place—breaking years of self-denial. Her body had already betrayed her. The damage was done.

Desire was dangerous.

Desire made you human.

And humans got killed.

She forced her mind to return to Eli Vega's stiff corpse rotting away next to her feet. Zeus stood at attention, whining the way he did when he wanted to know what their next plan was. They were supposed to leave, but something held her back. The lonesome night kept the docks quiet—abandoned but not empty. A few workers moved in the distance, silhouettes wraith-like, blurred by the mist-laced gloom. Von was grateful no one had been close enough to hear the silencer whisper death into the dark. Her eyes landed on the empty pine freight crate near the stern—roughly six feet long and two feet high. Built for shipping frozen fish. Or hiding a corpse.

Shipping labels sat stacked near the stern. She already knew who she'd send it to. Years of weight training had forged muscle beneath the surface, hardening her frame. Von was a hell of a lot stronger than she looked—strong enough for this. She dragged the crate across the slick deck, flipped it on its side, and pried it open. Its hollow interior yawned like a mouth waiting to be fed. Near the wheelhouse, a metal kill box sat built into the deck—standard gear for sportfishing, packed with ice kept solid by the below-zero Kodiak winter.

She scooped enough to line the bottom of the crate, packing it cold and tight like she was preparing a fresh catch for transport. Eli's body was dragged in and arranged with care. Aside from a foot of space above his head, he fit perfectly. Von added more ice to the top of his head, and before she could seal the lid shut, a staticky call came in through the radio. "Eli, this is Marchetti. You copy? They need you at Bay 4. Our shipment has arrived."

Von scanned the boat until she spotted one line from a shipping log that made her curious.

Authorized: Tony Marchetti

Von pulled out her phone and did a quick search. Marchetti's picture popped up. An article loaded beneath it.

"LAPD Detective Anthony Marchetti Terminated Amid Internal Affairs Probe."

She quickly scanned. Marchetti was accused of falsifying reports. Whispers of connections to a port-side fentanyl ring. Missing evidence. He'd gone quiet before charges could stick. And then he was just *gone*.

This haul wasn't for pescatarians—but for LAPD Homicide.

Von quickly scribbled a note intended for Detective Anaya Nazario, sealed it in a Ziplock bag to protect it from the ice, then tucked it deep beneath the body. She closed the crate, latched it shut, and filled out the shipping label—destination: the Port of Long Beach. When she was done, Von rinsed the deck clean—washed away every trace of blood and brain matter until not a single smear remained. Despite orders to leave it to the cleanup crew, she didn't trust they'd arrive in time before someone would discover the bloody mess. Sure enough, a familiar voice called out from the dock.

It was Rory Calloway—perfect timing.

"Hey Von, how's it going?" Rory said. "You helping out Eli? Anything I can do?"

"Could use your help on that forklift. Got a fresh batch filled to the brim."

"Sure thing!" Rory eagerly jumped on the forklift, and in no time, the engine sprang to life.

"Top priority," she said. "Needs to make the next outbound run."

Rory gave her a thumbs-up and slipped the forks beneath the wooden box. "Long Beach, right? That manifest's already loaded, but we've got room for one more."

"This is such a huge favor, thank you so much," she said sincerely. "I owe you one. Buy you a coffee at Kodiak Cup."

She watched as the crate rose off the deck—six feet of secrets packed in ice. Rory spun the forklift around and drove off toward the outbound stack, humming like this was just another day. It took all but ten minutes for the insulated pine freight crate to land where all of the other outbound cargo was stationed.

Rory came bouncing back, pleased with himself that he could be of service.

"Oh, and hey—can you keep this between us?" She put a hand on his shoulder. "I was supposed to man the forklift myself. Don't want anyone to think I can't do this job. Word gets out, and I could lose it, and I could use the money."

Rory made a zipping motion across his mouth. "One thing you can trust me on—I take secrets to my grave. Ain't known you long. Don't need to. Long as we're friends, I got your back."

"Well, I certainly appreciate it."

"Anytime," he said. "And I'll take you up on that coffee t'morrow. Best be headin' to bed if I'm to get up at four in the mornin.'"

She waved goodbye and waited until Rory Calloway was out of her line of sight. Just before she walked off Eli's boat, a trace of blood glistened between two deck boards. She grabbed a paper towel near the wheelhouse and thumbed it until it was clean. After wiping down the boat of her fingerprints, she whistled to Zeus. He'd been lying on his side, resting. She checked his ribs, gently pressing to see if they were broken. Thankfully, they weren't.

"*Lass uns gehen*," she told him, and he obeyed, following her off the boat.

Temperatures had plunged to below freezing, each steady breath curling into frosty plumes as they walked off into the cold.

Test passed. Yet she'd unleashed hell.

The crate was no longer her problem.

But it was about to be someone else's.

FOUR
THE ICE BOX DELIVERY

THE COLD MORNING haze clung to the harbor, the Port of Long Beach stretched wide—cranes looming like skeletal giants. Detective Anaya Nazario hugged her coat close to her, embarrassed that her spoiled SoCal ass considered fifty degrees cold. The longshoremen all looked the same: rugged, leathery skin from too many years under the unforgiving sun. Some sported flannel-lined canvas jackets, but many were in T-shirts and jeans, like their bodies had been forged by the elements, calloused by years of salt air and hard labor. Cold, heat—didn't matter. They were weatherproof, adapting to inclement conditions, built to endure whatever the port hurled at them.

But more so than the weather, it was the disorder that overwhelmed her. Containers were stacked high and scattered like child's toy blocks. Yet the dockworkers moved with practiced ease, as if they could decipher order within the chaos. Behind her, Wilmington and San Pedro buzzed to life. All around her, workers clocked in, trucks idled with diesel breath. To the west, the 1963 Vincent Thomas Bridge connected Terminal Island to San Pedro. It was the only suspension bridge in the Greater Los

Angeles area and a vital link keeping port traffic flowing like blood through a main artery.

Ocean Boulevard gate had been a nightmare—clogged with traffic all the way down to Pier D Street, where Detective Nazario and her partner, Detective Isaac Wilson, finally broke through. It was probably the reason her beau—and father of her child—Supervising Special Agent Blake Huxley, was late to arrive, having had to stay behind until their sitter showed up. But the morning rush hour didn't help. Brine and rust defined the Long Beach port, a kind of industrial charm that clung to everything. Yellow crime tape flapped in the winter breeze, cordoning off a fifty-foot perimeter in every direction. Frustrated port workers filled the air with their sailors' tongues, cursing the LAPD for shutting down the docks. A half-loaded forklift idled just outside the taped-off area, undelivered pallets still dangling from its forks. Behind the barricade, union bosses barked into the walkie-talkies, eyes cut with blame. They relayed updates while shooting death daggers at patrol officers— the poor grunts taking the bulk of the verbal abuse.

The main crate under scrutiny had been found dockside near Berth 55, tucked beside a rusted-out forklift and a busted fishnet, as if someone had hoped it would blend in with the rest of the forgotten. Nothing seemed out of the ordinary—except that it was addressed to her, which was unusual given the size. The crate stood tall and narrow, maybe as big as a large Christmas tree. The longshoremen would've ordinarily left the crate alone for the recipient to open. But the foul stench and blood oozing from its seams made that impossible. Based on her early morning briefing with Homicide Chief Trevor Johnson, it was enough to rattle a dock supervisor—who, against protocol, called in hazmat.

One of the hazmat techs peeled off his gloves, the top half of his suit rolled down to his waist—half-suited and moving with purpose. The rest of the team stayed back, talking among themselves, studying the crate like they were trying to decrypt a code.

The technician stepped toward her and Wilson, respirator clipped to his harness, gloves off, hood peeled back. "Detective Nazario, right?" he asked.

"And my partner, Detective Wilson."

"Well, the crate's labeled in your name," he told her. "Leaking blood. Didn't open it yet, but we scanned it with the VDN—"

"Viken Detection's Nighthawk HBI, you mean?" Wilson probed. "Portable X-ray thingy y'all use?"

The man looked surprised. "Correct—you're the first person that's gotten that one right. Not many do."

"Oh, I'm not that smart—trust me." Wilson laughed. "Ex-wife worked on the sales and marketing front for the VDN."

"Well, we scanned it, and that's why we called you in. The crate's a cold crate—also called an ice box or a fish tote. Insulated. Meant to hold ice-packed cod, not a corpse."

"And it's still sealed?" Nazario asked.

"Affirmative. Figured it's a crime scene now. Didn't want to contaminate anything. X-ray confirms that it's definitely a body."

They thanked the hazmat specialist and approached the crate. Latex-gloved himself, Wilson handed her a pair, and she snapped them on. The hazmat team had smartly rested the crate on its side as it was six feet tall and would be hard to reach, should someone need to crack the lid.

"You might need this," a tired dockworker said, handing her a crowbar. His skin looked like toughened hide. Even with latex gloves on, Nazario could feel the calluses on his hands.

Longshoremen didn't just operate forklifts, cranes, and towering straddle carriers—the massive mobile cargo-handling vehicles used in container terminals and ports. It was easy work, manning the machinery. However, the constant lifting of heavy freight, the hands-on container work, was what wore them down —the kind that slowly wrecked their back over time.

"Thank you," Nazario said, flipping the crowbar in her hands. Thin but incredibly weighty.

"You got it, or do you need my gorgeous biceps to pop her open?" Wilson flexed with theatrical flair—a pose that once might've been buried under layers of fast food and denial. His arms were impressively thin now, biceps barely registering a bump beneath his jacket. Post-heart attack glow-up, he liked to say. Down a hundred pounds and still milking it for laughs.

"How about I take the first swing?" she told Wilson. "You get the second pass if my arms decide to flop like noodles."

Nazario crouched beside the crate, crowbar clutched in her hand. Crimson streams oozed from the corners, staining the wood in random blotchy patches. The odor of decomp was faint, but present. A mélange of sulfur, ammonia, and that unforgettable sickly-sweet tang that promised human rot wafted into her nostrils, down her throat. She jammed the crowbar with a grunt, wedging it between the seam just under the closure, then cranked the handle down, forcing the lid to groan before it cracked. She gritted her teeth and forced it again.

A violent—*SNAP!*—split the air, and the lid broke loose.

Cold air hissed out, dense and unnatural—open just enough for her to peek inside.

Thick. Rotten. Like meat gone soft in the humid heat—but dulled by the cold, as if the ice was holding the worst of it back. Inside, the body lay flat. Arms at the sides. Eyes wide open, frost crusting the lashes. The skin had gone waxy and pale, pulled tight over sharp bone. A man. Mid-thirties maybe. Face frozen in a look that wasn't quite fear. Wasn't quite peace.

"Help me get this bitch open all the way," Nazario asked Wilson. They pried the top of the crate loose with the crowbar.

Humidity from the damp cold had softened the wood—moisture and decay had made it peel open like a coffin lid. They carefully set the wooden plank aside, so that they could closely examine the body without molesting the crime scene.

Blood covered his shirt, damp and semi-frozen from melted ice. Nazario carefully fingered the hole blown open in the center of his chest. A typical bullet entry wound was small—around 0.25 to 0.5 inches in diameter, depending on the caliber. But the shirt told a different story. The fabric was torn wide, maybe three inches across, blackened at the edges where the muzzle flash had kissed it. Threads curled back like burnt paper, framing the hole in a ragged halo.

The man looked Hispanic—his once olive skin now sallow with a bluish-gray hue. Nazario frowned, analyzing his features. He looked familiar, but she couldn't seem to place him. His name lost somewhere in her head.

"A good shot right to the heart," Wilson said.

"Hold up. Think I know this face."

"Was just thinking the same damn thing. Funny, he reminds me a lot of this DEA agent. Ran into him in South America on vacay. Since I'm a digital hoarder, I know I got it on the cloud somewhere." Wilson swiped through the photos on his phone. "Lemme see, let's go by the year...yeah, here it is."

Wilson showed her the picture. The man had a thin smile that didn't quite reach his hard eyes. Something shadowy beneath them, like his poker face, was hiding something insidious. He looked younger, more vibrant, more alive than dead.

"Shit. That's him. When did you say this was taken?"

"About five years ago. Met him at Cartagena, he was at some beach bar with a handful of other feds. Invited me to do touristy stuff. Hung out with him and his DEA crew for a day. Took this pic at that old Spanish fort—Castillo San Felipe."

Her mind began going through old case files like a Rolodex on fire. Then it hit her—"Elias Vega. That's him. Went by Eli."

"Yes—that's his name!" Wilson exclaimed. "Wasn't it stamped on all those files? The ones we worked on at them drug houses?"

"Yeah, that's how I remember him now. All those execution-style hits in East L.A. Ended up tied to cartel cross-border homicides between San Diego and TJ." Nazario spotted the Scientific Investigation Division's Chuck Whittier and Ellen Yang approaching from a distance. She waved at them. Though her mind was still distracted by the excitement of being able to identify the body.

"This old detective brain remembers now." Wilson tapped his temple. "His reports would always pop up all the time before he was sent to South America. Recall what the Feds used to call him?"

Nazario and Wilson spoke at once: "The ghost agent."

"Had a reputation for vanishing just before a bust went sideways," Nazario said.

SID's Whittier and Yang joined them. They were each dressed in navy tactical pants with cargo pockets for tools, Nitrile gloves, and windbreakers with the Scientific Investigation Division logo stamped on the back.

"Who had a reputation for vanishing?" Whittier asked.

"The dead guy," Wilson said with a laugh. "Can't vanish anymore."

"What're we looking at?" Yang nodded at the hazmat team. "Surprised to see hazmat out here on the Port of Long Beach."

"Cold crate. Looked suspicious. Kind that ordinarily hauls in frozen fish. Leaking blood. Had that funny smell you can't get out of your nose. Suspected it was a DB, but confirmed it using the VDN," Nazario said.

"Portable X-ray popped up a body instead of the catch of the day, eh?" Whittier added.

"Yup—from Alaska. No return address, just a fishery label—Kodiak Cannery, dated last week."

Whittier took out his Canon 5D, Mark IV and began taking pictures. "Good job with taking the top off the crate," he said, behind the lens.

Yang got to work immediately. She pulled out toothpicks and small plastic containers, swiping them beneath the fingernails. Prime spot for DNA—if Eli had managed to fight back.

"Have an ID," Yang asked over her shoulder, "or are we waiting to fingerprint him?"

"Elias 'Eli' Vega—former DEA." Nazario dropped into a squat, gaze level with the body. Then something caught her eye. It looked like a Ziplock bag. It was wedged just under the right arm, the corner of the plastic poking out, flapping in the ocean breeze.

"Wait...what is that?" Nazario pulled it gently, and it came free from behind the man's arm. It appeared to be a note.

"Good thing you've got gloves on. We'll need to dust it for prints," Whittier mumbled, snapping a picture of it.

"What's it say?" Wilson peeked over Nazario's shoulder.

They read the note together.

Nazario,

Don't trust anyone with a badge. He wore one too.

I'm sure you know who he is—former DEA. Dirty. Dead now.

There's another one in Kodiak, under Ryker's thumb. Former disgraced detective. Still breathing. Still hiding behind the law, he claims he's supposed to serve.

You'll know him when you find him. You always do.

—V

Nazario took out her iPhone and took a picture of the note for her own records.

Wilson whistled. "That your Serpent Woman, innit? What's her name—lost track of all her aliases. Damn heart attack put me on medical leave. Missed a real good one."

Huxley's voice boomed from behind them. "Dr. Wilder Agatha Friedrich by birth. Changed it legally to Von Schlange—'Schlange' is German for Serpent," he said. "Got a mean keloid running up her abdomen. Looks just like one, too."

Nazario lifted her head and kissed Huxley—brief, but intentional.

"Fucked her up—that near-fatal attack," Nazario finished Huxley's sentence. It had been the two of them, after all, who'd worked that case together. "Left her without a child. Unable to have kids. Scarred her—physically and mentally."

"Sure did. Went full femme fatale rage-mode after that," Huxley added.

"Don't mess with a woman you can't kill. She'll come back and *kill you*." Wilson chuckled, though it faded once he realized he was the only one laughing. "Sorry. Bad joke."

Huxley, with a gloved hand, reached for the note. "May I?"

"You may." Nazario handed it to him.

"Same handwriting. Can't forget it. Her signature—*Die Schlangenfrau*," Huxley said with ease. Being multilingual came easy. "Was on the folders of all the men she'd killed. Spacing's tight, snappy strokes, letters cut deep into the page—like she wanted the paper to bleed."

Huxley returned the note to Nazario. She sealed it back into the Ziplock bag and released it over to Ellen Yang. He drew closer to the crate and cursed under his breath, planting his hands on his hips.

"That's Eli fucking Vega. I was on an FBI-led task force that included a few DEA agents, and Vega was one of them."

"We were on a few drug busts that ended in homicides in East L.A. His reports always popped up. Seemed like he was damn good at his job until he flipped to the other side," Nazario said.

"Alright, real talk for a sec—how's this Serpent lady passin' notes like it's high school if she's workin' with some Black Nova shadow ops Avenger team?" Wilson said.

As hard as Nazario and Huxley tried not to smile, their faces cracked their hard surface, a grin spreading across their lips as they exchanged a glance. Wilson had that effect.

"Maybe they don't know," Nazario said.

"Was thinking the same thing," Huxley said. "This could've been a hit she was required to do, and she went rogue."

"So, what I'm hearin' is—Serpent chick trusts us enough to send us a message all the way from Kodiak—middle-of-nowhere Alaska," Wilson said, "when it could actually get her in a heap of trouble?"

Nazario and Huxley nodded in unison—some weird parenting telepathy that had started after their daughter was born. She blamed it on their surprisingly blissful relationship. Funny how living together with a baby, unmarried, no labels, turned out to be nothing like the smothering disaster her commitment-phobic ex-self had imagined.

"Risking her life—that's her MO," Nazario said. "Lives for it. No risk. No reward."

"Yeah, Von doesn't give a shit about rules. If there's a rule—she'll break it. And it is a good sign that she sent the little note," Huxley said.

"Well, shoot—forget the damn note. If her whole criminal profile's anti-authority, whether it's the law or this nut job secret Black Nova squad, who's to say she didn't just ship the body like it was a crate of fish? No permission needed, and sure as hell without their knowledge?"

A pensive beat dropped into silence, as Wilson's words chewed into her reasoning, tasked with the tedious job of trying to assemble this murder, akin to putting together Lego pieces. A kit of a castle. Disney-themed princess designs. The picture on the box looks easy, until you find yourself sitting in front of a pile of little parts, all needing exact placement. Then, after all the hard work, it gets taken apart. Legos go missing. Pieces scatter everywhere.

It was the one toy she absolutely hated as a child—and despised even more as an adult.

Too many pieces. Too much of a puzzle.

This case was like a Lego set missing the damn instructions—and they were the idiots told to build it anyway.

They stood near the crate, watching SID work. Cold curled off the corpse in slow ghostly breaths. The Long Beach port was teeming with crime scene professionals, a medley of busy longshoremen, and curious dockworkers pausing their labor to observe the scene. The coroner's van rolled in, adding to the crush, jamming the scene tighter. All the while, Nazario couldn't shake a single, brutal reality.

The body wasn't the worst part of it.

It was the message.

FIVE

THE FIRST ASSIGNMENT

THE ARCHAIC BRICK FIREPLACE, aged from years of neglect, had done a mediocre job of keeping the frigid cabin warm. By the early morning, Von awoke to her own breath, plumes of gray vapors escaping with each exhale, only validated by the drafty cold that settled bone deep. Ash was all that remained in the hearth, like a cremated body, brittle and weightless, ground into the cracks of old stone.

A tawny, thick fleece blanket had kept Zeus and her warm enough throughout the night, but not enough to thaw the chill that settled under her skin. She found a long-sleeved top and matching thermal leggings in the drawer that she had erred in skipping yesterday. Today, she wouldn't make the same mistake. After putting them on, she threw on jeans and a sweater, already feeling warmer. Von tossed more wood on the grate, lit a few newspapers piled next to the fireplace, and tossed them in. The wood immediately caught on fire, and an orange blaze erupted, defrosting her frozen fingers.

She attended to Zeus next, running her hands along his rib cage and softly pressing gently to test for tenderness. He didn't yelp this time, which was a good sign. When he rose, his legs seemed steadier than yesterday. He no longer struggled to stand, and the limp had all but disappeared. She put his canine snow jacket over him—a heavy-duty cover that protected his legs, chest, and back.

Von had the sudden urge to glance around the cabin for the second time since she'd arrived, and something caught her eye. It looked like a closet tucked away into the far corner of the living room, half-hidden behind a thick support beam. It was no wonder she hadn't seen it yesterday. The whole cabin was a patchwork of uneven angles and bad lighting, exaggerating the shadows that masked anything not directly in sight.

She opened it—and felt like an idiot. Inside hung a black, two-piece snowsuit she'd missed. Still, with the thermal top and leggings already under her clothes, she skipped the snow pants and shrugged into the snow jacket instead. At the bottom, there were snow booties for Zeus. She was glad she found them, as they'd protect her dog from the weather and tugged them on him.

Zeus trotted to the front door and began sniffing at the bottom. He scratched at the door and then sniffed again.

Von frowned. *"Was ist los?"* she wondered, asking Zeus what was wrong. He barked once, and just before a knock could land, Von swung the door wide. Her dog's senses and instincts were rarely wrong. Sure enough, the former Navy SEAL's tall frame stood before her. Early morning light kissed his jaw, sharpening the angles of his face. His skin, rich and bronzed, made his eyes seem lighter than before—a creamy caramel hue that softened the hardened seriousness behind them. His hair was lush and full, long bangs swept carelessly to one side, ending at a cleft chin that added an edge of rough charm.

Xander Holt was even more handsome than she'd remembered—too damn perfect for a man so dangerous. Caught momentarily off guard, Von scolded herself for growing soft. In her new line of work, she couldn't afford to get vulnerable. She didn't know what was worse: being dropped in a frozen rural ice chest with orders to execute fellow humans or standing this close to one whose presence was distractingly carnal.

It took her a minute to notice the two coffees he carried from Kodiak Cup. He held one out to her. "Red eye—black with a shot. Edith said it's the way you take it. Mine's a dead eye—black with three. Strong enough to make the lightweights twitchy."

"Guess you're no lightweight, then." Von took the coffee from his hand, fingers brushing against his—too brief, the fleeting touch burned like the fire that warmed the cabin.

He gave her a lopsided grin, one that transformed his face, civilized his features.

"Nothing gets my heart going," he said, low and bold, "except for a beautiful woman."

Heat coiled, rising through her body, flooding her cheeks with blood and blush.

"Well, then, won't have anything to worry about. Since we'll be working together," Von said, "looks like your pulse will stay nice and steady."

He sipped his coffee, his gaze locking with her steely gray eyes. Silence closed in around them, thick and heavy, until even time seemed to hold its breath.

"Oh...I don't know about that."

Is he flirting with me?

Stupid thought. Dangerous thought. She crushed it the moment it was formed.

After the attack, she'd ended a seven-year relationship, returned a two-carat ring, and, despite Bobby's pleading, never thought twice about severing ties. Von had never mixed business with pleasure, not when Damião wanted more than a business partnership. She would ordinarily shoot someone like Xander

Holt down with a curt rejection. Being direct—*a bitch*—always came easy. Her body would follow. The thought of being intimate with anyone never crossed her mind. Not during the years when her soul and every cell in her body wanted only one thing: revenge. She once had good men. The safe ones. The kind you proudly introduced to friends, to family—back when you still thought you deserved that sort of life.

This mysterious former sniper was as lethal as she was, maybe even more dangerous. She'd never met anyone like him—someone who had both a magnetic draw and a directness that matched her own. For the first time, she found herself unable to respond with snark. It had been so long since she'd even contemplated gifting herself any sort of sexual pleasure. Her mind never roamed to what could happen between the sheets, when the lights were dim, and it was just two people surrendering to their own desires.

"Pretty doesn't survive long in my world. A killer's ugly. No amount of flattery can change what I am," she said, but the force behind her voice bled out, the words slipping low, almost under her breath. "So, what happens now that I'm done with Eli?"

He tilted his head at her thoughtfully. Said nothing for thirty long seconds, which dragged like minutes. No words— just studied her with a slice of intrigue—a type of understanding that only one killer could offer another.

He finally broke his silence, words that sounded like he'd carried them for years.

"Every crime tells a story. But not every killer is the villain. What's ugly is letting real evil live without consequences." He paused, sipping his coffee. "And what happens now? You get your next orders."

"So, you here to collect me?"

He nodded once. "Your presence is required."

"Do I have a choice?"

"Negative," he said, then giving her a clipped nod toward the intended path before turning around and stalking north.

Without needing a command, Zeus trotted ahead, glued to Xander's side. Von closed the cabin door, coffee in hand, and fell in step, following them down a snowy path carved out by snowmobiles and the heavy boots of Alaskan locals. Xander kept a measured pace, never glancing back. Their earlier casual flirtation was left to freeze behind them, silence only broken by the crunch of boots breaking through six inches of fresh powder. The dock loomed ahead, salty essence of the ocean off the Gulf of Alaska grew stronger with every measured step.

Brine, fish offal, and kelp stung her nose, synthesizing with the clatter of dock workers and fishermen from the riggings at the harbor—each note adding to nature's ambiance laced with frigid beauty. Jagged, snow-capped peaks loomed in every direction, encompassing them like ancient sentinels carved from ice and stone. The longer they trod, the further the path entered the maw of the forest—the thick coastal woods populated by a family of Sitka Spruce towering nearly 200 feet tall. The trees loomed like beasts, their scaly, grayish bark and blue-green, one-inch needles forming a dense canopy overhead.

The scent of pine wafted into her nose, cleansing her lungs with each breath. Alders—other relatives—rose up to eighty feet tall, their oval green leaves curling in thick clusters, emitting a sweet, woody aroma. The western hemlock stood apart, its reddish-brown coloring screaming against the white tundra, branches draped in moss and lichen, like shoulders hunched under the weight of weather.

They continued farther down the gullet of pines and timber, winding up the path until at last they arrived at a 1,200-square-foot countrified bait and tackle shop, its corroded metal sign barely legible: "Gull's Bait & Tackle—Since 1954."

Von didn't know what to expect—but it surely wasn't a fisherman's go-to.

The moment they walked in, she was hit with the briny smell of fresh bait and the acrid bite of burnt coffee. A large saltwater aquarium near the entrance teemed with schools of minnows. A hand-painted sign above it listed all other available baits: herring, salmon roe, shrimp, squid, octopus tentacles, sand lance, clams, mussels, and—last but not least—chum. The walls were lined with professional-grade fishing rods, not the cheap kind made for weekend hobbyists. Shelves were stocked with spools of replacement line and every tool needed to fill a tackle box. There were Alaskan-logo T-shirts, all-weather gloves, and a rack of snow jackets near the back—the kind made for cold hellscapes like this one.

Behind the front counter stood a woman who looked to be Native American with copper-toned skin and a long braid that fell to her waist. She had high cheekbones and almond-shaped eyes that held a stare colder than the snowy temperatures outside. Though average in height—around five-foot-five—she was taller than Von's own five-feet-even frame. Despite her stature, Von had made up for it with years of weight training that turned her body into a compact weapon—lean muscle stacked over grit, carved sharp by discipline and rage.

"Sasha Redhawk." Xander turned to Von, breaking his silence. "Commander Cains's number one. Handles protection, high-risk breaches, and leads the cleanup crew."

Sasha didn't speak. She leveled Von with a blank stare, devoid of all emotion, yet heavy with one message: *don't fuck with me.*

"Von's our new asset," he said.

Without a word, Sasha moved to the window and flipped the sign to *Closed,* shutting out the world—and whatever came next, Von couldn't guess. Her mind kept circling one fact: Sasha was cleanup. And Von had already taken out the trash. After Sasha locked the door, Xander and Von followed her to the back. Past the rows of lures and a wide selection of plastic tackle boxes, a narrow hallway led to a back door disguised as a freezer unit. The door featured a small metal panel where Sasha swiped a key fob, and the door clicked open.

The meeting room was unimpressive. The cinderblock walls were a dull gray, stale with the smell of mildew. They appeared to absorb light from a large window, soaking up the natural light that streamed through it, framing a gorgeous view of the woods. A distressed wooden table sat in the middle of the room with matching chairs that looked as comfortable as sitting on a cement slab. On the wall, a dusty corkboard clung to secrets, covered with a yellowing map, shipping labels, and surveillance photos held up by pushpins. From somewhere above, the hum of a ventilation fan never quite drowned out the tension.

Commander Lucian Cain looked the part of his cover—jeans, thick red and black flannel, long-sleeved, with snow boots to finish the ensemble. He picked up his coffee and took a leisurely sip. He motioned for them to take a seat. The wooden chairs were even more uncomfortable than she imagined. How the commander could sit on his ass for however long in something so painfully unforgiving was beyond her.

"Congratulations on passing your test," Cain said. "How'd it go?"

"Think you know how it went."

Cain grinned widely. "I like your spunk, it suits you. But when I ask you a question, I expect an answer."

"Here's the real question: How in the hell did Eli Vega know who I was? Knew the moment he saw me at Kodiak Cup. Edith nearly finished the job—almost blew him away with her shotgun. For a motley crew that's supposed to be elite, you're not very discreet."

"You think we advertise? He was a loose end, and now he's just dead weight. Seemed like you did a good job of that. Weighing the body down with something. Is that how you got rid of it?" Cain leaned in and steepled his fingers. "We gave you very specific instructions to leave it for cleanup."

For the first time, Sasha spoke. "What in the hell did you do with the body?" she bit out through clenched teeth.

Von hadn't thought this far ahead, hadn't considered what she'd say, what excuse she'd give them. Her heart panicked in a run, thudding against her chest, palms went clammy. But before she could come up with some sort of fabrication, Xander surprised her.

"There were dock workers nosing around. We had no time to wait around and get caught by someone," he lied, "so I helped her out. Took the boat out to the middle of the ocean, used a few sandbags to get him nice and heavy, and dropped him in. He's fish food now. Wiped down the boat, simple as that—we're solid."

Avoiding his eyes, Von tried her level best not to look alarmed.

Sasha shifted her gaze between the two of them. "Never been a problem before. All you had to do was call me. It's my job to make sure they're disposed of the right way. Tethers have been known to break loose. Worse, what if he gets found by one of the deep-sea fishermen?"

"He won't be," Xander said with an extra air of confidence that unnerved her. It was almost like he knew exactly what was in the crate she shipped out.

"Sounding a little too cocky, Holt. That was a stupid move. It can come back on us when they're not disposed of the right way," Sasha lectured.

If Von had learned anything, it was that nothing ever came for free. Everything had a cost, and why Xander Holt was helping her was beyond her—but she had to find out the price. After a pensive beat, the commander turned to a locked file cabinet. He plucked a set of keys off his desk, unlocked it, and took out a folder. He handed it to her.

She opened it up, and while she didn't recognize the Italian-looking man in the picture, she recognized his name: Tony Marchetti.

"He's that former detective, huh?" Von said.

"How'd you know?" Cain asked, amused.

"Someone was radioing for him on the boat. Saw the shipping label with his signature—looked it up. Got fired for something?"

"He was once a rising star in the LAPD's Narcotics Division. Had a rep for results. Fast arrests, airtight reports, a knack for flipping dealers. Wasn't so good at covering his tracks, though. There were whispers of missing evidence. Unreported cash. And, of course, complaints about the use of excessive force. His house of cards came crashing down after Internal Affairs launched a probe into his ties to a series of suspicious ODs and botched sting operations. Body cam footage disappeared. Shit like that. Got stripped of his badge when they put it all together," Cain said, then added. "He's here now in Kodiak running muscle. We need you to gather intel. Track everything he does."

"Ryker's fentanyl pipeline is active and moving faster than we expected," Xander said.

"And am I supposed to keep this one breathing?" Von asked dryly.

Cain took a long sip from his coffee. "Kill only if necessary."

"Leave the body, or you'll slip up, and it could cost us big time," Sasha warned. "You don't know what you're doing—the both of you."

Xander threw her a salute, then said, "Walk you back."

Von stormed out of the shop with Zeus at her heels, leaving a trail of silence—and Xander, who followed close behind. The path through the forest held the chatter of gossiping birds, a cold breeze laced with the scent of pine trees. Each movement forward felt like stepping into a hush that had only begun to settle between them—nature breathing in rhythm, the world momentarily exhaling.

She held her tongue until they arrived at the cottage. Tension crackled, and despite wanting to let it go, the nagging unanswered question refused to let her stew forever. Von unlocked the cabin, its old rusty hinges squealing from years of winter erosion. Xander unexpectedly followed her in. She waited until he shut the door behind him before making her case.

She spun around and accosted him. "Why in the hell did you protect me back there?"

He didn't flinch. That was the first thing she noticed. Xander Holt gave her an unreadable stare, one that exuded an ex-military calm.

"I wasn't protecting you. I was protecting the mission," he said, moving to an old cabinet thick with dust from months of disuse. The cabinet sat incognito. She hadn't even noticed it enough to inspect its contents.

"So," she said slowly, "you gonna to ask me what I did with the body?"

He retrieved a matte black case, closed the cabinet, and then set the case on the table.

"It's my job to make sure you do yours." He opened the case, extracted a laptop, and then powered it on. "That's why I left the crate. See if you were smart enough to know what to do with it. My loyalty isn't to Black Nova or to the commander—but to the results. For Cain, your test was to kill Eli, but for me, it was more about understanding the ripple effect. He doesn't play well with the LAPD. Doesn't understand that we need them. That's where Cain and I...we don't quite see eye-to-eye. If Detective Nazario and her buddies are roped in, then we'll know if they'll try to bury the case to protect their own. We'll know who panics. Who tries to spin a cover-up—and most importantly—who else is dirty."

He motioned for her to come over, and she obeyed with some reluctance.

Xander maneuvered to surveillance footage of the docks. The black-and-white footage was grainy but visible. The screen indicated that Marchetti was at Bay 4 helping to bring in a new shipment of crates.

"New shipment of fentanyl's laced with something deadly—Xylazine."

Being a former veterinarian, Von recognized what it was immediately.

"That's a strong muscle relaxer I've often used in my clinic as a pain reliever. If it's cut with fentanyl, it could be deadly."

"Thing is, Ryker's batch is worse than the rest—Narcan won't bring you back if you overdose on his stuff. That's why I convinced Cain to onboard you as a federal asset rather than let your talents go to waste rotting away behind bars."

Von was stunned. So, it was Xander. He was the one that pulled the strings, saved her from a prison cell. A debt she hadn't asked for. She almost thanked him—*almost*. But the truth burned hotter: She was caged. Just in a bigger box.

They watched the screen as more dock workers helped off-load more crates. Tony paused to speak with a tall, looming man. He had an intimidating aura about him that she could see even through the pixelated video.

"That's Jaxon Ryker," Xander said. "We need to get closer. Time to go."

He closed the laptop and secured it back into the matte black box, locked it, and stowed it away in the cabinet.

"So, if you're going against Black Nova protocol—you're working both sides."

"And that's the other reason I wanted you on my team." His caramel eyes seemed to see right through her, *measuring*—not with judgment, but with unnerving precision. "You're now working both sides with me."

SIX

THE FIRST LEAK

NAZARIO WAS EXHAUSTED after a long sleepless night of insomnia; her mind kept rewinding back to the cargo she hadn't expected to receive. What made it worse was the *who* in all of this. Who was in the crate at the Port of Long Beach, and who sent it? Two factors. Von was reaching out—sending Eli Vega for a reason. And Nazario and Wilson had a reputation, had even earned the cute nickname "the clean team." Maybe that's why she chose them.

Now, they had the shit-job of trying to figure out if there were other badges who'd flipped to working for Jaxon Ryker. Von's note was a warning, one that left a bitter taste in her mouth. No detective enjoyed having to investigate their brothers and sisters in blue. But it had to be done. The alternative meant that more lives could be lost, especially since they didn't know exactly what type of drug Ryker was peddling. Augusta "Gus" Humphrey—her best friend, Captain on Gang and Narco—wouldn't tell her what was up. Not over the phone.

The text came in at 2:07 a.m: *Need coffee. Can't say it here. It's not clean. It's laced.*

That was Humphrey code: *This shit's bad.*

Nazario stared back down at the message again, and for much longer than she needed to, already deciphering what Humphrey meant. Ryker was distributing some new fentanyl strain, deadlier, meaner, not lab-pure. The kind of compound that didn't just get you hooked and high but killed you in the process. Though it wasn't so much the drug that gave her pause. It was the tone. Nazario had known her for two decades. Humphrey didn't get rattled easy.

She shook off the weight of the text. Whatever Humphrey had found would have to wait for their coffee date later that day. Wilson and she had an important meeting—federal this time. Buttoned-up, surveilled, and probably half-redacted. The Homeland Security Investigation's building rose twenty stories high with alternating horizontal bands of beige concrete and glass striping curved edges. Rounded corners gave the building an aerodynamic silhouette. Inside HSI, the hum of federal operations buzzed behind closed doors. The building stood like a guard, glass-skinned and watching over the bustling port below.

"This is the kinda place that you can hear a fart from across the room." Wilson laughed.

"Better not—you'll evacuate the building," she said, forcing a healthier burst of laughter from Wilson's belly.

Wilson had a point. They followed instructions and found the seventh-floor conference room. Nazario hated how quiet it was in there. No radios. No chatter. Just the low hum of servers and fluorescent light. It was the kind of silence that made you feel like you'd already said too much. A grizzled man in his mid-forties, with shaggy peppered hair and a scraggly, unkempt beard—just above code to keep the boss happy—didn't bother with a handshake. He lifted his badge: *Agent Saul Mendoza.*

"Mendoza. HSI. Don't think this'll take no more than half

an hour," he said, like a burnout in desperate need of a vacation. "Will answer what I can, but from what we've reviewed, there isn't much."

He heaved himself onto a leather chair and moved his thick legs until his beer-gut was trapped against the desk. His computer screen lit up the moment he moved his mouse, and the screen popped up on a wide-screen television.

"We're mostly interested in the port authority manifest. We know our federal asset with Black Nova signed off, but we're wondering if there were any consignees," Wilson said.

"Brought crime photos courtesy of SID in case we need to reference anything," Nazario said, lifting up her department-issued iPad.

Mendoza navigated the Central Business District (CBD), Automated Manifest System (AMS), and the screen displayed Eli Vega's journey.

Shipment Tracking: Internal HSI Dashboard

Carrier: MV Arcturus

IMO: 9583124

STATUS: DELIVERED – Port of Long Beach (04 days ago)

Container #: CAXU 918273-4

Route:

• **Origin:** Kodiak, AK (Port Code: USKDK) – Departed: Dec 1

• **Transit Port:** Seattle, WA (Port Code: USSEA) – Arrived: Dec 3

• **Final Port:** LB, CA (Port Code: USLGB) – Arrived: Dec 6

• **Customs Clearance:** Complete – Dec 7

• **Consignor:** W. Friedrich

• **Consignee:** *Not listed*

> • **Declared Content:** "Frozen Alaskan Cod – Food Grade"
> • **Seal Status:** INTACT at all ports

Wilson and Nazario exchanged a glance. Their eyes went to a single name: the consignor.

"Did you expect she'd actually use her birth name?" Nazario said.

"Sure did not," Wilson said.

"As you can see. The crate came in on the MV Arcturus, docked four days ago. Manifest says frozen Alaskan cod. Shipped from Kodiak." Agent Mendoza said.

Nazario furrowed her brows. "So, no consignee?"

"That was the most unusual part," Mendoza said, "about this shipment. Field was left blank, and yet customs still cleared it."

Nazario flipped through SID's crime scene photos. "No tamper marks. Seal was intact. She wanted it found."

"Even stranger—no digital entry in the terminal system." Mendoza navigated to another screen. He pointed to the list. Every crate popped up—except for the one from Kodiak labeled as frozen cod. "It's like the container showed up unscheduled. Only the manifest I just showed you, and that's it."

"Agent Mendoza, can you do us a huge favor and run the body through VICAP and DEA missing persons? We're ninety-nine percent sure we know who he is. We just need to confirm his identity."

Mendoza blew out a loud breath. "Sure—I'll run him through IAFIS and double-check DEA personnel records."

Twenty minutes later, the hit came through. Fingerprints matched Elias 'Eli' Vega. Former DEA. Long-term undercover in South America. Fired eighteen months ago. Official record cited "operational breach"—details sealed.

Nazario and Wilson thanked Mendoza and hurried to the elevators, the folder of what the agent had found, clutched under her arm. Once down on the first floor lobby, they cut across the plaza in silence.

Wilson unlocked the SUV's door and slid behind the wheel.

"We need to get a hold of his former partner—stat," Nazario told Wilson. She didn't wait for his answer. "If Vega was dirty and someone wanted him dead, that partner either helped bury him or could be working for Ryker."

Wilson nodded, pulling into traffic, eyes hard on the road. "She knew we'd trace it. The location. The timing. Von wanted us looking. To dig deeper."

"She's not just killing." Nazario raked a hand down her face. "She's talking to us."

———

Humphrey looked like life had taken a few cheap shots. Dark circles rimmed her amber eyes, told of a night without sleep again. Nazario gave her the fiercest hug before sitting down with her iced coffee. Despite her muscular, tattooed arms showing off strength, her best friend seemed to be at her weakest; a breaking point Nazario knew all too well.

"Still having those nightmares?" Nazario asked gingerly.

Humphrey surprised her, dropping her head in her hands. She burst into a sob that shook her entire body. Nazario couldn't remember a time she witnessed Humphrey cry. It wasn't that she was incapable of deep emotion; she was simply not one for tears. Not during her double mastectomy, as she battled cancer. She gritted her teeth and won the battle because that was Humphrey. Even during her wedding—while Nazario sobbed

like a baby, choking out words as she tried to officiate—
Humphrey was all smiles as she watched her now-wife walk
down the aisle in a gorgeous, strapless lace mermaid Vera Wang
gown.

"I keep reliving it over and over," her voice broke. "I couldn't
fucking see him. It was dark. All of a sudden, I'm getting three
to the chest. And Quinn doesn't know what to do. She knows
I'm still pissed about that article she wrote. I can't even sleep in
the same bed as her right now."

Nazario remembered the Ryker story Quinn chased.
Someone had sent photos of her and Humphrey together with a
note: *run it, and Humphrey dies*. Quinn ran it anyway—fear of
losing her job outweighed fear of the threat.

"She loves you. You've gotta find a way to forgive her. She
made a mistake. She was going to lose her job if she didn't
publish the article."

"And I almost fucking died!" Humphrey pounded a fist on
the table. "She broke my fucking cover. Ryker's men found out,
and they nearly killed me."

Nazario paused for a beat. Humphrey wiped the tears with
the back of an angry hand.

"Look, I'm the last person to give marital advice, but you
have to find a way to forgive her. You do, Gus. You just got
married. I've never seen you happier. If you can fight cancer and
beat it. You can fight for your marriage. For Quinn. For you.
Don't let this case be the reason it all ends. Don't be another
badge statistic. You don't have to be another marriage casualty
in uniform. Stats don't lie, Gus. Don't let yours end up there."

Nazario reached for Humphrey's hand and squeezed it.

"I don't want to talk about her right now." She swiped a
hand down her face until the grief dried. She pivoted the
conversation back to business. "The shit Ryker's moving? It's
not pure."

"What's it cut with?"

"Xylazine."

"Haven't been up on the drug scene. What the hell is it?"

"Veterinary sedative. Doesn't respond to Narcan, not the way Ryker's cooked it. We've been tracking it through Eastside sets for months."

"Eastside sets?"

"Gang cliques. My Gang and Narco team's been tracking them. Moving product out of Boyle Heights, El Sereno, Highland Park. Vario Monte 13 and the Hillside Locos—both working for Jaxon Ryker."

"Been a lot of ODs then? If someone gets a hot hit, EMTs can't revive them?"

"Yep. Dropping like flies. Street name's tranq dope—or the zombie drug, depending on who you ask. Whatever you wanna call it, Narcan won't save 'em."

Nazario had been working homicide for fifteen years. She'd transferred out of Gang and Narco so long ago. She'd been dealing with dead bodies ever since, instead of chasing live ones, peddling drugs. Things evolved quickly on the streets. New drugs were cut with so many new chemicals that elevated the escape, she'd lost track. Unless you were boots-on-the-ground in Gang and Narco, good luck keeping up with all the street-dope slang. They changed faster than they changed corners. But Nazario knew addiction. The craving. The need. She was an escapist too. Red wine was her exit of choice—only, she could never stop at just one glass.

By the time she finally got sober, she'd been polishing off two bottles daily. Never during the day, of course, she was the functioning alcoholic type. But she could very easily down at least fifty fluid ounces of red wine during the evening. Because she wanted to unwind. Because she had a bad day. Because her job was stressful. Because she had solved a case and wanted to celebrate. Nazario had plenty of excuses. Many times, she didn't need a reason to drink. But now she had a reason to stay clean. Being sober since her pregnancy felt good, but she always had that itch in the back of her head and knew just how easy it was to relapse.

Starting an addiction was easy.

Staying sober was the hard part.

Humphrey glanced around, like she wasn't sure she hadn't been followed.

"Think it's time we compare notes," she murmured. "You seen anything off in Homicide lately?"

Nazario hesitated. Then nodded once. "A crate came in off the Port of Long Beach a couple of days ago. The damn thing was sent to me. Labeled cod fish from Kodiak, Alaska—but it had that DB stink. Wilson and I show up, and hazmat's already on site." Nazario paused to take a sip of her latte. "Fluids draining out from the corners—obviously blood. Hazmat used their VDN X-ray to scan the crate. Definitely didn't show a bunch of fish. Popped her open. Ex-DEA. Frozen stiff. COD—took one to the chest. SID confirmed his identity from his prints. Eli—"

Humphrey leaned in. "Vega?"

"That would be him."

"Fuck. I knew the asshole. We worked the same joint task force. Narco often runs parallel with DEA—Operation Iron Net." Humphrey pulled air into her lungs, like she was trying to slow her heart from speeding. "Ran things by the book until he got sloppy. His name popped up during a few wire taps. Cartel chatter."

"And that's when he got fired? I'd imagine?" Nazario paused for a beat. "What we need to figure out is who else is working for Ryker. You know who his partner was at the time?"

"It's all making sense now."

"What is it?"

Humphrey stayed quiet. Two minutes dragged like a bad confession—slow, uneasy, and bound to get worse.

"There was a partner—officially linked to Eli. He disappeared before anyone could sit him down. People don't just walk away from a mess like that. If Vega was tangled, that partner knew where the bodies were buried. This stays between us."

She pulled out a thumb drive and slid it over to her.

"Gus, you're scaring me." Nazario examined the drive. "What's on this?"

"Remember when I said one of Ryker's men shot me?"

"Yeah, but he was wearing a mask or something. Never ID'd him. Got away."

"I think it was someone on the LAPD. Think it was a cop." She laced her fingers around her coffee. Nazario's heart sank. "Things have been different. Get weird vibes now at work. Like, I dunno, like I'm being watched. Like they're whispering. Like there's some dirty badges out there, and I don't know who it is. But I know enough to know too much. Part of the reason I can't sleep—get this feeling someone's been watching my house. Driving by. Can't explain it. Been doing this long enough to know that my gut, it's rarely wrong."

Nazario understood. "Von Schlange—our Serpent Woman —she's a federal asset for Black Nova. But I think she's working both sides."

"Heard about them. Some black-bag hybrid between the FBI and the CIA. No badges. Off-the-books operation. Answers to no one. Leaves no trail if they're moving bodies. Ghost-level shit."

"Well, she sent the body to me and this note. Said something about Vega being dirty and that there's another one out there in Kodiak."

Humphrey read it and gave it back to her. "Someone's dirty and you're not. That's why she sent him, and guaranteed Commander Lucian Cain has no idea she sent it." Humphrey pointed at the thumb drive. "Everything I could pull without tripping alarms. Off-the-books patrols, missing case files, IA flags that disappeared. People Vega was tied to, including his partner. Got a list of who I think might've flipped to the other side. Once you go down that road, start investigating them—you'll be on their shit list, too. You have to watch your back, Nazario."

"Not letting anything happen to you," she said, "and not letting anyone intimidate me."

But even as the words left her mouth, worry had already taken root—curling through her like smoke in the lungs. Her stomach churned with acid. Not fear exactly. Not yet. But the kind of unease that came from knowing something was off and that it wasn't done unraveling.

Just then, her phone rang: Wilson.

She let it go to voicemail. A few seconds later, he texted.

Wilson: *DB—scene's still hot. Think it's a cop. Texting you the address.*

"Lemme guess? Wilson?"

"Yeah, got another cold one." She rose to her feet and pulled Humphrey into the kind of hug that she knew her best friend needed. She whispered in her ear. "Body might be a badge. I'll fill you in if it has anything to do with Ryker."

"Start with Detective Clay Harrison. Young. Detective I. Got him on a short leash, but I've taken him under my wing. Three years in Gang and Narco—reminded me of myself back when I started." Humphrey handed her Harrison's card. "One of the good ones. Willing to talk. He was the one who compiled all the intel on that thumb drive."

"I'll be discreet," she promised.

In the car, Nazario contemplated her next stop. Before the next homicide scene, she had to go home. Pump first. Bodies dropped—motherhood didn't. She wasn't backing down. If someone thought a threat would force her into a cover-up—they picked the wrong detective.

A dead cop wasn't a coincidence.

SEVEN

THE END OF LOYALTY

SNOW FELL like ash from a burning world—too soft to bury the dread coiling beneath Von's skin. Despite its silence, flurries came down fast and hard, blurring the docks with alabaster layers that coated everything. Mother Nature seemed to whisper a warning of what was to come. Dread pressed against her internal alarm.

Something was coming.

She sensed it in the air.

The wintry landscape and heavy snowfall made each step soundless. She was wrapped in a Särmä TST M05 Snow Camo Jacket. The Finnish military-grade coat, sporting a white and gray print, had been designed for winter warfare and concealment in snow weather. Keeping her head up, Von's black balaclava kept her face warm and hidden. She was a ghost amidst the frosty terrain.

Following the directions, she found *The Silver Vow*, a sixty-foot Steiner Shipyard made of steel with a twenty-foot beam. With a six-crew capacity, the commercial fishing boat owned by Xander Holt was large enough and close enough to Tony Marchetti to set up surveillance without being noticed. Earlier that day, Von had tried to install *FlexiSpy*—an app that let her eavesdrop on conversations, activating audio remotely, even when the victim's phone sat idle.

But the Black Nova-issued phone was iron-clad—locked, firewalled, monitored.

After she sifted around, swiping through the phone, Von didn't expect to stumble upon her solution. In the security settings, buried beneath biometric options, a grayed-out toggle caught her eye. She tapped on it, but nothing happened. Then she long-pressed the side button past the power prompt and the SOS trigger—it populated, turning from gray to green, name populating—Phantom Vox. The dormant module opened to a screen, where a line of red text snaked across it:

Command mode enabled. Awaiting target.

Next to the text was a button: T-List

Clicking on it, a single name populated: Tony Marchetti

"Activate Recon Protocol" blinked on in red.

At first, she assumed the phone was for Black Nova to watch her, listen in on her every move, track her conversations. She figured it out quickly. T-list was short for "Target List." Then she understood that the phone wasn't for *her*. It was for *them*—the ones she was assigned to find, surveil, to kill. The commander wouldn't dole out the entire queue of the case roll. He'd likely put them out one file at a time. That's how you kept someone from connecting the dots. Couldn't risk her seeing the full scope. Too much access was too much power. Knowledge was leverage, one that Lucian Cain wasn't about to hand over.

Von had found Bluetooth earbuds in the cabinet that contained the metal box with the Black Nova-issued laptop. She put them on, and they immediately connected to her phone. Von had decided she would activate the recon button once she was on *The Silver Vow*. Approaching it first, as she and Xander had planned to avoid suspicion, Von made it on the stern. Zeus followed close beside her. They quietly descended the steps into the lower cabin, where a window aligned perfectly. Marchetti came into view just twenty-five feet away on a mid-sized cargo vessel at the starboard side facing her.

Von fished her phone out of her snow jacket pocket and navigated to Phantom Vox, clicked on T-List, and pressed the red blinking button with her target's name. It turned green—suddenly, voices boomed crystal clear in her ear.

An Italian accent came through in her ear. "Ryker's outta the picture, alright? He ain't here. I am. You answer to me. Want the tranq dope—you deal with me. Same supply, less heat. And none of this psychotic micromanaging."

Von figured it had to be Tony Marchetti since the spy app was connected to his phone, but she had to be sure. She found the AN/PVS-31 Binocular Night Vision Goggles hanging on the wall of the cabin. She plucked it up and focused it on her target. Marchetti was talking to a Hispanic man with serious features—a tight jaw, dark eyes like switchblades. The kind that held power. The kind that meant one thing: he wasn't someone you fucked with.

"We don't trust *gringos* with broken loyalties. *Los Cuervos* never forget," the man said, crossing his arms. "You ain't dealing with some *Americano* posers—little boys pretending to be some hard ass gangsters. You dealing with *Chihuahua* cartel, my friend. We eat you alive, and then we come after your big Italian *familia*. Pick them off, one at a time—have them for dessert."

Von, being multi-lingual, understood the cartel name—*Los Cuervos*. The Crows.

"C'mon, Salazar, you know as well as I that Ryker's been getting messy. Been fucking up. Got eyes on us. Not the FBI, CIA, or the cops—someone bigger. Some elite task force. That's all I know," Marchetti warned. "If they bring Ryker down—he's bringing your whole cartel down the drain with him."

Salazar considered Marchetti's words for a beat, then questioned, "You got a plug I don't know about? Where you pulling that from?"

"Used to be a top narcotics detective, in case you forgot. You gonna trust some sloppy-ass criminal—or you gonna trust intel from someone who spent years working dope cases, flipping dealers and running wires?"

Salazar rubbed his chin, thoughtfully. Then his serious expression cracked—he let out a short laugh and started clapping, mocking with intention, like the whole thing was a joke. Then his countenance dropped flat as stone. "*Los Cuervos* don't trust nobody. Trust is a loaded mother fucking word, brother. What makes you think we should believe someone who ain't loyal to his job—or to *El Fabricante.*"

Von filed away the nickname in her head.

"*The Manufacturer,*" Von murmured the English translation to herself.

Jaxon Ryker had to be who Salazar was referring to—but what the hell kind of tranq dope was he pushing? High-purity cuts, or some new variant that killed?

A shuffle behind her startled her. Von drew her P320 semi-automatic and leveled it at the noise. Xander raised his hands and gave her a lopsided grin.

"Easy there, *Trigger Queen.*"

Relieved, Von lowered her weapon and slid it back into the holster tucked against the small of her back. She didn't hear him step aboard his sportfishing yacht.

She took out one of her earbuds, wiped it with an alcohol pad she kept in her pocket—in case she had to use them to clear prints—and handed it to Xander.

"You found the spy app," he said, putting the earbud in his ear. "I'm impressed."

Xander leaned in close to her, his arm brushing up against

her. A warm current ran through her, like hot liquid melting the snowy terrain around them. She swallowed a breath, trying to keep her heart from accelerating. The sensation was unfamiliar to her, the way he made her feel when he was around her. It almost distracted her from her mission. He touched her hand, fingers grazing over hers as he slid the night vision binoculars from her grip. Xander put them to his eyes and adjusted the focus.

"Mateo Salazar," he said. "Runner for the cartel. The middleman."

Von filled him in, explaining, "Marchetti's turning on Ryker, trying to strike a deal."

Xander shook his head. "Got balls bigger than watermelons."

Marchetti's voice cut in. "What's it gonna be? You going down with Ryker? Better jump ship now. Telling you—there're eyes on us. Might even be watching as we speak."

Zeus growled and then began barking.

"*Was ist los?*" Von asked Zeus what was wrong.

POP! POP! POP!

Gunfire cracked from the west.

Zeus must've sensed it. He'd served in Iraq and Afghanistan with the Marines—trained to detect danger before it struck.

Xander and Von dropped fast, instincts kicking in. Wood splinters rained from a nearby boat that got in the way of oncoming fire. When the silence settled, they risked a glance through the cabin window.

Marchetti was down. Shot.

Salazar ducked low but managed to keep on his feet. More shots rang out, though Salazar dodged with the practiced precision of an athlete who'd learned to maneuver during a battle where warfare was second nature. He swiveled around and shot back in the direction of the live fire.

"Can you see anything?" Von asked. "Who's shooting?"

"No, can't see shit."

A shot rang out again, hitting a nearby dock worker twice in his chest. He dropped instantly; screams rang out in the night as nearby fishermen and longshoremen scrambled for cover. Salazar jumped into a boat that had been loaded with the crates Marchetti was managing—likely the drugs. He sped off, heavy snow flurries swirling around him as he disappeared into the darkness.

"We're clear," Xander said. "Let's check the bodies."

Von followed him out onto the deck, first checking on Marchetti.

His death was immediate, taking a clean hit between the eyes.

"From the distance that they were shooting—" Von started.

"Had to be a sniper," Xander finished her thought.

They moved to the second body. Xander checked the dock worker's pocket, pulling out an ID they didn't expect.

"Shit—he's no dock worker." Xander handed her the badge, emblazoned with the familiar bureau's justice eagle emblem. "FBI—Special Agent Gabriel Ordóñez."

"He was embedded. Did the commander know he was even here? Or was that another need-to-know no one bothered to mention?" Von bit out.

"Of course, FBI would be on Ryker, but this agent wasn't in the op file. My guess—Cain didn't know he was here either. Could only mean that Ordóñez was embedded deep. Too far in. He must've been so far undercover that he couldn't get out safely without blowing his cover. No way out without setting off alarms."

"And yet Ryker uncovered him before Black Nova did?" Von said skeptically. "What kinda organization are we if this Ryker bitch is five steps ahead of us?"

Xander looked to the west. Trying to get eyes on the sniper. "What makes you think whoever's perched up out there is on Ryker's team?" He swiped a hand down his face. "I think they're gone but can't see shit from here with all the snow. We gotta leave, don't think it's safe."

Shouts echoed from somewhere down the pier. A forklift reversed in panicked jerks as the operator powered it down and jumped out, running away from the docks in fear. Fishermen and others nearby began following suit. Sprinting to safety.

Zeus began to bark—a repeated staccato burst meant to warn.

Xander and Von locked eyes; danger had already claimed them.

In perfect timing, a quick—*POP! POP!*—sang through the chaotic night. Xander hit the deck fast, just as fire tore through Von's side: sharp, surgical, puncturing her ribs on the right side. A split second later—*POP!*—another punch ripped through her left thigh.

"Fuck, I'm hit," Von grunted, as she collapsed onto the frigid snowy deck.

The words came out low and strained, as blood already began pumping from the wounds, slowing her pulse, draining energy. The world tilted. Spun. An inky void clawed at the edges of her vision, dragging it toward its unconscious abyss.

"Stay down!" Xander directed and dove behind the forklift —still warm from the operator who'd abandoned it just seconds earlier.

Zeus barked once, eyes locked on Von, a sound loaded with loyalty—as if telling her, *Let me handle this.* No fear. Just a soldier who didn't wait for permission but acted out of love for his handler. Before she could stop him, he sprinted west in the direction of the sniper, moving at a speed she hadn't seen before, powering through the snow like he was a bulldozer.

"Zeus! Dammit!" Von shouted, then ordered, "*Nein! Komm zurück!*"—*No! Come back!*

It was too late, Zeus had disappeared, clearing the distance between Kodiak Port, and what Von could finally see as the snowfall slowed was the old Kodiak Pacific Processing. The 40,000 square-foot, four-story abandoned seafood cannery was once a booming plant that processed and preserved seafood. Though an illegal waste dumping scandal five years back had shut down the thriving plant for good. Half-boarded up and tagged with graffiti, eroded by Alaska's unforgiving weather, it now sat rotting as it overlooked the harbor 450 feet away.

Doing quick mental math, Von remembered that when she was a practicing veterinarian and dog trainer, she'd clocked Zeus at twenty-five miles per hour during combat exercises. The German Shepherd was an extremely fast runner. Twelve seconds. That's all he needed to reach the building, charge up the flight of stairs following the scent of the sniper, and locate him on the rooftop where the door had been left broken wide open for years. Von found the binoculars half buried in fresh powder on the ground next to her and lifted them to her eyes, grunting in pain, breath coming out short and shallow.

She could see the sniper—who Xander had thought had fled —still at his post.

A man in black snow gear, face unrecognizable. No one she'd seen walking around Kodiak. He fired a couple of more shots—*POP! POP!*—missing her head by an inch. Von army-crawled across the ground, leaving a crimson trail through the white earth. The cold snow seeped through her jacket and pants, easing the throb from fresh wounds, if only for a moment. Mustering up every ounce of energy she had left, Von staggered to her feet and ran, half limping, back to the boat, dragging her left leg like dead weight. She made it to the cabin below deck and collapsed against the bay window seat.

From the window, Von lifted the binoculars to her eyes, wiping blood from the lenses. The sniper took another shot at Xander but missed. The bullet ricocheted off the forklift. Von adjusted the focus on the binoculars just as Zeus leapt—jaws locking around the sniper's arm, knocking the rifle clean from his grip. Von understood now why Xander hadn't fired back. The former Navy SEAL most likely hadn't anticipated Zeus to be in the way and was probably waiting for the right time to pull the trigger. Just as the sniper turned his back toward them and Zeus was out of his line of sight, Xander took a single shot, exploding the man's skull like a melon under a sledgehammer.

The moment she knew the sniper was dead, the adrenaline siphoned out of her body like an open gas tank leaking fuel. Her body began to fail her, one piece at a time. Fingers lost their grip, dropping the binoculars as they slipped away, clattering to the floor. Legs unable to sustain weight, she turned from the window and slumped back against it. Eyes starved of cerebral blood flow to the retina, black blotches and flashes of light sparked like stars before a fading day. Palms turned clammy, a cold sweat spread across her paling skin as blood pressure continued to drop. Ears heard nothing except for a high-pitched ringing of tinnitus singing its tune. Mouth went dry, throat a parched desert thirsting for water. Entry wounds began to burn, returning the agony that had been numbed away by adrenaline, no longer able to protect her from the pain.

She was fading fast.

Blood soaking clothes.

Slow warmth spreading.

Thundering footsteps tore down the stairs, Xander's voice calling out for her, but her head couldn't obey her body's commands, couldn't turn toward him, couldn't answer. She forced down a sticky breath. Her mouth bone-dry. Throat closing. Von fought to remain conscious. She needed to tie a tourniquet around her leg, but the void taunted her, eager to drag her into its silent arms. If Jaxon Ryker hired the sniper—he'd silenced Marchetti for his betrayal—and she'd been next, no matter which side she was on.

In the end, loyalty and betrayal bled the same.

EIGHT

THE LAST HONEST BLUE

DETECTIVE ANAYA NAZARIO'S heart felt like it was getting ripped out of her chest. Stopping by to pump her milk, which was a necessity, was harder than she thought. She had pumped and stored the milk. But Ariabella wasn't having it—she wanted her mom. Not the bottle today. Her baby girl was fine before she laid eyes on her mother, wailing and squirming in Elena Cruz's arms, the babysitter who had been her lifeline.

It tore her insides seeing her daughter so distraught. She tried to soothe her, putting her to her breast, feeding her naturally, which is what she yearned for. The warmth of skin on skin instead of the sterile touch of a plastic nipple. Nazario looked at the time; it was twenty minutes in, and she had to leave. She handed Ariabella back to Elena, and her face contorted, cheeks flushed and wet. Her six-month-old loved more than anything to breastfeed, and Nazario wasn't about to stop because of work duties. Still, the demands of her job kept her away longer than she liked. The juggle was real. Hard. More painful than she could've ever imagined.

Huxley had texted her on the drive home, letting her know that he was already on scene. She let him know that she needed to make a quick pit stop at home. It was unbearable to see her daughter this way. Nazario almost wished she hadn't come home at all; it would've been easier on her little girl. But she needed to pump. Skip it, and she'd get mastitis. Nazario already had it three times—fever, chills, rock-hard breasts engorged with milk that had to be drained. Each time was an awful experience, one that had taught her to manage work and motherhood, but it was more challenging than she anticipated. Before Ariabella, she could push her body to the limit. Working around the clock, running past overtime, and letting her workaholic nature take over.

Now that she was a mother—one who'd chosen to breast-feed long-term—her body never let her forget. It knew when it was time to feed, when to pump, and store her milk. It told her to slow down. To savor the rare quiet moments when she could run home and hold her baby close. But when a homicide scene came in hot, she had to drop everything and go. That was the nature of her position as a homicide detective. And that felt like the worst kind of hell—torn between the job that demanded everything, and the one that mattered most: being a parent.

"It's okay, Mama," Elena said in a soothing tone that Nazario desperately needed. "Go, she'll be okay after five minutes. I promise you. Go."

Nazario kissed Ariabella on the forehead and jogged to her car, slamming the door harder than she meant to. Inside with the world sealed out, she dropped her head on the steering wheel and broke. She cried—deep heavy sobs that had been waiting since the day her sweet daughter was born. Tears she hadn't let herself feel. Not with cases piling up. Not with the badge she proudly wore. But now the iron bars around her heart gave way, and her body shook as everything she'd been holding in came pouring out. She was tough. Always had been. But the only person who could break her was a nineteen-pound little human she loved more than her own life.

Feeling like an emotional wreck, Nazario made it to the crime scene ten minutes late.

The four-plex in Echo Park had been blocked off with yellow crime tape and was already teeming with SID and the coroner—normally the ones too slow to the scene. Curious neighbors stood on their balconies, some outside, trying to catch a glimpse of all the action. Detective Wilson spoke with one of the neighbors, taking a statement out front.

"Thank you for your cooperation," Wilson said, to a young college-aged woman garbed in a UCLA sweatshirt and yoga pants. Caucasian. Dark hair in a ponytail. Apple face. Narrow brown eyes. Glasses. Nazario had a habit of memorizing clothing, faces—details the everyday civilian would ordinarily ignore. "I'll call you if I need to interview you again down at the station."

Her partner matched her cadence, stepping next to her as they headed for the front door.

"Four-unit complex. Single occupant per unit. No roommates, which surprised me. Took statements from all three."

"Anything?"

"One had gone out on an errand, the other went to work early that morning, left before they heard anything. Guy stopped by home for lunch, and the other fella returned after his errand. Came back home to a full-blown circus. Surprised to see the street lit up—patrol cars, SID van, coroner—the whole damn parade."

"So, they didn't hear or see anything?"

"Nope. But the young UCLA student said she heard someone scream and then heard a gunshot. She'd just gotten out of the shower. By the time she came out to see what was going on, the suspect had fled. Didn't catch the car or the perp. Called 9-1-1 and reported hearing live fire."

"And nothing suspicious leading up to this?" Nazario asked as they entered the apartment, where the homicide scene felt like a squeeze between SID's Whittier and Yang, and the coroner—plus his assistant—waiting on the investigation to wrap up before confiscating the body.

"Nothing out of the ordinary. Said Harrison was real quiet. Friendly. But he mostly kept to himself."

Nazario paused in the middle of the living room and pivoted to Wilson. "Hold up—did you just say Harrison? As in Detective Clay Harrison?"

"Yep. Apparently, he was young. About three years on Gang and Narco. Think he might've worked under Gus," he said. "Didn't you just have lunch with her? How's she doing?"

"Shit."

"What is it?"

Nazario lowered her voice, whispering so no one else could hear. "He was supposed to be our anonymous source. Had something to tell us. Knew who was dirty. Who might be working for Ryker. Gus told me that we should start with him."

"Looks like someone wanted to keep him quiet," Wilson mused. "C'mon, he's in his bedroom. Huxley's been studying the scene."

They walked through a hallway, past a bathroom, and made it to the bedroom at the end. The apartment was immaculate. Nothing out of order, except for one flip-flop that looked to have slipped off in the middle of the hallway.

"The front door was open," Wilson began, then pointed at the flip-flop. "Think he answered it and then ran to his bedroom to get his gun. Lost his house slipper along the way. Took a hit, point-blank to the noggin. Quick, execution-style."

Nazario entered the room. Decomp wasn't but three hours.

The odor was present, but not as strong as other homicide scenes she's investigated where the corpse had been marinating in death's grip for days.

Huxley was crouched low, analyzing the body. Whittier was spraying luminol in the main bathroom attached to the bedroom while Yang dusted for prints around the door handle, dressers, and walls.

"Hey," Huxley said, glancing up at her. "The ID of the body is Detective—"

"Clay Harrison," Nazario finished, snapping on her black latex Nitrile gloves. "I know, just came back from lunch."

She didn't say more, didn't need to. Huxley knew she was meeting Humphrey. He gave her a knowing look. "Did she give you anything on Harrison?" he asked, furrowing his brows.

Nazario leaned in, speaking low in his ear. "He was supposed to give up some blue—names tied to Ryker."

"Goddamn it," Huxley hissed, tone hushed. "Could've been a badge that killed him."

"She's spooked. Real scared. Wasn't herself. Said something about bad vibes at work. Like they know she's on to them," she whispered. "Word gets around, you know, and no one likes blue ratting out blue. Even the ones not on Ryker's payroll."

"We'll pow-wow later," Wilson said quietly, glancing around to make sure no one overheard their conversation. Even though SID didn't directly work with Homicide, they knew everyone, and they couldn't risk letting it leak that they were now having to do an internal investigation regarding members of their own.

Nazario focused her attention on Harrison. He was still in his pajamas, hand inches away from his department-issued semi-automatic. There was a black ring around the entry wound where the burn marks from the close-range shot had left its mark. Blood splatter painted the wall near his head—fragments of brain matter splattered the nearby dresser.

"No forced entry," Nazario said. "Someone knocks on the door in the early morning. He lets them in. Harrison must've known who the person was. But then he quickly realizes they're not there for a friendly chit-chat."

"Got no weapon on hand," Huxley said. "Runs back. Grabs his gun—too late. Perp fires at close range."

"And gets the hell up out before anyone can see them," Wilson finished. "Pretty sure they came in their personal vehicle. Would be pretty dang stupid to show up in a squad car."

"I would have to agree." Nazario stood up. "Ryker likes the clean hits. This has got his signature all over it."

She roamed the bedroom, scanning for anything amiss. But everything was where it should be. There was no struggle. The nightstand's drawer was open, likely where the gun had been. Whittier came out of the bathroom.

"It's a wrap for us," Whittier said, putting away the luminol in his bag. "Nothing at all in the bathroom."

"No prints anywhere, either," Yang said, gathering any DNA evidence she might've found on the body. "We took samples from under the nails, but there are no defense wounds."

"Yeah, it was an in-and-out job. No struggle that we could see. Nothing knocked over in here or in the living room," Nazario said.

"Which is a little unusual, given that there usually is a struggle," Huxley said. "Normally, something would get tossed to the floor during a jostle."

"So, it could only mean one thing, ladies and gents—no Wrestle Mania action. Harrison didn't get a chance to fight back. Had to've known the shooter. Killer got 'er done in one fell swoop. Slick—like he could teach a Master Class in Murder 101," Wilson said.

"Our thoughts exactly," Yang said. "Looks like they made your job real easy today."

"No shell casing, either," Whittier added. "Took it with them."

"We'll let you know if we find any DNA. Until the next time we meet again." Yang waved at them as she and Whittier strode out to their SID van.

Nazario, Wilson, and Huxley kept their mouths shut and waited until SID were gone.

"Let's split up and go back over the apartment. Triple-check to see if we might've missed anything," Nazario said. "Keep our thoughts to ourselves until we can talk in the car."

"Good idea," Huxley said. "I'll take the living room."

"I'll take the bathroom," Wilson said.

"I've got the bedroom," Nazario said.

Nazario crouched, scanning the floor again, then stood and let her gaze sweep the room one more time. Nothing. No drag marks, no overturned furniture, no blood splatter hidden beneath the dresser. Brain matter and blood had sustained itself in a tight arc around the head, staining the north wall just inches from where he lay. The bed was unmade, as if he'd been woken up from his sleep. Blinds were closed and hung straight, undisturbed. She moved toward the closet, cracked it wider—an assortment of blazers, button-up shirts, slacks, and jeans were neatly spaced.

C'mon, Nazario—what haven't you looked at?

She returned to the nightstand and examined the items. Under the lamp, a G-Shock watch lay face down next to his badge. A glass of water sat beside a bottle of melatonin, both drained halfway. Nazario picked up the bottle and studied the label. Thirty milligrams per tablet—one of the stronger doses you could buy over the counter on Amazon. Then a familiar book she'd read caught her attention. A battered copy of *El*

Narco: Inside Mexico's Criminal Insurgency, pages flagged, and margins filled with notes.

She carefully handled the book. Harrison must've read it dozens of times. Her gut twisted. She didn't know why, but something whispered inside that old detective part in her brain —*go through*. Chapter by chapter. Nazario sat on the edge of the bed, opened *El Narco*, and started flipping. Tabs. Underlines. Highlighted phrases. Scribbled notes in the margins. Harrison had worked the book over like it was a case file.

Then she hit Chapter Eleven: *The Fix Is In*

Nazario knew the chapter well. Yellow highlighter had marked a paragraph about police corruption, the kind that rots departments from the inside out. And then her heart stopped. She held her breath as she saw a note Harrison had written. Pen pressed down hard enough to break through the page.

If something happens to me, talk to Det. Tyrell Dawson. Don't trust anyone else.

Nazario stared at the words.

Not a clue—but a warning.

"We good to take the body, Detective?" The coroner stood at the door with his assistant, shaking her out of her spinning thoughts.

She swallowed a breath. "Yeah...we're all done."

Huxley and Wilson returned. "We got nothing," Huxley said.

"Not even dust. Harrison kept a mighty clean abode," Wilson said.

"We're taking off. Let us know if there's anything in his blood-stream or if anything unusual comes up during the autopsy," Nazario told the coroner.

"Report will be sent to the three of you," he said.

"Thanks!"

Nazario held her composure as they stepped into the hallway, the weight of Harrison's last words written down in the book still clinging to her like tar. She met their eyes briefly.

"What's wrong, Anaya?" Huxley asked.

"Why are we holding on to that old boring book?" Wilson asked.

Nazario didn't answer their questions; she stayed silent until they were safely in Wilson's SUV. She opened up the chapter, where her finger had been holding its place, and showed it to them.

"As I said in there, Gus told me to talk to him. That he was one of the good ones. Harrison helped her put together a list of potential badges that were paid off by Ryker—turned dirty," she said, digging in her blazer pocket and showing them the thumb drive.

"Holy bejesus," Wilson started, "what in the hell have we gotten ourselves into? Even the good ones'll start giving us the stink eye the moment they sniff an internal investigation's taking place."

"The bureau's gonna have a field day with this." Huxley ran a hand through his thick hair, upending it. "They'll definitely want to be roped in on this investigation. I'm afraid to know how many badges are working the wrong side of the law."

"We might not've found any DNA or prints, but this is something even better. He gave us a name we can work with. That's more than we had before." Nazario glanced out at the window, watching the coroner and his assistant wheel out the body bag on a stretcher. "Gus just told me to speak to Harrison —like two hours ago and damn it—now he's dead."

"At least Harrison's not the last honest blue," Wilson said, doing his thing, seeing the silver lining in a bad situation. "Detective Tyrell Dawson must've been trustworthy enough for Harrison to give up his name."

"He knew. Son of a bitch knew he was being hunted."

Nazario pinched the bridge of her nose. "He didn't leave this for SID. Not IAB. He left it for us."

"Not familiar with Tyrell Dawson. You guys know him? Heard of him?" Huxley asked.

"Nope, never met him." Wilson powered up the engine and put the SUV in reverse. "The LAPD and its departments have 9,000 sworn officers and 3,000 civilian workers, according to their last census. One of the largest municipal police departments in the U.S. That's 12,000 employees. Can't know 'em all."

"I don't know him either," Nazario said, "but it looks like we're fixing to get to know him."

As they drove away from Harrison's duplex, the neighborhood blurred past—Sunset Boulevard pulsing with taquerias, barbershops, old historic buildings, and the glow of neon signs over dive bars and indie record stores. A flash of Victorian rooftops from Angelino Heights broke the skyline, then faded. Echo Park Lake appeared briefly between buildings, still and silver under the dusk, paddle boats tethered for the day beneath the watchful gaze of the Lady of the Lake. A mural-covered wall slid past, then the flicker of a marquee outside The Echo. Farther off, the towers of Downtown L.A. stood tall, hazy with a film of yellow smog. They were each quiet, ruminating on Harrison's last words to them, scribbled in a book she almost disregarded.

The first order of business would be to contact Dawson and find out what he knew.

Dread consumed her as she stared down at the thumb drive in her hand. Soon, she would learn that as much as she wanted to trust the badge—honor meant nothing if the person behind it had already sold their soul.

NINE

THE CLOSE CALL

"WE NEED TO...WE need to get to that body," Von rasped, voice raw and low. "Rooftop. Old processing plant. Gotta ID him...figure out who he works for. If we don't, Black Nova gets compromised."

"Fuck being compromised," Xander snapped, scooping her in his arms and carrying her to the bed at the stern-facing wall at the rear of the cabin. "You're bleeding out. Priority one is making sure you don't die on me."

Police sirens punctuated the night, drawing closer.

"Zeus, he'll come back. Need my dog."

"We don't have time. Need to move the boat."

"Not without my fucking dog. We're not leaving without him."

Xander looked at his watch and then out at the cabin window. "Think I see him. He's got something in his mouth."

"Trained him for combat. Been deployed multiple times—embedded with the Marines—Iraq and Afghanistan. Knows how to identify what to retrieve," Von whispered, weakly. "Need something to stop the bleeding. I'd operate on myself, done it before. But I think I'm fixing to pass out."

"It's your lucky day. I had SQL—SEAL Qualified Training."

"TCCC?"

"Yep, Tactical Combat Casualty Care. Patched up a bunch of my men during Fallujah—second push, back in '04."

Xander grabbed a towel and rope. He folded the towel and pressed it against her ribs; she cried out in pain. Without needing to be instructed, her medical training kicked in. Von did her best to keep pressure on the lateral thoracic wound. He took a knife and cut the long rope, leaving enough to wrap around her upper thigh. Then he tied it off—tight enough to slow the bleeding, not stop it completely.

The sound of police sirens was closing in on them. Time wasn't on their side, though Zeus made his way onto the boat just before it was too late. He jogged to Von—blood splatter sprinkled his head, snout, and mouth. She'd have to bathe him, that's even if she survived the night. Xander closed the space between them and knelt to investigate what the German Shepherd had brought back.

Right hand pressing on her rib, the left palm opened. Zeus placed what looked like a black burner phone in her hand. She flipped it open. No code required. Von clicked on the messages — there were several text messages going back and forth between the sniper and his point of contact. A word stuck out to her: Deadeye. It had to be the sniper's code name.

She handed it to Xander.

He quickly checked the text messages.

POC: *Deadeye, what's the status?*

Deadeye: *M1 neutralized. M2 escaped. Snake's wounded. Still active.*

Xander looked up from the phone, turning white as the bitter snow.

"What is it?" Von gritted out through the ache coursing through her body.

The former Navy SEAL said nothing, shoving the phone in his jacket pocket just as blue and red police lights lit up the night, bright enough to shine through their boat. It sounded like there were at least a dozen squad cars out on the harbor. Xander sprinted toward the hatch and raced toward the helm. Soon, *The Silver Vow* was speeding away from the Kodiak Port and into the vast open ocean. The boat rocked and bounced by the speed, waves slamming against steel. Zeus nestled next to her protectively. Von kept pressure on her punctured ribcage, her left leg growing numb from the tourniquet.

Wind howled across the deck. Snow lashed against the windows, as the shoreline was gone, swallowed up by the night and the winter frosty storm—the whiteout turning their boat invisible. Twenty minutes later, they were far enough, where no sirens could follow. If they came, it wouldn't be by land. Xander raced back down to the cabin with what appeared to be a tactical camouflage medical bag. He set it down next to her and opened it up. Drowsy and listless, weakened by blood loss, she blinked at him—slow, unfocused.

"You going to tell me what's going on? You know something based on those text messages, don't you?"

He took out hydrogen peroxide and a stack of sterile gauze pads.

Instead of answering her, he said, "Let's get you out of that jacket."

She sat up and groaned, fighting through the pain. Together, they removed her snow jacket.

"Need the shirt off," he said, clearing his throat. Their eyes met—a flicker charged between them. Duty pulled them back, but the spark stayed. Undeniable. He breathed deep, as if trying to retain professionalism.

"I know," she said, "but I'll need your help."

"I've got extra shirts. Better cut it open, so you're not straining yourself."

He took the knife, and in one swift slice, cut the shirt open—fast and clean. Fabric peeled away, her bra did little to shield her large breasts from the cold—or from his eyes. Her breath went shallow, rising and falling against the freezing Alaska air. Goose bumps broke across her blood-smeared skin. It had made its way across her chest, soaking into her white bra, turning it crimson.

Xander was unable to hide his expression. More than being half-dressed—it was the scar. A thick, red keloid that snaked up her abdomen. Angry. Permanent. Few had seen it. Dr. Damião Sequeira had a reason—he was the one who'd performed the surgery. And so had three gangsters Von had once allied with to help track down the ringleader of a white supremacist group she'd eventually snuffed out.

His hand moved slow, deliberate. He traced two fingers along the scar, moving upward, following its path as if trying to map the pain beneath. She didn't stop him. Didn't speak. Just stared past him, jaws clenched, breath held. Von's eyes avoided his, avoided saying anything, as if the silence was safer than what might come if she broke it.

"I...I apologize." He paused, shaking his head. Hesitating, he said, "Can I ask?"

Eyes, raw and wet with emotion, finally met his. "Aryans."

"Aryan Nation Brotherhood?"

She nodded, and all she could say was a single word. "Retaliation." Tears rolled down her face, tears she hadn't expected. "I...I can't talk about it right now."

It was all she could say. Von couldn't bring herself to get into the details, that she was pregnant at the time. If felt like saying the words would break her.

"I'm...I'm so sorry. You don't have to talk about it." Xander reached for her face, wiping the tears from her cheeks. "If I ever see one of them alive, I swear—"

"You don't have to protect me," Von said, refocusing the conversation. "You better sew me up. Wouldn't be the first time."

"And you don't have to do everything alone," he said, taking the gauze and drenching it with hydrogen peroxide. He cleaned the wound. "I've seen a lot of ugly shit, especially during my deployments and I've never seen anyone carry their scar the way you do."

"I didn't survive for your approval."

"Whether you like it or not—you've earned my respect. And my protection." Xander took out the sutures and a Lidocaine injection. "That's non-negotiable. I'm not letting anything happen to you."

"You're not gonna be able to reach it. Better suture this one. Leg's a different story." Von watched him prep the Lidocaine. "And I don't need to be numb."

"I know you're tough. Wouldn't have made it through the hell you did if you weren't. But I'm fixing to numb your stubborn ass anyway—whether you like it or not," he said, injecting her side. She could barely feel the prick—nerves too shot. Body too far gone.

Xander moved to her leg while they waited for the Lidocaine to kick in.

"Can you help me out of this?" Von struggled to get her snow pants off. Xander untied the rope and eased the pants off. Blood from the entry wound to her side had pumped down toward her white panties, turning them bloody as well. Xander's eyes scanned her body, and his cheeks flushed before his gaze returned to her wound.

"At least my bra and underwear match," Von said dryly, trying to dispel the heat coloring her cheeks. "Well? You gonna numb me or admire the view?"

"You're not exactly making it easy to focus, you know," he said, voice low, eyes not quite meeting hers. He cleaned the wound on her leg and injected it, adding a double dose as he would have to cut it open.

He returned to the entry wound at her rib. "Do you feel that?" he asked, lightly pressing the wound.

She shook her head. "Can't feel shit."

"Good." He took out the sutures and began sewing. The entry wound was a bloody hole at the center of her right rib cage, the surrounding tissue inflamed with trauma, steadily oozing. "No major arteries were hit, thankfully."

It took ten minutes for Xander to close the wound. He was fast—focused—the kind of calm that only came from experience under fire. Von clenched her jaw against the pressure, though she felt no pain beyond the dull, persistent throb radiating along her right oblique. She watched him pierce the hook-like needle through the skin with careful precision, each stitch marrying the torn edges together until the wound closed. He tied off the last stitch and snipped the thread.

"You're better than most doctors I've worked with," Von complimented, coughing.

"Easier when there aren't mortars blowing up and bullets flying all over the place." Xander got up and strode to a small galley fridge and brought back a bottled water. He opened it and handed it to her. "You need to stay hydrated."

"Thank you," she said, and took a long drink. The cold water soothed her sandpaper throat like mercy—heaven in her mouth. She swallowed hard. Von hadn't realized just how thirsty she was until that first sip.

Xander sat back down and examined her left thigh. "Gonna need you to bend it a little, so I can take a look at your hamstring. See if it went through or not."

She bent it, groaning from the pain. Xander peeked on the other side.

"No exit wound," he said. "Gonna slice it open, but if I don't get clear visibility, then I think we're gonna have to leave it in."

Xander made a vertical line she thankfully couldn't feel. He took needle-nose forceps and started to dig; she could feel the pressure of the top rooting around in her thigh. Judging by his expression, Von was skeptical that the bullet could be removed. Thighs were made of dense quad tissue, and hers was nothing but thick muscle, potentially making extraction more difficult.

"See anything?"

He poured some hydrogen peroxide over it and dabbed blood away with gauze.

"Negative. It's lodged in there. Best to leave it in and close it up," he said, opening a new suture kit. He took the needle and started sewing the wound closed. In ten minutes, the wound was neatly stitched together. "Got ketamine if you need something for the pain?"

"I'm alright," she murmured, her head spinning, body searching for energy it didn't have.

Xander got up and went to a small closet, taking out towels and fresh clothes. He ran one of the towels under warm water and came back. She blinked slowly up at him, trembling from a cocktail of Kodiak's unforgiving weather and the misery of being shot twice. With a tender touch, Xander reached out, wiped the blood from her chest, her abdomen, and then down her thighs. But she felt the heat of it anyway. The cloth dragged against her battered limbs, dabbing light across the raw line of fresh stitches. The heat from the hot towel soothing her like an elixir, nuking the chill temporarily.

"Thank you," she said weakly.

"Wiped you down as best I could," he said, helping her sit

up and slipping a large thermal long-sleeved shirt over her. "Hope you don't mind wearing my clothes. It's all I've got."

"I'll take it," she said, breathing through the pain. He helped her into fresh snow pants and a jacket. They swallowed her frame, but they'd keep her warm.

Without warning, Zeus sniffed—then growled, scratching and pawing at the floorboards.

"You got something interesting beneath them boards?" Von asked, nodding toward Zeus.

Xander glanced over, brows furrowed. "Does he always do this?"

"Only if he found something—*big*."

"What the hell," he muttered, kneeling beside the dog.

"*Zur Seite gehen*," Von said, ordering Zeus to move aside.

"Far as I know, it's just emergency supplies—tools, a backup satellite beacon, maybe some spare fuel filters."

"Best double-check, because according to my dog, you got a whole lot more down there than wrench grease."

Xander fished a crowbar from one of the side compartments and wedged the tip between the boards. Wood creaked. With a grunt, he levered the panel free. He moved down the line—one by one, the remaining boards lifted away until a square hole gaped beneath them. The air that rose from it was stale, carrying a chemical accent that didn't belong.

"Holy shit," Xander said, reaching down below and pulling out what looked like a white substance plastic wrapped. "It's a brick. At least a thousand grams of tranq dope."

He reached down and began extracting brick after brick. There were a dozen.

"That's twelve thousand grams of fentanyl, cut with xylazine," Von said. Then leveled him with a look. "If you want me working both sides of LAPD and Black Nova with you— and without Cain knowing about it—you need to be straight with me. Did you know that zombie drug crap was down there?"

"Hell no." His voice hit hard. "Of course not."

"Does anyone have the key to this boat?"

"No. I've got one copy and that's on me at all times." Xander stood up and stormed upstairs to the navigation system located in the cockpit near the helm.

Von took the moment to whistle at Zeus. He trotted dutifully by her side. "*Gute Arbeit*," she said, scratching Zeus's head, letting him know that he'd done a good job.

He'd found the drugs without being ordered to, just like he'd stopped the sniper from killing her. It was the second time he'd saved her life. The first time, he laid his body on hers to keep her warm from the Casper, Wyoming frigid weather when she was nearly stabbed to death by the Aryans. She wouldn't have survived without him. The pressure of his one-hundred-pound body had helped to temper the bleeding. Without her dog, she would've bled out or frozen to death before the ambulance could get to her.

Footsteps thundered back down the stairs, Xander's face a mask of frustration and anxiety.

"The navigation log's clean. Engine hours haven't changed."

"So, the boat wasn't moved, wasn't used as a runner to transport the drugs."

"Exactly. Which means Ryker didn't drive it. Didn't need the keys. Didn't have to. Just needed access—long enough to lift the hatch and drop the bricks. The boards are worn. I've opened the panels hundreds of times. Anyone with half a brain, good at burying shit, would've found my little hiding spot in seconds."

Zeus went back to the compartment where the stash of drugs had been hidden and began to bark again. Xander returned to the hideout and looked down.

"Missed one. This one—it's fucking blinking." Xander lifted

the tenth brick out. A small red light blinked from a wafer-thin tracker embedded in the shrink wrap. "It's wired to a pressure-sensitive strip. Low-energy broadcast."

"Is it a bomb?" Fear flushed Von's face.

"Thank God, no. It's not for detonation," he explained. "But it's almost as bad. It's a geo-trigger."

"A tracking device?"

"Yep. Ryker probably chose my boat because I rarely move it. Haven't used it in a couple of years. This is the first time I've motored her off the docks. Put it on here in case I did. Keep track of the drugs in case it was found by some druggy, by the cartel, or by the cops."

"Or by Black Nova." Von gritted her teeth and inched her body until she was sitting at the edge of the bed, leaning in to get a closer look. "Out of all the boats docked at Kodiak Harbor, he picks yours? That's not a coincidence. Ryker would've known—everyone in this town does. I mean, Kodiak's not exactly a metropolis. *The Silver Vow* is yours, and he knew it."

Xander jostled in his pocket and tossed something at her.

She caught it in her hands—a small black burner phone.

"You got that detective's number?"

"Memorized. Why?"

"Send her another message—I know you sent her one in that crate."

"And what am I supposed to say?"

"Tell her about Marchetti. Warn her about the shipments of tranq dope to the Port of Long Beach."

"And I'm suspecting Cain doesn't know about the burner?"

"Nope—and we're keeping it that way. You're the last person Nazario hasn't written off. If this doesn't come from you, it turns into a war," Xander said.

"But why not loop Cain in on it?"

"Because Black Nova doesn't care about Ryker's body count

—we do. All they care about is containment. As long as he's dead and the pipeline's buried, they call it a win. But that detective of yours isn't playing cleanup. Nazario's chasing justice. She's gonna dig in the right direction—and when she does, she'll blow this wide open."

Von considered Xander's words, then quickly plugged Nazario's number into the phone, and saved it under contacts as Detective N. Von thought for a beat, staring at the screen. Without overthinking it, she began to type.

Von: *YSK—Marchetti's down. Sniper hit. Lead to the brain. Wasn't us. Looks like Ryker pulled the trigger. Disloyalty doesn't play well. BOLO: he's running tranq dope through the LB Ports.*

Her thumb hovered over the send button. Von hesitated, then pressed send—just as lights flared in the distance, cutting through the dark and spilling across the cabin window. A boat. Not a random fisherman. Moving steadily. And it was coming—straight for them.

Xander strode quickly toward the window and looked out. "We're not alone."

TEN

THE NAME HE LEFT BEHIND

OUTSIDE IN THE quiet plaza in front of the LAPD headquarters, Detective Nazario and Detective Wilson stood shoulder to shoulder in front of the LAPD Park Center Memorial Wall. Measuring 32 inches long and a width of 12 feet, 3 inches wide, the memorial brandished 2000 shimmering brass plaques, each set in shallow relief, angled just enough to catch shifting light. A deliberate arrangement of staggered rows gave it an artistic rhythm, drawing the eye to each name so that no fallen officers faded into the background.

Carved from collective loss, the memorial wall held a unique story. It was manufactured in Kansas and driven 1,600 miles across the country on a delivery truck, where it found its final resting place in front of headquarters. Nazario and Wilson watched as a worker carefully unwrapped a new pre-engraved plaque with name, rank, and the date they died on duty. The worker stepped up on a small ladder, took out weather-resistant epoxy resin with a caulking gun, added the adhesive to the back of the plate, and pressed it into place.

While Detective Clay Harrison had been killed off-duty and in his home, he'd earned his place on the memorial wall.

The moment the worker set the plaque in, the finality of the act gave a certain permanence. Someone wanted Harrison on that wall—among the blue. A wall that said his spirit lived on but made it clear: he was never coming back. Sadness sank Nazario's spirit, the kind of melancholy that swept over you when someone who stood for goodness was taken from the world too quickly. She didn't have to know Harrison to feel the weight of his loss settle deep in her bones.

Just a few feet away from them, three cops whispered among themselves. She'd forgotten their names, but not their faces. They glanced at the two of them sideways. Brief. Almost imperceptible. Someone untrained might've missed it entirely. Chalked it up as nothing. But not her. Nazario caught the tension in their shoulders, mouths pressed into tight lines. One shifted his weight; another crossed his arms. Their eyes narrowed—hard, cold—then their gaze sheared off too fast, the moment she met their glares.

Nazario cleared her throat and met Wilson's eyes.

Wilson smirked, voice dry. "Well," he whispered, "that wasn't subtle."

"Shit's already circulating—stinking up the air," Nazario said, voice low, "and I don't like it."

"They can kiss what's left of my ass."

Nazario raised an eyebrow.

"Weight loss perks," he muttered, deadpan.

The three beat cops started walking off—but not before passing close. Too close. The first two officers brushed past with just enough pressure to shoulder-check Nazario and Wilson as they went. When the third one shoved Nazario, she pivoted sharply, arms hooking the cop's wrist mid-stride. Not enough to hurt, just enough to remind them, like everyone else on the force knew, of her lifelong Taekwondo training that had earned her a fourth-degree black belt.

Nazario glanced at the officer's name on his uniform. "Do we have a problem, Officer Kendrick?"

"You shouldn't be digging your noses where they don't belong," Kendrick said.

"Excuse me, what did you just say?"

The cop winced as her fingers dug deeper into his wrist, a pressure point that made not only his wrist but his whole arm go limp. He yelped out in pain. The other two wore a look of surprise, not expecting Nazario's move. They shifted uncomfortably—caught between stepping in or backing off. Somewhere behind them, a police radio cracked into life. Traffic sang out in the distance, and then her phone started to chime—an incoming text message she'd been waiting for all day.

Could it be Detective Tyrell Dawson?

"Our noses are fixin' to follow the funk." Wilson gave them a genial smile. "So y'all best go home and take a bath, wash the dirt off you."

Nazario let go of the officer's wrist, and the man stepped back, massaging his arm.

"'Touch me or my partner again and we'll have a misconduct form filed on each of you before your shift's over," Nazario bit out.

"And that applies to anyone else stupid enough to try to intimidate us out of doing our sworn duty—the jobs we're trained to do." Wilson's smile widened. "So, y'all can go ahead and pass that along."

Huxley walked up and joined them as they'd planned. He clocked the tension the second he stepped into range. "What's going on?"

The supervising agent's massive size at six-four, two-twenty of pure muscle towered over the men like a giant. Nazario's reputation was in Taekwondo; his reputation stemmed from brutal, high-level MMA skills. Different styles. Same outcome.

Together, they were known to be the power couple no one wanted to test—or fuck with.

"They made deliberate contact. All three," Nazario said. "Figured a little fun intimidation would send a message."

"Kendrick gave her his signature shove," Wilson added, then said dryly. "Congratulations Officer Kendrick—you just made our list."

Huxley confronted them, stepping into their personal space. Accosting them. Nose to nose. He gave each of them stern eyes. "We're running an investigation, and we're not stopping until we find out who killed Detective Harrison. He was a damn good Gang and Narco detective with his whole life ahead of him until he was executed. More importantly, we will not stop until we find out if there are any dirties on Jaxon Ryker's payroll," he warned. "Do you officers have a problem with that?"

They stayed quiet, but Kendrick's posture frayed—shoulders too stiff, jaw too tight. He shifted his weight, like he could feel the ground starting to give beneath him, as though he wasn't sure who else felt it too. Nazario caught it. Riding the same detective radar wave, Wilson gave her a subtle elbow tap—covert enough for the others not to notice. The moment Huxley's eyes flicked between them for a beat, she knew he'd registered it too. Kendrick's body language went beyond tension. Beyond fear. It came from being found out.

"I asked you a question."

"No," one of them said.

"No, sir," another said.

The third shook his head.

"Good," Huxley said. "Next time you touch Nazario or Wilson, I'll be collecting your badges. Detective Nazario could take all three of you dipshits down on your asses before you can even blink. But if I hear that you—or anyone else on this force—so much as look at her the wrong way, I'll knock your teeth down your fucking throat and anyone else's who tries anything. That goes for Chief Johnson and Captain Gus Humphrey, too. We're going to find out who almost killed them—and we're coming for whoever did it. Pass it on. You and yours fuck with her? You're fucking with the wrong senior FBI agent. Federal muscle that'll take down everything and everyone in your chain of command. Got it?"

They nodded without a word, eyes down, like kids who knew better than to talk back.

Walking away, their arrogance collapsed into silence, their steps heavier than before.

"You alright?" Huxley asked, putting a hand on Nazario's back when they were gone.

Nazario inhaled deeply, raking her hand through her hair. "Wish you hadn't told them that we're conducting an internal investigation."

"They already know, Nazario. That much is obvious," Wilson said. "C'mon, you know word spreads around here like gasoline on dry grass."

"Wilson's right. They already know. Better we tell them to their faces that we're not getting punked. They're not intimidating us, Anaya." Huxley gripped her shoulders. "If we don't crush this now, who knows what's next? Bricks thrown through our home window. Warning notes left on our windshield. Death threats. It's not just you and me or Wilson. We've got a six-month-old to consider. Her safety. We needed to send a firm message, and I think we did."

Nazario conceded. "We've never had to investigate our own. Speaking of—haven't been able to get a hold of Detective Tyrell Dawson. But someone texted me—"

"Well, I've got good news. An agent I work with is good friends with Dawson. Convinced him to meet us. Highland Café in Highland Park—in an hour."

Nazario checked her watch. "We better hit the road and beat traffic." Nazario opened up an unread text. "If Dawson didn't text me, then I wonder who did?"

Nazario's breath caught in her throat.

"It's Von!"

"What did she say?" Wilson asked with urgency.

"Feel safer reading it once we're in your vehicle," Nazario said. They hustled to Wilson's Chevy Tahoe. Once inside, she pulled up Von's message and read it aloud.

"Marchetti's dead. Wasn't Black Nova. Von says it was one of Ryker's snipers who took the shot. Disloyalty got him killed." Nazario paused, then added. "Oh, and there's a BOLO—Ryker's running tranq dope through the Long Beach ports."

They idled briefly in the car, digesting the message.

Huxley was the first to break the silence. "Commander Cain said we'd have to follow their lead, but this is the first message from them. Seems a little out of place."

"Technically, it's the second message," Wilson plugged in the address to Highland Café in his navigation system and began driving in that direction. "Remember, the first one was the note Von left us with the frozen DB—instead of, you know, frozen *fish* like normal people ship."

"That's right, and if we follow the deductive criminal profiling and the inferential logic of Von's behavior—she most likely acted against Black Nova's protocols. They wouldn't ship a body to us. They'd take care of it on their own. That's how the CIA handles it. That's how they'd handle a corpse, too," Nazario reasoned.

"So, if she went rogue sending us the first message and now the text, then what you're saying is she must've acted alone?" Huxley said.

"Yep. I'm with Nazario on this," Wilson said. "I highly doubt Cain would've texted us."

"She must've sent this via a burner phone," Nazario said, then turned to Huxley. "Blake, is there a way we can find out?"

"Yeah, that's pretty simple. I'll get CAST on it. It's the bureau's Cellular Analysis Survey Team. They can get the CDRs, which would entail analyzing call detail records, checking the text metadata, and determining if the phone is linked to any known subscriber. CAST will also be able to investigate cell tower triangulation and get the exact location based on when the text was sent. Most likely, it'll show Kodiak, Alaska, where Eli Vega was shipped from," Huxley said.

"We care more about whether it was a burner," Nazario said, "because if it was, I'd assume it's a phone that Cain doesn't know she has. I'm basing that on how other agencies operate—CIA, NSA—they issue operatives custom phones. Encrypted, locked down, with modified operating systems. Strictly controlled for safe and private communication."

Huxley jumped on his phone. "Sending an email to my CAST contact. We should be able to verify the burner within a day or so once they jump on it. Won't take them long at all."

"They'll need my phone, right?" she asked.

"Once we confirm it's a burner, we can narrow down whether or not Von is doing her own thing. Basically, a female Jason Bourne with a dog," Wilson said.

"Yep. CAST is a digital forensics team and would need to extract data," Huxley said.

His lead foot zipped them down the 110 northbound, weaving and maneuvering through traffic with the expertise of a NASCAR driver. What would normally take forty-five minutes or longer with dreaded Los Angeles traffic ended up taking thirty-five minutes with time to spare.

"With as fast as you drive, I'm surprised you've never once got a speeding ticket," Nazario said, amused as Wilson smiled, huffing his breath on his nails and brushing them on his shirt.

"When you're as charming as me," he said, "you can talk your way out of one."

They pulled up and parked in front of Highland Café. Its gold font looked like the type-face one would use at a Tattoo parlor. The large glass front overlooked York Boulevard, a street widely known for its eclectic mix of eateries, shops, and cultural historic landmarks such as the 1963 Bob Baker Marionette Theater. Avenue 50 Studio was a non-profit gallery that focused on Latino and Chicano art, highlighting talented local artists.

On the same street stood the Los Angeles Police Museum, showcasing the history of the LAPD, featuring vintage police vehicles, motorcycles, badges, uniforms, and artifacts tied to the city's criminal history and law enforcement legacy. Visitors could view bullet-riddled patrol cars from the 1997 North Hollywood shootout—twisted metal and shattered glass that always left Nazario's stomach tight. The museum even had a copy of *The White Album* associated with the Manson Family murders. Nazario's favorite part of the LAPM was a replica of Alice Stebbins Wells's uniform, the first U.S. policewoman, honoring pioneering women in policing.

They climbed out of the Tahoe and strode toward the Highland Café—a laid-back corner spot with sun-faded brick, chipped blue trim, and the warm scent of fresh coffee, espresso, and pastries drifting out of the open door.

"Let's table the discussion for later. Gotta prepare to interview with Detective Dawson. I just hope he's not intimidated by the three of us," Huxley said.

"Either he'll open up or shut down," Nazario said.

They showed up twenty minutes ahead of schedule, but Nazario's assumption that they'd get their first was immediately disproven. Detective Tyrell Dawson was already waiting. His knee bounced manically. Eyes staring down into his coffee.

Hands clasped, released, then clasped again, like he couldn't decide what to hold onto.

"I'll order us some coffee, you guys go ahead," Huxley said.

Wilson and Nazario took a seat in front of the anxious detective and shook his hand, palms clammy, accompanied by a visible tremble. Dawson quickly retreated after the formal gesture and gripped his coffee cup, as if trying to hide his nervousness.

"Detective Dawson," Nazario began, "my name's Detective Nazario, and this is my partner, Detective Wilson—Homicide."

"I know who the three of y'all are—everyone admires Homicide's 'dream-team,'" he said, voice quieter and calmer than she'd expected. It belied his body language. Their meeting was the last place he wanted to be.

"That's a mighty nice compliment," Wilson said with a warm smile. "Surprised I made the cut. Pretty sure I'm just the referee around here."

"Don't sell yourself short," Dawson said with that same low, even tone. "You spit game—dropped some knowledge, talking down a man who'd already killed his wife and kids. Four hours, just you and a folding chair. That kind of resolve? You can't teach it. You're a natural. Either you have it, or you don't."

Wilson raised a brow. "You did your research."

"That's what I do," Dawson said. His knee continued to bob up and down beneath the table; Nazario could feel the vibration of his unease. Despite the detective's calm exterior, anxiety seeped out of the man's pores.

Huxley returned with three coffees and handed them off, knowing that Nazario and Wilson were opposites. She liked hers with cream and Splenda, and he took his black. He found a chair at a nearby table that wasn't being used and joined them.

"Hope I didn't miss anything."

"Oh, we're just getting to know each other. Making small

talk. Haven't started yet. I'll say, I'm mighty impressed with you," Wilson said, pivoting to their interviewee. "Detective Dawson, you know a whole lot about us, and we don't know much about you."

"All you need to know is that I came here to do the right thing."

"We're here because of Detective Clay Harrison," Nazario started. "He left us your name—think he knew he was a target."

"Do you know he was just killed three days ago?" Huxley asked.

Dawson closed his eyes and blew out a long breath. After a beat, he opened his eyes and met theirs. "Just found out today." He picked up his coffee and took a sip. It shivered with the shudder of his hand. His eyes turned moist, misting with emotion he couldn't contain. "Clay was a good man, my best friend. He was my brother. Went through the academy together. He was my best man at my wedding. The Godfather to my son. We were partners on patrol. Transferred to Gang and Narco the same year—stayed partners there, too."

"How're you holding up?" Wilson leaned in, hand steady as it settled over Dawson's shaky fingers. "I can't imagine what you're going through right now. To lose a partner, your brother?"

In that moment, Nazario loved how easily Wilson could tap into his compassion. He had the kind of empathy that disarmed the hardest cops—and the most dangerous criminals.

"Took a leave of absence. Put in the papers today. Captain Humphrey made it a priority—told me to go home. Was fixing to work this week and be off the next, but she said that work could wait. Said that my heart couldn't. That's why she's the best damn boss we've got. No bullshit. I'd follow her anywhere," he said with conviction.

It sounded like Humphrey, Nazario thought. Her best friend always prioritized mental health.

In their line of work, the job contributed to elevated rates of substance abuse, divorce, and suicide. Chronic stress degraded the body, impaired cognition, and eroded emotional resilience over time. Nazario knew addiction all too well. Being an alcoholic was the casualty of running herself into the ground. Since having her daughter, she'd stayed sober. But the itch was always there, tempting her to scratch it, to feed it, to help her numb it all away. In high-risk jobs—the military, firefighters, paramedics/EMTs, disaster relief workers, ER nurses, and doctors— you saw things you couldn't unsee.

You witnessed what many never would, and that shit stayed with you.

"Harrison was supposed to talk with us. Looks like someone got to him first. As I'm sure you've heard, we're working on the Ryker case. A DB showed up at the Port of Long Beach. A dirty DA. We suspect there are more within LAPD. Different departments. We're conducting an internal investigation. When was the last time you spoke with him, and were you aware Harrison was working on something big?"

"We never kept anything from each other. But he kept this from me. Had no idea why he suddenly became distant. Paranoid. Started telling me he thought he was being followed. Two days before he was killed, he came to me, made me promise him that I'd talk to you if something were to happen to him. I didn't know what it was about. Pressed him to give me something, anything to go by. How could I help if I was in the dark?" Dawson paused, eyes cast down at his hands.

"Did he finally open up and tell you what he was working on?" Wilson asked.

"He told me that there were dirty cops working for Ryker and that he thought he was on their shit list."

"Did he show you that list?" Huxley asked. "Any officers from Vice or Narco?"

Dawson shook his head. "He was afraid of retaliation. Afraid that if he told me, I'd end up dead. Reminded me that I was the one with a wife and a child to think about. Said he didn't have those types of obligations and responsibilities. Wanted to keep me safe. Protect me."

"Do you know if he hired a PI? Did he put a tail on the dirty cops?" Nazario asked.

"I know one thing. He was carrying around his camera, which was kind of unusual. We used to hang after work. Grab a beer, enjoy a boy's night out whenever my wife gave me the green light. But that all stopped a few months back. I asked him what he was up to, but he never let on. Makes sense now. Because if there's one thing I know about my partner, it's this— he was damn good at gathering intel. He wasn't the type to outsource what he could handle himself."

"There's a thumb drive we haven't reviewed yet. But my source believes Harrison had compiled whatever's on it," Nazario said, thinking about Humphrey—the one person she trusted to feed her truth from the inside.

"Knowing Clay, I'm sure it was all him. He wouldn't show me or let me in on it. If the intel was highly sensitive and dangerous, he'd never hire an outsider to help. He'd never ever risk an innocent life. The night before he died," Dawson's voice cracked, as he breathed through his nose to quell the oncoming surge of tears that welled in his eyes. "I begged him to spend the night at my place. Told him he could sleep on the couch. I was worried about him. Had this bad feeling. Couldn't sleep all night. He no longer felt safe at his pad. He said he couldn't risk something happening to my son. Was afraid danger would follow him into our home."

Dawson dug in his pocket and handed them a key along with a sealed envelope.

"That night, he gave this to me. Told me to give it to the three of you."

Huxley took the envelope and the key. "What's the key to?"

"He said the note would explain," Dawson said. Tears slipped down his cheeks. He dragged the back of his hand across his face, trying to hold the rest in. "Said it'd tell you what he couldn't."

ELEVEN

THE REDLIGHT PROTOCOL

A SPOTLIGHT SWEPT across the inky night, skimming across its choppy surface, shining through the cabin window as Xander glanced out, hand on his gun. The surge from the oncoming boat sent tumultuous waves slamming against *The Silver Vow*, pitching her violently to one side, forcing Von off the bed, where she smacked on the floor with a hard thud.

"Stay down here and keep your weapon up—cover your angle!" Xander shouted.

Von gritted her teeth through the pain, dragging her body up to her feet. Another wave pounded the starboard, causing her to stumble. She managed to find her footing as the boat rocked again. Her semi-automatic had been tossed near the hatch. She grabbed it just in time for another swell to hit, battering the sixty-foot Steiner Shipyard like it was some flimsy rowboat.

Gunfire erupted, slicing through the stillness.

The hell if she was staying in the cabin. Von climbed up the companion ladder, her left leg burning with each step, ribs throbbing up her right oblique as she clutched the railing for support and opened the hatch. A bullet flew toward her head;

she ducked in time for it to crash against the metal hatch, ricocheting off. Xander fired back but missed as the assailants dove for cover. Von waited patiently, aiming for the center console where she'd last spotted the goons. The moment one poked their head up at the center console—hesitating and unaware—Von took the shot. One round, straight through the skull. He dropped where he stood.

Xander spun around, eyes sharp. "Told you to stay in the cabin—you'll make your injuries worse."

"And I'm not some fucking damsel. I'm on the team for a reason."

"Damn good shot," he admitted under his breath.

"Watch out, their aiming for the engine!" Von shouted. Von and Xander shot back but the two remaining men took cover, aiming their AR-15s at the heart of the boat.

POP! POP! POP! POP!

Rather than shoot directly at them, the men opened fire—short-barreled AR barking over the water. Rounds tore through the hull and engine housing, hitting *The Silver Vow* where it hurt the most. The motor coughed, sputtering...and then died. They were adrift.

Xander sprinted to the engine, firing back at the two men.

"I need to clamp the fuel hose. Don't hit their engine—we may need their boat," Xander ordered, opening the engine panel. Smoke curled out. From above, a buzzing sound caught her attention, just as too much silence raised her suspicion. A temporary cease-fire didn't mean they were in the clear. Something was up. She tilted her head up and spotted a drone hovering above them.

"We got eyes on us. It's feeding them our location," she said, as the faint hum of the rotors divided the air.

The drone dipped lower, its frame bulkier than usual. It looked like a higher-end military-grade machine. And as it came closer, she spotted an olive-green object wired beneath. "Holy shit, they're not just tracking our location—it's a fucking grenade."

"Shoot it down before they detonate!" Xander shouted.

Von had already positioned herself before his frantic command. Without hesitation, she aimed and struck it at its fuselage at the center frame. It exploded in midair, its arms tore off, parts flew into the ocean, while others rained onto the deck. The direct hit slammed into the propeller blades as they showered onto the boat. The main body cracked, spiraling, and landing on the cabin roof with a heavy thunk.

Von charged toward Xander as best as she could, moving her aching body to help him as he struggled with the engine.

He dropped to his knees. "Hand me the toolbox, it's on the other side in the compartment under the bench."

She staggered to the bench, flipped it open, and grabbed the tools.

With her back turned, a loud thump vibrated the deck. The two men had made their way onto the boat. Von took the metal toolbox and swung it hard, hitting one of the men in the gut. He doubled over and fell onto the floorboards. Xander stood quickly and tried to take a shot, but the last man standing wrangled his arms around Von, putting the gun to her head.

"*¡Suelta tu arma!*" the man shouted. "*¡Suelta tu arma!*"

Von considered her options: take a bullet to her head, let Xander either try and take a shot or surrender his weapon—Plan C, take a chance and shoot him anywhere she had a clear shot. With her upper arms pinned and her gun still gripped in her hand, she calmly spoke.

"Do as he says," Von told Xander.

"Hell, the fuck, no."

"Drop your weapon," Von said, giving him a "trust me" look.

Xander cursed under his breath and dropped his weapon, raising his hands in the air.

"*Déjame ir y te mostraré dónde está la droga,*" she said, telling the man she'd show him where the drugs were if he let her go.

"*¡Tú también suelta tu arma primero!*" he said, ordering her to drop her weapon as well.

The second man stumbled to his feet, repositioning his assault rifle, the barrel of the AR-15 aimed at Xander's head. Von dropped the heavy metal toolbox on the man's foot, and his grip loosened. She spun around, shoved her gun to his heart, and pulled the trigger. He collapsed and was instantly dead. The second man shot at Xander, just as he dove for his gun, missing him by a few centimeters from painting the deck with his brains. In one swift move, she turned and—*POP! POP!*—slugged the last man standing, taking two to the belly.

He crumpled onto the deck, gurgling and writhing, coughing up blood.

Von stepped closer, racked the slide back, and shot the man in the head.

"You just proved yourself once again," Xander said, then, without wasting any time, picked up the toolbox and tried desperately to save his boat. "Might need your help."

She joined him, flinging open the engine hatch. A hybrid blend of pungent chemical fumes mixed with diesel fuel accosted her senses, burning her throat, hitting her nostrils. Coughing, Von covered her nose with the crook of her elbow. The engine was bleeding gasoline from the .223 caliber Remington that tore through the fuel line. Pressurized gases wheezed against the bulkhead like a dying animal trapped in steel. Xander stayed calm, hands moving with the expertise of a pit crew at a NASCAR event.

"Hand me the clamp," he said, and she dug into the toolbox

and gave it to him. He closed off the hose, using the clamp to slow the leak. Xander jammed the rag over the rupture, tightening the clamp until the seepage stopped. "The ignition coil is damaged. I'll have to hotwire the starter solenoid—hand me a flathead."

She slapped the screwdriver in his hand. Xander wedged it in the rectangular unit mounted near the engine—the starter solenoid. The metal bridged both the positive and starter terminals, sending a surge straight to the motor. The engine coughed twice, then roared back to life. Von grabbed a few more rags from the toolbox and helped him sop up the remaining pools of fuel that had pumped out of the ruptured hose.

Xander hoisted himself from the ground, stretching his legs from being in an uncomfortable position for too long. He rubbed his back, grimacing.

"You alright?" she asked.

"Injured my back."

"How'd it happen?"

Xander paused for a beat, eyes looking off in a distance, as if searching for the words.

"A mortar hit our tank in Afghanistan. Was thrown twenty feet," he finally said. "Had back surgery. It was a bitch to get through without pain meds. Saw too many soldiers popping them like candy—I'd rather grit it and bear it than get addicted to pills."

"Can't be easy."

"Nothing I've ever done in my life has come easy."

"What do we do with the bodies? I say we send them to Nazario again."

"No way. You've pulled that stunt already. Got away with it once, and without Cain finding out. Do it again and we risk blowing our cover. They may catch on to us, find out that we've gone rogue, working both sides."

"Got a better idea? I'd think they'd need to know about these two cartel goons."

"Smarter approach? We send her pictures instead. Agent Huxley will most likely run them through facial recognition software and can maybe ID them. Give them a job to do. We've already done ours. But we'll need to catch Cain up to speed. He'll know what to do with the dope. Send Sasha over. We need to build trust. How we do that is to let Sasha do her job—clean up the mess, dispose of the bodies however she sees fit."

Xander handed her the burner.

Von flipped it open, tapped on the camera icon, and took a couple of close-up shots of each man. She then selected the only message they had, which was to Detective Nazario, and considered what to say.

Von: *Cartel working for Ryker. Don't know them. Don't know their names. Tried to take us down. A boat owned by one of Black Nova Ops hid dope with a tracking device. Dropped them before they dropped us.*

Von then attached the images and showed the text to Xander. He gave her a thumbs-up, and she pressed send. She gave him back his burner just as his Black Nova-issued mobile, rang. It was a number he didn't recognize; Von could tell by the look of confusion on his face.

"Not sure who it is," he admitted, and then answered.

Since they were isolated in the middle of the ocean, Xander placed the call on speaker.

"Confirm comm security."

"Secure. You're on speaker, sir."

"It's been long enough. Would've expected a call by now." It was Cain, and he sounded like he'd been waiting for this call to go wrong. "What's the latest on Marchetti? Do we have the intel?"

Xander blew out a breath. "Package lost. Redlight Protocol is live."

"What do you mean lost?"

Von wasn't sure what Redlight Protocol was; she could only deduce that it must've meant some emergency status relating to a mission going wrong. "We mean that Ryker put up a sniper to take him out," she said. "Almost killed me in the process. Looks like they were aiming for Xander as well."

"Were you injured?" he asked, voice tight with fury. It was clear the commander wasn't concerned for her well-being, rather angry that her injury might compromise the mission. Angry that it potentially cost him time, resources, or deniability.

"I'm alright."

"You didn't answer my question—yes or no."

"Yes. They didn't hit any vital organs. But it hurts like a son of a bitch. Got me in the leg and ribs. I'm stitched up. I'm fine. It won't prevent me from doing my job."

"Good. Now what in the hell happened? Marchetti was supposed to be managing the dope."

Xander cut in. "He was working an angle behind Ryker's back. Trying to take the shipment for himself. Broker new terms with *Los Cuervos*. Mateo Salazar, the cartel runner, took off in the boat with the zombie drug when live fire started."

"Any intel on the sniper?"

Xander hesitated for a beat. Von recalled his code name: *Deadeye*. She also recalled the look on the former Navy SEAL's face. It was a look of recognition, a look that said he knew something, something he wasn't ready to share, and she wondered if he was going to open up to Cain.

"We took him down," Xander said. "But the attack...it was personal."

"And why would you think that, Holt?" Cain bit out. "Mind telling me what you're hiding? I'll find out either way. Best it come from your mouth because if I find out you're keeping sensitive information, it's gonna be your ass."

"He went by *Deadeye*—former SEAL. Petty Officer First Class Logan Rourke. He was under my command in Afghanistan. We were trapped in the valley. Hindu Kush mountains. Should have called off the mission, but I didn't. Our team split into two units. I led Bravo, and Rourke led Alpha. Taliban captured two of his men and executed them on video," Xander said, taking a ten-count to think, or perhaps gather the strength to admit wrongdoing. "Rourke was right, and I was in the wrong...and he never forgave me. I never forgave myself. Ryker recruited him for a reason. To get to me."

Von was taken aback by the story, but more than that, rattled by Ryker's reach, concerned about how he'd dug into Xander's past and found just the right man to pull the trigger. If the drug lord had that kind of resources and pull—who else was on his payroll? How many ghosts from Xander's past were lining up with guns? And what about hers? Could someone from the Aryan Brotherhood be working for Ryker, waiting to return the favor she'd paid in blood?

Reading her thoughts, Cain warned, "Well, let's hope that's the only pissed-off SEAL—because if you've angered more, the two of you won't be so lucky next time."

Xander put the call on mute and turned to her. "Don't tell him about the drugs."

"Wouldn't he wanna know?"

"Yes, and we're not telling him shit."

"What about the bodies?"

"Mention them and that's it," he ordered and then unmuted the call.

"We've got another problem," Von began, and then she filled Cain in on the two deceased cartel members who had tried to board *The Silver Vow*—omitting the drugs stashed on it.

"Are you certain that the drone had a locator on it?" Cain asked, sounding more irritated as the conversation continued.

"If it had a grenade ready to blow us up," Von said, "then I'm pretty damn certain it had a tracker on it."

"Since the boat is operational, you need to move. It's too risky to use the cartel's boat. Leave it there," Cain said, then added. "I've another task for both of you. One of Ryker's chemists vanished two hours ago. Her last encrypted ping was at Port Ashton Cannery Dock."

"You mean Prince William Sound?" Xander said.

"Yes. Move the bodies on the boat they came in on. Sasha will deal with them. Dock *The Silver Vow* at Port Ashton. I've got a guy that'll patch it up. We'll need it in case Ryker tries to move the next shipment by sea. You've already got eyes on him —and a boat that won't raise any flags."

"What about this chemist? What're you expecting us to do with her?" Von asked.

"If Ryker gets to her first, he'll kill her and bury the formula. This isn't any old type of zombie dope. He's cutting a new batch, making it unique. Stronger. More addictive. More lethal. We need to know how that formula works, so we can stop him," Cain said, tone emotionless. "Intercept. Secure. Keep her alive. Get her talking. If you don't move fast—I activate another asset. And clean the trail myself."

The moment Cain hung up, Von let Xander have it.

"What in the hell are we gonna do with the dope?"

"Dumping it. That's what we're fixing to do," Xander said. "We can't have this kind of shit on us. It's better that we get rid of it than have it out on the streets killing people."

"Don't think dumping it into the ocean is the right move. We'd have to weigh it down with something, but even then. It's toxic to the ocean. No way I'm letting you pollute the ocean."

"Now's not the time to get sentimental. Put your veterinarian, animal-loving ways behind you or come up with a better plan. Because knowing Cain, he'd want to destroy it anyway to contain the threat."

"And that's a mistake. Despite your loyalty to him, it's precisely why we can't fully trust his decisions. It's why you're doing this behind his back. Your gut tells you the same as mine. We send it to Nazario. Do you have a vacuum sealer and old spare parts?"

"Yeah, I use the sealer to preserve food, keep fish fresh—it also comes in handy when I'm trying to make sure my gear doesn't get wet."

"We double-vacuum seal it and mask it with motor grease, diesel-soaked rags. Pack it with spare parts. It'll throw off the scanners. An even cleaner way to do this—we bury it under ice and actual fish this time," Von said, though as a vegan, she hated the idea of having to catch fish and freeze them.

Xander rubbed his chin, working his jaw muscles as he weighed their options.

"This could be dangerous. But it can work. If we vacuum seal the dope and hide it under ice, it'll look like a cooler brick."

"Exactly."

"I've got empty crates, a trawling net, and a commercial ice maker on board."

"That's all we need."

They held each other's gaze—long and unflinching—just the heavy, unspoken question hanging between them. After a beat, Xander sighed. "Alright, let's do this thing. You rest. You've already strained yourself enough."

In the cabin, Von put fresh bandages on her side, then slipped her pants down to add a fresh wrap to her leg. Xander walked in, his eyes roamed over her, before flicking away—detached, casual. Heat crawled up her neck uninvited, her body betraying the disinterest she wore like armor, the autonomy and asexuality she'd spent years cultivating.

Xander searched the cabin, eyes avoiding hers.

"Trying to find where I left the trawling net," he said.

"Is this it?" Von looked behind her. "Think I'm lying on it?"

He leaned in close, his face inches from hers, lips a sheet away. "That's it," he whispered.

Von drew a breath. His eyes lingered on her mouth—like he might kiss her. Gasoline clung to him, but beneath it she caught a hint of leather and sandalwood. It stirred something carnal within her, making her wonder how he'd taste. But he grabbed the net instead and turned away. As he stalked off, she watched him go, pulse kicking harder now. They were in danger, not from Ryker or the cartel—but from whatever this was becoming, from a pull neither of them could control.

TWELVE

THE DEAD MAN'S MAP

Dear Detective Nazario,

If you're reading this letter, it means that I didn't make it. When I became a cop, I was sworn to a duty to honor the law and protect the innocent. I swore to a sacred vow that not only I'd uphold, but every cop who joined the force along with me would do the same. But I soon learned that I was naïve, seeing the world with rose-tinted glasses, never imagining that I'd be where I am today.

Never in a million years did I expect I'd fear for my life and not from the criminals I helped put behind bars, but from the very men who promised to seek justice and do their job of defending our society against evil. I knew coming into our line of work was dangerous and that any one of us could be killed in the line of duty. I had no idea our own brothers in blue would be the ones to take me out. So, if you're reading this, someone killed me before I could expose them, and that is why I need your help.

On the thumb drive that Captain Humphrey gave you is a list I've built over two years. Five names. All cops. One of them is behind my death. But the list isn't complete—there are two more names I kept off it because I'd just found out and hadn't had the time to update this. But they're in the lock box. So, seven in total. While I don't have evidence of this, I think there's enough intel I've gathered and enough threats on my life to know that it would only be a matter of time before they get to me. And Jaxon Ryker is the puppet master behind it all.

The key in this envelope is to my P.O. Box #216 at Iron-wood Vault on Church Street in Highland Park. Please keep the information private and only share it with people at the LAPD you absolutely trust. I hope you can finish what I started. All I ask is that you protect Detective Dawson with your lives. He has a family. Keep him out of this. The last thing I want is for him to end up like me—dead, with too many truths buried beside me.

Sincerely,
Detective Clay Harrison

DETECTIVE NAZARIO FINISHED READING the note aloud, leaving behind a somber silence in her wake. The silence settled in her home office until her six-month-old's hungry cry pierced the room, breaking Nazario, Wilson, and Huxley out of an eerie spell that had seized each of them. Words from a ghost, a dead man's map left behind.

Huxley stood slowly, the baby's cry growing louder, but nothing was more raucous than what was not said. The inevitability of having to uncover a list of dirty blue. Just how many officers were working for Ryker? One, two, three? Could there be more than four? It felt like a nightmare she couldn't wake up from. It carved a brutal line between right and wrong, placing them firmly on Team Good-Cop. A badge they would each wear proudly, but one that divided the force.

Suddenly, they were the narcs everyone hated—the do-gooders, even the so-called clean cops couldn't stand. No one liked cops who investigated cops. Nazario could sense a shift at work. Yesterday, the moment she and Wilson walked into their office, several officers went from conversing to turning off the chatter like a light switch and promptly striding out. They were told not to give her and Wilson shit. But ever since the memorial wall, the cold shoulders said plenty—and spoke louder than words ever could.

That was precisely why they decided to view the contents of the thumb drive and envelope in the privacy of her home office instead of at the station, where the atmosphere had quickly turned uncomfortable. Chief Johnson's no-nonsense, stern leadership didn't dissuade the officers from talking, from the rumors that began spinning. He'd even received a warning himself and shared it with them earlier that week.

Keep your narc detectives out of our business or start picking out your headstone.

Nazario and Wilson had grown worried. "Chief, maybe you just take that vacation you've been wanting," Nazario had suggested after reading the note that had been left on the chief's car window. "You've got four, five weeks of PTO you haven't used. Haven't even taken time off since before your divorce."

"I'm with Nazario on this," Wilson had said. "We love seeing your face every day, but we'd like to keep seeing it attached to a living body—if you know what I mean? I'm not trying to sound grim, but Harrison didn't listen either."

"I'm not letting them threaten me!" Chief said, slamming a fist on his desk. "They will *not* run me out of the job my Black ass worked too damn hard to earn."

"We're just worried—" Nazario began, but Johnson cut her off.

"And I will *not* let a bunch of grunt bitches intimidate the two most seasoned, best homicide detectives this department's got. Not happening. I'm fixin' to find out who wrote this note—and I'm taking their damn badge. Period."

Nazario swallowed a shaky breath, trying desperately to sweep the worry out of her head—but that dark, lurking dread she'd felt her entire career, when something bad was about to happen, wouldn't vacate. She'd worked plenty of tough cases—but this was the first time someone she loved like a father was in the crosshairs. Chief Johnson had been in her life since birth. He was Daddy's partner back in the day, before they'd risen through the ranks, side by side. A Black man and a Puerto Rican —pushing hard, bleeding harder, just to break the ceiling. Her dad had gone on to gangs and narco. Johnson remained in homicide.

They hadn't worn the same badge number in years, but their bond never broke.

Thirty years of friendship. Bound by blood, by loss, and the badge. Thirty years of partnership. Of knowing each other's moves before they made them. Thirty years of shared war stories, some they never dared tell. Thirty years of late calls, cold coffee, and holding the line. Thirty years of trust, one silence at a time. Thirty years of loyalty, even after the badge changed hands. Thirty years of laughs, arguments, and knowing when not to speak.

Thirty years of chasing monsters and standing shoulder to shoulder.

Thirty years of brotherhood. Then came the bullet that rewrote everything.

That's what made her father's murder hit Johnson "like the fucking roof collapsed on me," as the chief would often tell her.

It was why he was so protective of her. Nazario knew that Chief Trevor Johnson had lost a big piece of himself the day her father was gunned down. A piece of himself he'd never get back. But what he carried was Daddy's grit, his determination to always do the right thing, even among men who forgot what that meant.

Nazario wished Johnson were off somewhere, sending her postcards—keeping his head down until the internal investigations blew over. Instead, he was stubbornly holed up behind his desk, working late when needed, always just a call away when shit hit the fan. The man didn't know how to disappear. Not when everything around him was rotting from the inside. He stayed in the fire because, damn it, someone had to. Not for glory. Not for thanks. But because when shit broke loose, he was the one who didn't flinch.

The presence of her cooing daughter broke through Nazario's ruminations.

Huxley swayed their six-month-old. While she'd put on much-needed baby fat and gotten taller like her daddy, their daughter still looked like a tiny doll in his massive arms. He'd insisted Nazario keep pumping and storing milk so she wouldn't have to carry the full weight of feeding Ariabella alone. While Nazario was still breastfeeding, it helped to get the baby used to both nursing and bottle-feeding.

"Well, that's one dead detective who was more organized than some I've known alive. Shall we venture forward," Wilson began with a jovial smile, "and take a look-see at what's on the hard drive?"

Nazario powered on her laptop, connected a USB-C adaptor to the USB-C port on the left of her MacBook Air, and then plugged in the flash drive. "I'd rather not be looking at this," Nazario groaned, the weight of what they might find souring her belly. Huxley sat in a chair next to her, feeding the baby and watching her screen populate. Wilson stood looking over her shoulder. There were five names, three of which she recognized, and two she didn't.

1. Officer Ronnie Salerno
2. Officer Marcus Delgado
3. Officer Tyler Kendrick
4. Sergeant Vincent Greer
5. Detective Lila Mendez

The drive consisted of a root folder with five subfolders—one for each name. The detective had quietly compiled intel on every officer, including redacted IA summaries, internal complaint forms that had been wiped from official records, time stamped body cam stills, and off-the-record interviews.

"Salerno and Delgado, they're the two who'd tried to kidnap Ariabella," Huxley pointed out, "before they were killed by Von."

"Wait...zoom in on those surveillance stills in their folders, Nazario," Wilson said, and she did as she was asked. "Those pictures are dated two weeks before the abduction attempt."

Nazario analyzed the images. When not expanded, it was difficult to recognize the faces, but she pulled in for a close-up, she could see them clearly, and more importantly, who they were meeting with—Jaxon Ryker. They were being handed cash. This wasn't a spur-of-the-moment crime, rather financially motivated.

"Looks like Officer Kendrick had a reason to be jumpy when he shoved past us at the memorial wall," Nazario said.

She opened up Kendrick's folder. It was thin but damning: audio clips of locker room conversations with other officers casually mocking "The Clean Team"—which the three of them had been nicknamed.

"Wonder how long that Nazario bitch can last. Keeps

pushing like that, she'll be six feet under with her narc daddy," Kendrick said to one of his boys in blue.

Laughter followed. Then a new voice, unfamiliar, said, "Oh, how I'd love to do the honors. She's got it coming to her if she doesn't stop poking around. Her and that Fat Albert partner of hers."

More laughter and celebratory claps.

"Detective Isaac *Snack Pack* Wilson," Kendrick said. "Heard he's always stuffing his face with something—even on homicide scenes."

"Dude's got a stomach of steel and a mouth that never shuts up," someone cracked.

The audio clip ended, and, after knowing her partner of more than two decades, Nazario wasn't surprised by Wilson's burst of laughter. He never took himself seriously and very rarely took anything personally. That's why she loved him and why they were the complete opposite. During interrogations, Wilson's casual knack and relaxed conversational style balanced her cut-the-crap directness, making getting confessions easier when they worked together than when either went at it alone.

"Snack Pack," Wilson said with a hoot. "Now that's the one they got right!"

Huxley and Nazario exchanged a look, neither finding the moment funny.

The two remaining folders—Greer and Mendez—were unfamiliar, but the evidence was worse. Greer had pulled three separate OD cases from the system mid-report. Mendez, an IA detective, had flagged three early warnings on Kendrick—then buried them. And doing so revealed what Nazario hadn't wanted to admit to herself: the rot wasn't isolated. It was systematic.

She leaned back in her chair, hands on her head, brows raised, eyes wide, mouth hanging open. Nazario glanced up at the ceiling, as if searching for some version of reality where what they'd found wasn't true. Searching for answers other than the oldest motive known to man—greed. In all her years as a homicide detective, money always landed the number one spot as the reason why people kill. Make it look like an accident or a robbery gone wrong. Slip a little antifreeze in the unassuming victim's breakfast smoothie every morning and slowly poison them to death. Or make it quick—messy, personal—with the victim's own gun. Life insurance payouts were always a factoring influence, as if money would solve everything.

"Call Elena," Nazario started, turning to Huxley, "we need to find out what's in that P.O. box."

Huxley placed their daughter in her arms and called the babysitter. Elena lived only fifteen minutes away, so it didn't take long for her to arrive, which was one of the reasons they chose her. Proximity and a flexible schedule at a moment's notice were crucial in their line of work. The trio was off that day, but when it came to working on an important case—there was no such thing as a day off, especially given the fact that there were lives at stake.

Nazario couldn't dismiss the increasing worry, her concern over the chief's life.

Just as Elena arrived, Nazario dialed the chief to keep him in the loop. There was nothing he hated more than when they strayed on their day off without letting him know about it. He didn't mind if they put in some overtime; Johnson simply wanted to be kept in the loop. Another part of her used the call as an excuse to check in on him, especially given the fact that he was working from home today.

She put it on speaker. "Wanted to let you know—I realize it's our day off and all, but we're heading to Ironwood Vault up in Highland Park. Got a big lead we need to chase down."

"And you don't think it can wait a couple of days? Spend time with my grandbaby?"

"Don't think it can, sir." She filled him in on the note left behind—the dead man's map they'd been handed—along with what they'd uncovered on the flash drive. The key to the P.O. box might be the final waypoint they had before they'd get lost in an ocean of politics, cover-ups, and dirty hands.

"Goddamn it," Chief Johnson blew out a long breath. "I was hoping...hoping it wasn't true. Hoping we could be done with this internal investigation, close it up, and wash our hands of it."

"You know we can't do that now. This is way too big."

On the other line, the doorbell rang. Nazario could hear the chief breathing into the receiver as he walked to the front door.

"Not expecting a guest," he said. The door creaked open. "Can I help you?"

POP! POP!—loud, but not as loud as it should've been. Two gunshots, most likely fired through a silencer.

"Chief...*CHIEF JOHNSON?*"

The phone clattered to the floor. The thud of his body came next.

"I've been shot!" he cried out, the words distant, like the phone was no longer near his mouth as it slipped from his grasp and was on the floor out of reach.

"We're on our way!" she said with urgency.

Wilson dialed 9-1-1, and the operator confirmed that an ambulance and squad cars were en route to Chief Johnson's home.

"I've got the baby—go, go, go!" Elena urged, having arrived just in time.

"I'll drive," Wilson said, and they bolted out the door. Minutes later, they were flying down the freeway, portable lights flashing on the roof of the SUV. Wilson pushed the speedometer, weaving through traffic and taking side streets only he knew. They beat the squad cars and EMTs, arriving at Chief Johnson's house at record time. Luck—or maybe instinct —had worked in their favor. Huxley and Nazario's home was ten minutes out. Wilson, barely five. They were a tight crew, by choice and not just on the job, but in where they lived. Close enough to reach each other when it mattered most.

No matter how damn close they were, it wasn't close enough.

Now, they were racing time—and time wasn't on their side.

THIRTEEN

THE LINE THEY CROSSED

BY THE TIME Von had joined Xander, the two cartel bodies had been hauled away, loaded back onto the boat they'd arrived in. *The Silver Vow's* floorboards reeked of bleach instead of blood. The metallic scent had been scrubbed away, but the memory lingered. Xander had rigged the trawling net earlier, dropping it off the stern. It hadn't been long, but the waters this far north were thick with bottom-feeders—rockfish, cod, pollock.

As much as Von tried to rest, every time she closed her eyes, she saw them—boarding the boat, guns drawn. Her heart thumped hard against her aching rib cage. Gunfire. Bullets slamming. Fear coursing through her body, adrenaline taking charge as her mind raced to react quickly. But now that the calm after the storm had settled, every second came rushing back in vivid detail.

Despite physical and emotional exhaustion, sleep eluded her.

She reached for her phone, resting next to her on the bed, and launched the Phantom Vox app. It populated with that same text she'd seen the first time: *Command mode enabled. Awaiting target.*

She clicked on the T-List button, and her next target populated: Dr. Seung-ah Lee.

A picture filled the screen next to her name. A Korean woman in her mid-to-late fifties, with salt and pepper hair cropped to her shoulders and a serious disposition that leaned more clinical than warm. Von lifted herself off the bed and rubbed her throbbing temples, navigating away from the target list icon.

When she wasn't reliving every single person she dropped, flashes of live fire ignited again, crashing into her ribs, hitting her leg. She'd never had nightmares, never experienced PTSD until now. Breaking out into a cold sweat that made her shirt cling to her chest, Von struggled to her feet and joined Xander up on the top deck.

Xander glanced up at her, surprised to see her awake. "You don't look too good," he said, concern etched across his features.

Von scanned the deck. "Hope you didn't strain your back moving the bodies."

"I'll survive," was all he said. "You're white as a sheet. You should be resting."

"Every time I close my eyes I...never mind." She shook her head, holding back.

He put a hand on her shoulder, earnest eyes seeing right through her. "I still struggle with PTSD from that mortar blast," he admitted. "Nothing to be ashamed of. You wouldn't be human if our line of work didn't get to you. It gets to me."

"Then why do you do it? Why're you working for Black Nova? I don't have a choice, but you do."

Xander turned away, keeping his silence, avoiding her question, avoiding a response. He reeled in another fresh batch instead, the net sagging with motion. Fish writhed in a tangled mess, scales flashing like dull silver beneath the sunlight. Von caught the sharp tang of brine and blood as he hauled the catch aboard. She hated that they were trapped, hated that she was going against her vegan code to never injure a living thing. But they needed the fish.

Xander had the dope bricks double-wrapped, vacuum-sealed, and insulated with lead foil to throw off X-ray scanners. They sat neatly stacked at the bottom of the large, cold crate. He grabbed a bucket of ice and dumped it over them, burying the evidence in frozen silence.

"Grab the end of the net," he said, and she gripped it without hesitation. Her stomach knotted, eyes growing moist. Watching innocent living creatures sacrificed cut deeper than putting down the guilty. They tossed the fresh batch in, then Xander buried them in another layer of ice, smothering them under a cold sheet before sealing the crate closed.

An hour later, a long hour thick with unspoken tension, with Xander never answering her question about why he joined Black Nova, just letting the silence stretch like a taut fishing line straining under the weight—another boat finally appeared on the horizon. A rusted trawler with faded green paint pulled alongside, bumping gently against the hull. No words were exchanged. A single man stepped out—weathered, sunburnt, anonymous. He hoisted the crate with practiced ease, sliding it onto the dolly and then rolled it aboard without a glance back. Within minutes, the boat drifted off again, engine humming low as it cut through the swell, headed south toward the Port of Long Beach.

He stalked past her to the steering station and turned the helm toward the next waypoint.

Von hobbled behind him and sank into the farthest seat of the three-row bench behind the wheel. She hesitated, contemplating how to approach Xander, who seemed to be visibly shaken by her previous question. Curiosity got the better of her, and she couldn't help but ask again.

"Did I hit a nerve?" she asked gently. "Look, I didn't mean to cross a line—and if I did, I'm sorry. I'm just trying to understand why someone with your experience would break free from one government leash, only to take on another."

Xander stood at the helm, his hands gripping the steering wheel, jaw muscles dancing to the clench of his teeth. He set the boat on autopilot, then dropped into the last seat on the right. An empty chair sat between them—deliberate space, heavy with everything that had been buried, and everything about to surface.

He steepled his fingers together and glanced out at the ocean lapping past them. A vast, unbroken cerulean sea stretched around them—so endless it made their existence feel microscopic, like flecks of dust suspended in a breath. A place that could swallow them whole and leave not a single bone behind.

"I was part of Task Force Ember Cross. Our SEAL team was deployed to Colombia on a special counter-narcotics, counterterrorism task force. We weren't responsible for front line drug raids. It was a JSOC mission," he began, voice low, pensive.

"Joint Special Operations Command? They handle sensitive, high-risk missions like that targeted strike and raid on Bin Laden?"

"Yes, exactly. I led Navy SEAL Team 6—DEVGRU training and advising Colombian soldiers against FARC—Fuerzas Armadas Revolucionarias de Colombia. They're a well-known Marxist group founded in the 1960s, originally formed to represent the rural poor, to fight for land reform. But over time, what was meant to start out as something good, a revolution with a moral purpose, ended up turning into something deadly."

Xander rose to his feet, glanced at the NAVCOM panel—

autopilot engaged, trajectory clean. He opened up the mini-refrigerator, grabbed two West Coast IPAs, popped them open, and handed one to her. Von didn't drink. But after the gunfire, after nearly getting killed—after the bodies she had to drop just to make it out alive? Yeah, today she would.

Von took the beer. "Thanks," she said, then took a long drink, watching him do the same.

"We'd finally found the head of the cartel's brother—Álvaro Barragán. We had intel that his older brother, Tomás '*El Verdugo*' Barragán, the commander of FARC, was hiding out there, that Álvaro was protecting him."

"*El Verdugo*—The Silencer?"

"They called him that because everyone feared him. Cross him, and he'd wipe out your whole bloodline—no hesitation, no remorse. Didn't matter if it was your crew or your kids." He gulped his beer. "We were all shitting our pants. It was a dangerous mission, not because of the orders to eliminate him, but because of the potential casualties each of us might face. The fallout. I was especially placed in a vulnerable—"

"Because you were the one calling the shots."

He nodded, then continued, "Our intel was wrong. At one point, Tomás had been hiding out at Álvaro's, but he wasn't there that day. I had called in the orders to bomb the home after my commanding officer told me Álvaro's family was supposed to be at the market, but they were wrong. Álvaro, his wife, and two children were inside—they were all killed."

"Oh no," Von said, gripping the beer. "I...I hate to ask, but... what was the fallout?"

"I was congratulated for a successful mission. But none of us considered it anything but an epic fuck-up. I screamed at my CO, was pissed off that they lied to us. Got written up—called it insubordination. Gave two-shits about the write-up. Called Claire, my wife. All my men called their significant others. It hit us hard. The thought that we'd killed a mother and her children...it crushed us." Xander drained his beer and trashed it. Returned, face darkening. "Spoke with my son, Noah. He'd just turned four, and he was so excited that Mommy got him a bunch of Spider-Man stuff for his birthday. He loved Spider-Man. My little superhero." Xander stared down at his trembling hands, like they didn't belong to him. "A week later, I get a call from my CO. My wife and my son...they were...they were found murdered. My wife was raped before she was killed. They found my son in her arms."

Xander's head fell into his hands. His shoulders shook, and then a guttural, anguished cry escaped from somewhere deep inside. Shock riveted through her body, as her hand covered her mouth, and then unexpectedly, tears crawled down her cheeks. She'd expected something terrible had happened, but nothing compared to this. Without thinking twice, Von moved into the seat next to him, put an arm around Xander, and held him close. He turned into her, gripping her like he was drowning. The cold numbed away the ache where she'd been shot, but she could hardly feel it now. His face buried in her shoulder, wetting her shirt with grief. All she could do was hold him, let the torment leave his body one tear at a time.

Von cupped his face in her hands and drew his wet lips to hers. Their tears mingled in a shared moment between two souls who understood loss. Loss of life, loss of her unborn child, loss of his son who had his whole life ahead of him, loss of family, of hope. She kissed him deeply, their tongues finding each other, waltzing through sadness, through the dangerous circumstances that drew them together.

A spark ignited in her belly, filling her body, every single cell with a need that she'd never known until now. He kissed her back, hungry and yet at a leisured pace that was both deliberate and heartfelt. In his kiss, she could feel the ache of a man who had lost everything—and for the first time, dared to want it again. She could feel the despair she carried, and the pain he smothered—two broken things drawn to each other by damage neither of them knew how to name.

Their lips lingered against each other as they opened their eyes at the same time. Staring into each other, like scars that finally found their mirror. There was no awkwardness, no wondering if she'd made a mistake, if he made a mistake. Just two unlikely people coming together in shared pain, shared sorrow, shared trauma. Perhaps it was trauma-bonding that brought them together, or perhaps they were in the right place in their lives, in just the right moment to have finally found what neither knew they were searching for.

"It's been a very long time since I've felt anything else but asexuality. After the attack that almost killed me—the members of the Aryan Nation Brotherhood that knifed me up and left me for dead, left me unable to have children, left me to grieve the child I would never meet—it killed a part of me I thought I'd never get back," she said, tone as hushed as the wind. "Until now, I...I never thought I'd feel anything but numbness again. Thought I'd never be able to want a man ever again. When someone takes something from you, the scar never heals. Time adds to the heartache, time makes the pain more vivid, time doesn't heal the wounds as many say it does."

Von surprised herself with her own admission. Hearing the words aloud felt like freedom, freedom she hadn't had in a long while, freedom from the burden of carrying it around like a chain around her neck, weighing her down with a thousand pounds.

He brushed a hand across her cheek. Such a simple touch— yet it felt impossibly intimate.

"I've been abstinent since Claire and Noah were murdered. It killed something inside me, too. Something I thought I'd never get back. Claire was the total opposite of you, no offense."

"None taken," she said gently, gifting him with a warm smile.

"She went to church every Sunday. Was a deacon and part of the worship service. Had the voice of an angel. Claire taught Sunday school at our church and led a weekly Bible study group every Wednesday night while I was deployed. She was even Noah's classroom mom, volunteering to help out in the classroom every day. She was my rock, my best friend, my lover, my everything. So, when I lost her, when I lost my son—I swore I'd never want anyone else," he admitted. "I never mix business with pleasure. I don't date people I work with."

"It was just a kiss," she said, but the sting in her voice gave her away.

She avoided his eyes, suddenly feeling hurt, and didn't know why. He put a gentle hand on her chin and turned her face to meet his eyes.

"It was more than a kiss, and you know it," he said softly. "But I need to make you aware that Black Nova has a very strict rule: no emotional entanglements, no sexual relations with fellow operatives, no dating co-workers. It's a rule that I take very seriously."

"Got it." She swallowed the lump in her throat, voice returning flat. "Message received. Next time, I won't make the mistake of meaning something to you."

"I'm sorry, in the heat of the moment...I wasn't thinking clearly."

"No entanglements. No emotion," she repeated, robotically. "It won't happen again."

She finished her beer and discarded it in the trash.

"Look, I haven't shared that story with anyone," he confessed.

"Then I'll carry it with care," she whispered, then pivoted the conversation. "If you don't mind my asking: what happened with the head of FARC?"

"The murders of my family were done by one of the cartel members stateside. The cops weren't able to ID him. I had a surveillance camera mounted outside my home, but it was too dark to see his face. It lit a fire in me—in all of my men. We wanted to find the son of a bitch. But we could never find *El Verdugo*," he said, then added, "When I confronted my CO, he brushed off the murders of my family, and then that's when I retired from the military. To have my wife and child be killed, and my boss acts like it was no big deal, like I was burying some family pet instead of the mother of my child and my only son."

"I'm so sorry you went through that. That he had the balls to minimize such a horrendous event. I would've killed your CO myself," she said and meant it.

"But Commander Lucian Cain—he never minimized it. Had no idea who he was. When I first met him, I thought he was full of shit. Made me a promise that Black Nova would find the person responsible for murdering my family," he said, glancing out at the ocean slapping the sides of the boat. "I learned that Cain was a man of his word. He found the cartel member and took him out himself. Ever since that day, I remained indebted to him. Joined Black Nova to help stop the evil out there, those who often slip through the law's cracks. And it's why I...I wouldn't want to do anything that might jeopardize my job."

It landed like a punch to the gut. No one had ever called her a liability before.

"It makes perfect sense," was all she said, and then stood. "Gonna lie back down."

She returned to the cabin and found herself reliving the kiss, playing it over in her head—eclipsing the nightmare that had nearly gotten her killed. Just when she thought she'd never be able to close her eyes again without flashes of trauma, one kiss with Xander Holt silenced the noise long enough to let her drift off to sleep.

When she woke, they were anchored at Port Ashton Cannery Dock. Fishermen from all over the world came for the salmon runs, for the slaughter masked as sport. Von saw only loss—creatures ripped from the waters where they belonged. She forced the thought aside—her vegan conscience straining against it, as she drew in a breath at the stunning view. The silky-turquoise ocean was set against Alaska's rugged snow-capped mountains, with glaciers sprinkled about all around them like splintered gemstones from a god's forgotten palace.

Von limped up the stairs and onto the dock, Zeus trailing behind her. He had been really good at not having any accidents on the boat. So, as soon as he spotted land, he jogged to the closest tree and relieved himself. Xander was talking with an older man who looked like he worked with his hands. By the way he was gesturing toward the engine, she could tell the stranger was the boat mechanic Cain had set up. They exchanged a nod and a quick handshake. Then Xander turned and made his way back to her with a look that said he was ready for their next task.

"I didn't get a chance to look up our next target. But at least we're getting *The Silver Vow* a new engine courtesy of Black Nova. At least Cain's good on his promises," he said.

"Dr. Seung-ah Lee. That's the chemist. There's a picture of her, which'll help us with the search. Speaking of...where should we start? I'd get Zeus to find a trail if he had a piece of her clothing," Von said, opening up the app and showing Xander her profile picture.

"She looks like she doesn't want to be working for Ryker." He laughed, brightening up his ordinarily serious disposition. It made his latte-brown eyes shine in a refreshing way, as though the burden of carrying the loss of his family was forgotten for a fleeting moment.

"You should smile more," she said, and his cheeks flushed pink.

He cleared his throat, then redirected, "I know where we should start."

"Where?"

"Whittier—it's a small town here in Prince William Sound, about thirty minutes from here if we take the Anton Anderson Memorial Tunnel and have to wait, depending on when it opens. It's a toll tunnel and the fastest way."

"And if the tunnel's open?"

"Ten minutes."

"Do we have a car?"

Xander took a set of car keys from his pocket and unlocked the SUV from where he stood. It was a black Ford Expedition with limo-tinted windows, all-weather tires, and snow chains. Von was impressed. Commander Lucian Cain had planned ahead. What he hadn't planned, however, was for two of his operatives to have sent ten bricks—ten kilos straight to Nazario.

Now, if they didn't find Dr. Lee first, Ryker would bury the formula with her.

FOURTEEN

THE CHIEF GOES DOWN

THE DOOR WAS open when they got there, the perp gone. Chief Johnson lay in a pool of blood just inches from the doorway. It spread around, pumping out to the rhythm of his labored breathing. His chest stuttered—thin and distant, a whisper of life, fading fast. Two entry wounds: both in his abdomen. Luck was on his side—he hadn't taken one to the heart. But if they didn't act fast, they could still lose him.

The man who was more than her boss, more than a minority idol, more than a fierce leader whom she'd follow into a blazing fire if she had to. Chief Trevor Johnson was the father that she'd lost. Not a replacement for Daddy, but a stable male force who'd championed her own success, pushed her to be the best detective not because her last name was Nazario like her famous father, but because she'd made a name for herself, all by herself. But not independent of Johnson who always believed in her even during the dark days when she'd lost faith. He challenged her to attend AA meetings during the valleys of despair when her drinking grew out of control—when the disease of obsession, of addiction took hold.

While other superiors would've fired her long ago, the chief was there by her side, never giving up on her, never losing hope. Telling her she was stronger than alcoholism, stronger than the temptations to self-destruct. He stood for justice, not just procedure. He stood for moral conviction. He stood for truth, even when it bruised the blue. He stood for Black boys who feared the uniform. He stood for the neighborhoods, the ghettos forgotten by policy. He stood for integrity, even when it cost him friends. He stood for goodness—goodness that had been lost by so many who'd turned jaded by the job.

Chief Johnson was the glue that held Homicide together—without him, it was all just pieces waiting to break.

Nazario screamed out, "Blake, grab a towel from the bathroom. We need to apply pressure, or he'll bleed out. Wilson, pull the car up as close as you can. We're not waiting for the ambulance. We don't have time. They could be stuck in traffic."

Huxley rushed to the bathroom and snatched several towels.

"This is gonna hurt," she said and pressed the towels on Johnson's belly.

"Holy fuck," Johnson groaned, squeezing his eyes shut, writhing in pain.

"Hang on, sir," Nazario begged. "Hang on, hang on. Stay with me."

Wilson hopped into the Tahoe and backed it up. He popped the tailgate and dropped the back seats flat in one motion, then swiftly returned. "I'll take his feet," he said, "Huxley, grab under his arms. Nazario, keep his back stable."

They took their positions. Nazario placed her hand over Chief Johnson's and gently said, "We're gonna need you to apply pressure. Can you do that? Keep the towels down real good."

His hands, slick with blood, trembled as he pushed

Nazario's away, taking over—pressing down on the soaked towels with what little strength he had left. She braced his back, locking her hands beneath him as Huxley hooked his arms under the Chief's armpits, hauling him upright. Wilson grabbed the legs—one hand on each calf. No one spoke. They moved fast, carrying his limp mass toward the Tahoe.

"Put him down gently," Wilson said, and they laid the Chief across the folded third-row space. It was barely enough room, but it would get them to the hospital, and that's what mattered most. His chest rose—shallow but steady.

Nazario climbed into the second-row passenger seat. Twisting around, she said, "I got it from here, Chief. Relax. Just breathe. You're not done yelling at us yet."

The towel, once white, now bled red—like it had swallowed his pain, like it wept for him too. She remembered the day her father died—the exact moment her world split open. Two officers at the door, stiff in uniform, delivering the one truth, the news she refused to believe. It had already been bad between her and Mama when Daddy was alive. His death didn't just fracture the foundation—it detonated it.

"The hell if you're going to become a cop. You do, and I'm done with you!" Mama had screamed, her voice soaked in snot and fury.

Nazario didn't cry. Not because she didn't mourn. She was just too fucking angry to let grief take the lead. Rage settled in her chest like dry kindling—and it lit. Mama coped by pretending nothing had changed. Filling her time with church groups, tearing up floorboards that didn't need replacing, and swiping through online dates like she was shopping for toothpaste.

"You get to bring some loser home, fuck him in the bed you and Daddy shared—and I can't be a cop?"

The slap cracked before the silence did. Her cheek stung.

Her breath held. Mama shook, fists clenched, face twisted in a blend of grief and venom.

"If you follow his footsteps, you might as well be buried with him!"

Nazario stepped in close. Calm. Unflinching. "I'd rather be buried with him than live another day in this house with you."

That was the last time they spoke.

She was eighteen when she left, sitting on the porch of the only home that ever felt safe—her father's partner's house.

Trevor Johnson had just made detective—he'd lost his partner, but not the promise.

I'll look after your girl if anything happens, he'd sworn to Daddy.

Nazario sat on his steps all day, arms around her knees. Just sat there still as stone, watching the sun bleed out—waiting for the only man she trusted as much as her father to come home. The only one left she still believed in.

Now, he was fading right in front of her.

Eyes blinking slowly, groaning in pain.

Towels, a deep crimson, soaked in blood.

They tore down San Vincente, then veered east on Wilshire —Wilson wove through traffic, running lights, pushing the Tahoe past its limits. Every second mattered. UCLA Medical Center was the closest trauma unit, and they were racing against the clock.

"Wilson, can you manage calling off the ambulance," Huxley said, "or should I use my mobile?"

"I can juggle it." Wilson snatched the department-issued radio mic, hardwired into the center console—installed for emergencies like this. He thumbed the PTT button on the side and spoke fast. "Dispatch, this is Detective Wilson—cancel the ambulance. No time. We're transporting the chief ourselves.

GSW to the abdomen. ETA a minute away from UCLA. Notify the ER, STAT!" he said, urgency in his tone.

"Copy that. Ambulance cancelled. Alerting UCLA ER—critical gunshot wound, abdomen. Gurney prepped outside."

"Tell 'em to be ready. We're coming in hot. He's losing blood fast. And send SID out to Johnson's place. We'll need prints, photos, full scene processing."

Static cracked. Thirty seconds passed. Then dispatch came back on: "Trauma unit's been notified. Confirming—gurney's waiting outside for your arrival. SID's already at the crime scene."

"10-4." Wilson hung up the radio just as they pulled up in front of the ER at UCLA, three male nurses and a trauma doctor were waiting as expected.

"GSW abdomen—let's move! Get him on the gurney," the doctor shouted, and the three male nurses hoisted him on the gurney. "Two large bore IVs, Type and Cross, call the blood bank, FAST exam now. He's unstable!"

"OR's been called and prepped," one of the nurses said.

Another nurse quickly found Chief Johnson's vein and drew blood. "Sending this as a STAT lab order for blood type. Calling the blood bank."

"Have the blood ready, we'll need a transfusion. He's lost too much blood," said the doctor, and then turned to them. "What time was he shot?"

"About twenty minutes ago," Nazario said.

"We're getting him into surgery and conducting a FAST—a focused assessment—it's a sonogram to check for internal bleeding, so we can identify where he's bleeding out from and stop further loss," he spoke quickly. "Don't know how long the surgery will take, so you may be waiting for a while."

"We'll wait as long as it takes," Huxley said.

"I'll keep you updated when I can," he said and jogged back inside, tethered to the gurney by something heavier than duty.

Time hesitated, stalling under the dull hum of hospital LEDs, casting a cold, grayish-blue haze, that made the waiting room feel gritty, worn down by grief. The cheap chairs were ass-numbingly uncomfortable—standard-issue misery. They could've gone to Martin Luther King Jr. Community Hospital, once known as "Killer King" in South L.A.'s low-income Willowbrook. But that place would've dissolved whatever hope they had left.

If the Chief was going to make it, it sure as hell wouldn't be there.

Nazario had heard horror stories where a shortage of staff and worn-out medical personnel made the difference between life and death. The Ronald Reagan UCLA Medical Center, however, was dramatically different and known to be one of the top hospitals in the United States, especially for trauma care, surgery, and complex critical cases.

"It's been three hours already," Nazario complained, running her hands through her hair, upending it. She sat restless, fingers working against each other, gaze locked on the clock.

"He has to pull through," Wilson said, pacing. "Guy's tougher than all of the departments combined."

"He was bleeding out, Wilson. I had my hands on him. Felt the heat leaving him," she said, the weight of the grim possibility of losing the Chief pressed in—tight in her chest, cold in her gut.

Huxley stared at the door—the one that swallowed the doctor and nurses whole, taking all the answers with them. "Good thing the trauma team moved fast. Got here just in time. Could've lost him had we waited for the ambulance. UCLA's the best shot he has. They've got a great group of some of the best doctors in the world."

"Feels familiar—like Harrison all over again. People getting clipped for trying to expose the truth. We didn't get a chance to ask him if he got a look at the perp's face," Wilson said, checking his watch. He finally stopped pacing and sat back down next to Nazario.

"Highly doubt the shooter would've been stupid enough to show their face. Especially if they happen to be a dirty blue," Nazario said.

Her phone chimed. An incoming text message. Frowning, she wondered who it could be and clicked on the message.

"Hey...it's another message from our Serpent Woman," she said. "Glad that the bureau's Cellular Analysis Survey Team tracked the burner in Kodiak. It confirms she's working behind Black Nova's back."

Huxley, who sat to her right, and Wilson, on her left, both leaned in. They read the message quietly to themselves.

Von: *Cartel working for Ryker. Don't know them. Don't know their names. Tried to take us down. A boat owned by one of Black Nova Ops hid dope with a tracking device. Dropped them before they dropped us.*

There were two pictures of two bloodied bodies of Hispanic males.

"Sending you an email address. Email my contact, now," Huxley said, texting her the email address. "He's an FBI Intelligence Analyst. He'll put the photos through NGI, and they'll tag-team with the facial rec team over at LAPD. If they run the photos also through the LACRIS system—we'll be bound to get a hit between both software, so we can ID them."

In under a minute, she fired off the emails, photos attached, Huxley cc'd.

Just as she finished sending the email, her phone rang.

Huxley and Wilson gave her the same look of alarm, as if their guts were in sync. She checked the caller ID.

"It's Agent Saul Mendoza."

"From HSI?" Wilson asked.

"Yeah—from Homeland Security Investigations unit," she said, answering after the third ring. "Detective Nazario speaking."

"Looks like you've got another package," Agent Mendoza said. "Scanned it and looks like someone was thoughtful enough to send you enough pescetarian dinners to last you for the next month."

"Fish this time, huh?"

"Yep, but we won't know for sure until you open her up."

"Well, I'm at the hospital and might be here for another couple of hours. Emergency situation. I'm giving you permission to open it up."

"You sure?"

"Yes, I'm sure. If it's fish, you can keep it," Nazario said. "I'll stay on the phone."

"Opening her up now," Agent Mendoza said, as the phone rattled. A slicing sound, like a box cutter, came from the other end. "Well, it looks like it's fish this time. Guess I'll be eating lots of it."

"You sure that's all there is? The sender—my source—said something about stash found on their boat. Tranq. Planted."

"Hang on, digging toward the bottom...Holy shit! We got bricks." He paused, Nazario could hear him counting. "Ten total. Think it might be the tranq you mentioned."

Nazario recalled Von texting her about the dope that had been planted on a Black Nova boat. It had to be the drugs they found. "Call Captain Humphrey, Gang and Narco will need to be on it. Rope the FBI and DEA, they'll need to seize it."

"On it, Detective."

"And Agent Mendoza."

"Yeah?"

"Be careful. Only get involved with those in the division you absolutely trust."

"Got it."

Nazario cut the call, and yet her phone chimed once again with an email address. "Damn that was fast. Your intelligence analyst ID'd the two DBs Von sent pictures of as part of *Los Cuervos*— the *Chihuahua* cartel. Dangerous Mexican gang."

Wilson and Huxley inched closer. "Figured they were mixed up with the cartel. You've got another package?" Huxley asked.

"Thought I heard something about fish?" Wilson said.

"Came through the Long Beach Ports. Several bricks of tranq. It was planted in a Black Nova boat," Nazario said. "Agent Mendoza's on it, getting the DEA and the bureau involved. Told him to go to people he trusts."

Wilson whistled.

"Good call," Huxley said.

The person they'd been waiting for finally walked through the doors.

"It's the doctor," Wilson said, and Nazario stood quickly.

"I know you've all been waiting. It's always the hardest part. Chief Johnson took two shots to the abdomen, as you all know. One passed through the lower right quadrant and exited clean, but the second tore through a loop of the small intestine and fragmented. We found three perforations causing peritonitis, which in simple terms, means that there was a decent amount of contamination in the abdominal cavity." He paused briefly, glancing at them with purpose. "We resected about a foot of bowel, cleaned the area well, and managed to control the bleeding from a small arterial branch near the mesentery."

"Any damage to major organs?" Wilson asked, caution in his tone.

"Thankfully, no." The doctor rubbed his hands together. It might've looked routine to most, but Nazario was a detective. She'd seen that same switch in interrogation rooms. A nervous tick, disguised as habit.

He continued, "We did a primary anastomosis—reconnecting the bowels directly."

"Does he need a colonoscopy?" Nazario questioned.

"Wasn't a need for one. He'll be NPO for a few days—"

"Sorry, don't think we're familiar with that acronym," Huxley said. "What's it mean?"

"*Nil per os*. Latin phrase that means 'nothing by mouth.' Nothing to eat or drink—to give that area a break since it's been through significant trauma. We started broad-spectrum antibiotics to stay ahead of the infection." His voice turned low, more human. "He's stable for now. In the ICU, intubated. He made it through the hard part, but the next forty-eight hours will tell us if there's internal infection, leakage, or anything else we missed."

"Since you had to remove a part of the bowels," Wilson wondered aloud, crinkling his nose, "would he need a colonoscopy bag. Wait...colostomy? Y'know, that poop bag?"

Nazario shot Wilson a sideways glance—equal parts annoyance and amusement.

"Really?" Huxley said, glaring at Wilson.

The doctor raised a brow. "Yes and no. We did give him a colostomy bag for now—it's temporary. In a few months, if all goes well, it'll be reversed."

"A few months. That's a mighty long time," Wilson said.

"He's alive," the doctor reminded, sounding irritated, "that's what matters."

Enough about how the Chief would shit. Nazario leaned forward. Can we see him?"

"He's in PACU—post anesthesia care—so he'll be drifting in and out. Absolutely normal at this stage," the doctor said. "He's on heavy pain meds. You can see him, but he won't be fully coherent. Maybe a few mumbled words. He might open his eyes if he hears you. He won't be up for a real conversation. He does need his rest."

A voice over the intercom cracked overhead, announcing a doctor's name, followed by Code White. The doctor tilted his head toward the sound. Nazario knew that one—it meant a violent person was on the floor. She'd worked a case once where a woman shot her husband in the chest, then herself in the thigh to stage it as a robbery. She turned violent in the ER. That's how she remembered the code.

"That would be me," the doctor said, already turning. "Have any more questions, just ask the nurses—they'll do their best. Normally, we'd allow two in the ICU at a time, but I'll make an exception. All three of you can go in. Thirty minutes tops. He's in Room 8422, West ICU. Tell the nurse at the front desk you're with Chief Johnson."

As the doctor jogged off toward the chaos, Huxley strode to the front desk, and after five minutes, a nurse approached them.

"Here for Chief Johnson?" Huxley said.

The nurse looked at the three of them. "We're only allowed two visitors at a time."

"The doctor said he'd allow it," Huxley said.

"We'll be a half-hour max," Wilson promised.

"Very well then, follow me," she said.

As they trailed after the nurse, down the hall, Nazario felt the weight of it pressing in—the close call, the unknowns, the aftermath. The Chief had survived, but at what cost? The elevator doors opened with a soft chime, and they stepped in like soldiers walking into a war they didn't fully understand but couldn't avoid. Floor by floor, they rose—not just toward the ICU, but toward the new reality waiting for them behind a single door.

She braced herself, braced for the wires, the tubes, and the man beneath them.

Chief was a fighter—but the worst wounds weren't always ones you could see.

FIFTEEN

THE SEARCH FOR THE CHEMIST

THE ANTON ANDERSON MEMORIAL TUNNEL was carved into the Maynard Mountain, built in 1942 by the U.S. Army to withstand the extreme weather conditions of Alaska, when winds can reach up to 150 mph and winters would get as cold as -40°F. As the longest combined vehicle-railroad tunnel in the country, it connected the town of Whittier to the mainland. Since the tunnel was the only access to Whittier—it ran on the clock. Every thirty minutes, traffic reversed due to the single-lane road shared by vehicles and freight trains.

Just as they pulled up near the staging point, the gate dropped with a mechanical groan—blocking their path into the tunnel. Red lights glared on the side of the road, indicating that the tunnel was closed. Xander cursed under his breath, shifting the Expedition into park. The vehicle that had been waiting for them, courtesy of Black Nova, still hummed from the long drive off *The Silver Vow,* docked an hour ago at Prince William Sound, where it would soon have its bullet-riddled engine replaced.

"Damn it," he muttered, checking the dashboard clock. "We missed it by sixty seconds."

"So, the next chance is what—in thirty minutes?"

"Yeah, the schedule runs every half-hour with a fifteen-minute window per direction. The freight train has priority. So, when it's scheduled to run, it takes over the tunnel during its assigned slot."

"And both inbound and outbound traffic get paused?"

"Pretty much," he said, drumming his fingers on the steering wheel.

As they waited, a pressing question that had been nagging at her refused to leave her mind, weighing on her conscience. There was no better time to ask—now that the pandemonium had finally settled, but adrenaline still carried the mission forward. Honesty came easier than stillness, leaving no space for rehearsed answers.

"Since Cain took out those involved in your wife and child's murders, I have to ask—why work behind his back? You said it yourself—that you owe your life to the man."

Xander paused for a long beat, as though he was lost in thought, trying to choose his words.

"Why are you?" he said, turning the question back on her.

"Because in the short time I've known him, he's withheld vital intel that could save lives, intel that he claimed he'd feed the LAPD. Why would he bury proof that some cops were dirty?"

"He deems it outside of Black Nova's scope of operations," he began. "When I first started, I thought we'd be working closer with other agencies: FBI, CIA, and other police departments. I soon found out that Cain had ordered a partial blackout of intel surrounding Ryker's operations and drug smuggling."

"Why would he do that?"

"Senator Kenneth Braxton donates millions to a company called *Armtech Solutions*, a company that, on paper, is a private security firm. But in reality, they equip Black Nova with gear, surveillance tech, weapons, and other equipment we need to keep our operation afloat." Xander exhaled a long breath. "The senator's been using PAC money and campaign funds for an off-the-books kill team, which is essentially what Black Nova is, and if the public finds out, he not only brings himself down but exposes our operations."

Von listened intently, and then it all clicked, the pieces of the puzzle coming into place.

"Cain's protecting Braxton instead of the mission, isn't he?"

"I'm no lapdog. I signed up to protect people—not cover up for corrupt politicians," he said. "Don't get me wrong, we get our jobs done. But I don't trust that Cain will prevent more innocent people from getting killed, either by ODs from Ryker's tranq dope or by collateral damage."

"Cain would rather let people die just to keep Braxton out of the press?"

Xander nodded soberly. "Like you, I've followed Nazario's career. Earned my respect. The only way we stop Ryker is by leaking intel to Nazario. Braxton doesn't want to get caught up with exposing dirty cops. Worried about how it might threaten his political alliances. He's worried about campaign optics and his future in office."

"So, Cain doesn't want his funding source to go away, should he bring down the dirty cops? I thought Black Nova was government-funded?"

"Technically, yeah. But follow the money and you'll find private donors, political muscle, and a lot of people who don't give a damn who dies—as long as the fallout lands in someone else's backyard," he said, just as the light turned green. Xander put the SUV in drive and headed through the tunnel. "We're funded through back doors—black budgets, cutout companies, and people like Braxton. He's not the only one. Cain answers to them, not the Constitution."

Xander's words marinated in the silence between them. While Black Nova was doing the kind of dirty work no one else could stomach, cleaning up the world's worst messes, Cain had been compromised—serving politics instead of purpose. The commander was driven more by power and protection than principle. But wasn't that how D.C. worked? Budgets padded with pork, funneling money to private businesses under the guise of national interest. It wasn't new.

Once the tunnel opened, traffic wasn't bad. It took a short ten minutes to get to Whittier.

They checked in at a small, two-bedroom cabin located in a remote area of Whittier. Von was surprised to find that there were bags packed for them with the clothes they would need: one for her and one for Xander. The front office clerk was a gruff, burly man who looked like he worked outside in the cold winters. His face was a permanent shade of red, ruddy like the frosty terrain had charred his skin, leaving it weather-beaten and raw. His hands were dry and calloused. Voice, sandpaper-rough and just as uninviting.

Von clocked the stitched-on patch above his chest pocket: Lyle Gentry.

"Been here a while," Lyle said, voice like thawed gravel. "Don't recognize either of you. You're not locals, are you? How many nights we talkin'?"

"Can we take a week, or do you have the cabin reserved for another guest?" Xander asked.

"A week, huh?" he checked the computer. "Nope...don't have many visitors that stick around that long. You can have the cabin for as long as you need. Whatcha here for?"

"Doing some research. You say you've been here a while?"

"All my life. Can I help you with anything? Know all the best fishing spots. Some good ice fishing around Billings Creek Lake or near Portage Glacier. Both spots are some of the best ice fishing around. Catch ya some dolly varden, lake trout, and rainbow trout. Pick a good spot. Plenty of ice huts to rent that'll fit both of ya. Drill down into the ice and drop your line. And don't forget to pour a little Bailey's in your coffee to keep ya warm." Lyle said, a smile cracking across his weatherworn face—deep lines splitting at the corners of his mouth and brow, carved by too many cold winters.

"We won't be doing any fishing," Von said.

"Well, it ain't for everyone, that's for sure. There are glacier day cruises over in Prince William Sound, just gotta hop on back over through that memorial tunnel and make sure you check the schedule, or you'll be sitting around waiting for her to open up. On our side of the tunnel, there's plenty of fun stuff to do: kayaking, snowshoeing, checkin' out the wildlife like them sea otters, seals, and whales. Oh...and The Portage Pass Trail is a mighty nice place for a wilderness hike," Lyle said.

Xander took out his flip phone, fished for a photo, and flashed the image at Lyle Gentry.

"Since you seem to know everyone from around here," Xander said, "you recognize this woman? A Dr. Seung-ah Lee. Chemist. Scientist."

Lyle reached for the phone. "May I?"

Xander released the burner into the man's hands. Lyle tilted his head, observing.

"Don't recall the name. I'd definitely remember if a doctor came through these parts, but I do remember her face."

"Could she have used a different name?" Von said, already thinking in aliases.

She had been Frau Doktor Wilder Agatha Friedrich once—by birth, by degrees.

In Brazil, she'd morphed into Dr. Agatha Jones.

When survival demanded it, she became Luana Abraão.

But Von Schlange was born from blood, forged after the attack. That name didn't just mask the past—it replaced it.

Names were easy to change. Identity wasn't.

Lyle mulled over her question, then said, "Suppose—know for a fact she didn't use doctor-something when passing up through here. Korean lady, right?" The lines in his face deepened like old snow tracks. "Thing is, my wife's Korean, so I reckon that gives me just enough authority to take a decent guess."

"Yeah, Dr. Lee's a Korean chemist," Xander said. "So, she might've used a different name, but you remember that she stayed here?"

"Oh, yeah." He pinched the photo, zoomed in, then handed the burner back. Xander took it and stuffed it in his pocket. "Quiet. Paid cash. I remember that especially, since most folks use plastic. Stayed in Cabin Three. Can't forget that one—she left it spotless. Even washed the sheets herself. Did her own laundry in the guest washroom out back. Most folks don't bother. Neat like that tends to stick with you."

"Did she give you any indication," Xander said, "as to where she might've gone?"

"She said something about going to the AWCC—figured she was working on some wildlife project or study. Didn't give much detail, just said she'd be in and out a few days," Lyle said.

"AWCC? What's that?" Von asked.

"Alaska Wildlife Conservation Center—about twelve miles from here, but you've gotta head back through the Anton Anderson Tunnel to get there. It's out in Portage Valley, right off the Seward Highway. Big ol' place—does wildlife and conservation research. Bears, moose, bison, that sort of thing."

"Is that the only place she mentioned?" Xander said.

Lyle nodded slowly. "No, actually. She said she planned to stop by the WCC first. The Wildlife Conservation Center, and then she was heading to some lab fifteen minutes away. Can't seem to remember the name to save my life."

"You mean the Chinook Advanced Sciences Lab—the CASL—it's a small-scale marine lab, I believe," Xander said.

"Yeah, that's it!" Lyle snapped his finger. "She mentioned needing to run some lab tests. Kept it vague. Heard about that place. Always get the name all screwed up. It stuck in my head since hardly any locals go near it unless they're some pro, and that's how I knew she was...legit."

"You said that was her final destination?" Von said.

"That's what she said. Hope I was able to help a little." Lyle handed Xander the cabin keys.

"You helped a lot," Xander said, taking the keys.

"Cabin Seven. It's set back past the gravel road, near the edge of the forest. Has a propane heater, running water, and a basic shower setup—enough to live off-grid for the week. Quiet, out of the way. Locals say the signal's spotty, but it works if you stand by the north-facing window."

They thanked the man and climbed back into the Ford Expedition.

"So glad Cain had the sense to put snow chains on, or we'd be fucked trying to drive up these windy mountain roads covered in black ice," Xander said.

"That's the part I don't miss from when I lived in Casper, Wyoming. Driving on black ice can be dangerous," she said, then changed the subject. "You think she's still at the lab in Chinook? Wonder if she left that info with Lyle for a reason."

"Let's just hope Dr. Lee's still there. Don't know how long it takes to do whatever science experiment she was conducting." He drove toward the cabin, following Lyle's instructions. "And as far as what she told Mr. Gentry—it does seem a little too convenient. Maybe the doctor wants us to find her before Ryker does?"

"But why would she do that?"

"Simple: Ryker finds her, she's dead. We find her and we not only keep her alive, but we keep the formula alive, too."

"It wouldn't be very hard for Detective Nazario and the FBI's chemical forensics team to reverse engineer the dope we sent her."

"Yeah, but Lee wasn't just cooking formulas—she knows something Ryker doesn't want getting out. Recipes can be copied. Sure. But methodology? Ratios? The way the drug reacts under pressure? That kind of intel dies with the chemist. We need what's in her head—before someone else gets to it."

They pulled up to the remote cabin. The nearest neighbor was several hundred feet out—barely visible through the dense forest, far enough not to hear a scream. Someone could be buried out here, and no one would find them. Frigid temperatures and thick layers of fresh powder made it a lonesome, haunting oasis of white tundra.

Xander hauled their bags in and claimed the closest room to the front door. "I know you can handle yourself. But just in case anything happens, I'd feel more comfortable being next to the front door."

Von didn't fight him on the logistics.

The cabin was stripped down to the bare essentials. An old fireplace sat in the living room, flanked by a lounger and a couch that looked like they'd been salvaged from a flea market. The dining room was cramped, just enough space for a scratched-up wooden table and two mismatched chairs. The shared bathroom had only a standing shower—no tub—and the drain was rusted with age. The air carried a stale mix of burnt coffee and leftover ash from the fireplace, clinging to her nose. The windows were double-paned to block the frost, but the Whittier cold still seeped through, sharp enough to make her breath bloom in gray, vaporous plumes.

"Looks like the only heat we've got is that old fireplace," Xander said. "So, I'd suggest we sleep in our snow gear, otherwise we'd freeze."

"When should we head to the lab in Chinook?"

"Now. We can't wait," he said, "because if we do, she may be gone. That's if she hasn't already left Alaska."

"And what in the hell do we do with the doctor if we find her? Handcuff her and hold her hostage?"

"If we have to."

"C'mon. Seriously?" Von flung her hands up. "We can't make her hand over a formula she built with Ryker. What're we supposed to do—torture it out of her? We don't have to turn into the monsters we hunt."

"You drowned Walter Yang in his own fucking bathtub. Lit Darren Fischer on fire. Cut off Sean Martin's dick. And that's just the shortlist."

"That was different," Von said, through clenched teeth. "They were predators—part of a sex trafficking ring. Yang was an ephebophile buying teenage girls like they were stock. Fischer was a serial rapist. Martin? A textbook pedophile." She stepped closer. "Dr. Seung-ah Lee's not like them. She's a scientist, not a predator. Lee doesn't belong on some kill list."

"She's not innocent if she sold her soul to a drug lord."

"She's different than the other bastards that deserved to die," Von said. "I've got a moral code I abide by. That may sound stupid to you. But I do."

"I'm not advocating for waterboarding. All I'm saying—"

"You're accusing me of turning into the evil we hunt." Von inched close to his face. "Guess we both have something in common."

Xander stepped back, as though her proximity troubled something in him, something he didn't want to acknowledge, let alone face. Perhaps it was the mirror she held up without meaning to. One that showed his soul. His character. The thickening air. The heat. The tension. A nameless truth. A mirror that didn't just reflect rage or moral lines blurred by blood—but something messier.

Truth and fear stacked like bones.

Curiosity layered over distrust.

Respect layered over judgment.

It wasn't just that they were alike. It was the tension underneath—the way her silence made him itch, the way his precision made her want to claw through it. The heat between them wasn't just chemistry. It was a recognition too close for comfort. Recognition wrapped in danger. And maybe that's what unsettled him most. What unsettled her.

"We need her to open up to us," he said. Ironically, the one thing neither could do. "And that's what makes this harder. We need her to take a chance on us."

"Fine. But I'm not crossing a line I can't come back from," Von bit out. "I eliminate *real* threats—not innocents. I don't waste bullets on the wrong people."

Von waited in the SUV, jaw tight, pulse ticking like a clock wound too far.

The hypocrisy sat heavy in her chest, squeezing the air from her lungs. Neither Xander nor she trusted their own boss, Commander Lucian Cain, and now they had to convince a frightened, highly educated, rational woman that she should put her faith in two complete strangers—strangers whose jobs weren't just tied to an elite, black-level unit, but a deep-tier shadow ops division tasked with tracking and erasing people from the earth, leaving no trace behind.

Now, Von had one simple task: convince a stranger to trust her before someone else died.

SIXTEEN

THE LOCKED PAST

THE SANITIZED scent of near-fatality encased the intensive care unit, while lurid silence—broken only by the repetitive mechanical "blip" of machines—hung heavily, devoted to keeping Chief Johnson from slipping away. In this state, he'd aged ten years seemingly overnight. Deep stress lines rippled across his face like a complex roadmap. He wore it like a layer of cracked leather, raw from a career that never promised anything but danger and the chance not to make it home.

This once-sturdy sixty-five-year-old pillar of a man—steady, respected, devoted to the men and women who wore the badge—might've been taken out by one. It was a cruel irony. He was a man who never vacationed. He was a man who never took a day off—not because he was a workaholic, but because he loved his community. He was a man who lived to keep the streets safe. And now he'd been reduced to a disabled shell, a frame that no longer held the picture of strength it once did.

Nazario had never seen the chief broken-bodied, taken down in a medically compromised state, immobilized, and shot to hell. None of them had. Chief Johnson would want to get out of the hospital and get back to work as soon as possible. He would hate to be seen in such a vulnerable state and not because of pride, but because of how much he believed in being the one others leaned on. Because he was the kind of man who carried others, not the other way around.

Nazario and Wilson pulled up chairs on either side of the hospital bed, while Huxley stood at the foot, an edge of worry sweeping across his face as if sitting down would prove to be too still. The room was unnervingly quiet except for the ominous, continuous pulse of the ambulatory ECG monitor keeping track of the chief's heart. There was an awful type of tedium to it, like the steady *drip, drip* of a leaking faucet. Chief Johnson's chest rose and sagged, each ragged breath, hoarse. And then a low groan escaped his throat, as a hand weakly drifted to his stitched-up abdomen. The heart monitor began to drum faster, beeping louder.

A nurse strode in, pressed a few buttons on the machine, and the frenetic pulsing stopped.

"Is there something wrong?" Nazario asked her.

"He's in a lot of pain," she said, injecting the pain medication she brought with her directly into his IV.

"Is that morphine?" Huxley asked.

"No, it's Sufentanil—it's ten times stronger than Fentanyl."

Wilson whistled. "And how often do you give that one out?"

"We use it sparingly. Don't give it out that often. It's usually reserved for patients who had severe trauma to the body and require stronger pain management after a complex surgery," she said. "Chief Johnson's abdominal surgery was complex due to where the bullets punctured. Has the doctor explained our thirty-minute policy?"

Nazario nodded soberly. "Yes...yes, he has. We won't be longer than half an hour."

"Normally, we hold off on visitors until some of the post-surgery pain has been stabilized. While we're making an exception, we'd appreciate it if you limit the length of time you're here."

"Rodger that." Huxley saluted the nurse.

"I'll return in," the nurse began, then paused to check her watch, "twenty-five. Press this button if he's showing any type of distress. I don't always hear the machine going off, given I've got several other patients to care for."

Chief Johnson's eyes fluttered open, and he turned his head, movements slow.

Nazario waited for the nurse to leave, then said, "Hey, Chief, we've missed you. You came too close."

"Feels like a runaway train hit me at full speed," he said, voice raw-edged and gravelly. "I hate getting them pain drugs. They addictive as hell. Seen too many abuse them even if they hadn't initially planned to."

"Being an alcoholic myself, I never take them either. One addiction is enough for me. So, I totally get it. But, sir, you can't be in excruciating pain. If you have to take them to help you feel more comfortable and at ease, then that's exactly what you need to do."

"As long as you're in the ICU, there's no way they're gonna let you be in agony and not provide pain meds. Don't think you have much of a choice," Huxley said.

"You can try Tylenol and alternate between that and Ibuprofen every four hours, but I don't think it'll do jack. You're looking to be really uncomfortable and in a crap ton of pain for a while. Like several weeks," Wilson said, tone gentle. "Remember when I had appendicitis five years ago? Damn, no one told me cutting out a piece of your digestive system that looks no bigger than a three-inch worm was gonna be so effing brutal. Couldn't breathe, felt like someone was sitting on my chest. Thought my appendix grew back or something—turns out it was just gas. *Gas, folks!* Damn near crawled into the ER clutching my stomach like I was dying. Post-surgery carbon dioxide. Found out all I needed was a nice, big ol' fart."

The chief clutched his stomach, grimacing through the pain—but couldn't help it. A laugh escaped him anyway, unfiltered and genuine. Nazario tried to maintain her composure, lips tight, but the moment cracked her façade. She burst into laughter too, shaking her head. Even Huxley gave in—his smirk growing into a full smile, he clearly tried to fight and failed. Wilson had that effect on people. In a job soaked in blood, danger, and pressure, his timing was always perfect. Just when the weight got too heavy—he lightened it.

"Woo-wee," Chief wiped laughter-tears from his eyes. "You trying to kill me, Wilson?"

"I'd really kill you if you had to smell the gas I had to expel out of my butt."

They laughed harder, and this time Huxley's grin morphed into a chortle.

Once the lightness settled, Nazario was hard-pressed to ask a question that had been on all their minds since the shooting. "Don't mean to be a downer, but now that you're conscious...did you see who shot you?"

The atmosphere changed, equal parts curiosity and concern etched on each of their faces.

Chief Johnson was silent for a stretched-out beat, staring down at his ebony hands like they'd failed to protect him, failed to draw his weapon in time, failed to be ready for the attack that nearly cost him his life. He exhaled an elongated breath. "He was wearing a black ski mask. I thought I recognized his eyes— couldn't place a name."

"Any defining features? Anything at all?" Huxley asked.

"Single shooter. Average height. Around five-eight, maybe five-nine. Bulky, like he lifted weights. Green or hazel eyes. White dude." Johnson looked up at the ceiling, eyes misting.

"There was something in the way he carried himself. His stance —centered, squared off, elbows tucked. Not a civilian. That was a cop's stance. I want to be wrong."

"But if you're not?" Nazario asked.

"I dunno if I can protect y'all from our own. First Gus and now me." He met their eyes. "I can't lose any of you. There's a part of me that wants to bury the whole thing. Would be a whole lot easier than having to watch our backs."

"We've never gone down the easy road, and we're not fixin' to drive down it now," Wilson said, "and you don't have to worry about us."

"I think I speak for all of us," Nazario began. "We'd rather die doing what's right than to live doing what's wrong. No chance in hell are we closing this up, burying it, or looking away."

"They want to intimidate us. They want us running scared. But Detective Dawson handed us a possible lead," Huxley said.

Chief adjusted himself on the bed, groaning. "He was Detective Harrison's partner, right?"

"Yes, sir. There was a letter Harrison left in a sealed envelope, and a key to a private post office box. We're heading there after we leave here and checking it out," Nazario said.

"Thumb drive's got five names—all blue. Plus two bonus prizes off the record. Seven dirty badges. Two already dead. Guess karma's working the night shift," Wilson quipped.

"Officer Ronnie Salerno and Marcus Delgado—the ones who tried to kidnap Ariabella, right?" The chief grimaced, sweat dotting his forehead.

"Correct, sir. Five alive, excluding Salerno and Delgado. Harrison ran out of time to update the thumb drive. Don't feel comfortable saying the names here. Dawson was very helpful in passing along the letter and the key to the lock box. What's on the thumb drive is damning already. Afraid to see what's in the box," Nazario said.

She handed Chief Johnson the note that had been in the sealed envelope, along with the post office box key. Chief scanned it, reading it slowly, and once he was done, sighed. He closed his eyes, pinching the bridge of his nose.

"At least he wasn't naïve. Knew they were after him. Guess I was living in a bubble. Grew up seeing the good in people. My mama always taught me to treat a man by his character—not his badge. Thought our sworn duty meant something. Thought I'd know if one of our own flipped." His eyes drifted back to the ceiling like it held a truth he'd missed. "But Harrison saw it. He knew. A young, rookie detective—knew. And I didn't. That's what guts me a hell of a lot more than those fucking bullets that tore through me."

Angry tears crawled down his cheeks. Chief Johnson wiped them away, furious.

Nazario leaned in and reached out, clasping his hand in hers. "Remember when I took down Connor Morris? I was pissed at myself that I didn't draw my weapon. It was strapped to my ankle. I was running at full speed. There was so much fog off Santa Monica Beach that day. Everything was happening so damn fast." Nazario gripped Johnson's hand tighter, and he squeezed back. "I felt like I failed. Fourth-degree black belt in Taekwondo, and I had my meniscus and ACL torn. Was in a full leg brace for three months."

"Can't forget that one. You took him down, though. And that mother fucker was a former UFC fighter," Johnson reminded.

"But my knee wasn't the worst part. He nearly choked me out. I couldn't breathe." Nazario felt herself getting emotional just thinking about it. She swallowed hard. "Kept reliving that fight over and over. Caught the bastard but still felt like I'd failed. Like I'd lost my first fight. And Gus told me something I'll never forget. She stopped by when I was in the hospital and said: 'Don't go down self-misery road, detective—it's a dead-end.' And she was right. You can't beat yourself up for seeing the good in everyone. For believing in the good in all of us."

"That's why we love you," Wilson said with an affectionate smile.

"Well, I love y'all too, and I don't want anything to happen to any of you."

"The bureau's aware of the situation, and with what you told us about the shooter—it helps. You may not've seen his face —" Huxley started.

"But we can use his height, eye color, build, all that. We can use it. And hopefully the drive and what's in that locked box will tell us more," Nazario finished. "We'll be careful. But the one thing we won't do is let the motherfucker that did this to you get away."

The nurse came in, announcing her presence. "Well, hello, Chief Johnson. It's nice to see you awake. How're you feeling? We've got the hospital security guard sitting out front. Don't worry, it's someone we trust. The pain meds kicking in?"

"Appreciate it, but I'm not sure I trust anyone," the chief said wearily. "And I hate being drugged up."

"Is it helping with the pain at least?"

"A little, I suppose." Fingers dug into the mattress, holding on. "Still feels like I'm in hell."

"And you're going to feel that way for a while. We can try a different pain med if—"

"Oh, *heeell* no."

The nurse turned to them with a gentle smile. "He's been through a lot. I gave you an extra five minutes, but he's in a lot of discomfort and needs his rest now."

In the bed, Chief Johnson rolled his eyes to her back.

"I don't need no rest. Been laying up in this bed for too long," Johnson forced a holler—but it came out ragged, barely a rasp. His body betrayed him, voice thin and broken, even as his mind still burned with fight. A survivor's fury trapped in a frame that wouldn't listen.

"Don't be a martyr. Take the pain meds, they'll make the stay bearable. We'll visit again when we can and will update you when we look at all the intel," Nazario said.

He clutched her hand, words coming out in a paternal plea. "Please be careful—*please*."

Unable to hold back, she threw her arms around him and in a fierce hug, whispered in his ear, "We're taking them down."

———

Detective Nazario, Wilson, and Huxley were escorted into a back room that was steel-lined and windowless. The dull institutional light cast everything in a jade-blue hue, bleaching the space like a rose wilting under fluorescent fatigue. It reminded Nazario a lot of the hospital. Thoughts still lingered on Chief Johnson—sadness still lodged in her chest like a stone. The armored post office boxes stood in fortified silver rows. Unmoving, with secrets held inside, each holding something someone never meant to share.

"Here are all our secured units," the Ironwood Vault manager said.

"Secured, huh? What would be the reason," Nazario said, "that people use a secured post office area?"

"For high valuables. We have cameras and surveillance in addition to motion detectors and a top-notch security system to prevent potential theft," the manager explained. "To the right are numbers one through two hundred. To the left, two hundred through three hundred."

"We'll need to close this unit out once we empty it," Huxley said.

"I'm assuming neither of you is the owner." He paused, scanning the three of them. "I'm taking an educated guess based on your question. Sounds like this is your first time here, and I also don't recognize any of you."

"We're here working on a case. Detective Nazario—LAPD Homicide Division," Nazario flashed her badge, pointing to Wilson. "My partner, Detective Wilson."

Huxley introduced himself and then added, "FBI."

"I'll still need the owner's written consent to close out the unit," the manager said.

"Well...unfortunately, that's not gonna happen." Wilson clicked his tongue. "Unless you know a notary who specializes in the afterlife."

The manager furrowed his brows, knitting them together into a confused tangle.

"I'm not exactly sure what you're getting at," he said, Wilson's dry humor seemingly not clear enough. "If they can't be here in person, I can always send the deal agreement and closure paperwork digitally via email."

Nazario decided it was time to spell things bluntly. "The owner—Detective Clay Harrison is *dead*. As in no longer alive."

"As in...don't think he'll be checking his emails from the other side—bar the chance you believe in that sort of thing." Wilson beamed a friendly smile. "Unless ghosts have Gmail. I hear the service is...spotty."

The manager flushed. Pink shades of embarrassment rose up his pale neck and colored his cheeks, spreading like a wildfire doused in gasoline.

"I'm sure there's a death clause in place. Doubt we really need to go through the trouble of hunting down next of kin or the executor, do we? I mean, all to close out a post office box?"

Huxley said, although it sounded more like a statement, a rhetorical question.

"I'm...I'm very sorry to hear of his passing. I do normally require an executor, but I think I can make an exception and close out the account—effective today." He cleared his throat. "If you need anything, I'll just be at the front desk getting the process started and have it done by the time you leave."

"Thanks for your help," Huxley said to the man's back as he scurried off—like he couldn't get away fast enough from the awkward conversations of a dead man's locked past, a small metal box that might help them provide more details that would strengthen their internal investigation.

"One through two hundred to the right," Wilson said. "Since we're unit 216, we go left. I just love a little math and deductive reasoning."

They made a beeline to the left, scanning each box, and then stopping in front of 216.

Each flanked side by side before the box, staring at it for a ten-count, unsure of what they'd find. After what felt like a long beat, Nazario stepped forward and slid the polished key into the narrow lock, its teeth catching just enough to resist. A soft *click*. Unlike ordinary P.O. box places, Ironwood Vault catered to a select clientele. The kind of people who didn't ask for receipts. The kind of people who needed to secure property of high value, and not just monetary, but high-value intel—leverage. Access. Intel that could tarnish reputations. Lawyers. Occasional billionaires with a burner phone and a panic button. Fixers. Double lives that required the kind of privacy Ironwood Vault provided, a place that wasn't even searchable on Google maps.

No questions asked—just a key, a name that wasn't yours, and a box no one could trace.

Rather than swinging open, this box slid outward like a

drawer. Its metal surface glinted beneath the fluorescent hum. Nazario pulled it free, a tightness in her chest burning as bad as the curiosity about what they might uncover, burning as bad as the secrets Harrison had worked night and day for—worked hard enough to've been killed over it. She understood it now. Harrison couldn't turn away. What he'd seen chained him to the truth, and in the end, he sacrificed himself to bring it to light.

SEVENTEEN
THE RESCUE

THE CHINOOK ADVANCED SCIENCES LAB, just outside of Whittier—tucked in the shadows of Portage Pass, was exactly fifteen minutes past the tunnel as Lyle Gentry had said. They pulled up to a steel-framed structure designed to withstand Alaska's unforgiving winters. Its corrugated metal siding was rust-resistant and layered with insulated panels.

A standing-seam metal roof rose at a sharp pitch, fitted with ice guards to prevent snow from shearing off in slabs. The large windows were triple-glazed and mirrored with low-e coating. It appeared to be engineered to trap heat, shed condensation, and hold against the kind of cold that cracked lesser glass. It was a three-story structure with a modern, industrial design—steel-framed, angular, built to survive the elements. A sleek steel sign read *Chinook Advanced Sciences Lab*, the letters cut clean like a surgeon's blade.

They stepped out of the SUV, boots crunching and sinking under fresh powder that was deep enough to rise to their calves. Xander and Von stood for a beat, glancing up at the impressive science lab, a place that looked like it should've been in Beverly Hills instead of a remote location in Alaska. They walked in companionable silence, striding through the doors. Zeus, covered in snow, shook it off before following them in. Being a private facility, rather than a government building or the airport, there was no security checkpoint whatsoever. No full-body scanners, no metal detectors. Von found it odd that an advanced science lab wouldn't have any type of basic security system.

While there were cameras mounted outside and throughout the lobby, there wasn't even a security officer upon entry, making it easy for them to walk in armed with their SIG Sauer P320 semi-automatic weapons tucked along their waist. Their boots squeaked along the polished marble floors that must've cost a small fortune to outfit the expansive lobby. The facility felt equal parts high-end and eerily remote. Too quiet. Too sterile. The kind of silence money could buy—and hide behind. Locating the directory, Von wasn't surprised to find a list of labs.

The Chinook facility housed eight labs spread across three floors—enough to run a small biotech empire in the middle of nowhere. It made sense that they'd have cameras instead of actual security guards and magnetometers. They naturally started with the ground floor and the two labs that sat on level one: materials and containment testing. Each lab was secured with top-of-the-line access technology—a wall-mounted facial recognition scanner no bigger than a tablet, paired with a biometric palm reader about the size of a hand. Dual authentication, heat-mapped and AI-verified, just to open a door.

"Figures," Von said, breaking the silence. "Skip the outdated metal detectors and guards—sink it into high-tech. No way in hell is anyone getting into these labs without a fucking bulldozer."

There were no windows. Xander analyzed the door, running his hands along its edges.

He tapped once. "You hear that? It's solid steel."

"Looks like a regular door to me," Von said.

"Because they used some sort of polymer finish," Xander explained, "or coated it with a composite panel to make it appear like an ordinary door. But the core is steel."

"You mean, it's a ballistics-rated lab door? Can't shoot our way through?"

"Correct, not even bullets will breach this door. Typical handguns or rifles won't do it. A blowtorch would be needed for entry, and that shit takes time."

"How in the hell do we even find her if she's holed up inside one of these labs?"

"I dunno. But we should check the second lab on this ground floor and then scout out the second and third floors," he said.

The second lab was located on the first floor, on the opposite side of the building—the east wing, and there was no difference from the previous lab they'd investigated. There was the same reinforced steel door camouflaged to look like a regular door with technology for entry identical to the first lab.

"Let's take the elevator up and check out the other labs," Xander said.

"Seems pointless since we can't get in and we don't have a blow torch, but I'm not about to give up now," Von said.

They took the elevator up—smooth at first, the hum of the machinery steady in the shaft. Then suddenly a loud *BOOM* jostled the elevator, reverberating through the steel. The floor jolted beneath their boots. Overhead, the lights flickered, buzzing before snapping back on. Von slammed a hand against the cold metal—the same reinforced steel she figured lined every lab door in this place.

"What the fuck was that?" she snapped.

Xander hit the door control, stabbing the button with quick, precise jabs. Nothing.

"We've got company," Xander muttered, glancing up at the

panel. The elevator shuddered, climbing barely half a floor before grinding to a stop. The doors peeled open—not to a clean hallway, but to the split crawl space, maybe three feet of clearance. Xander didn't hesitate. He wedged his hands against the edges, forcing them wider.

"Guess we're climbing out of this bitch," Von said.

"Think there's enough space for you. I might be able to squeeze through. But I won't know until I try."

Another *BOOM* exploded through the air, shaking the elevator once again. Von braced her injured leg as she hit the wall. Zeus, who'd been stoic and fearless, was thrown back. He quickly recovered, jumping to his feet.

"Let's get him up first. He'll find her," Von told Xander, then turned to Zeus, switching to his native tongue and asking him to find the doctor. *"Finde den Wissenschaftler."*

Xander lifted her dog and pushed him through the crawl space. On the second floor, Zeus dropped to the ground, nose working, sharp instincts locking onto a trail. He didn't have a shirt or anything carrying the doctor's scent, but Zeus could still lock onto a human trace.

He turned to her next, extended a hand—and when she took it, Xander drew her closer to the opening. A strong arm slipped around her waist a little too low; his broad chest pressed against her back. Heat passing between them. She could feel the cords of muscle, catching the scent of him, aged leather and sandalwood. He placed both hands on her hips and lifted her with ease, as if she were no lighter than a sheet of paper.

"You good?"

"Yeah," she grunted as she gripped the edge of the elevator opening and crawled through, her shot leg burning from having to bend her knees. Xander jumped up off the floor and hoisted himself out of the elevator as if he'd done this sort of thing before.

There was a trail of bloody footprints that led down a hall.

Von and Xander followed it to a lab. Zeus was waiting for them, the door ajar by an inch, though it was too heavy for him to push his way through. The facial scanner appeared to be cracked, leaving only a black screen. Sparks flew off the hand scanner, its surface bloodied by someone's palm. Someone who was injured. That someone could very well be Dr. Seung-ah Lee. If only they could get to her before she bled out.

Pop! Pop! Pop!

Live fire sang through the air from a close distance.

"They're coming closer," Xander said, "think they're trying to break into the labs to see which one she's in. Shooting the biometric scanners. They must've shot at this one, but couldn't find the doctor. They're gonna return—we don't have much time!"

Xander pushed the heavy door open, and they entered the lab.

Von half expected the place to be turned over, smashed by bullets, but nothing had been touched. A waft of chemicals assaulted her senses; a metallic essence blended with a sour bite of ammonia. The fluorescent lights buzzed above, casting a harsh glare on metal workbenches cluttered with glassware: beakers, flasks, distilled columns, some still streaked with residue. In the corner stacked with sealed containers, a vacuum pump hummed beside a rattling centrifuge. Fume hoods lined the far wall, their vents clogged with grime.

There was a chemical locker that stood half open, shelves gutted. Barrels marked with faded hazard labels sat in puddles of slick runoff near a floor drain. Protective gear—masks, gloves—hung like abandoned skins on rusted hooks. Paperwork littered a workstation, scrawled formulas, and reaction notes pinned under a cracked clipboard. A refrigeration unit whirred softly, its door ajar, rows of vials stacked inside. In one corner, a terminal blinked on standby—screen locked, keys smudged. The place reeked of a rush job. Broken glass crunched underfoot. Whatever happened here, they'd left in a hurry. Or someone had never left at all.

Von closed it and glanced around, thinking the way the scientist might think. If it were Von and people were looking to kill her, she'd hide.

"Let's see if she's still here. She could be hiding," Von said.

"My thoughts exactly."

Von and Xander walked around, checking the bathroom and closets—nothing. They circled back and followed Zeus to the chemical lockers. He barked twice, scratching on one of the doors. Von wrapped her hand around the steel handle—powder-coated yellow, chipped near the base. She gave it a slow pull. Resistance. Not locked. Just jammed. She crouched, scanning the seam where the door met the frame. Classic three-point latch. The rods were likely wedged—top and bottom—either by rust, impact, or someone intentionally rigged it. Tapping once near the top hinge, she put her ear to it, listening. Hollow. A second tap lower and light a shuffle inside sprung to life, barely there. Bingo.

"Did you hear that?"

"Sure did," Xander said.

Leaning her shoulders in, Von applied steady pressure until the frame torqued.

"Do you have anything on you? Need to pry it open."

Xander took out a Leatherman Skeletool and flipped it open with practiced ease, retrieved the flathead bit driver, and wedged it behind the latch plate. One twist. The metal groaned. The top rod popped free. She yanked the handle again. This time, the door gave with a reluctant screech.

Wet, frightened eyes peered up at them. Dr. Seung-ah Lee

shuddered, raising her hands in the air. "Please, please don't hurt me," she begged.

"Not gonna harm you. We're here," Von said, "to protect you. But you've gotta trust us."

She shook her head. "I'm...I'm not going back. I can't go back. I can't go back to working for Ryker. If you're here to kill me, then you'll have to do it because I'd rather die than go back. Too many people have already died because of me."

"We're not the cops. We're not the cartel—and we're definitely not part of Jaxon Ryker's crew," Xander said. "We're here to make sure you're unharmed and that the formula isn't leaked."

The doctor, whose picture was of a leading professional in her industry, now appeared like a small child. She was petite enough to have fit in the chemical locker and smart enough to have evaded capture. Dr. Lee hugged her knees tighter to her chest, glancing warily at Zeus before returning her gaze.

Pop! Pop! Pop!

The sound of live fire came closer.

"We're running out of time. You must come with us. We have to get you to a safe location. Ask all the questions you want later," Von urged, extending a hand.

Suddenly, the doors to the lab slammed open with a rough kick.

"In here!" a male voice shouted.

"Shit." Von turned to the doctor. "It's now or never."

The doctor gripped Von's hand and crawled out of the chemical locker.

"Get on the ground and find cover," Xander said. Dr. Lee hid behind a steel lab table that would protect her against flying bullets.

A rain of live fire charged their way—Xander and Von hid next to the doctor.

Zeus, trained to hate guns and apprehend shooters, leaped out without warning, sprinting full speed at the gunmen. Von's heart slammed against her chest, afraid he'd get shot. Most of the time, Zeus took commands; other times, he defied directives and made decisions that could cost him his life. He'd risked his life countless times, but shoot-outs cranked the risk to lethal.

"Zeus," she shouted after him, "*komm zurück!*"

Disobeying her orders, he didn't come back.

Xander and Von briefly poked their heads up, shooting at the assailants while desperately trying to keep Zeus alive and provide him cover. Her German Shepherd wove with the expertise of a trained soldier—a military working dog embedded with the Marines and deployed to both Iraq and Afghanistan. He could sniff out bombs and disarm gunmen because she had trained him to do so. Most importantly, he had a fearless streak, one that didn't flinch during gunfire. During her veterinary years, Von had taught a dog training class, raising combat canines from puppyhood until they were ready to be dispatched to their handlers.

Zeus wasn't ordinary—brains and brawn fused into a creature who defied the limits of training, smarter than any dog she'd ever worked with.

Pop! Pop! Pop!

Pop! Pop! Pop! Pop!

Pop! Pop! Pop! Pop! Pop!

"Kill that damn mutt!" one of them roared. *Pop! Pop!*

Dr. Lee cried out, dropping to her knees, hands clamped to the crown of her head. Ducking low, Von thought she caught the edge of a whisper—pleading words, maybe a prayer coming out of the doctor's lips.

Von craned up, peaking to see where her dog was. The shots were aimed at Zeus, though they missed. Her German Shepherd had the instincts and speed to evade live fire, trained on battlegrounds. But here, the military-trained war dog might not be so lucky. It was only a matter of time before one of the bullets struck him.

"Sons of bitches." Von stood, her bum leg aching, as she rose from her crouched position.

"Where the hell're you going?" Xander questioned, frantic with worry.

"Saving my fucking dog—that's where I'm going."

Spotting another steel lab table closer to the shooters, she dashed toward it, raised her P320, and fired off a few rounds. One hit a man on the left—upper right chest. He screamed. Von shot him again, center mass. Blew a hole through his black heart. He dropped. One man down. She scanned the lab—two more men in black tactical gear, one ducked behind a chemical locker, the other wove between stainless steel tables with a SIG MCX Rattler raised tight to his chest. The Rattler—built for close quarters with a suppressed .300 Blackout punch—was perfect for tight rooms like this.

Shots sang from behind her, as Xander covered her, a shot hit the leg of the gunman who was weaving through the room. He gritted his teeth and stubbornly kept drawing closer, his shot leg limping forward. He'd get to her location very soon. Another shot from Xander's P320 hit the man in the right eye—blew out his socket, punched through his brain, cranial debris painted the walls as he crumpled to the ground.

Von kept moving—another target locked in. Near the door, a fourth shooter struggled with Zeus, her dog's jaws clamped around the forearm of his gun hand. Pain twisted across his face as he lost control of the weapon—it clattered to the floor. She didn't hesitate. *Pop! Pop!* Two bullets. More skull soup splattered the back wall.

Three down. One left—the bastard crouched behind the chemical locker.

"Hol' den letzten Mann!" Von ordered Zeus. *Get the last man!*

Zeus put his nose to the ground and began tracing the scent of the last Ryker henchman.

Xander and Dr. Lee jogged out of hiding, meeting Von at the closest lab table near the front entrance. *Pop! Pop! Pop!* Three shots cracked through the air—close enough to ruffle the doctor's hair, missing her head by half an inch. She ducked with a gasp as Von grabbed her arm and yanked her down behind cover.

Zeus darted toward the gunman, just as two more shots tore through the lab. The dog zig-zagged through the gunfire like a missile with teeth—fast, lethal, target-bound. The henchman stepped from cover, raising his weapon to unload. But Von and Xander were locked on. They fired. A storm of bullets shredded his torso, making his body jolt like a marionette. His finger clenched the trigger as he fell, sending wild rounds ricocheting off steel lab tables and scarring the floor.

Then—silence.

He hit the ground, twitchless.

"C'mon, we've gotta get the hell up out of here before more of them find us," Von told the doctor. "If they haven't already alerted their team to this lab before they were killed."

The doctor surveyed her surroundings—four corpses, blood pooling across the marble floors, walls streaked with gore and brain matter. Then she broke. Tears cascaded down her cheeks, shoulders trembling, her whole body quaking beneath the weight of post-traumatic shock. Terror.

"Not trying to be insensitive, but you've gotta move those legs. Save the tears for the car ride. We're out of time, Dr. Lee," Xander said, gripping her upper arm. "Where's the surveillance room? Where they keep all of the daily tapes?"

"It's...it's on this floor in room...in room 235, just a couple of doors down."

The surveillance room was indeed two doors down, a short walk away. It stank of old wires and ozone. Von closed the door behind them with a metallic clunk. No windows. No camera in the room itself. Just the low whir of servers and the soft glow of ten grainy feeds blinking across five screens in a grid of small squares. The doctor watched Xander with anxious eyes as he scanned the setup—standard rack mount NVR, off-brand but functional.

"Doesn't look like there's a cloud sync option," Xander said. "This surveillance system seems to be some local-brand."

"Lucky break," Von said. "Just hope you know what you're doing."

"Oh, I've erased plenty of footage. More than I can count." He pulled open the steel access drawer, found the drive bank underneath, and pointed. "You see, they're labeled by day."

He thumbed through the stack, found today's, and yanked it. It slipped out onto the control bay. Xander toggled to "manual overwrite."

"Huh...there's no password prompt. These people are more amateur than I thought," he said, selecting the footage for the day and then deleting it. Xander located the admin access panel and scrubbed the metadata index clean. "No one'll get this footage back. It's not enough to delete it because the forensic unit can recover deleted footage. That's why I had to manually overwrite to get rid of the metadata index."

"Good call," Von said, standing guard by the door, Glock raised. "I always thought all you needed to do was delete the digital file."

"It's more complicated than that," he said.

Von glanced down the hallway—no activity, at least not yet,

since she could hear faint sounds of approaching police cars. "Better hurry, got 5-o coming straight at us."

She glanced back at Dr. Lee. The chemist pressed herself into the corner, trembling. Her hands shook so hard she nearly dropped her glasses trying to wipe her face. An involuntary gag escaped her lips, turning away in time to vomit onto the tile. Acid and bile splashed near the baseboard. The room suddenly smelled of fear.

"Deep breath, Doc," Von said, low and firm. "Almost done."

Xander pulled the original drive, slid it into an empty plastic bag he found on the floor, and replaced the drive with a cloned feed that looped perfectly. Empty corridors. No faces. No bodies. No blood.

From far off—muffled but unmistakable—came the rising wail of sirens.

Getting closer. Fast.

"Whittier PD?" Von asked.

"Or Troopers," Xander said. "Either way, we're not sticking around."

He held the plastic bag that contained the old drive and nodded toward the exit.

Dr. Lee whimpered. Tried to stand, but her legs buckled— still hunched, still heaving.

They sprinted out of the building just as the sound of police cruisers drew near.

Von caught her elbow. "We leave now. Like Xander said, save it for the car ride. You can fall apart later."

Still trembling, the doctor nodded in compliance and finally began to move. They exited into the service hallway—boots quiet on concrete, red emergency lights pulsing overhead. The sound of sirens grew sharper, bouncing off the icy air outside. Another minute and the parking lot would be crawling. They slipped out the side exit into the dark, snow-dusted night.

"S-s-shouldn't we wait to talk to the cops?" Dr. Lee said.

"No!" Von and Xander said in unison.

Xander ushered the doctor into the back of the Ford Expedition, Zeus jumping in after her. Within seconds, they were peeling out of the driveway, taking a back exit to avoid being seen leaving the building. By the time Whittier PD arrived, the building would be empty. All evidence of their presence and the shoot-out, scrubbed from the surveillance footage.

A lie wrapped in silence—just enough to trigger bullets instead of questions—and now there were bodies on the ground to prove it.

EIGHTEEN

THE WRECKAGE

DETECTIVE NAZARIO HAD NEVER HESITATED in her twenty-five years on the force—not with any case, not with any perp, no matter how dangerous they were. She'd never experienced intimidation, not with the fourth-degree black belt in Taekwondo she'd earned by the age of eighteen. The detective was self-motivated, ambitious, earning an AA through dual enrollment by the time she graduated high school, which allowed her to fast-track.

She earned her bachelor's in criminology by nineteen and her master's degree in criminal investigations from George Washington University in just a year and a half. By twenty-one, she had completed her graduate studies and began her police career with the LAPD, following in her father's footsteps. Detective Lucas Nazario had been one of the best undercover Gang and Narco detectives the LAPD had. And throughout her career, she prided herself on being fearless—on taking down perps without the use of her weapon.

Detective Anaya Nazario was the weapon.

Though not even eighteen years of martial arts training had prepared her for this.

The moment they walked outside of Ironwood Vault, she could see the damage from the entryway of the private safe deposit suite twenty feet away, where they'd parked. The windows of Wilson's Chevy Tahoe had been smashed, including the front windshield. Shards of glass littered the asphalt. Dents of all sizes covered the body where the SUV had been assaulted. Both the brake and front lights had been crushed and damaged.

Spray-painted in white on the side of the vehicle read, "SNITCHES GET BURIED!"

Wilson whistled. "You almost have to respect the commitment," he said, dryly. "Smashed every window, dented every panel—this thing's got *personality* now."

While Nazario appreciated Wilson's sense of humor, the damage wasn't funny. Not to her. Not to Huxley, who flashed her worried eyes.

"I'm going back in, asking the manager for the exterior surveillance footage," Huxley said, jogging toward the door. "There's a camera mounted outside in the corner."

Wilson ran a hand along the caved-in door, squinting at the spray paint.

"Cool, maybe the footage caught which Picasso did it," Wilson said, with a chuckle. "Adds resale value. If you're selling to a demolition derby."

"This shit's not funny," Nazario said.

"Didn't say it was. Cheaper than crying. Humor's all I got left," he said, then let out another incredulous bubble of laughter. "Well, that, and a totaled SUV."

"Go on and laugh all you want. But I'm calling Whittier and Yang—we need SID to dust for prints. Take pics. We need this filed and documented," she said, already dialing SID's number.

"Doubt we'll see their faces on the camera or get any latent prints," Wilson said. "Worth a try, I suppose. But if this was from a dirty blue, they're not stupid enough to leave any evidence behind, and they must've seen the camera mounted on the building facing the parking lot."

Yang picked up on the second ring, just as the manager and Huxley walked out.

Shock riddled the manager's face. She overheard him saying something to Huxley, some sort of apology. "This tape is officially a part of our investigation now. It's evidence, and we'll need time to analyze it. We'll return it when we can."

"Don't think we need it back, and again, I'm very sorry this has happened. I wish I'd seen something, but I had stepped away from the front desk for a bit to do routine box checks and mail sorting in the other room."

The manager returned inside, and Huxley strode toward her, waving a surveillance tape in the air. Nazario lifted a finger, pointing at her phone. "Talking to Yang," she mouthed.

"Hey, Detective Nazario," Yang started on the other end of the line. "You don't call this number unless it's important. Everything alright?"

"Everything's far from fine." Nazario dragged a hand through her hair. "Will need you and Whittier. There's been an...incident. Wilson's Tahoe just got a full-blown facelift—courtesy of Mike Tyson. Don't think there's a single inch that didn't catch a punch."

"Oh boy," Yang said, then stalled for a beat, as if trying to figure out the best way to bring up the sensitive subject matter of their internal investigation. "You think this has something to do with your IA probe? If this is tied to internal, the timing is sus."

"Timing's certainly suspect. Need prints, DNA, anything that might've been left behind by our perps. Guessing blue and dirty. If this job was done by cops—they wouldn't be stupid enough to leave a trace of themselves behind."

An uncomfortable silence stifled the air. No one, regardless of what branch one served in, wanted to chatter about dirties within their blue family. It was akin to a mortal sin, a level of betrayal that you couldn't undo. A type of betrayal that went against your soul. It was the kind of gossip that could ruin your career, talk that could turn your best friends on the force into your worst enemies. It was the deadly unspoken rule that no one broke, even if there were lines crossed, even if there were paid-off patrol and bent badges.

It was shield loyalty. You backed the badge no matter what and stayed committed to the blue wall of silence, never breaking the code. You rode for your own. The ugly quiet made Nazario regret answering Yang's query. She shouldn't have been so honest. After all, Harrison and his partner, Detective Tyrell Dawson, had warned them not to trust anyone. Hell, Von Schlange—the Serpent Woman—had been the first to send a cryptic message she'd committed to memory.

> *Nazario,*
> *Don't trust anyone with a badge. He wore one too.*
> *I'm sure you know who he is—former DEA. Dirty.*
> *Dead now.*
> *There's another one in Kodiak, under Ryker's thumb.*
> *Former disgraced detective. Still breathing. Still hiding*
> *behind the law, he claims he's supposed to serve.*
> *You'll know him when you find him. You always do.*
> *—V*

Nazario stewed on those words: *Don't trust anyone with a badge.* Defensive, Yang finally spoke. Her words hit like a car slamming into a wall. Voice low and cutting, like it cost her, "How bad are we talking? The damage?"

"Well, we can't see out of the front window, and there's a nice note on the side—warning us that snitches get buried."

"They do, don't they?" Yang said, surprising Nazario. She always felt she could trust SID, and now, she wondered what team they were on: justice or self-preservation.

"Excuse me? I don't just think this was some random asshole off the street. This was internal. Maybe I told you too much, but it looks like you're more about silence than spine. Regardless, we need you here, and if we can't trust you to do this investigation, without fucking up the evidence to cover for your dirty shields—"

"All I'm saying, is that you start throwing shade, Detective Nazario, you better have more than a gut feeling. You know how fast that gets around. People hear you sniffing around your own —suddenly nobody returns your calls, your cases stall out, evidence goes missing."

Nazario gripped the phone in her hand.

Huxley called out for her. "Hey, Anaya, you need to come see this."

He used her first name, which meant it was something serious.

She turned her back to Wilson and Huxley, fingers clenching. Words came staccato and terse. "I'm not here to protect anyone's pension."

"Well, some of us are just trying to hold onto ours. You wanna light a match in a room full of gasoline? Fine. Just don't drag me or Whittier in it when it blows."

"If you're implying that you're gonna come here and clean up the evidence, then I'll do my job. Just as you should be doing yours. I'll get SID trainees out here if I must. If you're not willing to do a thorough investigation and gather what we need to put these fuckers behind bars, then I'll make sure there's another scientific investigation's lead doing the work you should've been doing. You're in charge of Scientific Investigation's Division, and if you can't do the right thing—I'll fight like hell to make sure someone else does."

"Look, I wasn't saying that I wasn't prepared to do my job. All I'm saying, is that going after dirty cops, you're risking—"

"I don't give a rats ass what I'm risking. I followed my father's footsteps to do the right thing. Detective Lucas Nazario was the best of the best. I hold no candle to my father. But he taught me one thing, and that one thing was integrity. They can intimidate me all they want, but I'll be damned before I go down without a fight. Now, get your asses down here and do your mother fucking job, or I swear to God, you won't have one by tomorrow morning."

"Detective Nazario—"

"Fuck you!" Nazario spat out, considering Ellen Yang's position, likely reflecting her partner, Chuck Whittier's stance.

Were they standing for something or standing aside? SID, the Scientific Investigation's Division, held a lot of power. It was their photographs, fingerprints, ballistics, trace reports—all the forensic evidence that could make or break a case. They documented the scene, sealed the chain of custody, filed reports. And if someone in that unit decided to look the other way, fudge a time stamp, misplace a print? A dirty cop's sins could disappear before they ever saw the light of day.

"There's right and there is wrong—and if you're hiding behind a badge, then you're no better than they are."

"Where's the address. Text it to me," Yang said eventually.

"Yeah, no. You're not getting the address. I'm done pretending you're one of the good ones. You and Whittier—you're either scared shitless or in on it. Either way, I'm not handing you anything. Lives are on the line. Lives that're dropping like flies over this tranq dope, this new chemical fucking concoction. So, no, no way in hell am I letting it bleed out because you're too busy covering your ass. We'll find someone else. Someone clean." Nazario glanced up, meeting Huxley and Wilson's inquisitive eyes. She white-knuckled the phone. "Don't text me. Don't call. Don't even breathe in my direction unless you start to remember which side you're supposed to be on."

Nazario hung up. Her jaw clenched, chest still hot from the last conversation. She quickly scanned her contacts and then found a junior recruit, fresh out of the academy. They'd barely begun shadowing the two senior SID techs who could now be tainted. No way in hell was she looping Whittier and Yang in on this. She needed someone pure. Someone who hadn't been in the game long enough to get dirty. Then she spotted the name, remembered it from a previous conversation with Humphrey.

Sierra Brooks.

Fresh out of the academy. Already turning heads in SID for her meticulous evidence pulls and airtight scene logs. She'd just started shadowing Whittier and Yang—still green enough to believe in the system. Still sharp enough to see through it. Nazario had only met her once, but she couldn't forget her. Captain Gus Humphrey's wedding—that warm fall night strung with lights and tequila. There was too much free booze—Nazario fought against the urge to pick up a drink. Brooks had worn a tailored navy suit, danced like she owned the floor, and gave a toast that made half the room cry. She was Humphrey's protégé, makeup artist, evidence tech, and goddamn truth-teller.

Her terracotta skin, deep and radiant under the patio lights, made her look carved from earth and light. Humphrey pulled Nazario aside that night and said, "This one? She's got a spine like rebar and a heart like mine."

Nazario found Brooks's number—waving off Huxley as he followed, who insisted that something was in Wilson's wrecked

SUV she *needed* to see. However, without a trusted SID tech, any note left in the vehicle meant nothing. They still needed fingerprints, photos, hard evidence—anything that could trace it back to the ones who did this, badge or not.

Nazario texted Brooks the address to Ironwood Vault and then waited five minutes before calling her.

Brooks picked up on the second ring.

"Detective Nazario? I got your text message."

"I need you," Nazario said. "Can you get to this scene, stat?"

"I'm not on rotation, but say the word and I'll move."

"Word. And don't tell Yang or Whittier."

"Copy that. What am I walking into?"

"A mess," Nazario muttered. "But you've got clean hands. I need eyes I can trust."

"Then you've got 'em. I'm en route."

Nazario ended the call and charged toward the wreck. "What the hell was left in the SUV?"

"A folder tucked under the backseat lining," Huxley said grimly. "It was meant...it was meant for us."

"As in you and me?"

"And Wilson."

"Shit." Nazario wondered how this day could possibly get any worse.

She moved toward the vehicle with leaden feet. Huxley snagged a manila envelope from Wilson's hands. The serious look on Wilson's ordinarily jovial expression made Nazario worry. No longer was he wearing his jokester face. Nazario peeled open the manila envelope, expecting evidence, maybe a note. What she found made her stomach bottom out.

Photos.

The first: Ariabella, fast asleep in her crib.

The second: Nazario and Huxley dead to the world in their bed.

A third—Elena Cruz, the babysitter, bottle feeding Ariabella in the living room.

All of them taken from inside the house. The angles were too tight, too precise to be through a window. The last photo was of Elena and Ariabella at a park, her daughter in a swing with a big smile on her little face. The person who took it had been standing close by, just a couple of feet away. Earlier that year, Nazario and Huxley had nearly lost their daughter when Jaxon Ryker's men had stormed into their home and attempted to kidnap their baby. Had it not been for Von, their only child might not be alive. But this time, this time these were taken by the very men she served with, dirty cops gone rogue, officers of the law who were supposed to be serving the community, now taking orders from a drug lord.

Nazario's hands trembled, rage flooded her chest like fire.

They hadn't just watched her family.

They'd been *inside*.

And then came the rest—just as violating, just as deliberate.

A woman in a cardigan, holding a grocery bag on a quiet front porch.

Aunt Maggie.

Wilson's aunt.

He always brought her up in passing, like a grounding wire. The one who raised him when no one else would.

Two more shots followed—one of her walking out of a church, another behind the counter at the food pantry where she volunteered on weekends. The timestamps were fresh—as in, *two days ago*, fresh.

They hadn't just watched her family.

They'd watched *his*, too.

No one was safe.

No line was sacred.

Huxley swiped a hand down his face, cheeks flooding with

the color of smoldering fury. He began pacing. First, Captain Gus Humphrey, her best friend—she takes three to the chest. Then, Clay Harrison gets killed. Then Chief Johnson nearly gets murdered. And now they weren't just coming after her, but threatening the lives of innocent family.

Nazario seethed, snapping, "How in the hell did they come into our home and bypass our fucking alarm system?"

"They had to've been watching our house, studying it. Must've been skilled enough to know how to turn it off," Huxley said. "This isn't the work of an amateur."

"It's the work of rot in uniform—corruption from the inside blue."

"Aunt Maggie's got alarms up the wazoo, too," Wilson said. "But it looks like they haven't been inside her house."

"Yet," Nazario bit out.

Just in time, Brooks pulled up with another SID trainee Nazario had seen around.

"Wow, it's like that, huh?" Brooks said, scanning the car with her eyes.

"It's someone from the inside," Nazario said, then warned her. "Careful, I'm now concerned for the safety of anyone associated with this case."

"Oh, they ain't about to threaten me," Brooks said.

"You sure you wanna do this?" Nazario showed her the pictures.

Brooks took a brave breath. "I'm here to do my job, Detective Nazario, and I'm not about to let some blue thugs run me off," Brooks said. "I've never let a negative experience dissuade me from joining the LAPD, not even after some of the bad ones used to rough up my brother—you know, the whole racial profiling."

Brooks turned and began tackling the SUV. While she and a fellow SID trainee started dusting for prints, Nazario hauled her laptop from the trunk. She'd hidden it smartly—wedged beneath the mat where Wilson's spare tire used to be. He'd taken it out weeks ago, told her straight-up: *If things go sideways, stash the important stuff here. Nobody checks for brains under a flat.*

Now she was glad she had.

Because whatever this was—it wasn't just vandalism. It was a message. And she needed answers fast.

"While they're doing their thing," Nazario said, "we need to check this second thumb drive."

There had been the one that Humphrey gave her, and yet a second one in Harrison's private lockbox.

"Right here and now?" Wilson said.

"Why not? We need to find out who made Harrison's list."

"Let's find out who these mother fuckers are," Huxley said, joining Wilson as they both stood behind Nazario, glancing over her shoulder.

Both thumb drives had a USB-C end that easily slid right into her MacBook Air.

They'd already gone through the thumb drive that Humphrey had given her with a list of five dirty cops, and now she wondered who else was involved. What other intel had Clay Harrison gathered?

The files weren't labeled. Just raw dates, folder dumps, and video files named with time stamps. Nazario clicked the first one. A grainy overhead angle lit up the screen—Detective Lila Mendez and Sergeant Vince Greer, full uniform, stepping into a warehouse they had no business in. At the bottom of the screen, a digital overlay glitched before it locked into place:

LAPD Evidence Storage—Restricted Access

Her stomach dropped. They weren't just dirty. They had the keys to the vault.

NINETEEN
THE CHEMIST SPEAKS

THE SILVER VOW'S engine rumbled low beneath them, steady as a heartbeat. Dr. Lee sat wrapped in a thermal blanket, knees drawn up, eyes still red and swollen from crying. She hadn't said much. Von didn't push. Xander stayed near the cabin's helm, watching the horizon. The sun sank behind the snow-topped Alaskan mountain terrain, sending crimson ribbons across the frosty horizon.

Von had to admit, she hadn't expected Alaska to be so breathtakingly beautiful. She also had to admit that the sunset's amber kiss against Xander's profile stirred something deep within her, a returning carnal urge that hadn't gone away despite all her efforts to bury it. Von redirected her thoughts. Somewhere back in Whittier, the Chinook Advanced Sciences Lab was most likely teeming with law enforcement by now. They'd barely made it out on time, escaping via a back road exit that prevented them from having to pass a slew of squad cars.

She'd seen trauma plenty of times in her life as both a veterinarian and a vigilante killer—but something about Dr. Lee's shaking hands, her body rocking back and forth, and that blank, quiet shock—it got to Von. Not because the doctor was fragile, but because she reminded Von of her own attack, years before she would transform into a paid assassin. Von kept one eye on the woman, the other on the coastline, while trying to avoid Xander's presence pulling at her like an undertow.

Von watched Xander and already understood what he was doing, having seen him operate the boat several times. From a distance, she studied him as he tapped the nav panel, punched in coordinates for Kodiak, and engaged autopilot. The console beeped twice, loud enough for her to hear, and then was locked in, charting the 170 nautical miles back to Kodiak, Alaska. He walked into the main cabin. Von never moved from the narrow table, one arm stretched along the bench. Xander joined her, sitting across from Dr. Lee with nothing but questions between them.

"We've got about eighteen, maybe twenty hours on water before we hit Kodiak," he said.

Xander folded his arms, pecs flexing in the most undignified way—like he didn't know exactly what that did to people. Frustration rippled through her. The hot, useless kind. How the hell was she supposed to stay mission-focused—complete a high-level op—when her supervisor looked like he belonged on the cover of a goddamn Military Thirst Calendar?

He had no right. None. And the worst part—he hadn't even done anything.

"Fixin' to be a long night," Xander added.

"It sure is," Von said, clearing her throat.

"We gonna sit here all night in silence," he addressed Dr. Lee, "or are you gonna let us in, let us help you?"

The doctor wiped her wet cheeks with the back of a hand.

"How'd you become involved with someone like Jaxon Ryker, and why're you running now? Change your mind on your...collaboration?"

"Do you have anything to drink? Like...alcohol?" the doctor finally said. Von raised a brow. A cocktail hour wasn't what she expected from Dr. Lee.

Xander gave Von a sideways glance, before returning his attention back to the biochemist.

"You sure?" Xander asked. "Got Knob Creek—whiskey. Also have tequila, scotch, and good ol' IPAs, American beer. Most people don't ask for booze when they're one panic attack away from a blackout. So, I'm gonna ask you again—you really want a buzz over water?"

"I'm serious. I need something—tequila, whiskey, turpentine —I don't care."

"Alrighty then."

Xander crossed the room, stepped into the galley, unscrewed the back of the cabinet under the sink. Out came a bottle of Knob Creek, wrapped like a weapon. Of course.

"That part of your field kit?" Von rubbed her chin.

Dr. Lee blinked. "Didn't peg you for a survivalist."

He twisted the cap, glancing up at them. A sly, lopsided smile spread across his full lips, and heat passed through her. Lips Von had tasted and wanted to taste again.

"Navy SEAL," he said. "We plan for collapse."

Xander filled the whiskey half full in a short, wide glass and handed it to Dr. Lee.

"Want anything while I've got my emergency vault open?" he asked Von.

"I'll pass," she said. Von was a teetotaler—she only drank when it served a purpose. Like the time she seduced an Army colonel only to kill him. Let him suffer for what he did. The colonel had been stalking his ex-wife, twisting the story so it looked like *she* was the threat. Von had moved to Brazil. Retired from vengeance. Hired a marketing director who'd fled to Rio de Janeiro, trying to escape her powerful ex. It was the first time

Von had failed, failed to protect an innocent life. Failed to keep her alive, failed to keep her safe from *him*.

So, Von did what she did best—she'd made sure he never touched anyone else ever again.

The doctor took a long sip of the Knob Creek before clutching the glass in her hands.

"Now, how did you get involved with Jaxon Ryker?" Xander asked.

"I was kidnapped. You and the whole world know it. It was playing on every news outlet."

Xander narrowed his eyes at the doctor. Any trace of empathy, gone.

"I've watched that surveillance footage hundreds of times. What caught my eye was frame 14:52, right before they shoved you into the van." Xander leaned in, accosting her personal space. The doctor shrank back. "It wasn't panic I saw. It was the way you looked at the man on your left. Then the man on your right. The smallest flick of the eyes. A nod. Subtle but intentional. And you weren't empty-handed, either. You not only had a laptop and a med kit, but a suitcase. Kinda strange to have your shit pre-packed during a supposed random kidnapping, don't you think?"

"I...I don't know what you're talking about," the doctor lashed out, the quiet composure dropping in an instant, replaced by a raised, defensive voice. "That wasn't in the media that aired. What played was exactly what happened."

Xander tapped his phone screen and held it up to Dr. Lee without warning.

"I've got the full version. The version that didn't make it on the five o'clock news. Frame 14:52. You're looking left and then right. You see that nod? An insider, nonverbal conversation was taking place. That's why it was cut, and the false version was leaked to the media."

Von's eyes narrowed. She hadn't seen this footage. Not in the reports Cain gave her.

"Like I said, you weren't empty-handed. See the laptop? The medical kit? The suitcase? I actually think you had three or more suitcases based on what I think I see in the trunk of the car."

Von studied the trunk. While the windows were tinted, it wasn't limo tint. It did appear as though there was more luggage in the back.

"Most people who are genuinely abducted," Von said, "don't have a quick 'grab and go' suitcase waiting for them."

Xander lowered his phone, gaze sharp. "So, tell me, Doc. Was that really a kidnapping or a staged abduction to throw authorities off your trail, a trail that leads back to Jaxon Ryker and an intentional alliance with the drug lord?"

Dr. Lee took another large gulp of her whiskey.

"You've already made up your mind," Dr. Lee snapped. "So, what exactly do you want me to say? Huh?" She crossed her arms too fast, too defensive. "I looked to the left and then the right? I nodded? Maybe I did. I can't remember now. That was over two years ago. A lot has happened. Would you think clearly if there were armed men throwing you into the back of some SUV?"

"Oh, so the kidnappers had a suitcase on them? For what reason?" Von said.

"I don't know. How do you know it was mine?"

Von turned to Xander.

"She's lying through her teeth. She had every part in this, and I wouldn't be surprised if the whole thing was her idea," Von said.

"Neither of you were there. You didn't live it." She let out a shaky laugh. "Go ahead and play detective. Decide whatever fits the story you've already written. Your theory. Why would I leave a good job to work for a drug dealer?"

"People do crazy shit all the time out of boredom. You were stuck in the same role for twenty, thirty years. The biochemist everyone looked up to. Someone who always did the right thing, and you got sick of it. Needed a change. And when you were offered to lead this synthetic drug development and the cash was better than anything you'd made as a biochemist—you took up his offer," Von said.

"And maybe, just maybe, Ryker claimed that you'd be a part of a new synthetic drug, one that would be unlike anything out there. Maybe that excited you more than the money. You said yes. But you didn't realize it would be a new strain of zombie dope. Didn't think so many people would OD on it."

Dr. Lee took another long gulp, swallowing the remaining whiskey.

"Care for seconds?" Xander asked.

"Please."

Xander grabbed the bottle of Knob Creek from the hidden compartment under the sink and poured her a generous help-ing. He wisely left the bottle on the table between them, just in case, and they waited patiently for Dr. Lee to speak, for her to provide the answers they needed.

She took a sip of her whiskey and blew out a long breath before beginning.

"I was a part of a new drug research project, a neuroprotec-tive compound called Nexatryl-X It was originally designed to treat traumatic brain injury—TBIs in soldiers and athletes—a game changer for post-concussion syndrome and early-onset dementia. Our target response was for the drug to regenerate neural synapses via synthetic peptides, mimicking brain-derived neurotropic factors—BDNF." Dr. Lee said, pausing for another drink. "Originally, during phase two of the trial, it was claimed that Nexatryl-X improved cognition and reduced neural inflammation in eighty percent of patients."

"Wow, those are great results," Von said. Her background in veterinarian medicine had always made her appreciate doctors of all kinds—the science, the ethics, the burden of it.

"Yes, they were. Everyone was ecstatic until I discovered the raw EEG and neuroimaging data had been selectively culled. Patients who suffered side effects such as seizures, hemorrhaging, and hallucinations were quietly removed from the final dataset." The doctor turned to look out at the ocean lapping past them. "I also found the compound degraded body temperature in an unusual way. It was unpredictable, releasing toxic metabolites in certain genetic subtypes."

"The release of toxic metabolites, that issue reminds me of acetaminophen in cats. They lack of glucuronyl in transferase enzymes. Things like Tylenol can't be metabolized, because it can break down into toxic metabolites. So, it sounds like there was a toxic metabolite buildup in certain case study participants," Von explained.

The doctor's brows rose, as a look of surprise spread across her face. "How do you know so much about the subject?"

"Let's just say I used to wear a white coat too—before I traded it in for something...less forgiving," Von said. "I spent enough years in veterinary medicine to know how fast a compound can turn. Especially in the wrong body."

"That's...quite a career change," Dr. Lee said, eyeing the gun strapped to Von's hip.

"I'm sensing a repercussion for being a whistleblower," Xander said.

Dr. Lee nodded wearily, taking a longer swig of her whiskey. "Helix Point Labs buried the claim—because Nexatryl-X was co-funded by a defense contractor and a Big Pharma giant, Caridynex Therapeutics. Instead of being protected, they essentially created a false entry to put in my employee file. I was accused of misconduct, citing a minor protocol deviation I made early in the study, claiming that I took processing samples off-site due to equipment failure. My name was pulled from the final paper, and I was removed from the project. What hit even harder was the fact that I was blacklisted. No institution would touch me after that."

"Why were you in Helix Point Labs at the time of the fake kidnapping if you were fired?"

"They gave me two weeks to wrap up another research project I was doing—a cutting-edge experiment focused on synthetic hormone mapping for perimenopausal and menopausal women. It was designed to safely regulate hormonal imbalance in a new way. Nothing like what's currently on the market, whether it be over the counter or prescribed," she said.

"So, you were pissed off and decided to stage this kidnapping? Why pivot to the extreme and go from being an award-winning, decorated biochemist to working for a dangerous drug lord like Jaxon Ryker?" Xander said, his confusion mirroring her own.

"I could ask the same to the both of you? I don't know who the two of you work for, but it looks like you're in a dangerous profession as well," Dr. Lee countered.

"Doesn't matter who we work for," Xander said. "What matters is you're still breathing—which means you're on a need-to-know basis, Doctor. And right now, you don't."

"So, why flip to the dark side and why the change of heart now?"

Dr. Lee finished her drink and plunked it next to the bottle on the table.

"I needed a change. Obviously, doing the right thing hadn't worked. I wasn't able to make the same amount of money because word spread fast within the science community. One minute, I had a great-paying job, and the next, it was gone. Just like that. Suddenly, that mark on my career changed everything. I even tried to get a teaching job, but each place I'd applied to turned me down, and I couldn't help but feel their retribution ran deep. They dragged my name through the mud. It turned my entire life upside down."

As if she were trying to steady the pace of her heart, the doctor breathed deeply through her nose, then exhaled out of her mouth.

"Min-jun, my younger brother, was really smart, but wasted it all the moment he started taking that zombie drug. I asked him who was his supplier. He refused to give Ryker up at first. But I found out on my own. Hired a PI and found out about Jaxon Ryker's operations. So, I went to him and offered my services for a high price. Didn't think he'd be able to pay me more than the lab did. But he did. He hadn't worked with a biochemist with my kind of expertise. It didn't take long to convince him."

She reached for the bottle and poured herself another glass. Von considered that the doctor must have a high tolerance since she didn't remotely appear to have a buzz. In fact, she spoke like any other sober person instead of someone downing her third generous helping of whiskey.

The doctor continued, "I knew based on Jaxon Ryker's eagerness to have me on his crew, that I had a bargaining chip. So, part of our agreement, my 'employment package' if you will, was for his men to stop selling Min-jun the dope. He readily agreed. I was trying to protect my baby brother. Min-jun had agreed to enter rehab if I paid for it, and I honestly thought things were finally going to look up for me and for my brother. I had work that paid very well, work that was morally questionable. But at this point, it wasn't just about my survival—it was all about the well-being of Min-jun, who was hooked on a very dangerous drug."

"Is Min-jun clean now?" Von asked, leaning in. Elbows resting on her knees.

Dr. Lee chewed on her inner cheek, looked down at her hands as tears began to crawl down her face. "Three weeks ago, I found out that Min-jun had checked himself out of rehab after several months of staying clean. He started using again, only this time he started taking the more potent version of the zombie drug that I had created." She took a long drink, then continued, "Like the others, he OD'd. His roommate tried Narcan—"

"But it didn't work because this new strain is unresponsive to Narcan," Von finished.

The doctor nodded. "EMTs arrived quickly, but there was nothing they could do. I...I killed my baby brother." Her voice shook as a swell of pain and tears came rushing out. "I killed him. I knew what I was doing when I created the drug. Despite the risks, I made it anyway. I took orders from a drug dealer, ignoring all the internal warnings my brain tried to fire off like flares. I disregarded my conscience, and now he's...he's dead. *Dead!*"

She covered her face with her hands. A sharp pang of pain stabbed Von in the heart.

When Von had taken revenge on the men who had cut her open, leaving her inches away from death, causing her to suffer a miscarriage and leaving her to be unable to have children, Von had taken retribution out on the men connected to an illegal sex ring that had caused it all. And all her vengeance came back to haunt her. Samantha, her little sister, had suffered scars from being kidnapped and sold to wealthy, disgusting sexual predators. They found out who she was and targeted the one person

Von loved more than anyone. For payback, they murdered Sammy, and it was all her fault.

She understood Dr. Lee's agony.

Von, too, had killed her baby sister.

Now, they had a job to do. She and Xander had privately discussed what they'd do with Dr. Lee, and after hearing out the doctor, Von was even more determined that their solution was their only choice.

"What...what're you going to do with me? If you kill me, I'd be...I'd be grateful. I don't deserve to live. Not after what I've done. After Min-jun's death, I left Ryker, and no one leaves him. If you don't kill me, he will."

"Here's what we're fixing to do. We're flying you back to Los Angeles, and you're gonna speak with Detective Anaya Nazario and Supervising Special Agent Blake Huxley. You're gonna give them a bargaining chip, just like you did with Jaxon Ryker," Von said.

"What bargaining chip? Even if I give them the formula, my life's ruined. If no one would hire me then, they'd certainly not do so now. After I volunteered to work for a drug lord."

"You're not gonna say a word about the plotted abduction. From their standpoint, you were abducted and missing for two years. You tell them that you'd be willing to give up the formula on the condition that they clear your name. That they expose the research study that was manipulated, and that a part of your demand is that Helix Point Labs rehires you," Xander said.

Dr. Lee didn't respond. She just stared past them, eyes hollow like she was already halfway dead. Von didn't blame her. Grief like that didn't just hollow you out—it rewired your bones. But deals had to be made, and they didn't have the luxury of mercy. Somewhere in Los Angeles, another batch was already hitting the streets. Another Min-jun. Another Sammy. Another innocent life hooked on a new, more powerfully engineered strain of the zombie drug—the tranq dope. Von sat, jaw clenched. The past was unchangeable.

But the body count didn't have to keep climbing, not if she could stop it.

And if Jaxon Ryker wanted to finish what he started, then she'd be waiting.

TWENTY

THE DEAD DETECTIVE'S LEDGER

DETECTIVE NAZARIO DIDN'T EXPECT to see who came in behind Detective Mendez and Sergeant Greer into the restricted evidence cage—but once she did, the pieces fell into place and hit hard like a steel-toed boot to the sternum.

SID Unit Supervisor, Chuck Whittier.

And right behind him, Supervising Criminalist Ellen Yang.

They walked as if they'd done this hundreds of times, as if breaking the law had become second nature. Whittier scanned his badge like it was just another Tuesday night, while Yang stepped past the threshold and glanced straight up at the camera —then flipped the hallway lights off. She'd done this before. They'd done this before.

The timestamp: 2:14 a.m.

The badge logs had been wiped. But Harrison's backup drive had caught it—silent, undisturbed, buried in a private locked box he'd left in case something happened to him. Mendez entered first, face turned just enough to hide behind her collar. Yet, there was no mistaking that it was her. The footage cut there. When it picked back up again, twenty minutes had passed. The lights flicked back on. And Greer was carrying out a file box—plain, unmarked, no barcode, no chain-of-custody form.

They didn't log it. They didn't explain it. They just left.

Whatever had been in that evidence room was gone now. Removed. Scrubbed from record.

This wasn't a mistake. It was cleanup. And SID had their hands all over it.

"I would've never suspected Whittier and Yang," Wilson finally said.

Nazario filled both Huxley and Wilson in on the tense conversation she'd had with Yang and the reason why Yang and Whittier weren't at the scene.

"Was wondering why Brooks and the newbie trainee," Wilson said, "were combing through the charred corpse of my ride—*may she rest in pieces*—instead of the two OGs."

"It makes sense now. There's no way Mendez and Greer could have access to the restricted evidence storage area without the keys," Huxley said.

"Hang on, I thought that was the end of the clip. Guess I must've paused it. There's another fifteen seconds or so remaining." Nazario pressed play.

Still inside the precinct, in the service corridor, Detective Mendez and Sergeant Greer stood chatting with Whittier and Yang—Whittier still holding the box he'd essentially stolen out of the SID-controlled evidence vault, a storage cage that was a high-security, restricted-access area that not just the average beat cop couldn't touch. Even senior-level LAPD leadership in charge of whole departments didn't have the power to simply waltz in and waltz out without significant petitions for authorization prior to entry.

There were these rules for a good reason: to prevent evidence tampering.

Then Detective Mendez took out a letter-sized envelope and handed it to Whittier. Sergeant Greer followed suit, handing Yang a similar envelope. The two SID supervisors opened their "gift" in unison. Cold hard cash. They counted it, as if to ensure it was all there before returning it to their respective envelopes.

Greer turned and pointed at the camera. Nazario didn't have to hear the exchange to know what the sergeant was discussing. He was concerned about the cameras. Yang waved him off with a hand and said something. Nazario zoomed in on her lips and played it back, pausing frame by frame. "Did you catch that?" Nazario asked Huxley and Wilson.

"Sure did, it looks like she was saying 'don't worry'—Whittier and Yang are too seasoned to've left the tapes lying around for anyone to find," Huxley said.

"Guess Harrison didn't trust the system either. Looks like he backed up the backup—just in case Chuck Whittier got deletion-happy. I mean, hot damn," Wilson mused, "the man left us a ghost file. That's some thorough detective work right there. Six feet under and still out-performing half this department. Bet Chuckie-Cheese thought he was scrubbing the only copy—what a rookie mistake for an OG who outta know better."

Nazario scanned the screen, trying to discover anything she hadn't already checked.

Two more folders stood out: UNFILED_1, UNFILED_2.

She started with the first one and clicked on the UNFILED_1 folder.

Inside was another folder: ARCHIVE.

Another click.

NO TAG.

Then came the fourth and final folder: 6MO_SURV_TRACK.

Nazario glanced up, briefly checking on Brooks and the SID

trainee's progress. They were still working the wreck—Brooks photographing the undercarriage while the trainee measured the size and depth of each impact with a forensic scale. The L-shaped ruler was used to measure and document size, depth, and spacing. The standard SID tool in crime scene photographs was typically placed next to tool marks, dents, or blood splatter to provide an accurate scale reference in photos. Evidence markers ringed the car like yellow teeth, and the scorched frame still seemed intact in places. After photographing the undercarriage, Brooks knelt, collecting debris near the rear axle—likely searching for accelerant residue or remnants of a triggering device.

"They're doing a helluva better job than Whittier and Yang," Nazario said, returning to the contents of the thumb drive.

She right-clicked the folder and scrolled down to the "Get Info" tab.

"5.62 gigabytes, 1,821 files," Nazario muttered. "Looks like Harrison archived a shit-ton of footage. It's gotta be more surveillance videos based on the size of the folder."

Once she opened up the folder, her detective gut had been right. Nearly two thousand short video clips were organized by date and timestamp. She began with the earliest date, a video taken six months prior.

Huxley frowned, pointing out, "That date—it's the day Ariabella was born."

"Oh yeah, it is," Nazario said, clicking on the video.

Her mouth hit the floor. It was footage taken of her asleep in the hospital, Huxley passed out on the guest chair next to the bed. Shot on a mobile device, the person videoing walked over to their newborn and picked her up. He began rocking her gently, bobbing her up and down with gloved hands. Nazario paused the footage and rewound it, trying to decipher who the person was, but there was very little to go by. He was wearing black sneakers, though the brand and the size were hard to make out.

Judging by their large hands, she knew it was a male holding the baby, ruling out Mendez.

"Are you fucking kidding me!" Nazario slammed her fist down on the raised cement edge beneath her.

"Jesus *surveillance-footage* Christ," Wilson said with exasperation. "We're way past dirty cops. This dude's got balls bigger than the budget shortfall in this department."

Nazario's eyes widened, realizing what this meant. She clicked on another footage: she and Huxley walking out of her OB appointment, walking the baby during maternity leave, shopping at Carter's Babies & Kids in Antioch, just thirteen minutes away from Huxley's Brentwood home. What was most alarming was that in most of the footage, the person filming was in the same room, building, or sometimes mere feet away.

They were followed everywhere. To the park. To work. To the gym. Chatting with Elena, their babysitter, before going out on a rare date night. It was an equal opportunity, intense tracking of their daily life from sunup to sundown. No one was left out. Huxley was monitored to the FBI headquarters, speaking to colleagues on a lunch break outside the office, running before work with their daughter in a jogging stroller they paid too much money for.

There were a handful of Chief Johnson, too—less frequent but telling. A late-night meeting with the three of them at HQ. Alone in his office past midnight. Even one where he was talking to his lawyer during divorce proceedings at the attorney's private office.

"If it's a cop—which, let's be real, it is—they've got full

access to the station. Recording that stuff would be as easy as stealing a stapler. But inside a private lawyer's office? What'd they do—pretend to serve him papers and ask for a tour?" Wilson said.

"They must've walked in," Nazario said, trying to plot out how such footage could've been taken, "and asked the receptionist if they could use their restroom."

"The receptionist lets them in, they walk past the conference room—and with those glass windows, it was easy for them to casually raise their phone and press record," Huxley said. "They looked like they were in a deep discussion. Lawyer doesn't break eye contact, and neither does the chief. Was probably too distraught and stressed out to pay attention to anything other than what his lawyer was advising him to do. Divorces are messy. The person walks by, gets what he needs, and then walks out. Easy as that."

"Y'know, now that I'm looking closer, the video doesn't have the same quality as the rest—the ones that looked like they were shot on a smartphone. He or she—and there's only two *she's* that Harrison flagged—Detective Lila Mendez or SID's Ellen Yang. Based on the thumb drives, there were seven badges listed. Only five are alive and can be our perp," Wilson said. "Minus the two deceased that tried to kidnap Ariabella before Von took them out."

"Well, they all might've played a part in filming them and then saved it all in some shared folder. Harrison then found a way to access them—saved a duplicate copy of the folder without letting them know he had it," Nazario said.

"Or they found out he had it and killed him over it," Huxley said.

"That's exactly what happened!" Nazario snapped her finger.

"So, door number one: Detective Mendez. Door number

two: Sergeant Greer. Door number three: Officer Kendrick. Doors number four and five: SID's Whittier or Yang." He squinted at the screen. "One of them likely used one of these itty-bitty hidden cameras mounted somewhere on their chest. Could be as small as a button. Hell, they make pen cams now. All they had to do was book an in-person consult with the lawyer, make up some excuse to hire him, time it around Chief Johnson's appointment," Wilson said. "Now let's get to mine. Pretty sure I'm in that folder somewhere."

"You sure are." Nazario felt the fatigue deep in her bones. The sheer effort behind all of it—the fear, the intimidation—was exhausting. Not only was it emotionally draining, but outright frightening.

Wilson's videos were just as invasive. Following him to his Aunt Maggie's house. Going to church with her, not because he was a Christian, but because he could never say no to his aunt. Going grocery shopping, arguing at a drive-through speaker at Jack in the Box, standing in line at the 7-Eleven with three kinds of beef jerky and a Monster drink, feeding pigeons outside a courthouse, and talking to them like they were people.

"I'm actually shocked that they didn't get one of me taking a shit," he said.

Classic Wilson humor. Only this time, Nazario realized, what they all had, that the laugh came second to the gut-punch of realizing someone had been watching them live their lives—frame by frame. Nearly two thousand files of cataloged surveillance footage of Chief Johnson and three of them.

They'd quickly gone through one hundred twenty clips, each ten to thirty seconds long—in just under an hour. However, they still had 1,701 left, which meant at least fourteen more hours of watching, scanning, and trying not to lose her mind.

"We're not gonna get through all of this now. Need another fourteen hours," Nazario said, exasperated. "Why do this?"

"Well, they tailed Chief Johnson because they needed to know his daily activity in order to put a hit on him," Wilson said.

"So, we're next." Nazario closed her eyes and pinched the bridge of her nose.

"That's a good possibility," Huxley said. "This isn't just intimidation. Wilson's right—they studied the chief's moves, which made it easier. They knew when to strike. We need to get patrol on our home. One for Wilson, one for us, and one for Chief Johnson."

"That's not gonna work. None of them wanna get involved, especially when they know we're eyeballs deep in an IA." Nazario opened her eyes. "Word has already gotten around. First Gus got shot, then Harrison's murder, and now Chief Johnson's close call. No one wants to end up dead or snitching out their fellow blue family."

"So, what's in that other folder—unfiled *número* two," Wilson said.

"We're about to find out," Nazario sighed, and like the UNFILED_1 folder, she clicked on the UNFILED_2 folder.

Inside was another folder: ARCHIVE.

Another click.

Yet another folder with no tag, just like the other one.

The fourth had a label that alarmed her: EXCTRACTION_NOVA_LEE.

She opened it up, and this time, there were three videos instead of hundreds.

Each video had been labeled by the order of events, at least that's how it appeared.

LEE_LAB_ABDUCT_1

HARRISON_CAIN_2

HARRISON_FINAL_3

She started with the first video. A petite Asian woman sat at the lab bench; eyes pressed to the microscope's eyepiece. She adjusted the fine focus knob, then shifted the mechanical stage to refine the specimen's position. There was no sound except for a lower-third in bold white lettering that appeared at the bottom of the screen: Dr. Seung-ah Lee.

"Seung-ah...pretty sure that's Korean," Huxley said. Being a multi-linguist, Huxley was fluent in English, French, Spanish, Russian, German, and even spoke conversational Mandarin. When it came to language, Nazario never questioned him.

"Oh, our scientist is definitely Korean. Was married and divorced to three." Wilson spoke from personal experience, which Nazario equally couldn't dispute. "Probably should've picked a different country after divorce number two," he added dryly.

Suddenly, the doors burst open. Dr. Lee stood abruptly.

Three masked men came storming toward her—sending beakers flying as they surged forward, upending equipment without ever slowing down. Dr. Lee panicked, frantically searching around, desperate to escape, but there was nowhere for her to go. Given that the doctor had been perched at a microscope in the back of the room, the only way out was past the three intruders.

Within seconds, two seized her upper arms while the third shoved a black cover over her head. Kicking and struggling did very little good. Dr. Lee's small frame was easily manageable, as both men were much larger. The video cut to them exiting the building, hallway cameras followed their activity until they disappeared out of the front doors. The video cut to their final escape into a Toyota with the biochemist already in the vehicle. The SUV idled at the curb like it belonged there—just another blacked-out 4Runner in a city full of them. Stripped of chrome, roof railings, or decals—every surface was matte black, swallowing light instead of reflecting it. Every window was tinted deep enough to blur faces, illegal even by L.A. standards. She could barely see Dr. Lee in the back. It no longer looked like a family car but a hunter—quiet, ordinary, built to blend in and vanish without a trace.

The video finished as the camera mounted outside captured the vehicle speeding away.

Just when Nazario thought the video was complete, a news clip had been spliced in toward the end. A news broadcaster showed the same clip they'd watched, and this time, there was sound.

"Three unidentifiable men stormed into Helix Point Laboratories off of West Adams near USC. Helix Point Laboratories is known for its cutting-edge research in biochemical applications, specializing in neurochemical modeling and synthetic compound testing. Based in Mid-City Los Angeles, the private, state-of-the-art facility has quietly partnered with major government research and pharmaceutical companies. Just yesterday, surveillance footage captured a brazen breach of the lab, during which a highly respected scientist was abducted—a chilling incident caught on camera." The video cut from the broadcast showing the abduction, to past media clips—Dr. Lee at conferences, panel discussions, and award ceremonies, poised and articulate.

She was a rising star in biochemical research. A smart, calculated snatch by Jaxon Ryker.

The broadcaster continued, "Dr. Seung-ah Lee, who earned her Ph.D. in biochemistry from Harvard and went on to become a leading mind in synthetic compound development with multiple patents to her name, was believed to have been abducted under mysterious circumstances. A prominent researcher in neurotoxicology and former NIH fellow, Dr. Lee was widely regarded as one of the brightest minds in advanced drug synthesis. Her work has been cited in over a hundred peer-reviewed journals and earned her the National Medal of Science shortlist just last year."

The video cut to a press conference just outside of Helix Point Laboratories. Nazario's eyes narrowed as the press conference came into focus. A cluster of microphones. Flashing cameras. And there—behind the podium—stood Detective Clay Harrison. She leaned toward Huxley and Wilson.

"That's Harrison. Was a Detective Level I in Gang and Narco. Why in the hell was he up there speaking?"

"Usually, they'd have someone from Major Crimes," Wilson added under his breath.

"Or at least a goddamn PIO," Nazario bit out. "Public Information Officer, they handle all the media shit."

Huxley didn't blink. "He was probably first on scene. And smart enough to recognize this wasn't just a missing persons case. If he started connecting the dots—that her abduction might be narcotics related—they'd keep him close. Let him have the floor. Throw him to the wolves. No one likes these fucking press conferences where a million goddamn questions—all of which you can't answer due to tight investigations, red tape, and regs—are being thrown at you. Why not shove an eager, green detective in front of all them flashing cameras?"

Nazario's jaws clenched. "This has everything to do with what Dr. Lee did for a living."

Huxley nodded. "Think about it. She was a synthetic drug expert. Worked with multiple pharma companies. NIH, too. Everything Jaxon Ryker would need to build his so-called zombie drug. Only if he had Lee's hand in it, I'm betting his strain is deadlier than anything else out there, more addictive. That's why we're seeing so many ODs. With Dr. Lee in his pocket, Ryker would have everything he needed to perfect the formula. She's not just a target—she *is* the formula."

The camera panned back to Harrison, who adjusted the mic with an unsteady hand. His jaw was tight. Shoulders drawn in. He scanned the crowd like he wasn't sure if he was supposed to be there—or if someone would yank him off mid-sentence.

He cleared his throat. "At approximately 8:42 a.m. yesterday morning, our LAPD officers responded to an alarming call from Helix Point Laboratories in the Jefferson Corridor area. Upon entry, the lab appeared to've been breached, and Dr. Seung-ah Lee—an employee at the facility—was unaccounted for. Surveillance footage has since confirmed she was forcibly removed by three unidentified individuals, believed to be male, masked, and armed."

Harrison paused, glancing briefly off-camera. A barely visible twitch in his left eye.

"Given Dr. Lee's background in biochemical research and her known work with synthetic compounds, the Gang and Narcotics division is assisting in this investigation. We are pursuing multiple leads that suggest her abduction may be tied to the ongoing spread of a lethal new synthetic substance on the streets of Los Angeles."

He shifted his weight, one hand clenching the note cards he never looked at.

"We are coordinating with state and federal partners. Anyone with information on Dr. Lee's whereabouts is urged to contact LAPD's anonymous tip line."

Another pause. His lips parted like he might say more—but he didn't.

Instead, he gave a tight nod and stepped back from the mic.

Nazario watched him fade behind the cluster of command staff and crisp uniforms—like he didn't belong and knew it.

"He looked scared," she said quietly.

"Hell, I'd be scared too. He knew them dirty blues were after him. This press conference—it made him a bigger target," Wilson said.

"Or...he was guilty," Huxley replied, "guilty of uncovering the truth."

Nazario clicked on the next video labeled: HARRISON_CAIN_2

Harrison positioned his desktop camera and made sure it was recording before answering the phone. This one was a short video, not lasting more than two minutes.

"Saw your press conference," Cain said. "Good work, except you looked like you were about to shit your pants."

"I did what you asked. I'm following all leads involving Ryker. And now there's a missing biochemist. You never mentioned Dr. Lee, but you had to've known who she was and why she'd be important to Ryker. You promised me you'd protect me. Make sure I'd be safe."

"Oh, I'm familiar with Dr. Lee, and if he's shipping her out here to Alaska, I'm fixin' to find her. Now about your safety... think now's the time to getcha into hiding. New ID, new life, new everything. You'll have to hang up your blue hat. But you can find another trade. It's the only way I can ensure your safety. I can't control who in the LAPD might decide to take you down, and I mean take you down for good."

"All I ask is that you find Dr. Lee and keep her safe. If she dies, the formula goes down with her."

"Have you considered my offer?"

Harrison paused for a beat. "No way in hell am I giving up on this investigation. I've put too much time into compiling all my intel, intel that can take these fuckers down. Dirty cops that're working for Ryker. Cops that I know. Cops that I've gone to lunch with. Attended their wedding. Bought them gifts when they had babies." He blew out a breath. "They betrayed their oath, their oath to work for the people, for society, to protect and honor the law—"

"Fuck honor and law, Clay. Do you wanna live or are you fixin' to die? 'Cause if you keep going down this moral road you're on...I'm not gonna be able to protect you. I can't keep you alive."

"I'd rather die doing the right thing," Harrison said, voice quivering, slamming down the phone.

The last and final video tore Nazario's heart right out of her chest. HARRISON_FINAL_3 video was all but thirty seconds long.

Clay looked ragged. Dark circles rimmed his eyes. He looked like he hadn't slept in weeks.

"If you're watching this...I didn't make it. I could've disappeared, could've dropped this whole case, taken up Lucian Cain's offer, to start a new life, have a new identity. But I couldn't. I can't." He stared at the camera, eyes tired. "Dr. Lee's still out there. And I think Ryker plans to kill her once she gives him what he wants."

Tears formed but didn't fall.

"You wanna finish what I started? Then take this evidence and burn their empire down. No mercy. No hesitation. Just clean justice."

A long beat passed. They were watching a dead man's diary. When it came down to right or wrong, he made his stand. He chose conviction. Even if choosing right would end his life. He'd boldly chosen virtue. Detective Clay Harrison had been exceptional, one of the rare good ones. Someone with true nobility. Someone society needed. Someone the LAPD needed.

Nazario's eyes misted, lips quivering with emotion.

And then she absorbed his last words, words that stuck to her soul.

"I'd rather die doing the right thing than go on living only to become the monsters that we're supposed to take off the streets." Harrison's eyes glanced away to an open window, like a man about to be executed. "Like I said...if you're watching this, I'm likely gone. I'm...I'm a dead man. But you're not. So, finish it. Expose them. All of them."

Tears he'd been trying to fight finally fell down his cheeks.

"We didn't become cops to become criminals."

TWENTY-ONE

THE CLOSE QUARTERS

THE NIGHT DRAGGED ON, endless with intense anticipation, as the boat carved its way through the black waters off the Alaskan coast. Fourteen hours back to Kodiak and nowhere else to rest. The sea breathed in long, rhythmic swells beneath the hull, wind skimming cold across the deck like fingers brushing across the nape of a neck.

The cabin lights flickered against the press of the darkness and the ocean tide; low clouds smothered the stars. There were two staterooms, each with a full-sized bed. Absent were the bunk beds she'd half-expected or the solitude of an empty nook. All the seating areas were too small, too uncomfortable. Dr. Lee had already been given the smaller room. After drinking four glasses of Knob Creek and having had a heavy, soul-weary conversation, the taxed biochemist retired to her room.

Von considered chugging coffee and forcing herself to stay awake, but she couldn't escape her circumstances. She couldn't escape the first man in years to make her want. The first man to raise the heat from her body despite the bitter Alaskan cold. The first to make her ache—not just with tension, but with a need she didn't recognize. He was the first man who caused a war within her, the battle between her mind wanting to push him away and her body begging to have him closer. The first who made her aware of her own skin, of the way breath caught when he was near. It wasn't just attraction. It was so much worse.

He made her curious.

He made her imagine things—emotional messy things, tender things, things she had no right to crave. She had built an entire identity on being untouchable, untaken. Now she'd have to lie in a narrow bed with the scent of him clinging to the sheets, sleep beside a man who drove her mad with sexual curiosity—wondering what it would feel like to give in. Not just to the heat. But to him entirely. To the heart. Von had never given her mind, body, and soul to anyone.

Now there was just one bed and too little space between them.

Physical exhaustion pulled at her, but so did a deep churning desire to ignore all the rules, to ignore her mind, and tear down the walls that kept her isolated from desire. Part of her wanted to remain stoic, asexual, and keep Xander at arm's length. But if she had to admit to herself, perhaps the reason she's remained without a real relationship, the reason she never let anyone close to her was because deep down she didn't think she deserved love. Not when she was a killer.

Von stood leaning against the railing, looking out at the waves knocking against the boat, tired as hell and too chicken shit to go to bed. The cold night didn't do much for the flashes of heat that coursed through her. A single emergency surgery had put her thirty-something body into early menopause. Hot flashes were common, but she wondered if what she was feeling had less to do with a hormonal imbalance and everything to do with Xander Holt.

Von checked her watch: 12:34 a.m. She'd been running on

fumes since 5:30 a.m., but sleep hadn't come. Xander was still restless, and she wondered if he was delaying for the same reason. Von had passed him up on her way out of the bathroom. The sixty-foot Steiner had a small marine shower that was barely wide enough to lift her arms. It felt incredible taking a hot shower. She was grateful that they used dissolvable stitches, which allowed her to get the area wet. Metal walls beaded with steam, carrying the scent of soap and something faintly masculine—traces of Xander still clinging to the air. She told herself it didn't matter who used it last. But her skin remembered.

He'd waited patiently until she was done before taking his turn.

Now she was unsure what she was lingering out on the deck for. She glanced up at the dark velvet sky—the hush of waves licked the hull. Finally, the stars had come out, faint and fractured behind the mist, like someone had cracked a mirror and scattered light across the heavens. But that wasn't why she was still out there. The sea breeze chilled her skin, brushing back her long bangs and sending frosty kisses against her freshly shaved scalp, exposing her serpent tattoo inked on the right side of her head.

She could've gone to bed. She should've. Instead, she stood there barefoot, letting a light sprinkle of snow ice her numbing feet. Moonlight rippled across the water as the new motor purred nearby. Misty curls of steam whispered out from beneath the door. Xander was in the shower now, taking his turn. Von spied the empty glass and whiskey calling her name. No, she didn't drink, but tonight she gave herself some grace. Von walked the glass over to the galley, washed it out, and walked out back onto the deck, where she poured herself a glass.

A part of her rational mind tried to tell her that she was on the deck enjoying the scenic landscape. A part of her mind tried to explain it away, insisting that she was waiting until her anxious nerves settled. Maybe she'd wait to go to bed until after she had a drink. Von sipped, the warmth of the whiskey coated her throat and spread through her body like a slow-burning flame; her mind attempted to find more excuses for avoiding sleep. And then there was the possible truth, stripped of excuses.

Just maybe she was waiting to catch him stepping out of the shower.

Von took another sip of the whiskey, letting it press a false calm into her nerves—a sharp hush beneath the surface, like silence layered over a scream. The door creaked open, and her brain shouted at her to keep her eyes to herself, but the desire inside disobeyed, and she turned to see Xander walking out of the bathroom with nothing on, but a loose towel wrapped around his tapered waist. She watched him walk into his room and close the door. Part of her wished he wouldn't put his clothes back on. Von took a longer swig of her whiskey, lost in her thoughts, procrastinating like a schoolgirl with her first real crush. Before her body collapsed from exhaustion, she'd eventually have to lie down. She couldn't stay awake forever.

"Thought you didn't drink?" Xander's voice made her jump. She didn't hear him walk up from behind. "Sorry for scaring you."

"It's a once-in-a-while kinda thing."

"Gonna check the navigation, make sure that everything's set. Why don't you go on, take the bed."

"And where are you gonna sleep?"

"I'll take the floor, no big deal. Had to sleep in shittier situations during deployments. If I can sleep in Iraq and Afghanistan with mortars and live fire around the clock like a bad sound-track, I can sleep on my boat's floor."

"I don't think that's an option, given the floors are freezing, even with the heat on," Von said, wondering to herself if she was really concerned about the weather or if she was trying to convince him to share the bed.

Xander leaned in closer, watching her with curious eyes.

"You actually concerned about my well-being or is this about something else?" he said, his question mirroring her own.

"What *something* are we talking about?"

Xander smiled—slow, knowing. "You tell me."

Von took another sip. The whiskey was warm. Safer than the look in his eyes.

"I promise to keep my hands to myself," Von said, finishing the glass. "I know you're all about the rules. The no-fraternizing with fellow operatives."

Xander raised a brow, a lopsided grin playing across his handsome lips. He drew closer, just inches away. Lips close enough to test her resolve.

"Is that your subtle way of saying fraternizing might be on the table?"

"Might be," she said, the corner of her mouth twitching. "But I don't do halfway. If you're gonna break the rule, you better be damn sure it's worth it."

"I've been breaking a lot of rules since you've come on board," Xander defended. "I mean, we'll be sending Dr. Lee to Los Angeles instead of delivering her to Commander Cain."

"To be fair, he said to keep her safe. He said nothing about handing her over to him." She started for the captain's cabin. "And we go halves—I take one side of the bed; you take the other."

The door creaked open on weathered hinges, groaning like the ship itself was tired of the cold. Von stepped into the captain's cabin—dim, spartan, but unexpectedly warm. Honey colored light licked the cabin walls. Half a dozen white candles lined a built-in shelf above a customized desk. On closer inspection, they were fake—which made sense. A hard wave could easily knock real ones down and start a fire. Even so, the imitation candles cast a soft, steady glow, a halo over old nautical charts, a folded blanket, and a full-sized bed dressed in deep navy covers—no creases, neatly made, as if he honored everything he touched, from the uniform he once wore to the bed he now slept in.

It said a lot about his character, how the room was a lot warmer, more inviting than she'd anticipated. The space smelled like cedar and something faintly him—soap, salty air, and cologne he hadn't worn in years but still clung to his clothes. Von realized she hadn't packed for nightwear. She slept naked, but in Alaskan freezing weather, she'd need something other than bare skin. The desk chair had a thick black classic pullover hoodie draped over it—oversized, maybe his, possibly forgotten. On the left chest, it had the Navy SEAL Trident emblem embroidered in gold thread. She stripped out of her clothes; nothing was left but her panties. At five feet even, Von was petite, though years of weight training had carved her into a lethal, tight machine—chiseled like a statue built for war. Small, silent, deadly.

Without thinking, she pulled the sweater over her head. It hung loose, soft, falling past her hips and down to her knees. As she brought the collar to her face, she caught it—a faint ghost of perfume. Feminine. Unfamiliar. It clung to the seams. A woman's scent. Faded, but still there. Still *his*. Von didn't care—it kept her warm. But it made her wonder. Made her wonder who it truly belonged to and if she'd crossed a line. Then again, she had shit to wear. This sweater was the only thing keeping her from freezing throughout the chilly night.

The floor was cold beneath her bare feet, but the room...the room felt lived in.

A small, framed photo sat at the desk. She crossed to it, drawn by an unidentifiable pull she couldn't name, a pull that was foreign to her. Von picked up the framed picture. The glass was cool to the touch. A woman smiled into the wind, dark blonde hair sweeping across her face like sea grass caught in a current. Her eyes weren't just looking—they were reaching, soft with a joy meant only for the one behind the lens. Beside her, a little boy stood beaming.

She remembered his name...*Noah*.

His hair was a cascade of golden waves, wild and full, like a sunflower mid-turn toward the sun. He had Xander's caramel eyes, but with a penetrating depth—an old soul staring out from a four-year-old. But the smile, that open, radiant thing was all his mother's through and through. The beach lapped behind them as the sun's beams showered them in golden hues.

She didn't hear him at first—only noticed the shift of air behind her. Xander stood in the doorway, arms at his sides, open and watching. He didn't move. Watched her with the picture gripped in her hands. Didn't ask her to put the picture down. Just said, "That's them."

Von gulped, clutching the picture of Xander's wife and child, two souls whom he'd loved and lost. Guilt flooded her. She felt as though she had invaded something sacred. Her voice came out low. "I'm sorry." It wasn't pity. It wasn't a question. Just a simple line dropped between two people who knew what it meant to lose everything and keep moving anyway.

He drew closer. Von moved to set it down, but he placed his hand over hers—steadying it, as if it weighed a hundred pounds and she couldn't carry it alone.

"Noah loves the beach...loves to make sandcastles," he said, and she noted he'd spoken about his son in the present. They were still alive in his heart. He glanced down at the sweater.

Von swallowed, growing increasingly uncomfortable, and not because he'd done anything wrong, but because she felt she was reading his private diary, invading something deeply personal. She should've kept her clothes on and gone to sleep. Instead, she'd taken liberties with his private things, his private life.

"Again, I'm sorry. I don't have anything to sleep in, and I saw the sweater—"

"It was the last thing she wore. I haven't washed it. It still smells like her," he said, causing blood to rush to her cheeks.

Mortified, she added, "I'll take it off. I can sleep in my clothes. I mean it, I'm really sorry."

She slipped her hand away from his and set down the picture.

"You...you don't have to keep apologizing." His hand traced the length of her arm, fingers lingering on the sleeve—like he was trying to feel his wife through the fabric she once wore.

Von could sense the yearning, the loneliness without his family, the helplessness of being unable to bring them back, the anger, the sadness, and the heartache—a mélange of emotion so raw it clung to the air between them, wetting his eyes as he sucked in a shaky breath. Quiet tears trickled down his cheeks.

Boldness swept away the last of her hesitation, leaving only the aching desire to give him what he mourned most—a fragment of his wife, if only borrowed through her. She reached for the half-empty bottle of Love Memoir by Iman, his wife's perfume. Von caught the familiar scent, it clung to the sweater. She sprayed it once on the fabric, then misted each side of her neck, and finally her wrist—rubbing them together.

The scent was warm the moment it reached her—like a memory exhaled. First came a soft burst of bergamot and blackcurrant, light and citrusy but tethered by something sweeter, almost creamy like sun-warmed skin. Then the florals unfolded: jasmine and rose layered with a powdery hush of orris, delicate but grounded. And beneath it all, the scent deepened—vetiver's smoky earth, the musk pull of patchouli, and a whisper of vanilla that clung like an afterthought, or a promise.

It didn't just smell like a perfume. It smelled like missing someone.

The tears she wiped away were replaced with a fresh set. Almost numb with the pain, Xander let heartache wet his face, eyes fixed on the sweater like it was the only thing keeping him breathing. The perfume still hung in the air—warm, floral, with that faint, rich note she now knew by heart. Von stood there, feeling the weight of it all press between them. She wasn't the type to step into someone else's grief, but she understood it— how you'd do anything to feel the person you lost, even for a second.

She took a slow breath. "I'm not her. I'm not trying to be. But if this helps you remember what it felt like to have her close, then for tonight, I can hold that place—for you, for her, for your son."

Silence. The kind that closed in around them. Von didn't push it. If he wanted this, it had to be his choice. A shaky hand found her arm, the grip soft but sure. He drew her in until her chest brushed his—but it was all his grief-worn body could manage. His hand slipped back to his side, both arms hanging, fists clenching and unclenching like he didn't know if he should, or could, let her in and really touch her.

Von knew she had enough strength for the both of them, enough courage, empathy, and heart to be what he needed, if only for this night. She wrapped her arms around him and held him against her. His lean, muscular frame towered over her. At six-one; he was more than a foot taller, all coiled power and precision. Xander's head fell against the crook of her neck, inhaling a long, deep breath, as if he were breathing in his wife. Last came his arms; he lifted them with the weight and heaviness of someone carrying years of memories that hurt to touch.

The warm, solid cage of his arms were like bands of tempered steel, closing around her. He stayed there, face hidden against her neck until the trembling in his shoulders eased—but his hold didn't. Xander's breath hitched. A low sound escaped him, something between a sob and a sigh as he held her tighter, afraid to let go, afraid she'd vanish. His mouth fastened to her neck in a kiss edged with teeth. He bit down lightly, sucking just enough to leave warmth blooming under her skin, as he blurred the line between tenderness and hunger. Her mouth fell open, head tilted back, letting herself open up to him.

Fingers dug into his back as his mouth continued up her neck, and hot liquid current raced through her. Breath came in shallow pants, dizzy with equal parts raw desire and emotion that flooded her senses. His lips found the spot just behind her ear, tongue tracing a slow line that sent a shiver skittering down her spine. A moan she'd been holding back escaped. His lips continued planting tender kisses along her jaw, on her cheek.

When he finally looked down at her, candlelight set his eyes aglow—no longer shadowed, but molten gold against his bronzed skin. It was a sharp contrast to the thick sweep of his hair, dark as fresh-brewed espresso. Rimmed red and misted with emotion, his eyes searched hers. Not just for her, but for the ghost she was letting breathe through her. His hand found her face, a rough, calloused palm brushing her cheek, thumb skimming over her mouth.

"I...I told you I'd hold that place. I just need to know...is it me you want, or her?"

He held her with his eyes for a beat too long, enough to make her wonder if she'd made a mistake—yet every part of her ached for more. Then he leaned in where his mouth found hers, tongue slipping past her lips, tangling with hers in a slow, hungry dance.

His hands slipped under the sweater, bracing her hips. He

picked her up as if gravity had let her go. She wrapped her legs around him, the sting of the bullet that had torn through her left quad flaring hot before the frigid Alaskan air dulled it. Pain gave way to something else—the rush of a rare moment where she let herself be a woman with needs and desires. Her hands tangled in his hair as she kissed him like she'd never kissed anyone else. Soul deep, an ache that she felt in her bones, an ache for more, an ache for what she'd lost, what he'd lost. For a heartbeat, they were two beings bound in a dangerous world that had forged them into weapons—and the walls they'd built came crashing down.

He crawled on top of her, mouth still on hers, less tender, and more desperate, as if he could devour the space between them and still need more. Her fingers found the buttons of his flannel, shoving the fabric over his shoulders. Beneath it, he was all heat under a thin thermal. He yanked it over his head like it was choking him, eyes never leaving hers. Von's hands found the cargo pants he wore—simple, stretchy waistband. No clumsy buttons or zippers. *Thank fucking God.* She yanked them off his hips, rough. Xander shoved free of them and tossed them aside. Black boxer briefs clung to him, tight in all the right places.

As he stood watching her with heavy breaths, her eyes stayed trained on his. Von stripped off the sweater she treasured—the one that meant everything—and let it fall to the floor. Cold Alaskan air brushed over her skin, making her shiver. The one thing that had kept her abstinent for so long came rushing back. It wasn't her bare chest or the gray boy shorts that made her feel vulnerable, but the red, snake-like keloid scar that ran from her diaphragm down to her pubic line.

She turned her head away, hands covering her belly.

Von hadn't let anyone see it. Maybe that was why she'd stayed single—unable to fully be intimate without shame. She felt the bed dip under his weight, the heat from his skin chasing away the cold. Alaskan winter had nothing on the heat of being exposed—her scar lay bare for him to see.

"You're the...second person who's seen it, not counting my parents and sister," she said, quietly, head still turned. "I can't...I can't have kids. Wanted to be a mom my whole life." Her voice cracked. "All of my female parts were gutted out. No frozen eggs. My sister offered hers before she was killed...even offered to be my surrogate. This all started when she was kidnapped a couple of years before my attack. Sex trafficking ring. Many minors were sold to wealthy men. Sammy, she testified against them—the Aryan's. My ex-fiancé did as well. Then one was released from prison, he—"

"They came after you, didn't they? Payback for your sister. They attacked your fiancé?"

"I came in after work and...and I found him in a pool of blood. He was on the floor in the kitchen. They stabbed him, but he survived it. I should've taken up Sammy's offer. I decided I'd kill those motherfuckers instead. But it never made the pain go away. They killed my sister to get back at me. Maybe she'd still be alive. Maybe I'd be a mom. I was...I was p-pregnant when they attacked me, so I know what it's like to lose a child. My baby, she would've been seven—same age as yours—if he were still here."

A single tear escaped before she could stop it. That was all she'd give.

His fingers caught her chin, turning her face toward him. Xander's eyes glistened with emotion. He gently took the hand shielding her scar and moved it aside until that snake of a scar lay in open air, for his eyes only. Eyes that held a kindness she hadn't seen until now.

"Von," he murmured, "I can't imagine what you went through. And I'm...I'm honored that you shared that piece of yourself with me. But you gotta know, you don't ever have to hide from me...not ever."

He cupped her face, wiping away the tear with his thumb.

"For what it's worth," he said, "I haven't been with anyone since her. The anger...it ate up something in me. Everything soft. The parts she evened out. The parts that made me better."

"It's been years for me," she replied, then smirked faintly. "Unless you count the man I seduced to kill last year."

His mouth twitched into a quick, surprised laugh—a laugh that lit up his face, and for a moment, chased away the pain. Chased away hers, too. Xander ran a finger lightly over the scar, starting between her breasts and stopping just before her pubic region. Then he bent down and pressed his lips to her abdomen, where the baby would've been. Without a word, he drew the thick navy wool blanket over them, lay beside her, and kissed her so softly she thought she might cry again.

He kissed her deeply, slowly, and she savored every second —tasting the scent of freshly washed skin, feeling his calloused hands from years of training against her flesh. They parted, his breath brushing her lips. "Can I just hold you tonight?"

"I kill people...I don't cuddle," she whispered against his mouth, drawing another laugh from him. She loved that laugh— the way it transformed his whole face. "You...you sure it's me you want?"

He rested his forehead against hers. "I want to hold you. Not my wife. You, Von—if you'll let me?"

A knot formed in her throat. She hadn't expected he'd choose her. "I'd...I'd love that."

He drew her in, and she rested her head on his chest, listening to the steady rhythm of his heart. It soothed her. Their bare skin pressed together under the weight of the blanket, warmth pooling between them. Von had never been this close to someone she hadn't slept with—and somehow, it felt more intimate than anything she'd ever known.

TWENTY-TWO

THE FIRST FLIP

NAZARIO AND WILSON sat at Chief Johnson's bedside. He looked better—color in his face returned, voice steady—but the doctors were keeping him longer than he wanted. Ten days in ICU, and now the general ward. For a man who'd spent his life in control, the tubes and beeping monitors were an insult. Huxley had the day off. She'd pushed him to take it. Their six-month-old needed him home, especially after the threats against their lives.

The photos had changed everything—images of the baby, taken without them knowing, proof that someone had been that close. Too close. Huxley wired the house like a bunker: cameras in every room, security system upgraded to military grade. Wilson did the same, and they'd also arranged to outfit Chief Johnson's place, too. Extra eyes needed to be everywhere—living rooms, the nursery, porches, the fucking bathroom—every angle covered.

They couldn't trust patrol to watch their backs, not when they didn't know who else was dirty beyond the names Detective Harrison had left behind. Wilson's Tahoe was already retired, its battered body like a warning label. Ryker's message was loud, clear—no one was untouchable. Huxley kept loaded guns stashed across the house: one in the living room, another upstairs by the bed, one strapped to his side even in sweatpants.

It was a shit way to live—Kevlar at work, Kevlar at the grocery store, Kevlar while rocking the baby to sleep. Kevlar in bed. Cameras in every corner. Always watching, because someone out there was watching them. They'd even brought a bulletproof vest for the chief.

"Detective Nazario, we're not going to be able to put that vest on our patient," the nurse had said earlier.

"And why the hell not? He's stitched up, ain't he? Would you rather him be safe or dead?"

"Got hospital security squatting right outside his door like you suggested, and we've also limited his visitor's list to only the three of you: you, your partner, and Supervising Special Agent Huxley. Just like you requested. But what we're not fixin' to do is strap a heavy vest over his trauma sites. We still need access to those entry wounds. In case he bleeds. In case of infection. We need to make sure the stitches are intact. The list goes on and on," she'd firmly said. "Now, I'm gonna give y'all a half hour. Okay? My patient needs his rest."

"Fine. Then I'd like to still keep this vest next to his bed in case he needs to grab it. And Chief Johnson's gonna need his gun, too. This is non-negotiable. We've reason to believe there're some really dangerous assholes targeting us. We're involved in a very dangerous case where our lives are at stake. They're not only trying to threaten us into silence, but they're trying to kill us." Nazario thrust a hand at Johnson. "Look what they did to him. Those bullets...they were meant to *murder* him."

"We don't allow guns—"

"You're gonna make an exception. You *have* to." Nazario gritted her teeth. "All it takes is for your security guard to go for a piss break, and someone slips in. It's that easy. Your efforts to keep Chief Johnson alive will be wasted in the time it takes to flush the goddamn toilet."

"We don't let just any hood rat walk up in here."

"They're not anyone you might think. We're not talking your average thug. These people we're talking about, they're your neighbor next door. All smiles. Polite. You'd never know different. The worst of it—these are dirty *fucking* cops I'm talking about. And they can very easily persuade the front desk to let them in with a flash of their badge. You feel me? And that's all I'm allowed to say."

"Mmh, baby, I'm from Compton...I done seen what y'all can do when you got a badge. Seen plenty hide their racism behind the mighty law." The nurse folded her ebony arms across magenta scrubs, the bright fabric bold against the smooth, dark tone of her skin.

Chief Johnson stayed silent. Silent out of duty, to remain as a united front. Always. They hadn't told him about the threats—not yet—but he trusted them enough to let them talk. The worry carved lines into his deep brown skin, each one telling a story. Not just concern. Fear. The Chief understood exactly how far the danger had climbed.

The nurse thought for a long beat, then planted her hands on her hips. "Alright. Keep the gun and the vest in the nightstand. I won't say a word if y'all don't. But I'm risking my job, ya hear me? We keep this on the DL. And it's the last thing I'm fixin' to do for y'all. Now you've got twenty minutes before you gotta get up on out, so that my patient can rest." She paused at the door, turned around, throwing last words over her shoulder. "And dontcha worry. Been dealin' with dirty cops my whole life—they ain't touchin' my patient."

They'd waited until the nurse left before giving Chief Johnson the rundown.

"What'n the hell're we up against?" Chief Johnson finally spoke.

Wilson took out his phone, swiped through photos, and then handed his boss the phone.

"Ain't no accident they did you like that. That's a love letter from the wrong side." He returned the phone to Wilson.

"They're talking to us," Wilson said, "and they're using bullets for punctuation."

"Last we was talkin' was 'bout Harrison's thumb drive and that lockbox." Chief Johnson reached for a bottle of water on the nightstand and took a sip. "Whaddya got for me?"

Nazario went through the list of the cops Harrison had tracked that were working for Ryker, starting from Officers Ronnie Salerno and Marcus Delgado, the two who had been shot and killed by Von when they tried to kidnap Ariabella. Then there was the frozen body that was shipped in and addressed to Nazario at the Port of Long Beach, Eli Vega, former DEA agent flipped to the wrong side.

"Oh, I remember, Salerno, Delgado, and Vega—the DB shipped in some fish crate from Alaska," Johnson said.

"We also crossed paths with Officer Tyler Kendrick—saw him jawin' with his buddies by the memorial wall. Wilson and I, we paid respects to Harrison when his name was added to the wall. Kendrick brushed past me hard, like he was sending a message. So, when his name showed up on Harrison's list, no shock there. But two others went further—bold enough to break into the evidence cage," Nazario said.

"That restricted access area?" Johnson said. "Who? They can't just waltz up in there."

"Sergeant Vincent Greer and Detective Lila Mendez," Wilson said.

"Don't know 'em too well, but I believe they both work in

VICE—sometimes overlapping with Gang and Narco on some of the cases," Johnson said.

"Yep," Nazario said. "They took evidence out of the restricted storage area. Harrison had surveillance footage. Caught them right in the action."

"But there's more. You wouldn't believe who let them in," Wilson said.

"Please tell me it ain't someone we work with on a regular?" Johnson said.

"SID's Ellen Yang and Chuck Whittier."

Chief Johnson blinked. Then burst out into an unexpected laugh.

"Alright—that's cute. I know y'all are trying to make me feel better. You got me, that's a good one."

"If it's a joke, Mendez and Greer brought props," Wilson said, "two envelopes, small bills, and a timestamp."

"This isn't an episode of Punk'd, sir. They're both involved," Nazario said.

"What in the actual fuck?" Chief Johnson adjusted himself on the bed. "C'mon, you shittin' me right now. That can't be right. Ain't no way. Those two? Been working with them most of my career. They straight. Straight as arrows."

"Straight as arrows back then. Today, they curve where the money flows," Wilson said.

"They were on camera, Chief," Nazario said, then laid out the tense call with Yang—how she'd pulled in two junior SID techs she knew were clean, because she couldn't trust Yang or Whittier anymore. She wasn't about to hand them a scene and watch the evidence disappear when Wilson's SUV was laid to rest.

"This is bad. This is *real* bad," Chief Johnson swiped a hand down his face and leaned back against the pillow. "And I'm stuck in this motha fuckin' hospital for at least two more weeks."

"We've got enough to file a warrant on each of them. But if we arrest too fast, we lose the handler," Nazario said.

Chief Johnson shifted against the rails, one hand guarding the IV line. "I'm not lying here and doin' nothin' while this all burns down. Got my phone and that's all I need. Here's what we're fixin' to do. Gonna call my DA contact—Shaniqua Carver."

"This district attorney, you trust her?" Nazario asked.

Chief Johnson plucked his phone from the nightstand. "Didn't have a father around, so I took her under my wing. Was there for her when she graduated from law school. If she leaks, I'll know before the ink dries."

"Who're we starting with first? I say we go for the youngster —Officer Kendrick, the little douche bag might open up before the veterans do," Wilson said.

"Good call. He's young. Broke. Not built for prison math. You pull him quietly. Show him only what you need to get him to flip. What do we got on him?" Johnson asked.

"Voice recording of him talking shit with some of his friends —locker-room stuff," Nazario said.

Johnson took another sip of water before setting the bottle down. "Anything incriminating in the audio recording?"

"Apparently, I'm 'Detective Snack-Pack.' Adorable. Then he promised Nazario would be six feet under with her 'narc-ass dad.'"

Chief Johnson narrowed his eyes at Wilson. "I'll allow the Snack-Pack joke. The other part's a viable threat. What else we got—what're the three write-ups?"

Nazario rolled her thumb along her jaw. "One: VICE caught him off-duty soliciting a sex worker—logged as 'counseled' and buried. Two: after he was involved in a cruiser fender-bender, he refused a mandatory drug screen and vanished five days on 'sick.' Three: Kendrick showed up at an

OD call with pinpoint pupils, found sealed packets of tranq dope in his locker—Ryker's product. He's not just on Ryker's payroll, Chief—he's on Ryker's dope."

"So, he'll flip," Chief Johnson said. It wasn't a question.

"Oh, I don't doubt it," Nazario said.

Chief Johnson grunted in pain as he tried to get comfortable. "Show him only what you need. The recorded threats. The three buried write-ups. Offer him a lawyer and a path he can live with."

Wilson took out a Ziplock bag of sliced apples and plunked a piece in his mouth. Johnson raised a brow. "Wire?" Wilson muffled between crunches.

"If he bites, you wire him for one routine hand off. Don't arrest at pass—you follow that envelope. I want the courier and whoever counts cash on the other side." Johnson's jaw set. "And if Kendrick points at anyone for my shooting, you get it on tape and you get it corroborated. Don't want 'I heard'—I want who, what gun, what cover," Chief Johnson said, scrolling through contacts on his phone.

"You calling that DA contact now?" Nazario frowned.

"And why not? Lock the doors," the chief ordered.

Nazario strode to the hospital door and locked it, then quickly pulled up a chair next to her boss. Chief Johnson lowered the volume just enough for the three of them to hear and then put the call on speaker.

A woman answered in a brisk tone. "You better not be dying, Trevor."

"Two holes says I qualified." He glanced at Nazario and Wilson. "This line, it isn't clean. Heads-up only."

A beat. "Go."

"Fixin' to do an interrogation, need to keep it tight. Just my people involved, the ones I trust—Detective Nazario, Detective Wilson, and Supervising Special Agent Huxley. Nobody else.

You won't be in the room—but you'll get the interrogation after. By law, it'll be on record."

"Judge?"

"Your fastest, someone who won't leak."

"Cortez. I'll prime him for sealed warrants if your intel sings."

"Shaniqua, you'll hear from my detective. We're sitting on dirty badges."

"Say it plain, Trevor."

"Cops. One put two rounds in me. Don't know who it was yet. But they're threatening my team now."

"Got it. This call didn't happen," DA Carver said. "Bring me clean papers—sworn affidavit, timestamps, stills, bank summaries—hand-carried. Proof. I can get it sealed in an hour."

"You'll have a packet in two. We're aiming to flip Officer Tyler Kendrick first—young patrol, compromised. He's taken cash runs for Ryker, and he's using Ryker's tranq dope. He can give us the courier, the payment cadence, and who pulled the trigger on me."

"Good. Add a proffer memo spelling that out—what Kendrick offers and what you're asking in return. Face-to-face only, phones go in a box."

"Understood."

"Knock on my door when one of your detectives is in the building—I'll line up Judge Cortez."

"Appreciate it."

"Bring proof, not smoke," the DA said and then hung up.

"You really think we can squeeze all that intel you promised to Shaniqua Carver, your district attorney friend?" Nazario rose to her feet, and Wilson followed.

"Yes. How do I know this? The two of you are the best. Make sure to keep Huxley in the loop. We need the feds on this, since we can't trust our own. Now, go before my nurse comes back and decides y'all are violating visiting hours."

———

An hour before he finally caved and walked into the FBI's interview room—where Huxley and Wilson waited with Nazario—Kendrick spotted them outside of his apartment and immediately went chalk-pale. Though he tried the tough-guy routine, it fell apart fast. Detective Nazario was already wound tight; the threats had stacked—on Captain Gus Humphrey, on Chief Johnson, and now on her, Huxley, their six-month-old, and Wilson.

Ryker's people, or the dirty badges, had both her and Huxley on edge. He was off-duty but wouldn't stay home. Huxley buckled six-month-old Ariabella into her carrier and came anyway. In the room, the baby slept under the vent's hum while Huxley sat beside Nazario, one hand on the car seat handle, the other flat on the table. No sitter. No day care. Not with this heat.

They held the meeting at a private FBI interrogation room because the LAPD headquarters had been compromised. Way too many cops already knew about the internal investigations, and the gossip spread like fire. As Kendrick sat before them, letting the clock chew through five minutes of silence, she thought of the F-150's dented hood and the instant he realized they had him.

"Don't know why the hell you're both here," Kendrick had said, "but I need you to get the fuck outta my way—I'm late." He shoulder-checked her and strode to his beat-up '08 F-150 XLT Super Crew. Whispering under his breath: "Stupid cunt."

In one swift move, Nazario recalled hooking an arm under his, pivoting her hips, and then dumping him over her shoulder.

He'd slammed hard face-first on his sun-faded black hood, the metal buckling under his weight.

"You've had three strikes against you," Nazario said through clenched teeth. "This is your fourth."

He'd tried to turn around, arms swinging wild. She dodged and drove an elbow strike to his jaw. With her left forearm, she pinned him down hard against the back of his neck. He gasped for air. Nazario's right hand wrenched his wrist up behind his back at a bad angle—another inch and the joint would go.

Wilson had kept his iPhone recording it all, catching the action. "Here are your options. Option A: You come down to the FBI headquarters, and you answer some questions. Cooperate."

"And if I say fuck off, fat ass—not gonna happen?"

Wilson laughed. Nazario pulled his arm back even harder until she heard a snap.

Kendrick cried out in pain. "You just broke my fucking arm!"

"I'll break more of you if you don't stop with the smart-ass bullshit," Nazario warned, "and answer the questions."

"Option B: I blast this video to every supervisor, every rookie, every vet at the station. And then, I send it to my contact at the local news. Next, it gets uploaded onto every social platform, stacked with your tranq dope from the locker, the prostitutes you were caught with, and that little fender-bender you caused while you were high—plus we expose that attempt to hide it all," Wilson said with a smile. "It goes viral, you resign, and after you become a viral sensation, you'll be lucky to mop floors on the graveyard shift at a strip mall."

Now, Kendrick sat nursing a broken arm in the interrogation room along with a bruised ego. He glanced up at the clock on the wall and then back at them, narrowing his eyes. When five minutes of silence stretched to ten, Nazario played the locker-room-shit-talk tape. Rewinding the part when he was caught threatening her life.

"*Wonder how long that Nazario bitch can last.*" Kendrick's voice on the recording rolled out. "*Keeps pushing like that, she'll be six feet under with her narc daddy.*"

Wilson plunked down various images of the young officer with prostitutes, several images of tranq dope found in his locker, and finally a report of the car accident that Kendrick had been involved in. Redacted words from the report. Nazario snagged the document and read it aloud.

"Kendrick presented objective signs of narcotics (pinpoint pupils, limited light response, slowed psychomotor.) HGN negative. Probable depressant/opioid," Nazario said, then added. "So, you ready to cut a deal or are you willing to go down. Who're you willing to protect when they're not willing to protect you?"

"They might've covered for you before, but that ends now." Huxley lifted their whimpering daughter out of the carrier and fed her a bottle of breast milk, voice flat. "You and your buddies put my daughter on a target list. You threatened my family. The woman I love. So, here's your choice: cooperate—wear a wire and walk out tonight—or I bury you in federal paper: stacked counts, no deals, no daylight. I take this packet to the U.S. Attorney, and you rot under a mountain of *federal* charges."

"I'm not wearing some fucking wire." Kendrick's knees began manically bobbing up and down. "If Greer or Mendez find out, they'll talk to the boss, and when they do—I'm *dead*. And what do I even get if I talk?"

"Perks package includes *alive*. Health, dental, and continued breathing privileges." Wilson grinned. "Plus, the only insurance policy Ryker can't void."

Nazario leaned in, steepling her fingers. "We're not here for your head—we want the hand on your leash. Give us Greer and

Mendez: name, number, meet spot. You wear the wire; you walk out tonight. DA Carver can put the terms in writing. All you need to do is pass a polygraph. Because if you shot Detective Clay Harrison, tried to kill Chief Johnson, and Captain Humphrey—the immunity deal's off the table."

"I didn't shoot no badges. Don't know who did it, either. I'm the rookie, remember? You really think they'd trust me with that intel? Don't know who tried to take out Captain Humphrey or Chief Johnson, and I sure as hell don't know who took out Detective Harrison. I'll do your polygraph, and I'll pass it." Kendrick met their eyes. "But the one thing I'm not fixing to do is go down with them. Wire me the fuck up."

TWENTY-THREE

THE DELIVERY

THE EARLY MORNING sun cut through the Captain's Quarters with a burst of deep saffron and tawny blooms that licked the walls with the rise of the sun. Von woke first, tucked against Xander's lean frame, all corded muscle and steady heat, the kind that radiated and made her forget the cold. The night had been an unexpected moment of bliss—a breach in both their defenses, brick by brick, crumbling until nothing stood between them. Now, she wondered if she had the strength to rebuild once more, summon the compulsion to raise hers again.

Von changed into her cold-weather clothes in the bathroom and slipped out into the kitchen area. The small galley sat just forward of the salon, a narrow strip of counters bolted tight against the port side. A stainless-steel sink, gimbaled stove, and a compact drip coffee maker were wedged in beneath the portholes. Von moved in the tight space like she'd done it before—pulling a dented tin from the overhead cabinet, scooping grounds, and setting the pot to brew while the hull creaked around them.

The sharp, earthy scent of fresh coffee curled through the galley. 5:14 a.m. Glowing on her watch face. The world hadn't stirred yet, and for a moment, she felt alone, like the ocean around them had swallowed all that remained. She'd half-expected Dr. Lee to be up, but then Von recalled the amount of whiskey the doctor drank. Enough to take the edge off, an elixir that allowed her to sleep in. Von took her coffee mug up on the deck and sat on the flybridge bench, watching the sun awaken the heavens, early morning sunlight spilling across the water.

While Von tried her best to think of anything else but last night, his lips against hers came rushing back. The way he tasted like mint, the heat of him warming her skin. Flesh against naked flesh. The hunger was deep, unguarded—like he'd been starving for her. But was it truly her he'd wanted, or was it his wife, the spirit of her relived through Von, wearing her perfume, the sweater she'd last worn?

When Xander closed his eyes, was it Von he was holding, kissing, or the ghost of his wife?

Her thoughts swirled, pulling her under like a strong current—she didn't hear his footsteps until he was there. Xander sat down next to her with a cup of the morning brew in his hands, hands she wanted on her skin again, hands she yearned for. If only another touch, another caress. Strong yet gentle, in his arms, she felt safe, felt like she'd come home.

"If you're making coffee, I think I'll keep you around."

"The best way to start the day."

"Did you sleep well?" he asked, eyes still on the horizon.

She sipped her coffee. "Better than I have in a long time. You?"

He turned to meet her eyes. "First time I didn't have a post-traumatic flashback. You...you make the nightmares stay away," he said, catching her off guard with his sincerity.

She gulped; a rush of emotions flooded her body. Unfamiliar.

"I don't...I don't honestly do that. Haven't slept in the same bed with a man since the attack. Like I said, I was engaged—and yeah, he was there, too. Sure, he got stabbed. But he got to keep all his working parts, while I...I lost everything. So, I broke it off. Things weren't the same after that."

"Thank you for trusting me with that. I know you don't hand out pieces of yourself easily. And for what it's worth—I haven't done this either. Not since my wife and son were killed."

Von watched the ocean race past, its vastness swallowing the horizon. Out here, they were nothing more than a fleeting speck against an endless expanse, two shadows carried over the skin of the water. In that moment, it felt as if the sea held no one else—only them, suspended in its boundless embrace.

Before courage left her, Von felt the need to clear her conscience. "It wasn't my intention to play your wife, just wanted...wanted to give something back, something you've been missing."

He brushed his hand across her cheek. "I buried her a long time ago." Xander leaned in and whispered in her ear. "It wasn't her I saw last night...it was you."

His face hovered close, close enough that a breath could bridge the distance.

Desire spread through her like a flame racing over kerosene. Filling her body with an urge for more, for honesty, the kind of honesty she couldn't face before. She'd built her new vigilante life on autonomy, on the pride of remaining in strict, disciplined control. But with Xander, every ounce of restraint had been dismantled, hard shell splintering into pieces she couldn't put back together.

"Last night, I liked it," she said, tone hushed, lips a sheet away, "more than I should have."

"I wouldn't mind a repeat of last night."

She broke away, the heat between them snapping like a live wire cut loose. Cold air rushed in where his nearness had been.

"I don't think that's a good idea. I shouldn't have...shouldn't have let this happen. We've got a mission, a job to do. You said so yourself that there's a strict rule against it." Her voice carried discipline she didn't feel, the words betraying her true desires. "If Commander Lucian Cain finds out—"

"Fuck him." Xander's jaw was set, voice low and rough. "I don't give a damn if he finds out. I'm done being his loyal lap dog."

Von's pulse stumbled. She gripped her coffee mug tighter, as if the heat there could steady her. "If it wasn't for him, they wouldn't have caught the killer who murdered your family. You were the one who told me that. I don't want to be the reason you're out of a job. I don't want to be the reason you lose the only thing you've got left." Her voice thinned. "I'd hate to see you lose more than you have already."

Von charged back to the galley, the deck groaning under her boots. She scrubbed her coffee cup harder than she meant to, scalding water biting her fingers. Fury—at herself—burned hotter than the rinse. Following the rules. Doing the right thing. Since when had that ever been her way? If she caved in, if she let herself have what she'd been starving for, Black Nova might consider it a breach and send her to prison. And what would they do to Xander?

Too many unknowns wedged themselves between them, jagged as glass.

The risks were clear—but walking away felt like handing over the one thing she'd been denying herself for years. After the blood and the near-death and the endless hunt for predators, she'd made herself mission-focused to the bone. No room for passion. No room for the simple, healthy need to be touched, to be wanted, to be loved. Anger churned with regret.

She couldn't take the words back, couldn't afford to change her mind. Nothing good would come from making Xander her lover.

So why did it feel like she was losing?

For the remaining six hours of the journey to get to Kodiak Benny Benson State Airport, silence settled between them, broken only by the low hum of the engines and the slap of waves against the hull. Each retreated behind their own walls while the boat carved a steady path, the cold bite of the air thickening with unspoken words.

Dr. Seung-ah Lee's nerves showed in the quick flick of her gaze, the restless shift of her weight. Kodiak's airport was much quieter than Von expected, with fewer travelers. The hollow echo of announcements carried through near-empty halls. Only a handful of vacationers moved through baggage check, which made the lines go quicker. Shadowing Dr. Lee to the security gate—the last point they were allowed—Von and Xander turned to the biochemist for one last conversation. Von had hoped the doctor would open up more.

Lee hitched the strap on her carry-on higher over her shoulder. "Why haven't either of you asked me for the formula?"

"Because it'll instantly paint a target on our backs," Xander said, "and we don't need that."

Von's hand rested on Zeus's head, fingers brushing over coarse fur. The dog leaned into her touch, a soldier at her side. "I have to ask, what makes you more valuable than the rest of his lab?"

"Ryker, he has one other chemist. She can't replicate my formula exactly—not without me. But she's clever enough to reverse-engineer, run pieces of the synthesis, a crude version, a highly unstable, sloppy copy, lethal in all the wrong ways. It won't have the same precision, but it'll still kill. That's why Ryker keeps her around."

"Even more reason to send you to Detective Nazario," Von said.

"Do you...do you trust her?"

"She's the only cop we trust right about now at the LAPD," Von said.

"Nazario will know what to do with the formula," Xander said. "The FBI's in play—they'll lock it down, trace the supply chain, make sure Ryker can't produce it again."

"I don't know if I'll be safe anywhere," Dr. Lee admitted. "He'll find me, I just know it."

"If you keep moving and follow the plan," Von said, "you'll last long enough for us to end this."

"That doesn't exactly make me feel better. Sounds like you're saying there's no guarantee I'll be safe."

"Nothing's ever guaranteed. We kept you breathing this long, but once you're in L.A., we can't promise it'll be fine." Xander said.

Von's phone buzzed. She glanced down—Commander Lucian Cain. Dr. Lee let out a sharp breath and stepped into the security line. Von and Xander watched until she passed through the body scanner. Once her bag cleared the belt, they turned their attention back to the missed call.

"Lemme guess? Cain?"

Von nodded. "Time to face the devil."

The Rusted Anchor was a low-lit dockside bar tucked between a weather-beaten bait shop and a cannery warehouse. The exterior was chipped and salt-stained. A neon anchor flickered at the window. Inside, the air smelled of old wood, fried halibut, and beer. The local dive bar reminded Von of pubs in Casper, Wyoming. Nets hung from the rafters and a wood-burning stove clicked in the corner, struggling to push back the chill that leaked in from the harbor.

Cain claimed a half-moon booth in the far back, away from the dartboard and jukebox. The seat was cracked, the table scarred by years of initials carved into it. His hands cupped something likely strong; its amber liquid glinted under the incandescent lights. Xander and Von slid into the seat across from him. A cocktail waitress in skinny jeans and a low-cut V-neck shirt with *The Rusted Anchor* logo—a large bass frozen in mid-splash—stretched across her right breast, eagerly approached the table.

"Can I getcha another Scotch, Commander?"

"So as long as it's that fourteen-year-old single malt Oban," he said.

"Absolutely." She smacked her gum, turning to Von and Xander. "Anything I can getcha?"

"Club soda with a lime," Von said.

"Oh, c'mon, you can drink something stronger than that," Cain said.

Von ignored the commander, turned to the waitress. "Just the club soda."

"IPA, something local will do," Xander said.

When the waitress left, Cain's friendly smile vanished. He took a sip of his scotch, getting right to the biochemist. "So, I'm assuming you recovered Dr. Lee successfully? What did you do with our asset?"

"We kept her safe, that was your order. And she is in a safe location," Xander said.

"Safe as in where exactly?"

"Los Angeles. Detective Anaya Nazario's the only person in the LAPD that we can trust right now," Von said.

The commander's face darkened, heat rising under his skin like a furnace under pressure. His jaws locked so hard a vein stood out at his temple. "You made a call without me. Now the doctor's on the grid, and Ryker will smell it. LAPD's hands are filthy. Nazario won't know who to trust, and neither will you," he snarled.

Zeus sat up beneath the table, sensing the tension. Von stroked his head, trying to ease him.

"She sure as hell wasn't safe here, not even in our hands. Not with Ryker here. The formula is the last thing we need. We didn't ask for it. Otherwise, we might be next on Ryker's hit list. We made an executive decision, and we stand by it," Xander said, voice low and metered.

The waitress returned with their drinks. Cain thanked her and tipped her a twenty.

Xander took a swig of his beer. Von squeezed the lime in her club soda, idly swirling the straw as tense silence settled between them. The commander seemed to be contemplating Xander's words, weighing the risks.

"Alright, you make a valid point." Cain nodded. "But I'm not so sure Nazario can protect her, keep her safe."

"It's out of our hands. If there's a hit on her, she'll give Nazario the formula—hopefully, before they take her out," Von said.

The Rusted Anchor buzzed with the low drone of fishermen and locals, the air thick with fried bar food and beer. Cain nursed his scotch, still in quiet contemplation. Xander's Alaskan IPA stood sweating on the table beside him. Von sat rigid, her glass untouched, Zeus crouched underfoot, eyes glinting whenever the door creaked.

The door opened, and hushed silence seemed to ripple through the bar.

Jaxon Ryker stepped inside. His tattoos poked out from his wrists, curling up his neck, covering his knuckles. He had a looming presence, a slow and steady gait that held intimidation in every step. Crowds parted, giving him space.

"Speaking of...we've got company," Cain said for their ears only.

A low murmur swept across the bar. Zeus sat up again, a growl curling from his throat as Ryker approached and dragged a chair over. He straddled it backwards, forearms resting heavy across the top. Von had expected his men at his back. But Ryker didn't need them. The room bent around him, his presence alone enough to dominate.

"Funny thing," Ryker said, voice leveled with danger. "A prized piece of property of mine disappears, and suddenly I find the three of you talking shop over drinks in Kodiak. What are the odds?"

Cain didn't so much as twitch. He took a sip of his Scotch. "If you came here for small talk, you picked the wrong table."

Xander leaned forward, all sharp edges. "She was never yours to begin with."

Ryker's mouth twitched into a smile. He enjoyed testing them. His gaze drifted to Von, but she was already stroking Zeus's head, who hadn't stopped growling since the man sat down.

"The chemist is mine. She belongs to me, and I'll have her back. Alive or dead," he warned, losing his smile.

"You didn't lose her, Ryker. You kidnapped her. She wasn't your property—she was your prisoner," she said flatly.

"We all know that was the story we fed to the media. Truth is, she came to me. Begged me to be on my payroll. So, when I find her, and I will find her, you'll see what happens when people betray me," he bit out. "Her cold, dead body will sing louder than any formula."

"Walk away, Ryker." Cain's face twisted into a mask of restraint, fury coiled tight beneath the surface. "Before you find out what happens when you strike at something that hits back harder."

Ryker's smile turned into a loud chortle; he kicked his head back, thoroughly amused.

"I've got more eyes and ears out there than your itty-bitty crew. After I'm done, you'll see who holds the power—Black Nova or Jaxon Ryker," he said and walked out, leaving the room colder than when he'd entered.

Fumes seemed to seep out of Cain's pores. Color rushed up his neck, rising to his cheeks, blotchy and red as raw meat.

"He thinks he's invincible. Thinks he's God. Wait 'til he bleeds like any other man." Cain downed his Scotch and slammed the empty glass on the table.

"What's the next play?" Von asked.

"We're gonna hit him where it hurts," Cain said, nodding to her phone. "Next target's live and loaded."

She opened up the Phantom Vox app and hit the T-list icon.

Dr. Nadia Volkov—early forties, a blunt blond bob cut to her ears, framing ice blue eyes.

"Ukrainian scientist. Another bright mind willing to work for Ryker. She's his only other biochemist. We cut off the head of his science branch—he'll have nothing left. Can't cook the dope without one of them," he said.

Volkov must've been the scientist whom Dr. Lee was referring to.

"With Volkov gone, he'll have to keep Dr. Lee alive," Xander said.

"Exactly." Cain steepled his fingers.

"He'll come hunting for her," Von said.

"Then may the hunt begin," Cain said. The ominous blessing rang loud in her ears. But Von wasn't thinking about Ryker. She was already picturing the face of the scientist she'd have to find—*and end.*

TWENTY-FOUR

THE STING OPERATION

DETECTIVE ANAYA NAZARIO and Detective Isaac Wilson would never be called out on a drug sting operation, not when homicide stuck to the body side of things. But this time it was different. Since Detective Harrison's murder and the frozen corpse of the dirty DEA agent—Elias 'Eli' Vega—the bodies and the dope overlapped. Harrison's death had threads running straight through dirty cops on Rykcr's payroll.

That meant they were in and part of the sting.

She'd put in her time with Gang and Narco, long enough to know she wasn't built for it. Worn down by the sight of kids barely into their teens—eleven, thirteen, fifteen—pressed into service as runners or dealers. Used up and discarded. Worse were the girls, groomed and sold off, lives gutted before they'd even begun. Vice might've owned trafficking, but when gangs ran it, Gang and Narco got pulled in. She'd rather chase corpses than watch another child ground into ash. Too many young lives burned before they ever had a chance. Homicide was brutal, but at least the dead weren't still suffering.

It'd been a hot minute since the last time she'd been on a sting operation.

Gang and Narco were running the ops, but Captain Gus Humphrey had vouched for them to sit in—especially with Nazario's past experience. Working alongside her best friend of almost two decades was a rare treat, though nerves crawled her skin. Stings always carried weight. One wrong move and everything could go sideways. But if tonight went right, they'd have them—Detective Lila Mendez and Sergeant Vincent Greer in cuffs, finally where they belonged. Bagging Mendez and Greer was just the start. Next up: SID's lead techs, Chuck Whittier and Ellen Yang—if the two forensic specialists were smart enough to flip.

To avoid any other LAPD blue—dirty or clean—from sniffing around, they had ordered Kendrick to the FBI headquarters instead of Narco Division. In a cramped back room that smelled of burnt coffee and sweat, an IA tech yanked Kendrick's shirt up. Sweat slicked his chest, running in nervous rivulets, while Sergeant Manual Alvarado—an internal affairs agent—checked his watch, lips tense. Kendrick twitched enough that one of the techs had to blot him with a rough hand towel.

"Settle down, or nothing's gonna stick," the tech muttered.

"Ten minutes to wire him," Alvarado cut in.

Kendrick's eyes darted anxiously around the room—Nazario, Wilson, Huxley, Captain Gus Humphrey—packed in with the IA pair. Seven bodies in a room built for three.

"Don't know why all of y'all gotta be in here," Kendrick grumbled.

"Making sure this goes down the right way," Nazario shot back.

The tech clipped a lav mic to the inner seam of Kendrick's shirt, threading a thin wire down his torso. He taped it flat against his sternum, then anchored it with surgical strips across muscle and ribs. The transmitter pack was slipped into a low-slung chest holster, snugged tight to keep from shifting. Every move was tested—shirt tugged, arms raised. No rustle, no crackle.

"Pig's sweating like a busted hydrant. Surprised he passed the polygraph." The tech swiped another streak before pressing down the final strip.

"Don't matter. As long as it's done and everything's clear in our ears," Humphrey said.

"Say something in the mic, Kendrick," Nazario ordered.

Each of them wore a wireless earpiece, the faint hiss of an open channel filling their heads as they waited.

He cleared his throat. "Check—one, two, three, four."

Static cracked, then settled. The voice in their wireless earpieces came through crisp.

"Nice and clean," Huxley said.

"Clean here, too," Wilson said.

"Same," Humphrey said.

"Crystal," Nazario said.

———

Captain Gus Humphrey and Detective Tyrell Dawson, Detective Clay Harrison's former partner, were parked in the command vehicle, closer to the Vernon Cold Storage building—an old, abandoned shell that hadn't seen a pallet of goods in over a decade. Everyone still called it that, though the freezer units had long since been gutted and stripped of copper.

Wilson took the driver's seat while Nazario rode shotgun. A block east, Huxley and another FBI agent had their own post, logging time stamps like it was any other op. From the IA van down the street, a tech confirmed, "Audio's holding, mic's hot."

"Hold positions," Humphrey's voice came over the tac channel. Cool, clipped, and nothing but command. "Nobody moves unless I give the word."

"Rodger that," Wilson returned with a smirk. "Statue mode engaged. Somebody cover me if pigeons show up."

Humphrey laughed into the mic.

The sting was already in motion when Kendrick rolled into the lot, the hulking brick shell looming like a carcass under buzzing sodium lights. Loading bays sat dead and rusted, weeds splitting through cracked concrete. Nazario took out her binoculars. Kendrick was parked where Mendez had told him—beside a gutted freezer unit, its metal skin tattooed in layers of fluorescent yellow and pink graffiti, colors burning loud against the dark, bright enough she could see it from her perch.

"Two incoming," Alvarado announced.

Headlights sliced across the dark lot. Two sedans crept in slow and easy. Mendez and Greer had come separate—smart move. Less heat that way. If anyone clocked them leaving the station at the same time—or even pulling out from home—it'd look wrong. Safer apart. Nazario lifted her binoculars. Beside her, Wilson lifted his own.

Kendrick got out of his vehicle and stood in front of the headlights. Mendez and Greer met him, lights still on to dispel the inky night and provide visibility.

"The dope must be within the vicinity," Nazario spoke into the mic.

"Thinking the same," Humphrey returned.

Voices came through Nazario's earpiece.

"Pop your trunk," Mendez ordered.

Kendrick frowned. "Thought we were loading the dope in your ride?"

"Change of plans. You're the mule." Greer cut in. "We keep our cars clean—fast out if it blows."

"And what about me?" Kendrick moved with believable hesitation.

"What about you?" Greer snapped. "We keep to the script.

You lifted the stash off some tweaker—busted him, and brought it in. Easy enough, since you're always nose-deep in the shit anyway."

"Quit dragging, rookie, or we hand the brass your little hooker-and-dope secret," Detective Lila Mendez said, her threatening tone contradicting her polished, by-the-book exterior.

Nazario had underestimated Mendez, hadn't realized how full-thug she could get.

The young officer picked up his pace and popped his trunk. "Now what?"

"Now you help us gut this old freezer." Mendez took out a set of keys.

The detached, retired frozen storage unit was the size of a shipping container, forty feet of dented steel scarred with graffiti. Heavy steel double doors were cinched shut with thick chains, a rusted padlock biting through the links.

Mendez unlatched the lock.

"Get ready to move in," Humphrey said.

Wilson eased up in his Tesla Model Y—an upgrade from his old Tahoe. In L.A., it blended like background noise, nothing out of the ordinary. With the headlights off and the engine silent, the car ghosted into position, unseen, unheard.

Kendrick blinked at the stacks inside the gutted freezer. One look at Kendrick's face told her everything—the freezer wasn't just stocked—it was stuffed to the ceiling.

"Holy shit. There's no way all this is fitting in my fucking trunk."

Mendez smirked. "Relax, rookie. We just need you to move two bags."

Kendrick grabbed one by the strap, nearly grunting at the weight. "Christ—how much tranq dope is in this?"

"Twenty bricks each," Greer said flat, like it was nothing. "Forty kilos. That's your haul."

Kendrick hooked a duffel under each arm, lugged them to the trunk, and dropped them in before slamming it shut.

"Trunk's loaded." Kendrick stepped back, his gaze flicking toward them—casual enough to pass, but not clean enough for Mendez.

Her eyes narrowed. "The hell you looking at?"

"N-n-nothing. I'll do the drop—"

She fisted his shirt and yanked it up. "You fucking snitch!"

"Goddamn it! Move, move, move—go, go!" Humphrey barked into the earpiece.

Humphrey and Dawson surged forward, guns high, voices cracking like thunder.

"Hands up! LAPD!"

Kendrick bolted, diving behind his car.

Then everything fractured.

Greer snapped first—wild, jittery. His pistol screamed, muzzle flash strobing the dark.

Nazario and Wilson jumped out of his Tesla and sprinted toward the action just as bullets ripped into concrete—chips stung her face, dust clouding her eyes. Metal screamed with ricochets, sparks spitting off car doors and the steel frame. Every shot felt way too close; the air itself shredded around her.

Nazario picked up her pace, being the fastest runner on the force, she left everyone in the dust: Humphrey, Dawson, Wilson, and even Huxley. Her breath came out in short bursts under the Kevlar. Mendez sprang out from her cover, shooting once in Nazario's direction. She ducked just as the bullet whizzed by. Then—Greer's eyes found her. This time, he didn't miss. *Pop-pop.* The world blinked white. Two blows to her chest, sledgehammer force.

Vest hit, she was slammed backward, striking the cement with a hard thud.

It all souped together, a muffled blur, like sounds trapped under water.

Heartbeat too loud.

Air—get air—

Somewhere through the haze: "Anaya!" Huxley's voice, raw, pulling her back.

She clawed herself upright, legs answering before her head. Years on elite track teams—high school, college—her body still remembered. Runner's body, runner's will. Nazario pushed forward, accelerating, lungs screaming.

Pop!

Another flash—she was hit again—her shoulder lit up on fire. Left side. Hot liquid spilled down her arm, escaping from her body. She was closest to Greer and Mendez. Too close for her team to risk a shot. The tunnel narrowed: just her, the Sig, and Greer's silhouette retreating, wild-eyed.

She drew in a breath—hands steady, aim precise.

Bang. Bang. Bang.

Three sharp kicks. Greer folded, stomach shredded, blood gushing dark. He writhed, hands useless against the holes as he groaned in pain.

"Get the fuck out, Mendez!" Humphrey bellowed.

Mendez crawled out slow, venom in her stare. Eyes locked on Kendrick like a blade before she dropped her weapon, and it thudded against the ground.

"Ambulance! Now!" Humphrey barked. "Wilson—stop the bleeding. Keep him alive."

Nazario caught Wilson out of the corner of her eye, ripping off his sweater, slamming it down on Greer's stomach. Blood swallowed the fabric.

"Don't worry, Cap," Wilson muttered darkly. "I'll patch him up—long enough for a jury to finish the job."

Greer wailed, animal, desperate.

Wilson pressed harder, merciless.

Then Huxley—sudden, grounding, her safe haven—his hands warm on her face, brushing back damp hair. His voice cracked. "Anaya...talk to me. Where?"

"Left shoulder," she grunted, low. "Vest caught the rest."

Her arm throbbed fire, blood trailing down her wrist. Still, her Glock 22 stayed firm in her right hand. Still ready.

The radio crackled in her ear. IA tech's voice, clipped, urgent: "Dispatch, IA One. Officer down, life-threatening. Second officer wounded. Roll the medics, multiple units, Code 3—Vernon Cold Storage."

The scene swam in and out—powder smoke, sirens distant, Greer bleeding out, Mendez cuffed. Concrete stank of iron and cordite.

Nazario's sleeve was slick with red, shoulder burning hot. Still on her feet. Still in the fight.

"You sure you're alright?" Huxley asked.

"I'm fine. At least it was my left and not my right arm," Nazario said, breathing through her nose. "Should be an in and out procedure. Get the shell case out, get a few stitches. Should be home by tonight. Greer, on the other hand—"

"Would've killed him myself. But I do hope he lives through it. Can't wait to testify against the asshole in court," Huxley said.

Two ambulances screamed up, lights cutting through the inky night.

IA Sergeant Manual Alvarez cuffed Mendez and shoved her into the back of the van, locked her behind the prison cage, while two EMTs rushed Greer, gloves already slick as they clamped hands down hard on his gut, barking for more gauze as they heaved him onto the gurney.

Nazario staggered toward the old freezer, pressing her right hand hard against her torn shoulder, blood running hot between her fingers.

Huxley intercepted the second set of EMTs, holding up a hand. "Give her five," he said, voice firm. Nazario caught the look he gave them—no panic, no coddling, no savior swagger. He knew she could grit through and handle her shit. He wasn't about to let anyone drag her off for a shoulder wound while the scene was still hot. God, she loved him for that.

Humphrey and Dawson were already eyeing the stash.

"Holy shit," Humphrey muttered, scanning the pile. "Five duffels, easy."

"They said twenty bricks a bag," Dawson added. "Two already in Kendrick's trunk. Five here makes—"

"A hundred and forty bricks of this tranq dope, zombie drug shit—and it's a new formula. Not even Narcan can shake an OD out of it," Humphrey said.

Nazario counted fast, her chest still heaving, left arm burning. "Seven duffels...one forty keys. Wholesale? Forty million, give or take. And on the street?" She exhaled. "North of eleven. Maybe sixteen."

"That's a lot of dope," Dawson said.

"And a whole lot of fucking cash," Humphrey said, then snapped out of the moment, turning to Nazario. "Girl, get your ass back over to those EMTs and get that hole patched up."

Wilson strolled up, Greer's blood painted to his elbows. "She's tougher than Greer, Cap—but I'll make sure she gets into that ambulance before I need a hose-down."

While Humphrey and Dawson loaded the dope into their SUV, Nazario was already on her way to the hospital. No waiting rooms, no paperwork shuffle—the badge cleared the path. Within an hour, the casing was out of her shoulder, stitches tight and clean, pain dulled by a haze of meds.

When Huxley and Nazario pulled into the driveway, the house looked quiet, the porch light throwing a warm pool across the door. Normal. Too normal. Inside, their babysitter Elena hovered by the entryway, wringing her hands. Their daughter's toys littered the rug, cartoons muttered low on the TV— just another night.

Except Elena's eyes were wide, anxious. "I'm sorry," she whispered, "but she insisted on speaking with you."

Nazario's chest tightened. She followed Elena's glance toward the dining room.

Someone sat at the table, framed by the low overhead light. Shoulders trembling. An Asian woman, mid-to-late fifties. Familiar Korean features Nazario recognized from the briefing photos.

Dr. Seung-ah Lee.

Two years gone. Kidnapped. Vanished. And now Dr. Seung-ah Lee was in their house—eyes wide, terrified, as if death had followed her inside.

TWENTY-FIVE

THE WOMAN IN WHITE

VON SPOTTED her first through the glass: a pale figure bent over the bench, lab coat ghosting under the harsh fluorescents. Dr. Nadia Volkov—the woman in white, alone, unaware she was already marked for death.

Tucked away near the Trident Seafoods Cannery—a massive processing hub with rusting docks and enough steel to choke the horizon for decades, Northern Processing & Packing had been abandoned. Locals ignored it, wrote it off as another failed business.

Von knew better.

Ryker had gutted the old cannery and raised a lab inside its bones. Once, the place had frozen and boxed salmon by the ton. Now the conveyors were still, the air carried the spirit of brine beneath the sharp bite of chemicals. The walk-in freezers hummed with a different purpose—Ryker's drug lab built on the carcass of a fish plant. The fact that every local had forgotten about it made it a brilliant move on Ryker's part.

Von and Xander followed Zeus's lead, as Cain had given them a white lab coat that'd been worn by Volkov. She didn't know how he managed to possess it, nor did she ask. It was the golden item she needed. Von slipped the folded fabric, dulled with Volkov's scent, to his nose. One sniff and Zeus had his snout to the ground, ears pricked, body tight with focus as he followed traces of Dr. Volkov. Without her dog, they'd have been utterly lost. The building was a labyrinth, corridors looping back on themselves, stairwells ended in locked doors.

The building rose five stories, gutted and rebuilt so many times that the halls stretched into shadows, storage rooms opened into more storage rooms. It felt like a place meant to swallow intruders whole. Von and Xander could've wandered for hours before finally breaking into the lab.

They breached the lab in silence. Sterile halls twisted them left, right, left again—a maze of white tile and steel doors. Without Zeus, there was no way in hell they would've found it, hidden on the third floor. Large panes of glass faced them, thick enough to stop a bullet, letting them peer inside.

Dr. Volkov was hunched over a steel workstation, her goggles pushed up, hair damp with sweat. A flask glowed over a hot plate, vapors fogging the glass partitions. Preoccupied, she didn't see them as Von tried the door. "It's open," she said.

"Probably wasn't expecting someone to find the lab," Xander stroked Zeus's head, praising her dog in German, telling him he was a good boy. "*Guter Junge.*"

Von lifted a brow. "Didn't know you spoke German."

"I speak several languages. Interpreter in Afghanistan—Dari, too."

The more she learned about Xander, the harder it became to ignore the pull.

"You ready?" she asked.

"Let's go."

The door swung open with quiet ease, hinges barely whispering. For a heartbeat, Volkov didn't react. Bent over her bench, shoulders hunched in that white coat, she looked like prey, an easy target. Maybe she hadn't heard them. Or maybe she wanted them to think that. Von brought her weapon up—too late. Volkov spun, pistol already in hand, eyes hard and cold. The woman in white wasn't cowering.

She was waiting.

"*Hol' sie dir!*" Von ordered Zeus to get her—but he was already moving, halfway to Volkov before the command left her mouth.

He met the scientist in a vicious sprint, clamping down onto her calf. A bullet fired out of Volkov's gun, clipping Von's ear. Blood streaked down her temple, ran down her cheek, dripping off her jaw.

Xander shot back just as Volkov ducked; nearby beakers and test tubes burst and speckled the ground with fractured glass. Having better aim and control of her weapon than they anticipated, Volkov's next round tore through Xander's shirt—missing his bicep by a fraction of an inch.

"Shit, I've been shot." Xander said, words clipped between breaths. "Somebody's been at the shooting range."

"Damn it. Where?"

Xander showed her—lower abdomen.

"Put pressure on it," Von instructed.

Von returned her attention back on to her dog. Zeus let go of Volkov's calf and found her gun arm, biting hard. The scientist barely flinched—grip firm on her weapon. With her free hand, she slammed a punch into Zeus's face, sending him flying.

Fucking bitch.

"Got her head in my line," Xander breathed weakly, focusing his semi-automatic on the scientist, wincing from the gunshot.

"Don't you fucking do it. Put pressure on your wound and don't you dare try to play soldier right now. She's mine."

Von charged forward, taking long, wide strides. Zeus wasn't

down for long. The moment his guardian marched forward, he was back on his feet, meeting her fury, having her back.

Volkov didn't have time to shoot. Von was already on her. With her gun hand, she smacked the scientist across her face. Zeus sprinted into the action, clamping down on her hand, stubbornly clenching the gun. The scientist wailed out in pain, fingers loosening, releasing the gun. The pistol clanked onto the floor.

"Don't you ever touch my dog again," Von warned.

Dr. Nadia Volkov hit the floor, back thudding harshly onto the linoleum. She put her hands up, trembling. "If you kill me, he's not going to stop. He'll replace me. Rebuild another lab."

"Let him try." Von pressed the barrel of her SIG at the center of her forehead.

Volkov bared her teeth, voice dripping with venom. "Cain sends some lapdog to pull the trigger—outsource the trash?"

Von thumbed the hammer back, the click cold as steel. "Black Nova says hello."

Boom!

The woman in white lay still. Von lowered her gun, mission complete.

———

They raced away from the lab, taking side streets only Xander knew. She drove, while he gave instructions on where to turn until they were safely back in her cabin again. Same old thin walls, same draft sneaking through the cracks. It was a cage dressed in timber. Before they left, Von snapped a picture of the dead scientist and texted it to Cain.

In under thirty seconds, his reply came through: *Great work. Sasha's on the cleanup. Take two weeks off, you've earned it. Check Phantom Vox in a couple for next steps. Location?*

She texted back, warning him of the maze they'd have to go through to find the lab.

Von: *Northern Processing & Packing. Place is a fucking maze. Would've been lost w/out Zeus. Lab's on the 3rd floor...left on the first corridor, right, then another left. All the way down.*

Cain: *Thx will pass it along. Enjoy the downtime...you'll need it.*

Von scrolled through her contacts and found Dr. Lee's mobile. She sent her the picture of Volkov and a quick text.

Von: *Don't get comfortable. You're all that's left now.*

She slid her phone away after texting Cain, the silence pressing around her. A forced break, she mulled, considering his words. Why would she need the time off? It sounded like a warning.

Then a low sound broke it—a moan from behind. At first, she thought the old wood was settling beneath her boots. But it came again, rough, pained. Von turned. It was Xander. That's right, he'd been shot. But the black snow jacket he wore concealed the blood, almost making her forget. He'd been quietly muting his pain until now.

Zeus nosed closer, scanning his body before stopping at Xander's lower left side—just above the groin. A thin whine broke from the dog's throat. Not a good sign—he knew exactly where Xander had been hit. The shepherd could track bombs, weapons, people by scent—and he could detect injury. Hell, he could even warn when someone was about to have a seizure.

"I need to look at your wound."

"It's fine...I'm fine. I've survived worse." Xander's eyes glazed over, movements slowing. He looked like he was about to pass out. He swayed unsteadily as he tried to walk.

"Whoa, whoa, whoa...you're not going anywhere."

"I'm fine...I'll...I'll take care of it."

"Not alone, you're not." She held his upper arm and led him

to the bedroom. Von unzipped his black snow jacket, and once it hit the ground, her eyes widened. Long-sleeved white thermals were now soaked with blood near the base. Left lower quadrant. The doctor in her kicked in; the years of experience operating on animals returned in a flash.

Xander slumped onto the edge of the bed, skin ashen and pale.

"C'mon, lie down, lie down. Nice and easy." She eased him back, and he scooted to the headboard, squeezing his eyes shut, wincing in pain. "Deep breaths. Don't you dare move."

She turned and reached for her medical bag in her closet. Von never went without it in case she needed to patch Zeus up or herself. She'd only ever stitched herself up once because the bullet had hit her shoulder where she could reach.

Von worked fast, taking out scissors. She cut his shirt open, from the waist to the neck. Peeling off the shirt, she was careful not to force him to move any more than he needed to. The thermal slid off his shoulders and under his back. She dropped the shirt in the trash bin and returned to her medical bag, retrieving a scalpel, suture, and a 2% lidocaine vial—left over from her vet days, but just as effective on human flesh.

"Numbing the area with lidocaine. It'll work fast. You won't feel a thing in about a minute or two." She injected the lidocaine near the point of entry.

"Thank you," he said. "Don't have to help me, you know."

"You helped me. Why wouldn't I return the favor." She looked at her watch and when it was time, she pressed lightly on the wound. "Feel that?"

He shook his head no.

"Cutting you open just a little. Need to look inside, see how far deep we're talking about."

She made a vertical incision, snagged a needle-nose forceps, and poked it into the wound, opening the wound wide enough to get a glimpse.

"Good news, I can see the bullet. Looks like a shallow wound. The angle was just right, and your snow jacket was thick enough to soak up most of the punch. You're real lucky."

Finding the bullet, she caught it with the needle-nose forceps and tugged it free, metal dark and slick. She let it fall into a tray with a hard *clink*, then threaded her suture needle. In under five minutes, she had the wound disinfected, closed, and bandaged.

"Done already?" he asked, color returning to his face. "Wow, that's gotta be a record. And I actually feel like myself again. Don't feel a damn thing."

"And you shouldn't for at least two to four hours. Gave you lidocaine with epinephrine."

Von forced herself to focus on the wound, not on the man. His chest was right there, bare under her hands, every line of muscle defined in the glow of the cabin light. Not unnaturally roid-large, but muscular in a natural, functional way—carved by years of discipline. It was maddening how close she was, how much she wanted to look when she needed to think. He was perfect and dangerous in a way she hadn't braced for.

Her hand grazed over the bandage, not to examine the injury, but to feel, to touch him. She swallowed, snapping off gloves sticky with blood, and tossed them into the trash. Von avoided his eyes, suddenly finding it hard to breathe.

Xander's voice came low. "I should probably go." A pause. Eyes finding hers. "But what if I told you I want to stay?"

"You...you probably shouldn't be driving."

"That's not what I meant."

"And you were just shot, I'm not so sure you should be doing anything other than resting."

"Every time I walk into a room, I'm ready to die. Tonight's

the first time since my son and wife were murdered that I've actually wanted to live—for something. For someone," Xander said, reaching for her hand. "I don't want to rest. I want you."

Von forced herself to meet his eyes. "It'll take a week for you to heal. As long as it took for me."

Xander gave her a rough laugh. "Fuck a week."

She shook her head, voice low. "Then at least give it a day. I'm not doing this until a day's passed."

They did just that—let a day pass. He needed it, though the wound would take weeks to mend. Her own gunshots hadn't healed, and his certainly hadn't either. So, she waited, keeping her distance until he drifted to sleep. Only then did she curl in behind him, body close but careful. By the next morning, the lines between restraint and want had blurred.

As she awoke to the sunshine filling the cabin, the first thing she felt was his hands wandering up her thighs, clutching her against his chest. His hands were large, strong, rough with calluses—yet the way he laced his fingers through hers was nothing but gentle, pulling her closer, inviting her into him. She wanted to fight it, yank free, but for once her body and mind were aligned, neither wanting to let go.

"Do you feel okay?" she asked, breathless.

"I'm not waiting a fucking week," he said against her lips. "A bullet isn't stopping me from being with you. It's been a night, and that's all I need."

"But you've been shot—"

"And so have you. We're still here, Von. Still breathing. And all I want right now is you."

Von found herself moving closer as though a current had caught her, carrying her straight to him. His heartbeat set the rhythm, and hers couldn't help but follow. She curled next to his right, uninjured side, heat radiating from flesh despite the biting chill that drafted through the bedroom. He opened his arm up like a doorway into safety he didn't offer anyone else, offering the part of himself he never let go unguarded. Xander folded her in, bracing her against him until there was no space between them.

He brushed a hand against her cheek, touch devastatingly tender, catching her by surprise.

Her eyes never left his as she stripped off the thermal shirt and snow pants. He freed himself from his jeans, careful to avoid bumping into his wound, gaze locked on her every move while she unsnapped her bra. Bare-breasted now, nothing left but white boy shorts clinging to her chiseled abs—her body all discipline and raw femininity.

The habit to hide returned, her hand instinctively tried to conceal the keloid scar that ran up the length of her abdomen like a red python.

"Come here," he whispered. She lay back down beside him, her hand still covering part of the scar—too long, too brutal for her to hide, even with both hands. He gently drew her fingers away as he had before. "Every inch of you is beautiful. Especially this. I see the survivor. I see the woman who refuses to break. I see you. And I want you."

"We're...we're breaking the rules," she breathed, a low warning.

"If this is wrong, then let me be wrong with you." He cupped her face, jaw tight with need. "Goddamn it, I'd rather risk everything than to lose this moment."

She leaned in, drawn like a moth to a blazing flame, and ever so softly brushed her lips to his—feather light. It was a whisper of a kiss that answered his gentle caress and incredibly kind words with action. His lips parted, tongue sliding to meet hers, and a familiar insatiable hunger erupted—catapulting the rhythm. A ravenous need drove them, the kiss deepening. Two starved souls who'd surrendered pleasure for duty too long, unable now to forfeit their humanity. He moaned, hands roaming her curves, until they found her breasts, kneading with deliberate urgency.

Her body tingled, as though it hadn't been touched for so long that the memory of intimacy had dulled—until now. Their lips parted, both breathless. Xander kept his eyes on hers as his hand roamed, following the path of the serpent scar down the length of her torso, hands slipping into her briefs. He slid two fingers into her, slick with desire, and moved—deep, steady. Von's eyes closed on their own, hands clutching the headboard. Her head fell back as a rough sound escaped her throat.

She writhed, breath quickening, as his fingers drove her higher. His lips grazed her ear, voice rough, commanding: "Come for me, Von."

Every nerve lit, every muscle tightening—she was right there, ready to fall—when she caught his wrist, forcing the rhythm to break.

Von met his eyes, panting for air. Her fingers unclenched the headboard, and her hand boldly found his large manhood, hard with want. His eyes were fixed on her like gravity as her hand went beneath the barrier of fabric. Her fingers curled around his thickness, stroking him with a steady, measured pace. There was something intimate about staring into his golden eyes, keeping hers pinned on his, as she pleasured him, watching his mouth fall open, his chest rise and dip.

"Not without you inside me," she said. She let him go just as he was about to break, holding him back so he could savor it—so he could finish with her, deep inside, the way she needed.

She shoved off her boy shorts and helped him out of his. Suddenly, they couldn't move fast enough. Finally free of the last piece of fabric, a barrier between them, Xander surprised her when he rolled on top, hovering over her.

"Your wound—"

"I'll survive."

He pinned her wrists above her head with one hand and slipped just half of himself inside her with the other. He stretched her past her limits, the fit almost unbearable, almost perfect. The sheer size of him left her straining, every inch of her tight around him.

"Fuck—you're so damn tight," he growled, voice ragged. His eyes squeezed shut, breath shuddering as he tried to hold on. Opening his eyes, he watched her as he pushed himself deeper until he was all in. He stretched her further, almost intolerable. She winced as a sharp sting burned through her.

"Are you...are you alright?" he asked, making her feel like a virgin.

She swallowed a shaky breath and nodded. "I've never been dominated before."

She could feel all of him, easily the largest man she'd ever taken, and even without movement, he filled her so perfectly it felt like their bodies were carved to fit this way. Her womanhood clenched around him, gripping him with fierce precision, hot and unyielding.

"Do you want me to dominate you?" his voice husky.

"I don't give up control. But with you—I want to," she said, then dared him with a single command. "Dominate me, Xander. That's an order."

He shifted, moving from pinning her wrists with his palm to threading his fingers through hers. Then his clasp strengthened, locking her arms down with power, so she couldn't move. She sucked in a sharp breath. To her shock, it was the most erotic sensation she'd ever known.

His grip was fierce, almost possessive, his fingers intertwined with hers, keeping her arms pinned above her head, out of reach from touching him. After a long beat of stillness, his hips rocked in slow circles—lingering deliberately, sliding deep, giving all of himself to her, and then sliding out. It was the casual cadence of his movement, the tender ease of every step. The way he pushed back in just as steady and unhurried. It was torture. His eyes never left hers. Von's body began to tremble beneath him, the gradual torment of his pace unraveling her control. The contradiction had her nerves on fire—extreme power and tenderness, a rhythm that undid her more than violence ever had.

He leaned in, tracing her lips with his tongue. "I need your hands on me," he whispered, words spilling hot against her mouth. His grip eased, releasing her fingers, and instead he cupped her face. Von's arms slid instantly around him, nails grazing his back, fingers threading into his hair, tugging him closer as his lips claimed hers. He lowered himself onto her, chest to chest, skin burning, sweat slicking the heat between them. Von shifted her hips beneath his weight, one hand sliding to his hip. She pressed, urging him deeper until he sank fully inside her.

He groaned, bodies locking tight, her rhythm catching his as his breath hovered over her lips, heat colliding, mouths so close they shared the same air. Her mouth slackened, gasping. He slid out slow, only to drive back in—harder, deeper until her whimper broke free. She clenched against his girth, his hiss tearing out raw as his hands gripped her bottom, burying himself to the hilt. Again, he moved, slow but deliberate, every stroke dragging her higher. She wrapped her arms around his back, fusing him to her, pressing every inch of him against her body. He dipped to her ear, thrusting deeper.

"I want to stay inside you," he rasped. He slid out just far enough to tease, pausing to lock eyes with her—daring her, waiting.

"Then stay, Xander." Her body clenched, voice breaking. "Stay until there's nothing left of us."

She dragged her hands down his hips, pressing him in, rocking beneath him until his back arched and he hissed her name. "Take me. Please," she begged.

The plea ripped out of her before she could stop it. His response was brutal—driving into her with a force that shoved her back against the headboard. The dance started slow, controlled, then built into a frantic pace. He wrapped her against his chest, face buried in her neck, his hands cupping her ass, guiding her, moving her to his rhythm. Her body arched, bowing under him, until his hand slid lower—fingers slithered down her stomach until they found her clit. Xander's thumb circled, slow, deliberate, then faster, vibrating against her as his thrusts quickened, syncing to her ache, to her need.

"I want to hear you say it," he growled. "Say you want more."

"Please, Xander...don't stop," she gasped. He moved like he knew every secret of her body, biting her neck, sucking hard as he pulled all the way out, pausing too long, then plunging back inside, deep and merciless. Her nails raked his back as he found the perfect pace—stretching her, making her tremble beneath him.

"Come for me, Von. Come for me," he begged. His thumb pressed harder against her bud, circling fast, relentless, until her body seized. She screamed, release tearing through her like an electric current, crying out his name. Xander's mouth crashed to hers, swallowing her cry as his own release tore out of him—an animalistic growl ripped through his chest as he poured himself into her. Still inside her, he collapsed against her, weight heavy, chest heaving, lips dragging across her temple. His breath shuddered, uneven, like he was holding something back.

"It's been years." His voice cracked soft and quiet against her ear. "Not since her."

Von stilled beneath him, arms tightening around his back.

At once, his shoulders bobbed, body trembling and not from pleasure but from pain as his body betrayed him, damp emotion slid down her skin where his face pressed. A sob, raw and guttural, broke free from his chest. It was a cry she'd never heard from another soul, a deep anguish. A man breaking open, letting go of something he'd buried so long ago it almost destroyed him.

He clung to her, fingers biting into her flesh as though she were his life raft in a storm. Von didn't speak, only stroked her fingers through his hair, gentle and tender. Letting herself be his anchor. Letting him unravel without judgment. Holding him close and realizing, with a sting she couldn't name, that for the first time in years she wasn't holding a weapon.

She was holding a man.

TWENTY-SIX
THE INTERROGATION

THEY HAD LET Dr. Seung-ah Lee sleep, having had a stressful and exhaustive five-hour and forty-five-minute red-eye flight from Alaska to LAX. But Nazario shook Dr. Lee awake at six a.m., feeling bad about having to do it. Guilt tugged at her for a beat, then she shoved it down. She and Huxley had a pressing, back-to-back interrogation—Detective Lila Mendez and Sergeant Vincent Greer—and there was no chance in hell Nazario was going to miss it.

"I know you're tired, but we can't keep you here. It's not safe. Too many eyes on the LAPD. Too many dirty ears on the line. I'll be putting you in a Bureau safe house this morning, it's the only way to keep you alive," Huxley said.

"But first, we need to have us a little chat." Nazario leaned in. "Why did you show up at our house, and who sent you?"

The doctor shifted uncomfortably as she used proxemics manipulation—an interrogation tactic that deliberately invaded personal space to unsettle the subject. Closing the gap between a detective and the subject in question unnerved them. It often heightened psychological pressure, asserted dominance, and made the interrogator project confidence.

Despite Lee's story that she'd been kidnapped against her will, Nazario's gut was warning her. Something was off about the kidnapping. She'd sensed it the moment she watched the footage. She couldn't trust Dr. Lee. While she couldn't prove it, Nazario tried a tactic detectives often used. Act as if the investigation team had evidence that they didn't in order to cough up a confession. Get to the truth.

"Why don't you start with the real story. We have reason to believe there's more to the lab kidnapping," Nazario said, Huxley shot her a knowing look, recognizing the ploy.

Dr. Lee's eyes widened, as if she was shocked by the amount of information they had on her. She slumped her head in her hands and then said, "I was fired from Helix Point Labs after a synthetic drug gave participants of the trial terrible side effects. I blew the whistle, and they falsified a paper trail, claims of personal misconduct. Worse, I was blacklisted from the industry. They gave me two weeks to wrap up my current scientific research."

"That's why you were there the day of the kidnapping. You staged the whole thing because Ryker offered you more money than you earned working in the lab, didn't he?" Nazario said.

"I reached out to him. Told him what I could do for him. My background in neurochemical modeling and synthetic compound production was of great appeal to him. It didn't take long to be on his payroll. And, yes, he paid me well. But quitting Ryker after all the ODs was something no one does. Once he has you, whether you initially volunteered to do the job or not, there's no going back. There's no way to return to a cleaner life. Because I'm the only one who truly knows all the steps in the production of tranq dope—he'll try to find me, extract the formula, however necessary, before killing me. He can try to replicate the drug with other scientists, but it won't be the same. He can lose customers if they don't like the new batch. It could be even more deadly. There're too many things that could go wrong."

"You were pretty damn bold to flip from being an award-winning biochemist to going off to the dark side. But I can see how not being able to find work in your field would've narrowed your options." Huxley steepled his fingers, eyeing her. "So, who sent you? Someone helped you get out of Alaska. No way you escaped Ryker solo. We think we know who that someone is, but we need confirmation."

"Von and Xander. Direct order from Black Nova at the very top of the food chain."

"Why would Von spare you, hmmm?" Nazario asked. "Why would Black Nova keep you alive, the person responsible for this new, deadlier strain of tranq dope that's killing people out in the streets?"

"Because I'm the only one left that knows the entire formula, the cooking methods, the whole process from the very beginning to the very end." Dr. Lee logged into her phone, opened up a text message, and slid the mobile to Nazario. Huxley peeked over her shoulder. "Dr. Nadia Volkov. Ukrainian biochemist. Also received her Ph.D. in biochemistry, as I did. She knew most of the formula, but I was careful to keep some things to myself in case this would ever happen."

They studied the image. It was a clean shot to the head. A blonde, mid-thirties woman in a bloodied white lab coat lay limp on the floor.

"I could see Von taking Volkov out. Smart move from Black Nova. Hitting Ryker where it hurts, crippling his production supply. Probably scrambling to find a replacement. Whether it's the same formula or not." Nazario handed her back the phone.

"So, you privately kept a tight production pipeline when you cooked up each batch. Truly surprised you managed to do that with Volkov present. What you're saying is—it was an insurance policy move, so that what you had was too valuable. Bought yourself time. Bought yourself your life. He can't risk killing you now that you're the only one with the keys to his empire," Huxley said, checking his watch, then turning to Nazario. "I'd better move her to the safe house. Wouldn't want to be late for the interrogation."

Nazario nodded, then asked, "Did you give Von, Xander, or anyone else in Black Nova the formula?"

Dr. Lee shook her head. "They didn't want it. Afraid that they'd be targeted, killed over it—and they most certainly would've been. Von specifically asked me to hand it to you, that you were the only one she trusted, said you'd keep it safe."

Dr. Lee reached around her neck and unclasped the necklace. "Platinum, not silver or white gold. Had to ensure that it didn't tarnish. Custom-designed."

She placed it carefully on the table. Nazario picked it up—heavier than it looked. Dangling from the chain was an antique-style oval locket, its surface etched with delicate cherry blossoms, a single diamond gleamed at the center. Nazario brushed her thumb across the design, then pressed the tiny button hidden along the side. A soft click. The locket opened. Inside, instead of a pressed flower or family photo, a hollow compartment held a micro SD card fitting flush against the inner wall.

"It's small and could easily be lost. And if it's in a standard SD holder, it'll be the first place anyone would look, too easy to find. I'd keep it in the locket until you're ready to turn it over to the proper chain of command—just to be on the safe side," Dr. Lee said.

"Thank you, this has been immensely helpful," Nazario said.

"Got everything you need?" Huxley gestured toward her two large roll-style suitcases, which looked to have been in the doctor's life since her college years. Scratched and dented, they had the character of old friends. It told Nazario a lot about Dr. Lee—that she was equal parts practical and disciplined. She lived efficiently, valuing functional over excess. Just two suitcases were enough to hold everything that mattered.

Huxley kissed Nazario goodbye. "Meet you there. Hug baby girl for me."

"Elena will be here in an hour."

As he escorted Dr. Lee toward the door, she paused and turned around. "Please...stay safe, Detective," she said, and then vanished out the front where Lee would be taken to a safe house that even she wouldn't know. Huxley would never dare tell her because it would jeopardize the safety of not just the doctor, but the detective as well.

Nazario clasped the pendant in her hands. Its antique design was beautiful. The platinum material reinforced every part of the pendant, from the firm clasp to the hinges, and finally, the hidden chamber that kept secrets. On the surface, it looked like nothing more than a keepsake. But in truth, it carried the formula for the most lethal new strand of tranq dope—data worth more than gold, more dangerous than any bullet.

———

The IA wing had its own corridor directly in the LAPD HQ and officers lining the lobby, glancing away deliberately as Nazario, Wilson, and Chief Johnson walked in. Security scanners loomed at the entrance, and surveillance cameras were positioned in every corner of the building. Against the morning haze, the Police Administration Building held an ominous presence. The moment the three of them walked in with Chief Johnson limping along with a cane, voices hushed, dropping quick, more eyes cut away.

"Pay no mind," the chief said for their ears only.

"Yeah, sure, Chief. I'll just pretend that half the department didn't look at us like we ran over their grandma," Wilson said.

Nazario didn't give them the satisfaction of a glance. The lobby, ordinarily buzzing with uniforms and chatter, felt off—air thick, whispers low, sideways glares darting at them when the three weren't looking. "Fuck 'em all," she snapped, charging forward, Wilson at her shoulder, Chief Johnson trailing like a watchful shadow.

An IA sergeant in plainclothes met them at a secure metal door and swiped them in with his keycard. "Sergeant Marco Santori," the Italian IA agent introduced himself. "Yous got more of us on yous side than yous know. Some of us, we still know right from wrong, haven't lost our conscience—and we sure as hell don't stand with cop killers or those that shoot at their own."

Santori stuck out his hand, and Nazario shook it, giving him a nod.

"That's the nicest thing anyone's said to me in this building —and I once got complimented on my donut choices." Wilson slapped the sergeant's shoulder. "For a second, I thought we'd have to start wearing Kevlar just to check our mail."

"Know this, Chief," Santori began, turning to Johnson. "What those *cazzos*—assholes in plain English—pulled was all kinds of wrong. Evil, straight up. We're hoping yous put Mendez, Greer, and every other son of a bitch tied to this behind bars. They don't deserve to wear a badge."

"Appreciate it. Guess not everyone wants us dead." Chief Johnson exhaled loudly. "Just ninety-nine percent of 'em."

Once through the metal door, the air turned sterile, altered, as if oxygen had been filtered of humanity. Lined with white-washed walls, the hallways stretched on, more black-eyed cameras following their every move. Every footstep squeaked against the waxed linoleum floors. The rest of HQ felt more human, more like a collaborative, harmonious team. At least it had before Jaxon Ryker popped up on the street and began flipping cops. However, the IA wing felt as if its coldness was operationally normal—unity bled out, replaced by suspicion, replaced by their number one rule: never trust anyone.

As they were ushered into a box room, Nazario noticed that there were no half-dead plants, no sociable chatter around the coffee pot, no mess hall with fresh bagels, crude jokes, and friendly banter. Just cold light and the knowledge that every inch of the place was wired to catch the truth in a twitch or a swallow.

The room was windowless. One-way glass on one side. A table bolted to the floor; chairs made for discomfort. Fluorescents washed everything pale. On the table sat a recorder, its red light waiting, blinking, ready to pin their words in permanent ink.

Chief Johnson carefully lowered onto a chair, resting his cane against the wall. Nazario plunked down next to him, nursing her left shoulder, the uncomfortable stitches reminding her that it was a fellow blue who'd tried to kill her, causing rage to fuel through her. She was not about to miss this interrogation. Wilson dropped into the chair beside her. The silence pressed down harder than any question that might surface.

They'd arrived just in time.

IA Sergeant Manual Alvarez waited inside the interrogation room, posture rigid, the kind of cold anger only betrayal could fuel, carved across his face. He didn't raise his voice; every line of his jaw said he wanted blood. Huxley stood in the far corner, arms crossed over his massive chest. At six-four, broad as a doorframe, he looked less like an FBI supervising agent and more like the executioner waiting his turn. The Huxley men were all built that way—big, towering, born thick with muscle as if they'd been training since birth. Huxley, though, was the tallest and most imposing of them all, the kind of presence that made the room shrink.

Captain Gus Humphrey was no less imposing. Muscles from years of throwing iron in the gym, her frame carried the weight of someone who'd never backed down from a fight. Both arms were sleeved in black-ink tattoos, scars from working undercover ran through the ink like hidden fault lines, reminders of fights the tattoos could never cover. Humphrey had always carried herself with blunt confidence of a woman who didn't need to tell anyone she was tougher than most men— she'd already proven it a hundred times over. It was a trait that made her wife, Quinn, fall in love with her.

Nazario had known both Humphrey and Huxley for two decades. Once, she'd feared living with Huxley—together with their child, just not married—would sour the bond between them. It hadn't. If anything, it fused it tighter. He wasn't just her partner. He was her lover, the father of her daughter, and the one person who would burn the world if she asked.

Alvarez broke the silence first. "Agent Huxley. Captain Humphrey. Don't expect me to go easy on those two traitors. I don't give a damn what whispers are crawling through HQ— Internal Affairs isn't in the business of shielding dirty blue. Not after this."

Huxley's jaw locked, eyes lifted to the mirrored glass dividing them from the interrogation room. He couldn't see her, but Nazario felt him find her anyway. "She's the mother of my child," he said, voice taut. "The love of my life. Had it not been for her vest, she'd be on a slab right now. The Bureau doesn't let that slide."

Humphrey leaned forward, voice a snarl, not a whisper. "And let's not forget—they damn near killed me and Chief Johnson. Like they killed Harrison. Can't prove whose finger was on the trigger, but we all know dirty badges had a hand in it.

And now they come for Nazario?" Her jaw set, muscle jumping. "Then it's war."

Huxley and her best friend rushing to her defense made her eyes burn. The truth was raw—she could've been killed. But there they were, loyal and unflinching. Love and danger, pain and devotion—always the razor's edge she lived on, where life and death tangled together.

The door buzzed open. Sergeant Marco Santori—the same officer who'd escorted them in—stepped through, this time with a prisoner in tow. Detective Lila Mendez was the first to enter, shackled, swallowed in county-issue orange. The cheap canvas couldn't erase her ego-driven cop swagger, but her eyes betrayed her—a flash of fear, then defiance. Greer would be interviewed separately. They'd figured Mendez would be easier to break.

The shootout had left no room for doubt. Both had opened fire on fellow officers, the weight of the charges too heavy for anything less. Caught with one hundred and forty keys of tranq dope stacked in an old freezer storage. No drawn-out first round of interrogation. No friendly "cop courtesy." The second the smoke cleared, IA had them in custody. Federal charges—narcotics trafficking, attempted murder, conspiracy—were already stacked and waiting.

They weren't in a squad room anymore. They weren't cops. They were inmates. Held in federal holding block until special watch—the only place dirty blue could rot before their trials chewed them up.

Mendez's lawyer followed in behind her in a sharp suit and noisy, polished Italian leather shoes that demanded attention. He sat down, plunking his briefcase on the floor next to him, and took out a legal pad and a pen.

"Sergeant Manny Alverez, Internal Affairs. Captain Gus Humphrey, Gang and Narco. Back corner, Supervising Special Agent Blake Huxley—FBI," Alverez introduced them to the lawyer. "Interrogation will be on record, meaning it will be recorded."

Alvarez pressed a button on the digital recorder.

The lawyer tapped his pen and nodded once, cracking a thin smile that seemed as if even that small performance drained him.

"First of all, I think I speak for everyone in this room that we could see Sergeant Greer letting greed drive his fall from grace. But you, Mendez? Someone who'd had a spotless record. Someone the PD trusted?" Alvarez froze her with a hard stare.

"Guess women aren't supposed to be bad, huh? But it's expected out of Greer? I find your train of thought a little sexist," Mendez said.

"You're not helping yourself. Sit back and stay quiet," the lawyer scolded his client. "I tell you when to talk and when to shut the hell up. That's why I'm here."

"I've bagged more dope slingers than I can count—but one hundred and forty keys of tranq? Enough dope to wipe out half of this city on ODs," Humphrey said.

"Opened fire on fellow police officers. You're not walking out of this, no matter how much money you're paying your fancy defense council," Alvarez said. "Question is—how many years you want to add on? Could be looking at life—"

The lawyer cut in. "My client shot once and missed. She wasn't the one who was the main shooter, that was Sergeant Greer."

"Firing her weapon even once at a fellow officer counts," Humphrey said.

"What if we told you we have evidence that puts her at the homicide scene of Detective Clay Harrison?" Huxley said, and Nazario knew it was a bluff. They often used stretching the truth to scare out a confession. But Mendez, being a detective herself, would likely not fall for it. "More evidence that she was involved in other shootings: Chief Johnson and Captain Humphrey suffered near-fatal attacks."

"That's fucking bullshit! You've got nothing on me. Nothing!" Mendez burst out, despite her training. Nazario was surprised. She'd expected that Lila Mendez would display a little more control of her emotions. "Could've been anyone. Ryker's men or someone else he flipped—"

"Keep it together, Mendez. I mean it—shut up now and stay that way until I tell you when to speak," the lawyer warned.

Alvarez leaned in and began firing off questions, questions that prompted Mendez to shut down as expected.

"Where's Ryker now? Who was your last point of contact?"

Mendez glanced at the lawyer, as if asking for permission to speak. He nodded.

"No comment."

"Who were you running protection for? Which port?"

"No comment."

"Who else in LAPD is on his payroll?"

"No comment."

"Where are your kickbacks being funneled? Shell accounts? Cash drops?"

"No comment."

"Who gave the order to kill Harrison, and attempt to kill Humphrey, Johnson, and shoot at fellow officers in case the pickup with Kendrick went south?"

"No comment."

"Where was Kendrick supposed to drop off the dope?"

"No comment."

Alvarez paused for a beat and sat back, blowing out a raucous breath.

Huxley walked over and slammed his fist on the table, accosting her as he got inches away from her face.

"You really think Ryker's gonna save you? He won't. You're

expendable. The second you got caught, you stopped being useful," Huxley said. "You're really okay with spending the rest of your life behind bars?"

Mendez started to shake, eyes darting away, as if she hadn't fully realized the consequences of her actions until this moment.

"Guess I made a mistake. Got in too deep. There's no turning back now," she said, words shivering out hushed. Anger switched quickly into worry, lowering the volume of her voice.

"Are the drugs only going through the Port of Long Beach, or are there other drop-offs? If so, where? C'mon, if you don't say it, Greer gets a shot at a potential plea deal instead of you."

Mendez laughed, though her eyes welled up with emotion, anxiety making her cuffed hands tremble. "He'll never talk."

"Last chance. Give us something," Humphrey cut in. "Remember why you became a cop to begin with. Remember the vow you made. Remember that at one time, you were on the right side of the fence."

The words seemed to sting, a tear crawled down Mendez's cheek.

"All I'll say is that the shipments don't end here. You think L.A.'s bad? You haven't a clue where it goes from here," she said.

"Which states and which ports?" Alvarez asked.

"No further questions. We're all done here." The defense attorney stood abruptly. Mendez, however, moved slowly, as though every inch of her body was weighed down by the chains of her choices and the consequences she was now facing.

They stalked to the door, frustration filling the room as the team was left with no answers.

Mendez paused at the doorway, shoulder angling back just enough to cut them a look. Her lips curled into something between a smirk and a sneer. "You'll never catch him. Not in this city."

TWENTY-SEVEN
THE LAST GOODBYE

THE EARLY MORNING rays cut through the cabin window, washing the walls with pale golden and soft pink hues. The cabin was quiet except for the sound of his breathing. Von stirred, the weight of his arm still heavy across her waist. For one impossible second, she let herself imagine this could last—two killers pretending to belong in a bed instead of a battlefield.

Xander shifted behind her, lips brushing against her shoulder, peppering light kisses up the nape of her neck. He held her with a force that startled her—not careful, not restrained, but fierce, like letting go might undo him. Von had never been held like that. Men wanted her before, but this was different. This wasn't a conquest or even lust. The grip bordered on desperate. As if she held the key to his survival. She let him hold her with conviction, let herself feel it deep within her soul.

Tenderness she hadn't expected from him, from herself, startled her. It spoke louder than any declaration. She hadn't expected herself to mirror his gentleness, hadn't anticipated that this was what she'd needed, been waiting for all her life. Every kiss, brush of his hand screamed what neither of them had said aloud: *love*.

"Did you sleep well?" Von laced her fingers through his.

"I always sleep well with you," he whispered into her ear. "You bring me peace I hadn't had in a long time. It's like you erase everything ugly and replace it with beauty, with hope."

His words prickled her skin, sending goose bumps across her flesh.

"You're not so tough after all. Nothing but gooey on the inside."

"And it's all your fault," he said, and they shared a laugh.

She turned to face him. Her long bangs fell forward, partially covering her gray eyes. He brushed the wayward hair back, his finger brushing against her face. "I don't regret this. Not for a second."

Her throat tightened, and before she could censor herself with old defense mechanisms, the words tumbled out of her mouth. "Neither do I."

They lay there for a beat in companionable silence, sharing a moment, staring into each other's eyes without a shred of awkward morning-after vibes. For just a heartbeat, she let herself believe it—that this was real, that it was hers.

Then the phone lit up on the nightstand.

Xander's arms shifted. He reached for it, screen glowing against his face. Von saw his expression harden, the warmth draining from it. His jaw clenched as he lingered for a moment, then set the phone down, screen still glowing, the lock not yet sliding back in place.

He turned and kissed her. "Would you like the shower first, or can I take it?"

"Go ahead. I'm not planning to wash you off," she said boldly.

"I'd say you're gooey on the inside, too." He gave her a lopsided smile. Her eyes followed him as he walked naked to the bathroom.

"And it's all your fault," she returned his words to him.

The bathroom door closed, water hissing through the pipes. The phone remained on the nightstand, its glow dimming but still visible. Von told herself not to look, that it was none of her business. But her body betrayed her, hand reaching out, snatching the phone up before it locked her out.

The words burned as she read them.

Cain: *Never forget who delivered the man who killed your wife and child. You owe me. This assignment is mandatory.*

Von got dressed, the words spinning through her mind. What assignment was necessary?

She made coffee in the kitchen and took Zeus out for a potty break, something in her gut dreading what the message meant. Why was Xander the only one to be sent the cryptic text, but she was not? They've been working on assignments together up until that point. Von checked the Phantom Vox app, and there were no new targets.

As she perched herself at the dining room chair, Xander finally came in with wet hair and smelling of soap. When she slid a mug of coffee across to him, he accepted it with a quiet nod.

"Von," he said quietly. "We need to talk."

"I...I know. I looked at your phone. I'm sorry," she said, sipping her coffee. "Just checked the app. Got no new targets. So, I have to ask...what mandatory assignment is Cain talking about? I thought we were both teamed up to go after the target?"

"I'm not allowed to discuss it. The order...it's a solo mission."

"What? How come?"

"I wondered the same. I dunno. Cain has his reasons. But I think...I think he knows more about the change in our relationship than he's letting on."

"So, he's punishing us?" Von stood, raking her hands

through her hair. She didn't expect to be so hurt, to feel like part of her would die without Xander being in her life. The thought of not seeing Xander every day, not being able to wake up beside him, not being able to kiss him or make love to him. The thought that she was losing someone when she'd just found him, ripped at her insides worse than the attack that left her barren and near death.

Xander slowly approached, his roped chest pressed against her back. He wrapped his arms around her waist and pressed his lips against her shoulder. "Believe me—I don't wanna go either."

She spun to face him. "Then don't. Don't go. Tell him fucking no."

He brushed a hand across her cheek. "You know I can't do that."

"You're a grown man. You can do whatever the hell you want." Her voice shivered, eyes growing unexpectedly wet. Von had spent years hardening her shell, years stewing in rage, revenge coursing through her, eating away at any tender emotion. But something had changed in her. Something that made her remember who she was before the attack, before her sister went missing and was forced into an illegal sex trafficking ring, before Sammy was later murdered. Something had tapped into Wilder Agatha Friedrich, her birth name, her old, pure identity, untainted by violence and trauma.

Xander opened her broken soul and filled it with the one word she couldn't escape, couldn't push away, or bury, no matter how hard she tried: *love*. She dared not say it, not now, she wasn't ready. It was too soon. But every cell inside her knew what it was, and she wondered if he felt it too. Wondered if he would miss her when he was gone, wondered if he'd reflect upon the night they shared as a magical moment that had changed them both. Wondered if his heart would ache without her.

Xander leaned in and kissed her deeply just as tears crawled down her cheeks. Her wet face pressed against his in a deep, yearning kiss—tongues hungry, desperate, ravenous, as though they wanted to savor this last moment together, bottle it in their hearts, and never forget.

They parted, breaths mingling, forehead against forehead. He thumbed the tears from her cheeks. "Last night was...it was incredible. I loved my wife, but we never shared an intense bond. I've never felt this way about anyone."

"I've been searching my whole life for you," Von admitted, voice trembling. "You can't leave me."

She'd never been this bare, never let anyone see her break. Tears felt strange and foreign to her, a weakness she buried the night she almost died in Casper, Wyoming—bleeding out in the snow after the vicious stabbing that carved more than scars. Since then, Von had hated men. All men. Every face blurred into the sneers of her attackers. She knew it wasn't fair, knew it was wrong, but trauma hardened her into stone, fueled by rage so deep it became her marrow.

And yet, in Xander's arms, the stone cracked. Pain that she thought was permanent slipped away. Anger she'd clung to dissolved into something she hadn't dared imagine: *hope*. A fragile, dangerous hope of a life not defined by scars. She pictured a home together. A child, maybe, through surrogacy—a family that could stitch closed both her loss and his. For a flicker of time, she let herself see the possibilities of healing, of love returned.

But the moment carried teeth. Because now it was being yanked away. How long would he be gone? Would she ever see him again—or had she just tasted a future that would vanish before it began?

Then the question that had been burning a hole in her spirit, finally slipped out. "When do you leave?"

"Now. My flight's in an hour and I want to make sure I get ahead of the long lines."

"How long have you known?" Her fists ached to beat his chest, but her body betrayed her—arms locked around his neck, eyes burning with hurt. He flinched, the movement pulling at his wound, but he held her tighter anyway.

"About a week," he whispered. "I'm sorry I didn't tell you. I thought I could stay away from you, thought I was strong enough to fight this. That it would be easy to...to leave you. But every night, I imagined what it would be like—being with you. Touching you. Making love to you. And last night...last night was more than I ever let myself dream of." His forehead stayed pressed to hers, lips hovering just a sheet away. "I want you to have something."

He pulled away for a beat, digging into his pocket. He took her hand, pressing a ring into her palm. The metal was warm from his skin, heavy in a way that wasn't just weight. She glanced at it. The ring was titanium, scuffed along the edges, the surface carved with a SEAL Trident—the eagle, the anchor, the pistol, the trident itself. Worn smooth in places from years of use, it wasn't jewelry. It was history. *His history*.

"This has been with me through everything," he said quietly. "BUD/S—Basic Underwater Demolition/SEAL training. Hell Week, when they tried to break us. Iraq. Afghanistan. Black Ops. Nights I didn't think I'd see daylight. It was on my hand the day my wife died. Every scar I carry, this ring carried with me."

She swallowed hard, staring down at it. "Xander, I can't take this. Besides, it won't fit."

"It will. Had it sized for you," he said, surprising her. He'd thought ahead.

Her breath caught. "I don't understand. Why?"

"Because the Navy gave me dog tags. Numbers. Blood type. Rank. That's who they made me. But this ring—this is me. And now, it's you."

He plucked it from her palm and slid it onto her ring finger, the metal settling like it had always belonged there.

He leaned in, voice rough but steady. "Cain can send me anywhere. But as long as you wear this, you'll know where I am. And I'll know you'll find me."

She stared at him, the weight of the ring and his words sinking in. "Find you?" Voice laced with confusion. "What does that even mean? Why would you need someone to follow after you?"

"Because Cain can bury me under cover and silence. Missions no one tracks. No one admits exist." He held her hands in his. "But if I'm gone—really gone—you'll know I didn't just walk away from you. If I don't return in six months, that means something's up. I could be in danger, or the mission could be compromised."

"Nothing's gonna touch you. If you disappear, I'll tear the world apart to drag you back. No matter where, no matter what. That's a vow." She wrapped her arms around him, and they held each other for a long beat.

"I have to go," he whispered in her ear. He kissed her one last time, bruising her lips with an ache that penetrated her very being. Saying goodbye without words. And in his kiss, she could feel that what they had wasn't surface, but something etched past flesh and blood, into their souls itself.

He parted from her reluctantly. "I've gotta get back to my cabin, get my suitcases. There won't be a day when I'm not thinking about you. Please...please find me."

Xander bent down and rubbed Zeus on the head. "Take care of her," he said, and then Von watched the one fate had finally given her, the man she'd waited a lifetime for—only to be torn away—walk out the door.

The moment the door closed, Zeus whimpered as if he knew Xander wasn't coming back.

Von slumped onto the couch, and suddenly, a stream of tears she thought she could fight off came rushing out. She buried her face in her hands and wept as though death had claimed her life. After an hour, she cleaned herself up and decided she was going to confront the commander himself.

She charged in, slamming the door open, as frosty air rushed through Gull's Bait & Tackle. Von stormed into Cain's office. He leaned back and took a swig of his whiskey, a fat cigar hanging from his lip. He glanced up and shut his laptop, and she could only assume it was for the same reason he'd forced Xander away, the same reason she was not privy to the location of the mission.

Secrecy was a priority.

Zeus charged forward, inches away from his leg, baring his teeth as a low growl escaped his throat. Cain eyed the dog wearily, raising a brow. He scooted his chair back, trying to put space between himself and the lethal dog. Von didn't play around. She racked the gun back, metal snapping loud in the silence, and then drove the barrel into Cain's heart, pressing down hard. It barely got a rise from him.

"Where the fuck is Xander? What did you send him to do and where?"

Cain eyed the ring on her finger, recognition shifting across his face. "Cute, he left you a parting gift."

"Where the fuck is he? And why's my target list empty?"

"Was giving you a couple of weeks off, remember?" Cain

glanced at the gun, then back at her. Unshaken. "Holt is in the field. Doing work that can't wait."

Von raised the gun, centering the barrel at the middle of his forehead. "Then tell me where."

Cain grinned a thin, smug smile. "And what would you do? Drag him back? Distract him? You'd rather ruin him than let him finish."

Zeus snarled louder, the ridge of his back bristling. Von bared her teeth in return, voice a blade. "You don't give a damn about human life. To you, Xander's disposable—hell, we all are. But sending him out alone?" Her fists curled. "That's not strategy. That's a death sentence. Even street cops know the rule— you work in pairs, or you don't come home. You strip him of that, you're not leading, you're killing. And if you put him in the ground, Cain—" Her eyes narrowed, voice dropping low. "I'll find him. And I'll come for you, too."

Cain leaned forward, letting the barrel dig into his skull. "Danger's the point. If he survives it, he proves himself. If he doesn't...he wasn't built for this."

Von's jaw locked. The gun stayed steady, surgical hands, cold and unshaken. The silence thickened, and Cain owned it. When he spoke, his voice was steady, but beneath the calm throbbed a menace that promised consequences.

Von holstered the gun. A warning not to mess with his master continued, as Zeus's growl turned up a notch.

"I don't believe you can do it—find him. You get reckless when it's personal. And this...this is personal. Maybe, just maybe, that's why he was sent—*alone.*"

Von's eyes flashed with anger. "What're you saying? That's my assignment, isn't it?"

Cain took a puff from his cigar and dropped the ashes in a nearby coffee cup. "Assignments are fluid, Von. Consider this a test. But I doubt you'll pass—because caring clouds your aim."

Von snapped her fingers, and Zeus returned to her side.

"Then watch me."

"One more thing...your next target will be uploaded this week. I need proof."

"Of what?"

"That you're still a weapon and not a woman pining over some man who's long gone. A man who prioritized his job over his feelings, prioritized duty over you. Question is, can you?"

Her eyes burned through the haze between them. "I know what you're doing. Trying to pit us against each other—I see it. But don't act like you know him. You've met him in briefings. I've bled beside him. You want to test loyalty? His doesn't crack. And neither does mine. If you think dangling doubt is enough to shake me...you don't know me either."

Von stormed out into the icy cold, snow flurries clinging to her lashes, needling her skin, melting into her heat. She felt the world try to strip her bare, but her mind held fast, tethered to the one man she couldn't let go.

———

She slid into the SUV, the leather stiff with cold, circling her fingers around the steering wheel until her knuckles whitened. The chill bit into her flesh, but it was nothing compared to the frost spreading inside her. Von let her forehead fall against the wheel. The thought of Xander gone clawed at her ribs, an ache she couldn't outpace.

Her breath fogged the windshield, ghosting and fading, just like the image of him she tried to hold onto. Suddenly, her burner phone pinged with a text message. No one knew the number, not even Xander had it memorized, and so the only other person who could've been texting her was Detective Nazario. But it was unlikely.

The detective never initiated contact with Von first. Von contacted her. She wondered who it could be, secretly wishing that it was Xander, but knowing he was on a mission. He wouldn't compromise it by reaching out to her this soon. It was likely she wouldn't hear from him at all. She looked down at her phone.

Unknown number: *Yo, Von, I'm in town.*

Von: *Who the fuck is this?*

Unknown number: *Blackdragon6*

Von stiffened. It couldn't be. She muttered under her breath: *Fucking Jefferson Pierce.* The hacker had once been her ghost in the machine, helping her hunt the predators who stole her sister and forced Sammy into a sex ring. The courts had let those men walk, but Von hadn't. She made sure they never hurt another girl again. Pierce's trail of digital breadcrumbs had led her to every last one. Without him, she might never have found them—never avenged what they'd done when they slit her open and left her to die.

Instead of prison time, the FBI put Pierce on their payroll when they realized that they could use his special set of skills.

Von: *What the hell are you doing here?*

Unknown number: *Relax. I'm on the Ryker case. Meet me at Kodiak Cup in an hour, first round of caffeine's on me.*

———

The coffee shop was half-empty, the hiss of the espresso machine filling the quiet. Von kept her Black Nova phone on the table but didn't touch it. Pierce stirred his coffee, calm and unhurried. They caught up in fragments—Pierce sharing bits about his FBI work, Von admitting to the strain of working with Black Nova. But her mind wasn't there. It circled Xander, the absence gnawing at her.

Pierce's presence dulled the edges of solitude, but only slightly.

"I can't say I'm surprised that they tapped you to jump onto the Ryker case," Von said.

"He's not as easy to find. Took me a minute to find you. Everyone else in Black Nova—impossible to track."

"Then how'd you find me?"

"Detective Nazario gave me your burner. I can usually crack anything. But that Black Nova phone and the laptop they issued to you—*impossible*."

Von's heart dropped. "Shit, was hoping you could help me track someone. He could...he could be in danger."

"Xander Holt?"

"Yeah," she said, staring down at her coffee cup, heat rising to her cheeks.

"Wait...you're in love with him, aren't you?"

Von didn't answer. She couldn't deny it even if she tried.

Pierce caught her hand and examined the ring. "That's new."

Von started to slide her hand away. "He gave it to me. Said something like I could find him as long as I had it."

"Hold still." He angled his head, watching the band on her finger like he was lining up a shot. He didn't say anything. Just studied. Turned her wrist a fraction with two fingers. Back again.

"Take it off," he said at last. "Lemme see it."

The scrutiny made her chest knot. "Not happening."

The look he leveled at her wasn't asking. "Trust me."

Against her better judgment, she slid the ring free and pushed it across the table. Pierce turned it, tilted it toward the light. Nothing unusual to her eye—just scratched titanium—but something in his expression shifted.

He set it carefully down, met her gaze. His voice dropped.

"Von...this isn't just a ring."

Her pulse jumped. "What the hell 're you talking about?"

He tapped the edge with his thumb. "There's tech in here. A secure chip, some kind of low-power transmitter. Hand me your burner."

Von gave it to him. Pierce moved through the phone's settings, checking the connections before his attention shifted to an app called Weather Cast.

"What is it?"

He held up the screen. "This app. It's connected to the ring."

"I don't get it. It's a weather widget. Tells you if it's going to rain or be sunny. So what?"

"It's camouflage." He opened it, revealing a global map. A green light sat motionless over Kodiak Airport.

She paused for a beat, then burst into laughter. "C'mon. What is this, *Mission: Impossible?* Some paranoid sci-fi tech bullshit?"

Pierce didn't laugh. "M2M. Machine-to-machine communication routed through a relay server."

"English. I have no idea what you're saying. Why is the weather app displaying a map? I don't get it. It's a tracking device?"

"Not exactly. The ring's the middleman. It's a hardware authentication token."

Von stared at him blankly. "In layman's terms, Pierce. Layman's terms."

"The ring links this app to his phone."

Von looked back at the green dot on the map. "You're saying that's Xander?"

"His last known location."

"How is it tracking him if it's on my finger?"

"It isn't." Pierce looked up at her. "The ring's not the tracker. It's a hardware key."

"A key to what?"

"To his location feed. The secure chip in the ring unlocks the connection and gives your phone access. His phone sends the coordinates. Yours receives them through an encrypted relay."

She looked from the map to the ring. "Then why isn't it moving?"

"Looks like he has a kill switch on his end. The feed was manually cut at the airport, so the app froze on the last coordinates it received."

"But the ring still works?"

"The ring never stopped working. He cut the connection from his phone. If he reactivates the feed, his location will appear here again." Pierce pointed to the map.

"When he's...when he's in danger?"

The room shrank. Von snatched the ring back, closing her fist around it.

"How do I...how do I find him if you can't?" Her voice shook.

"Keep it on your finger. Monitor the app. Until he turns the feed back on, all you can do is wait. I'll try to find another way. The ring might be your best shot."

She needed space to think, so she cut the meeting short and promised to stay in touch. He assured her he'd hit her burner to keep it on the DL—well clear of Cain's prying eyes and ears.

Outside, the air was colder than it should've been. She turned the band in her palm, thumb brushing the edge Pierce had examined. Weathered and scarred, the ring looked like it had survived wars and carried life and death in its metal skin. The Trident etched into its surface. Something personal. Something his. Now, it read differently in her hand. Not just a vow, but a device. Not just affection, but circuitry.

Was it even about me? Or was it about access, tactics, survival?

She slid the ring back onto her finger. The metal settled against her skin like it had always belonged there, cold and heavy. Betrayal tangled with something else, something she wouldn't name without tearing herself open.

Whatever it was—symbol or signal, promise or ploy—he'd chosen her to wear it.

TWENTY-EIGHT

THE WARNING

DETECTIVE LILA MENDEZ had been right. The second Sergeant Vincent Greer entered with his lawyer in tow, Nazario saw it plain: he wasn't going to talk. His eyes were shards of ice; every step forward radiated a swagger that dared them to break him. He sank into the chair with a sneer carved across his face, then swept a deliberate stare over each interrogator—Alvarez, Humphrey, Huxley. The silence stretched, thick and hostile, until Alvarez finally cut through it.

"I would wipe that smug look on your face, or maybe you need a little reminder. Attempted murder of a peace officer, PC 664/187(a). Assault with a firearm PC 245(d). Discharge of a weapon in public, PC 245(d). And don't think we forgot the dope—HS 11352 for trafficking, plus further enhancements for weight." Alvarez leaned in, steepling his fingers. "Every single round you fired adds decades. Stack it all up, and you'll never see daylight again."

Huxley remained standing. Nazario knew he was the fitness type who preferred standing desks above sitting down. But the agent also liked to use his massive size in both brawn and height as a source of intimidation. In most cases, it worked, but not today, not with Greer.

"It's simple. All you have to do is give up Ryker's location and the location of the drop points, who else is involved, and maybe we can discuss a plea deal," Huxley said.

Greer glanced at his lawyer. "Permission to answer."

"Granted."

Greer slid his eyes to Huxley. "Charge me whatever alphabet soup you want. And a plea deal?" he scoffed. "You and I both know the jury'll eat me alive, and when they're done chewing me up and spitting me out—the other inmates will kill me. They hate cops—"

Gus cut in, "We can get you in PC."

Greer broke out into laughter. Head cocked back like he'd heard a funny joke at a comedy club. "Don't you get it? Ryker's got reach. Don't matter if I'm in protective custody. I speak, and Ryker'll get somebody on the inside—I'll be shanked in a week. You want me to give you Ryker? Probation will be a death sentence. A shank in the yard, a bullet on the outside. You might as well dig me a grave. His men'll put a bullet through my head. Either way—I'm a dead man."

"Witness protection. New name. New face." Alvarez said, "We can make that happen—if you give us Ryker."

"Witness protection?" Greer let out another round of amusing laughter. "Not with Ryker. Not when he's got cops on his payroll. He'll find me and he'll bury me."

Huxley leaned in, palms pressed on the table, face inches away from Greer as he loomed over him. "You think silence buys you time? It doesn't. Ryker won't protect you—he'll kill you anyway, just to cover his tracks. You've been caught. You're no longer an asset to him. In fact, you're a weak link he'll have to cut. You and Mendez are now a liability. You're a dead man walking, Greer. Only question is who pulls the trigger—Ryker, or the State of California. You've got one chance to choose who you want holding the gun."

"My client's safety is my top priority." The lawyer finally spoke. "Snitching doesn't just shorten his life—it ends it. Prison's a risk, but there's at least a chance. Witness protection? Please. My client's right. Ryker has cops, guards, even feds in his pocket. You want him to talk? That's suicide, and you all know it. Put him in protective custody, and you're handing his name to the very people who want him dead. We're not falling for it. No one can protect him on the outside, especially if he gives up Ryker. My job isn't to gamble with his life—it's to keep him breathing."

Humphrey drew closer, tattoos shifting as her fists pressed to the table. "Listen to me, Greer. You think Ryker's men care about you? You're a pawn. He'll leave you rotting, same as Harrison. You've got one shot to flip the script—right here, right now. Give us something, and maybe you walk out of this alive. Stay loyal to Ryker, and you'll die nameless in a cage. That's your choice. Yours."

"If you're serious about protection, it's not for IA or LAPD to promise." The lawyer stood, and Greer followed suit. "You'd need the U.S. Marshals, WITSEC-level clearance. Until I see something in writing from them, my client won't answer another word."

Alvarez got up from his chair and stood in front of the door. "C'mon, Marshals don't hand out miracles, Greer. You think they'll take on a dirty cop who shot at his own? Not a chance. You want to walk out of prison alive—this room is your only shot."

The lawyer snapped his briefcase shut. "Then we're done here. My client invokes his Fifth Amendment rights," he said. "Now, get out of our way."

Nazario studied their faces. Alvarez, Humphrey, and

Huxley seemed to watch with the same sense of desperation as she felt. The door clicked shut behind Greer and his lawyer. What little hope they'd carried bled out of the room with them. Harrison was still dead. Ryker was still breathing free air. And the streets were still poisoned—his tranq flooding veins, dropping bodies with every hit.

By 2021, overdose deaths in Los Angeles County had doubled. The brass answered by creating the Overdose Response Task Force (ORTF)—July 1, 2022—mandating homicide units to roll out on ODs when dealers could be tied to the body. Prosecutors had gone on record: push fentanyl, kill someone, you'd face a murder charge. But since Ryker's new tranq strain hit the streets, numbers had tripled. Every corpse was another nail in her city's coffin. Nazario burned to pin every one of them on him—if they could just smoke the bastard out.

Humphrey, Alvarez, and Huxley filed into the observation room with her and Wilson.

The air was already heavy when Wilson's special phone buzzed—the line patrol only rang when it smelled like homicide. The room fell silent. They all watched Wilson lift the receiver, waiting for the verdict in his gravel-tinged voice.

"Whatcha got for me?" he asked, skipping the formalities. "Another one, huh? Uh-huh...unusual how?" Wilson glanced at Nazario and the rest of the watchful eyes in the room, shrugging his shoulders. "Can't say over the phone? Well, alrighty. Be there in fifteen. Oh...and don't worry about calling ORTF. We'll fill them, but only after we've investigated the scene. Thanks."

"If we're calling ORTF, it could only mean it's another OD," Nazario said.

"Yep, but the patrol on duty was...I dunno...shaken up by it. Wouldn't give me anything about it. Said we had to see for ourselves," he said. "They texted me the address. Real sketchy area—Watts."

"I gotta get back to my office. Write this interrogation up," Alvarez said. "If you can even call it that. Whittier and Yang won't be showing up on any scene anytime soon. You'll be working with Sierra Brooks and her assistant."

"Met her, she's good. How'd the interrogation with them go? Give up anything at all about Ryker?" Nazario asked.

"Negative. Whittier and Yang are benched—unpaid administrative leave, stripped of field clearance until IA finishes. And yes, already ran them through the room. Tried to squeeze them. Both invoked the Fifth. If we prove they opened that vault, it's obstruction and evidence tampering. They won't come back from that. They're looking at criminal charges. Anyway, lemme know if you find anything interesting at the scene," Alvarez said.

The call gnawed at her. Patrol never whispered around a routine OD unless the scene was bad. Real bad. Whatever waited at that scene—it had patrol spooked.

———

The first thing that hit Nazario was the soul-ripping wail of a woman's cries piercing the night. It flooded her ears, punched through her chest, splintering her heart into a million shards. She'd been on plenty of devastating crime scenes, but instinct— two decades of experience—told her this OD would haunt her.

Neighbors lingered outside their dilapidated homes, smoking cigarettes, swigging booze, some brazenly passing joints. Chipped paint. Dead grass. Sagging roofs and barred, grime-streaked windows—Watts' dangerous ghetto and its urban decay on full display. Yellow tape cordoned the scene, squad car lights washing everything in red and blue.

At the curb, a white coroner's van loomed—stark as a coffin on wheels.

Nazario led the way, ducking under the crime tape with

Wilson and Huxley in tow. Inside, two officers tried to console the woman, but when they couldn't penetrate through her grief, one of them approached while their partner stayed next to the woman and met them.

"The body's down the hall on the far left," he said. "I've been trying to talk to the mother, get an idea as to whose tranq it was, but she's inconsolable."

The mother? Oh, no. No, no, no.

As they walked down the hall, Nazario's heart began to speed up, dread filling her to the marrow with every step closer. When they stepped inside, the new SID lead, Sierra Brooks, was finishing her sweep. Nazario deduced that she'd already circled the room with her camera—shots of the body, the clothes on the floor, the take-out boxes, the bent spoon that was used to get high. Her assistant moved slow and precise, gloved hands lifting baggies, swabbing a desk for residue, and then sealing everything in evidence envelopes.

Even on an OD, the process was the same: document everything, because you never knew what detail would flip the narrative from an accident to a homicide. Regardless, it was a homicide, and Ryker was the one who'd pulled the trigger. Then Nazario spotted the body of a young boy, and her heart sank even deeper.

Brooks nodded at them. "Gabriel Cruz. Twelve years old. Only child. We think the tranq was his mom's, Carmen Cruz. Single mother. History of drug abuse. We won't know for sure until we talk to her. After she calms down," said Brooks.

"What makes you think it belonged to Miss Cruz?" Wilson asked.

"Found another stash in her socks drawer," Brooks said.

"We'll have to arrest her on possession and murder. Maybe Carmen will be ready to cough up the name of her dealer, and we could drop the second-degree and hit her with Penal Code 273a—child endangerment causing death," Huxley said.

The conversations blurred all around her as Nazario walked slowly over to the body, gut clenching. Brown skin, wiry frame, a child with his whole life ahead of him. In all her years, this OD cut close—Hispanic, too young, like the neighborhood boys she grew up with. Like family. A depressed needle sticking out of his arm. Another life gone to poison on the streets, and now Watts had just swallowed another life whole.

This time it was a child.

"He was just a baby." Nazario's voice shook, then turned to Brooks. "Did you happen to bag any Narcan?"

"It was next to the body," Brooks said. "Surprised it didn't work."

"This new strain of tranq doesn't respond to Narcan—and that's exactly why it's so damn dangerous," Huxley said.

Nazario swept the room. There were various rap artists on the walls. A Nintendo Switch on the nightstand. The TV was on as a movie of Scar Face played in the background.

"Was there a cell phone anywhere?" Nazario asked.

"Mom said he had a phone, but we couldn't find it," Brooks answered.

Nazario opened the drawers with gloved hands. "Let's look for his cell. It's gotta be here somewhere."

Huxley looked into the closet, and Wilson sifted through his bookbag. Nazario dropped to her knees and looked under the bed. There were piles of dirty clothes on the floor. She dug through them, and at the bottom was his phone.

"Got it. It was under the clothes. He must've dropped it," she said, handing it to Huxley.

"I'll get DFE on it right away," he said, bagging it. "Since we're dealing with Ryker, we need a step ahead of LAPD's DEU. FBI should examine it just in case he knew the dealer."

"Good call," Nazario said. "Our digital evidence unit's good. But it's hard for them to crack the code to get entry into the phone. I'd trust one of your digital forensic examiners to handle it. Better get Carmen's phone, too. If it really was her stash, she must have her dealer's contact."

"We wanted you to see the body first before taking the needle out of his arm," Brooks said.

"Appreciate it, Sierra. Thank you." Nazario raked a hand down her face, breathing deeply through her nose. That familiar squeeze in her chest returned, slow at first, then crushing—clamping down on her chest until every breath felt borrowed. Panic rode shotgun with anxiety, crawling up her throat, buzzing in her skull, the same relentless wave that hit every damn time she worked a case this brutal.

Huxley noticed. He put a hand on her back. "You doing okay, Anaya?"

She nodded. "Trying to breathe through it."

"Don't know about you guys, but I think I need a beer after this. How about we head to End of Watch. Unless it'll trigger you, Nazario," Wilson said, then whispered, "Would hate to be the reason you relapse."

"It's a good idea. I'm down." She dug into her blazer pocket and popped two Gabapentin for the anxiety attack that could sometimes be debilitating. "I'll stick to club soda."

They stayed a little longer, going through everything SID gathered, searching in Gabriel's room and his mother's in case SID missed something. However, Brooks and her assistant had done a thorough job. By the time they were done, the grieving mother had settled down. Nazario's heart turned to ice, knowing that Gabriel would still be alive had it not been for her drug habit.

Huxley waited until Carmen had calmed, then pressed her.

Sure enough—it was her stash her son had found. After the confession, he ordered the beat cops to arrest her. The mother didn't resist. Anguish—or maybe guilt—kept her still. Carmen seemed to quietly accept her fate, as if whatever sentence awaited her could never compare to the life sentence of losing her son.

———

Chief Johnson surprised them by showing up at End of Watch, a popular local bar that most LAPD officers and FBI agents frequented. After almost being killed, Nazario didn't expect the chief to go to a popular bar where some of the dirties would show. She should've been worried, but after Gabriel Cruz's OD, she didn't give a fuck who glared at them.

For the most part, the patrons at the bar seemed to mind their own business. But there were some that leaned in and began talking in hushed tones, glancing their way. Wilson, Huxley, and Johnson ordered beers, and Nazario stuck to a club soda. She wished she could have just one drink, but she never could.

"Maybe we should've picked a different bar," Wilson said. "At least one where we don't look like the punch line before happy hour."

"They can all go to hell. Let them stare at the two best detectives and the best federal agent in Los Angeles County. Y'all have done one helluva job," Chief commended.

"We still don't have Jaxon Ryker, though," Nazario took a sip of her club soda, wishing for a moment she was Jesus and could turn it into red wine.

"Tell me about the OD."

"Oh, god." Nazario let out a long, weighty breath, eyes

closing as she pinched the bridge of her nose. She felt Huxley's strong hand massaging the back of her neck.

"That bad?" Johnson said.

"Twelve-year-old Hispanic kid. Gabriel Cruz. Father's out of the picture. The mother, Carmen Cruz—single mother with a drug habit," Nazario informed.

"My guess, the boy probably watched his mom shoot up," Wilson said.

"So, he found her supply and decided to try it for himself," Johnson finished.

"Seems that way. We confiscated the kid's phone and the mom's. I'll be handing them over to one of my digital forensic examiners. Mom gave us her password, but we don't know the kid's yet. DFE will definitely crack it open—just in case we find something of use. I doubt it. More gold in what's in Carmen's phone," Huxley said.

Chief Johnson took a sip of his beer. "We're close. Real close. I know you're a go-getter, Nazario. Know you feel like you failed, but you didn't. You all didn't. This OD—it was tragic. This is exactly why we've gotta get Ryker for murder. Cause that's what this was. He killed that boy. Mom did, too."

"Got a good feeling we can get her to give up her dealer— and if we do, I'll buy us a round at a bar where half the room doesn't want us dead," Wilson said.

They went over the case piece by piece, making sure nothing slipped past them. Dealers moving product beyond L.A. More badges gone dirty. The murder of Detective Clay Harrison. The hit on Captain Gus Humphrey and Chief Johnson. Wilson's car, trashed.

But in the back of Nazario's mind, one image wouldn't let go: that twelve-year-old boy. Eyes glazed in milky film. Lips purple. Skin gone ashy blue. Needle buried in his vein. An hour later, she knew if she didn't leave now, those thoughts would drive her to pick up a drink. Her excuse was stronger: a six-month-old waiting at home with the babysitter.

"Probably should turn in," Nazario said, checking her watch. "Gotta get home to the baby."

"I'm good to go," Wilson said, his beer long finished. It always surprised Nazario how people could nurse a drink for an hour or two. She'd have finished a bottle of wine by then.

"Well, I'm sure as shit not staying here solo. Best get moving, too, before I catch another round," Chief Johnson muttered, tapping the plate of his vest. "Kevlar can't stop one between the eyes."

"Please don't say that, sir," Nazario said.

Huxley flagged the waitress, dropped his card, and closed out the tab. "Drinks are on me."

They filed into the night, scattering toward their cars.

"Hug the baby for me!" Johnson called.

"Will do, sir!" Nazario thumbed her car fob. Nothing. Tried again. Still nothing. Then—time slowed. A light blinked three times on the dash.

Huxley's eyes widened. He shouted, voice raw: "GET DOWN! GET DOWN!"

Wilson turned, confused, "What did I miss—"

Chief Johnson went pale, dropped flat to the pavement.

Nazario finally saw it. Realized—too late.

BOOM!

Orange flames engulfed her vehicle as it exploded, jolting it off the ground and slamming it back down. The blast swallowed the night, turning metal to shrapnel, asphalt to crater. Nazario hit the ground hard, lungs burning, smoke stinging her eyes. Wilson's screams asking if everyone was okay got lost beneath the roar. As the fire ate what was left of her car, one truth seared into her mind: this wasn't just a warning. If she'd buckled her daughter up into the backseat tonight, her daughter would be ashes.

Nazario knew right then and there—no badge, no shield, no one in this city could keep her family safe. And her family wasn't just her daughter. It was Wilson, Humphrey, Chief Johnson, and Huxley—the last of the blue she still believed in.

And now—this was war.

AUTHOR'S NOTE

The *Serpent Series* was born out of both imagination and bloodline.

My uncle, Nicholas Estavillo, made history as the first Puerto Rican in New York City to rise to three-star rank in the NYPD. A decorated Marine and graduate of the FBI National Academy at Quantico, he earned honors such as the Combat Action Ribbon, Vietnam Service Medal with Bronze Star, and the Vietnam Gallantry Cross Unit Citation. Over decades of service, he commanded Manhattan precincts before becoming Chief of Patrol in 2002—breaking barriers and leaving a legacy of strength, discipline, and integrity.

My father, Jose Estavillo, served his country as a career Airman in the United States Air Force and later as an officer in U.S. Customs and Border Protection, where he trained at the U.S. Customs Academy in Glynco, Georgia. He retired in Florida with his wife, carrying with him the quiet resilience and sense of duty that continue to influence the characters I write.

My mother immigrated from Korea to the United States, carrying with her a fierce will to survive and rebuild. Because of her, I grew up in a trilingual household—English, Spanish, and

Korean—an upbringing that gave me a layered way of seeing the world.

As a Puerto Rican–Korean author, I write thrillers from a perspective shaped by two distinct heritages, each rooted in survival, resilience, and pride. In spaces where BIPOC voices are often overlooked, my family's story is proof of what it means to rise in systems not built for us, and of the strength it takes to break through.

Detective Anaya Nazario—and other characters like Von Schlange—carry that same lineage of resilience. They fight within systems never meant for them, yet refuse to bow or break. Their survival, like my family's, is an act of defiance and strength.

This series is, in part, my way of honoring them both. And to my surprise, readers have embraced it too—the Serpent Series was acquired in a multi-book deal, reached over 24,000 downloads in its first year, and even found its way onto the BookRaid bestseller list in the thriller category. That support reminds me every day why I keep writing.

Your reviews help keep the Serpent Series alive. If you liked this story, sharing your thoughts on Amazon or Goodreads would mean the world.

— S.Z. Estavillo

ALSO BY S.Z. ESTAVILLO

The Serpent Series

The Serpent's Bridge

The Serpent Woman

Twilight of the Serpent

The Serpent's Order

ABOUT THE AUTHOR

SZ Estavillo has been passionate about writing since childhood, with a defining moment in second grade when her teacher predicted, "You're going to be a writer someday." Her biracial heritage, being half-Korean and half-Puerto Rican, deeply influences her book themes. As a staunch advocate for diversity and inclusion, SZ works tirelessly to amplify the voices of underrepresented and marginalized communities within the publishing industry.

SZ is not only a feminist whose principles echo throughout her works, but also a true crime aficionado, having devoured every episode of true crime on networks like Discovery ID and

Oxygen. Her interest in justice is deeply rooted in her family history.

Balancing her roles as a devoted mother and an enthusiastic digital marketer, SZ brings her professional expertise into her personal passion, amassing over 100,000 followers on social media. She uses her platform to inspire and uplift the writing community with motivational and positive content. Along with her two children and two dogs, she enjoys the simple pleasures of family sushi outings in their Fresno home.

If you enjoyed this book, consider following her on social media or posting a review. Your support helps extend the reach of voices that matter. Thank you for reading and being part of this journey. Stay tuned for her upcoming books in the Serpent Series.

Please follow SZ Estavillo:

Goodreads: https://www.goodreads.com/author/show/49349032.S_Z_Estavillo
X: @szestavillo
Instagram: @szestavillo.author
TikTok: @szestavillo.author
Facebook Page: https://www.facebook.com/sonyozofiaestavillo

A small press bound by the belief that every voice matters.

Sign up for our newsletter to learn about new releases and more.
https://oliver-heberbooks.com/subscribe/

Follow us on social media:

facebook.com/oliverheberbooks

instagram.com/oliverheberbooks

amazon.com/oliverheberbooks

youtube.com/@OliverHeberBooksPublisher